TORREY FLOWERS
THE LAST CRY

The Last Cry (Urban Fiction)
By: Torrey Flowers aka Ravenion Nalls

Cover Image by: Torrey Flowers
Cover Design By: Jazzy Kitty Publishing

Logo Designs By: Andre M. Saunders/Leroy Grayson
Editor: Anelda L. Attaway

© 2011 Torrey Flowers 1-653565140
ISBN 978-0-9830548-9-4
Library of Congress Control Number: 2011937649

For Worldwide Distribution, printed in the United States of America. Published by Jazzy Kitty Greetings Marketing & Publishing, LLC dba Jazzy Kitty Publishing. Utilizing Microsoft Publishing and adobe software.

This book may contain strong language, may not be suitable for children under the age of 12.

DEDICATION

To all the people that believed in me; Yolanda Denise Stroud, Eric "EJ" Jones, Angela Lashun Hawkins, Latasha Talley Strong, Toccara Holiday, Corneilus Holiday, Ray Talley, Rashida, Anthony, Brooksey, Rayzen, Kerry, Jimaine, Richard Sr., Richard Jr., Amy, KeKe, Damon, Mario DG Yola, Amber and Grandma Mildred.

To all my real homies; Will, Nick, Carey, Gary, Shahid, Yiyie, Bg, W. W., Bruce, Lil Jeff, Scar, Mia, Moan, Hickey, Antonio Blackmon, Emmitt, Drop, Cuzo, Timmy Lee, Major N, Troy, Wyhid, Ace, Country Slugger, GF, YMF, GD, Bloods, Crips, Pittsburgh, Toney Coney, Cut, Brad, Tuck, Baby Young, Mal, Fly, Plug, Polo, Dual, Gary Kinder, D, Stokes, Mike Deezy, Mike Henderson, Patman, David Baker, Calbra, Robert Jenkins, Tony Jenkins, Enoch, Ismeal, KB, Big D, Bankhead, Jerry Trigger, Jerry Lee, Dred, Pleasure, Bo Hog, Ms. Lango, Ms. Vincient, Ms. Dixon, CeCe, KD, Mr. Walker, Ms. Walker, Pooh, Brandon Cindy, Country M. Hightower, Nino, Duke. Lil Man, Unc, Tray, Mark B, Ray, Tylon Sweet, Kenny, Jit, No, Dog Nuts, DJ, Goldie, KeKe, June, Latoya, Carla, Tyesha, Malata, Nat, Silky, Hanson and Geanva, Tasha, Twyla, Keke, Nikki, Sabrina, Jazmine, Dwayne E, Suspect, DavidA, Aries, Smiley, M. Sapp, Chuck Brinkly, Larry Hunt, Phillip Odom, Mr. O.W, Yung Bookieball, Harpo, Cortez, Cee Durden, Saulsbury, Webster, Brisco, Hall, Turner, Mack, Wright, Watson, A. Huges, Hosa Strong, Swamp out of space but not out of luv... My homies.

Thanks Tay for letting me use your phone, you are a buster.

TABLE OF CONTENTS

SUMMARY

The Last Cry

By Torrey Flowers aka Ravenion Nalls

Main Characters:
Juan Ellis
Natasha Middle
Sonya
Smokey
Leo Nikko
Ike

Juan Ellis, a local street dealer finds himself in a robbery, in which he kills one of the robbers. After being captured by the police the next day, he finds his faith in the hands of 18-year-old Natasha Middles. Natasha holds a possessive love for him and goes to her grandfather Honorable Judge Harold Middle for help in hope that Ellis would finally notice her and give her the relationship she dreamed of.

After getting out of the murder charge with the help of Natasha's grandfather, Juan turns her way. Finally her dream comes true and they engage in a relationship; she dreams of becoming a lawyer and Juan an Atlanta kingpin. The two were destined. Natasha's father tore the two away by putting her on the college campus. His dreams of taking over the City of Atlanta were born by departing from their relationship. Juan and long-time friend Ike sold everything and started their drug business. Becoming well known, until Ike got busted by an undercover cop, he had to carry the business himself. By pulling a hit for a Detroit kingpin, he became more powerful with their help.

Finally the Fulton County police convicted him on a murder charge that he didn't do. Finding peace in the arms of a white officer, he learned more about himself and his relationship with Natasha grew. Natasha's hiding her pregnancy caused him to believe she and Ike had become lovers after Ike's release. Natasha's father and grandfather got Juan out and he saw the two together. Blaming God for all his hardship and failure, Juan promised God that the world will feel his pain.

Contacting Tony, his Detroit employer, Juan finds out that Tony is his uncle. Tasha calls Tony and tells him about the baby and reunites with Juan. Tony dies because he didn't want to do a hit for the mob boss. Tasha and Ike get hit by a tractor trailer and get put in a coma. His son is born premature. Sworn to avenge Tony's death, Juan hooks up with Sonya and the BFM and promises to relocate the gang. So, they take out the mob leader and get over 4 million in drugs and money.

Sonya turns out to be a Federal agent with an assignment to bust the gang, but falls in love with Ellis. She lists him as her snitch and turns the gang against him. After robbing some Cubans for a large amount of cocaine, Juan Ellis flees to Africa to get his name and prints changed over. He attended to his family avoiding the gang. Sonya makes attempts on Tasha's life and tells the gang that Juan is snitching. With the Feds and gang after him, Juan flees to Cuba and finds favor in Nikko, the Don of the underworld.

Nikko sends him back with a 65-man army and watches his dream come true and his life end. The Middle whole family dies from a revenge of an inmate and his son gets kidnapped.

CHAPTER 1
The Beginning

It was a warm sunny day; the trees were lush with their new leaves. The flowers had just bloomed, tears rolled down Natasha Middles sleepy face as she looked out her bedroom window. She said to herself, "To most people this would be a beautiful day. Why am I feeling so ugly? Why do people hurt one another? It's like happiness has no meaning. I can't tell what's real or fake, who's out to hurt me and who's not. Love is driving me crazy; I guess everyone isn't meant to be happy. Especially me!"

She stood from her king size bed, still wearing her white sundress from the day before. She turned left out of her room and walked down the hall, slowly wiping the tears from her eyes with both of her hands. As she walked into her kitchen looking at the brown cabinets which hung on the wall straight ahead of her, she turned to her right and opened her Maytag refrigerator looking for something to snack on. With success, she found a ham and cheese sandwich wrapped in saran wrap on a plate. She got it, reached on top of the refrigerator, grabbed a bag of sour cream and onion Lay's chips, took a glass from the sink and poured some apple juice.

She walked to her well-kept living room containing white flowery walls, black leather sofa, and stainless solid white carpet and a JVC entertainment system. She turned to her CD player which sat next to the sofa in the center of the living room. She wanted to find something that would take her mind off of Juan's situation. It was still hard to believe that he was sent to prison to serve 20 years for a murder he didn't commit. She placed "Kenny G live" in the CD player. As the jazz tune filled the room, she relaxed on the sofa and tried not to think of him.

He was so sweet and so young, everything she had always wanted. But he was also a drug dealer, robber and now a convicted murderer. She remembered when she first met him. It was a rainy day on May 12, 1991. She remembered it well because that was the day he sent her home crying. She wrote it in her diary. She was 16 years old and on her way to the corner store when he passed her and pulled in the parking lot of McPherson Super Market in a gray 84 Cutlass with reverse eight chrome wheels. She wondered how he could he be so young and driving. She had heard some of the girls in school and around the neighborhood say he was 15 years old. But she never had a chance to come face to face with him.

She ran into the store wearing a white Boss outfit with white shirt, white shorts, some white Sketchers shoes with no socks and a gold ankle bracelet on. She noticed as walked past that he was playing a Pac-Man arcade game that sat next to the entrance. He had on some blue sport jeans pants with both legs pulled up, a blue Nike short sleeve shirt with white checks all over it. She didn't want to stare him down, so she went her way but kept a close eye on him. She started getting things for breakfast: eggs, grits, milk, bacon and so on. He stepped to the counter and asked for some triple zero bags and razor blades, things he needed to cut up and sell drugs. He turned around from the counter and looked at her with no interest. But to her, Juan seemed like a person with alot of confidence who would be interesting to know. He just seemed different. To be honest, he was different. He was a drug dealer, a street thug, which really turned her on. She had seen him riding around before, so young and so free. So she decided to introduce herself.

"Hi. My name is Natasha. What's yours?" He responded, "Child go head on now, you're too young and still a momma baby."

She got mad because he didn't even know her and he just chumped her off. With a commanding tone she asked, "How could you say that about me when you don't even know me?!"

"I've checked you out before, you stay on Marbut. You don't suppose to be in this hood; your pop is a lawyer so that makes it simple, you're not my race."

He smiled and started to walk off when she grabbed his right arm.

"What! Nigga, I'm just as black as you. We're both Pecan tan. I'm 16 years old, 91 pounds. So how can you say we're not the same race? I don't have a pointed nose, sho don't have blonde hair. I have the same puffed lips as black people."

He only smiled and jerked his arm away. What he meant was she's not hood. So he told her to take her suburban ass back around the corner before her momma came looking for her eggs. Those words sent her home crying to her momma Nancy and she stayed with her for 2 years. Every time she heard his car booming down the street she'd think about it. Hearing a girl who he'd just slept with talk about how he bought them this and that made her remember. She used to wonder if she gave him some would he look at her different. Then she used to always tell herself she wouldn't be any different from the rest of 'em. But he finally broke on her 18th birthday; he had gotten in some trouble. All she knew was when she looked out her window, she saw him being handcuffed and put in the back seat of a Zone 6 police car.

She ran down the steps and out the door in her black night gown, asking the officers what he had done. The white slim officer continued to get in the driver seat while the black muscular officer opened the door to the passenger side. She hit the window and asked him what happened.

"Are you trying to get arrested young lady?" The black officer asked. She looked into his big brown eyes, at his puffed nose, full goatee and pulled away from the window.

She asked, "What has he done so quickly? He's been with me all night. He just left about an hour ago. What could he have done so quickly?"

"He's a suspect in a murder that happened last night."

"I just told you he was with me all last night."

"Well ma'am I guess I'll be seeing you at Fulton County Jail."

She looked at him and seen the hurt in his eyes and told him not to worry, everything would be okay. He dropped his head as the car pulled off. She ran into the house and headed for the phone that sat on the end table next to the black and gold velvet sofa. She was wondering who she could call, maybe someone from her daddy's law firm or her granddaddy. Before she knew it, her finger was already dialing a number. It was her grandfather, Honorable Judge Harold Middle. He'd been a judge for 12 years in the superior court. He loved his family, especially his only grandchild from his only child. As the phone rang, tears fell down her cheeks. She couldn't even begin to understand why she was crying or why she was helping him; 17 years old, always in trouble or doing something stupid. She thought she wasn't his race. She thought about hanging up the phone. The more she thought about his words the more she wanted to hang up. Then again, she really hoped that maybe this would get them closer, give them a chance to have a real conversation.

"Hello?" His voice sounded heavy.

"Granddaddy! Granddaddy! They locked up my boyfriend for nothing!"

She yelled through the phone, "He didn't do nothing granddaddy! He was with me all last night. I let him in through the back door when my momma went to bed. Granddaddy, he was with me. He didn't do nothing! Please get him out! You're a judge; I know you can get him out. He didn't do nothing! He was with me."

From the sound of her voice he knew she was hurt and telling the truth. She was crying and crying out in love. He was hurt because she never called him for anything like this before. Plus, he knew she wouldn't be involved with someone who'd kill someone. It hurt him to hear all the pain in her voice.

"Well baby, first we have to see what his charges are. Then, we'll see if they'll give him a bond. After that, we'll meet and see who'll take the case. I'll try my best to speak on his behalf. What's his name?"

"Juan Ellis."

"Well I'll make some calls and see what I can dig up. Don't worry yourself baby girl, I'll try my best. Hopefully he'll be home, although I can't make any promises. All I can do is try. Just focus on your education."

She raced up the steps to her bedroom, the first room on the right. She grabbed her blue jeans and slid into them and put on her white t-shirt from the chair that sat in front of her king size bed. Underneath the chair were a pair of low cut white Nikes. She slipped in them and ran back down the steps. Grabbing her purse from the same end table the phone sat on, she ran out, slamming the door. The window shook from the sharp closing of the door. She took her keys from her purse, locked the door and jumped the two steps, almost stepping into her mom's freshly planted lilies which were just starting to bloom in the first week of May. Jumping in her blue 1993 Acura, she cranked the sounds of Toni Braxton's *"Breathe Again"* which filled the car with sound. Strawberry fragrance started blowing from the air conditioner. She was backing out when she thought about which direction to take, either the short route to Maynard Terrace where there are no lights or traffic, or Moreland with its ongoing lights and traffic. She decided on Maynard Terrace, she took Maynard Terrace to Garnett Street where the Atlanta Police precinct was. She parked in the lot across the street from the B&O Bonding Company.

When she reached the entrance, she ran into a slim, black male officer and asked could she see "Juan Ellis." The officer pointed to the black female officer at the desk. She walked to the front desk and asked her if she could see Juan Ellis.

The officer replied, "If he's the one they just brought in, he's going through booking. I'll have to check with the detective, because I think he's going back upstairs."

She left, returned five minutes later and pointed towards the glass double doors. Natasha walked up very slowly, trying to figure out what to say to him. As her mind wandered, she saw that they were already face to face. He looked at her from behind the glass with the phone in his hand.

She sat on the stainless steel stool and picked up the phone.

"Girl, you don't give up do you? I knew you would be down here. Please tell me what do you want from me? Why are you even here?"

You could see the frustration on his face.

"Well, I know you didn't do it, at least that's what my heart tells me."

He wanted to tell her, her heart was wrong. He killed a man in a drug deal. He dropped his head. The deal went down behind the laundry mat with Vic and Moe. He knew it was a setup when CJ walked up asking for a light, because no one knew the deal was going down. When they refused CJ the light, Moe pulled out a gun and said you already know what time it is, don't make this no murder scene. He thought about the 56 thousand he had in his book bag. He was about to lose a three kilo deal, probably his life too, because they know he'll hunt them down and kill him. He smiled and threw the book bag at Moe, pulled his 380 out and shot Moe. CJ and Vic backed up. He unloaded the clip at them. They started running. He took the clip out, put it in his pocket, reloaded and started shooting again. Vic didn't have enough time to close the trunk, so he picked the book bag up, grabbed the dope out the trunk and ran down McPherson Ave to the corner store. He jumped in his white '98 Oldsmobile with the deep-dish gold Dayton rims. He turned his wood grain steering wheel and slapped the car in reverse. The sound of Eightball and MJG's *"Coming out hard"* thumped as he sped down McPherson Ave again, turned left on Maynard Terrace and then turned on to the expressway. He headed west on I-20, towards his apartment in Grady Homes.

"Anyway, my heart dropped when I seen you, being put in that police car."

He interrupted her, "Lady, what do you want from me? I'm not your type. I'm a ghetto nigga. You're supposed to be chasing an Uncle Tom with a future, not me. This is my future in and out of shit like this. That's why I told you, you're not my race, because I'll only fuck up your life. So why don't you be on your merry way, because you being here ain't making my situation no better. You ain't making me happy because you're coming to see me. This ain't gonna make me like you because you're down here."

She slammed the phone against the window and started to get up, but something pulled her back down.

"Dammit Nigga! You act like you're the only one in this damn world and the whole world is against you. If you stop being hard on me you'll see I came down here to help you if you'll just listen and give me a chance to explain myself. At least me being down here should mean something to you. Do this mean anything to you?"

"Can you get this through your thick ass skull? I don't fucking like you! I don't need your help! I've been on my own my whole damn life. I don't have no family. I've been getting in and out of trouble on my own. I haven't had no help. It's not meant for me to have any help. My parents died when I was two. You know what the sad part about it is? I don't know why God let 'em die. So why should I care whether you're down here or not? See I'm a street nigga and bad shit happens to street niggas. We always come up with something new. So I wish you'll leave so I can figure out a way to get myself out of here."

She smiled because she knew he needed someone to listen to him and she just learned a little about him: he was alone.

"Juan, listen. I am your way out of here. My grandfather may be the judge you go in front of. I told him that we were together last night. So he's gonna try to help you. I'ma bail you out soon as they set bail for you. I know now that hardroll is just a cap, a wall to keep people out. You're used to one night stands and being alone. I don't see nobody else coming down here to your aid. You had to be happy to see me because if you wasn't you would've been got up and left. You just wanted to let some of that anger out."

He thought about what she said. It made sense. He didn't give her enough time to explain why she was down there. He couldn't tell her he was sorry because her plan might not work. He smiled at her and said, "You're right. I didn't give you a chance and I'm sorry. You need to stick around because I'll be going to court in a few hours, or you can go tell your story to the detective. Hey! Why are you helping me after I dissed you?"

"I'm gonna leave now and go talk to someone. When I come back on your next visit try to be a little nicer. While I'm gone think about what's happening to us, a relationship."

He smiled and thought to himself, she's trying to blackmail me into a relationship. This bitch is psycho. But he knew he had to play it cool to get her story.

"Yeah! Yeah! Shawty us a relationship, go on and handle business and we can be together when I get out or write each other till I get out. One way or another it will be an us. By the way Shawty, what's your name?! I forgot."

"Natasha Middle. I'll be back in an hour."

He smiled and looked at her when she stood. She was fitting those jeans and you could see her black bra through the white t-shirt. She was cute and fine. He just didn't know why she was chasing him. He hit the window with the phone. She turned around and looked. He put his left hand on the glass. She put hers on the glass, also kissed her two right fingers and put 'em to the glass. He did the same. She smiled as she walked away to find the detective that was handling his case. She was smiling because they were finally seeing eye to eye. She knew she had to do everything she could to make things right. She was winning the fight. She walked into the homicide unit and asked a tall slim white male who was the detective handling the Juan Ellis case. He pointed at the heavy built black detective named Tim Jones. He was walking toward them, so she stepped in his path and stopped him. She introduced herself and got straight to the point.

"How can you prove that he was with you around 11:30 last night Ms. Middle?"

"My grandfather sir, he's Judge Harold Middle, he'll prove to you that he was with me last night. Do you want me to call him?"

"Yes!"

With no hesitation she called and handed him the phone as it rang.

"Hello, Harold Middle here."

"Hello Judge Middle, Detective Jones. I'm sorry to bother you at home but your granddaughter is down here giving a statement about her boyfriend Juan Ellis and she said you can verify that he was with her last night."

"Well last night around 11 I saw her let him in through the back door. I wanted to say something. Then I thought about it. It's Friday night, she turns 18 in the morning, so I let it be. She's a grown lady after 12. We can't tell her what to do anymore. You know how that goes detective. Now what time he left I can't say because I went to bed and when I woke up this morning she was screaming and hollering. That's all I can say because that's all I know, Mr. Jones. I hope I've been some sort of help to you."

"Thank you sir, you've been very helpful to us." He hung up, with a smile on his face. Her eyes widened in anticipation.

"Natasha, your grandfather's story ran jammed up with yours. We have no choice but to let 'em go because he wouldn't make no statement. I'll have him down in a few minutes."

As he walked out, she went to the pay phone outside of homicide by the elevator and called her granddaddy.

"Granddaddy you did it! You did it! How did you know what to say?"

"I just took your words, checked things out and put them in my own words. Remember, I wasn't always a judge."

"Thank you granddaddy. You're the best."
As she hung up and started to turn around he ran up to her and kissed her. She was so happy it was their first kiss.

"Now that's what I'm talking about. Stand by your man till the end. You pulled it off. Let's ease up out of here."

"Okay." She replied with a big smile on her face. As they walked off they were hand and hand swinging their arms. Soon as they reached the parking lot he let her hand go.

"Okay Natasha, I owe you one."

"But where are you going?"

"I got things to handle. I'll call you, okay?"

"How can you call me when you don't even have my number?"

"I said I'll call you."

She watched him walk away with tears in her eyes; her plan hadn't worked at all. She got in the car feeling used, cranked it and drove off. The music didn't even matter to her. She couldn't believe a person could be so heartless. Then she remembered what he said, "You being down here ain't gonna make me like you." She didn't even notice that she was speeding, driving dangerous through lanes. But she made it home safely. As she walked through the door, her mom told her she had a phone call.

"Who was it?" She asked who it was again, not giving her mom time to answer. Really not even caring; she had her head down walking through the living room.

"I don't know, he didn't say much. All he said was he'll call back later." Then she said, almost passing her momma, "If I'm sleep wake me up."

Nancy pulled her brown dress to her knees and reached out to her.

"Come on baby and tell momma what's the matter."

She sat on the sofa next to her and put her face in her lap and started crying.

"I got played."

"Baby what's going on? Daddy called talking about that boy Juan. Something about him being arrested for murder and you saying he couldn't have done it because you let him through the back door last night? Baby what is it about that boy? Why are you so caught up in that boy? Don't drive yourself crazy about that boy. I thought you go with Eric, he seems to really like and love you."

She looked up at her and said, "Momma, he just want to have sex, I'm not ready to have sex just yet. I want to get married. That's how I'll know it's special. So if a man marries me, then he'll get the goods; until then, its mine to keep."

Her mom laughed and said, "Let me get to your time and age. Girl its' 93, you're 18 years old, you better wake up. Okay, let's just say Juan comes along; start kicking it with you and he tries you?"

"Even though I love that boy, I'll tell 'em the same thang: No sex!"

"And he'll tell you 'No Juan.' You can't expect that boy to drop his lifestyle for you. He's not gonna do it! He's not! Baby, you've been behind that boy too long now! Leave him alone because if he see you're after him, which a blind man can see, you're gonna lose. You're gonna lose your belief because your need and want gonna over take your better judgment. Besides you're a white girl to him. You're not his race, remember?"

"That's not what he meant. I'm not ghetto; Hold up mom, the phone is ringing." She looked at the caller ID and said, "It's not him its Eric."

"Hello Eric!"

"How you doing Tasha? Listen, we've been together for 18 months and I feel like we're getting nowhere. I don't understand you or know what else to do to prove my love for you."

"So you're saying you want to break up?"

"Yes. It's not that I don't love you or anything."

"I know! I know! I know!" She looked at her mom and came bold with her next statement.

"Yeah I kinda figured you'll be breaking up with me because we haven't had sex. You feel like you've done all you could but it's not good enough. I don't see nothing wrong with this. Goodbye Eric, good luck with your new girlfriend." She hung the phone up; turned to face her mom, put her hands on her hips with a big smile. Nancy dropped her head because she knew she was gonna get the 'I told you so!'"

"Like I said, he was about sex; I can see through people like that. I'm going to lie down if he calls wake me up." He never called. It was like he didn't even care about her getting him out. He didn't have feeling for anyone but himself. Now it was Nancy's turn to give the 'I told you so' look after seeing her baby walk around with her head down. She walked in her room. Natasha was laying in the dark at the foot of the bed and her momma sat down and rubbed her on the back.

"I hate to say I told you so. But I told you so. It's been three days and that boy ain't the least bit concerned about you."

"Yeah mom I finally understand, he don't like me he's all about himself. Here it is 11:30 pm and that phone hasn't rung and said 'Hello this is Juan.'"

"And it ain't! So I trust now that it's over?"

"Momma! He can't call he don't have the number. I just got played and tricked myself." A rock hit the window. They looked at each other, wondering who'll be throwing rocks this time of night."

"Tasha."

"Momma, you heard that?"

"Heard what?"

"Tasha!"

"Heard that!"

"Tasha… Tasha!"

"Baby it's coming from outdoors. Look out the window and see who it is."

"Don't walk away, here I come! Juan hold up, here I come. It's him!" She took off running down the steps with her nightgown on.

"Tasha! Tasha! I know you hear me, don't go out there with no clothes on. Girl, put something over that gown. Tasha you hear me? Your daddy will shoot me and you both if he pull up and see you half dressed. Tasha!" Nancy ran down the hall and steps behind her but Tasha wasn't listening. She was running to her love. When she swung the door open, she was surprised to see him sitting on the step.

"Why didn't you call me?"

"It wasn't right to call you."

"What do you mean it wasn't right?" She had one hand on her hip waiting for an answer. He looked up at her red gown, nice tits standing out and answered, "You didn't call me; you came face to face, so I had to face you."

"Well, thank you very much. Juan I like you. As a matter of fact I'm in love with you. I just want to show you realness. I know you don't have a family and no one loves you. But that don't give you a reason to dog me out. You're like scrooge; all to yourself."

"Shawty I'm not rich, so I can't be like him."

"You're rich in love, in your heart and you don't want nobody to share your wealth, to share you. There's more to life than selling drugs and one night stands. Life is love and love is life."

"So now you're a philosopher. Allow me to enlighten you on life. Life is like a boarded slave ship, people bowing down to satisfy God, to make it to paradise. But we here have to satisfy ourselves because everybody who's praying for Heaven ain't going so I live life as is."

"And what's that?"

"Hell! Were in hell already; drugs, robbery and murder, sin in general. So tell me what's in your heart? And where do you stay in your heart?"

"You and I want to stay in yours!"

"Is that right?"

"Juan stop being hard on me, just accept me for who I am!"

"And who are you?"

"I am Natasha Middle. I'm 18. I start college in 3 months. I'm gonna be a lawyer. Juan I'm a good girl who only want to be happy. I want to make you happy. I want to get to know your heart. Please accept me. I'm a Christian and I believe in prayer. To show you God hears us every night, I pray for you and my prayers have been answered because you're sitting here with me now. I love you Juan, I love you because I know there's something more to you than this." They sat there in each other arms in silence. She turned to kiss him.

"Shawty, don't. I'll only hurt you. Let me be your friend."

"Well let me worry about that." She didn't want to open them up to an argument about love and his concept about him being bad for her. She kissed him to respond; he responded harder. Tears rolled down her eyes. She didn't want to open them. This was like a dream come true, a vision in the darkest night. She had done it. Won his heart in hope of the small time they now shared.

"Juan, do you want to meet my mom?"

"It's late my Shawty; I'll catch up with her at another time. Right now Shawty you belong in the house. It's late and your chest is open. So ease on in the house and call me in the morning. Here are my numbers; my home phone and cell." He handed her a piece of paper from his pocket.

"Take care of my home."

"Okay."

He left. She ran in the house screaming and jumping.

"Momma I did it! Momma I did it. He's mine. I won his heart over. I beat him! I won!"

"I see! I see! He sounds very smart from what I heard. Now it's up to you to strengthen the both of y'all. Only you can make it work. Maybe

God is using you to strengthen and mold him."

"I will momma! When is daddy due in?"

"Tomorrow!"

"I'm gonna tell him to help Juan get a job. Momma, he don't have no family so help me reach him."

"I will baby. This may be a blessing for us all."

As she prepared for bed, she asked the Lord what to do. Not to her understanding her heart told her to give her all to him. She smiled and closed her eyes.

CHAPTER 2
The Fall Out

"**L**ook at my little princess. Wake up baby girl, Daddy's home!" She looked up hugged him and said, "Daddy what time is it?"

He was sitting on the right side of the bed with a blue and white Tommy shirt on and Nancy was standing smiling with a white sundress on.

"10:30. Why?"

"I got to make a phone call."

"You're not happy to see Mr. Richard Middle, your daddy?"

"Don't be silly, I'm always happy to see you return from a hard day's work."

"But princess, I've been gone for two weeks. It's alot I got to tell you and give you for your birthday." He handed her a 20 inch herring bone necklace with a gold cross with 5 diamonds on it around the edges and one in the middle. She smiled, hugged him, kissed him on the left cheek, widened her eyes and said, "Thank you daddy!"

"Now let me tell you about the case. It was 20 million dollars insurance."

"Hold up daddy, not now, I got to make this phone call."

"Can't it wait?"

"Richard, your baby girl isn't interested in hearing about cases no more. She got a thug in her life."

"Eric is a thug? Why I thought he was okay and had a bright future."

"No! Not Eric, Eric is no more, they broke up yesterday. She finally got Juan in her life." He looked at her with a look of betrayal. She was sitting up with the cover over her lap. Her head leaning against the head rest. Then he turned and looked at Nancy standing at the end of the bed. He stood away from the bed, looked at both of them in disgust. He hated that boy. He tried to be polite when he spoke because she was grown now, but he couldn't.

"Hell no! I won't go for this. That boy ain't nothing but trouble. Riding up and down the street playing that loud music, selling drugs in the projects. You think I don't know about that boy. Nancy, I told you a long time ago that we should've moved to keep her from guys like that. But no! You didn't want to sell this house. 'My momma left me this house and this is where I want to stay.' Look at what this house has gotten us now, our daughter is in love with a no good ass thug who ain't got no future, will probably distract her from going to school, trick her, get her pregnant and leave her. HELL NO! I won't go for this! I thought he hated you anyway!"

He was boiling and she knew it. She just slid down and put the cover over her head. Nancy broke the silence.

"He did hate her until she and your father got him off a murder charge."

"Got him off a what! Princess I'm gonna ask you one time, what is it about that boy?"

"I love him daddy."

"You love him?! You don't even know him."

"My heart knows him." She took her head from under the cover and grabbed the phone. She dialed the number he had given her.

"Who are you calling?"

"I'm calling him so please be quiet. I'm 18. I can date who I want to. Daddy, just believe in me, believe in my judgment and help me make him realize love is real. Will you help me?" It took all he had to say yes to her, but he did. She was his only child and he'd do anything to make her happy. Plus he knew he couldn't stop her. All she'd do is sneak around with him or probably move out.

"Hello Juan. It's me."

"Me who?"

"Tasha."

"Shawty, don't you know you're not the only one who calls this house. Beside I don't know your phone voice. What time is it?"

"It's 11 o'clock... Juan? Juan? I don't believe this, he hung up. Don't y'all say nothing."

"Why are you calling him back?" Richard asked.

"I'm fix 'en to give him a piece of my mind. Hello Juan? What in the hell is wrong with you? Listen, I'm not weak and I'm tired of you playing me for weak. I'm a human and I have a fucking heart. I'm not fix 'en to kiss your ass just for you to talk to me. I've went down this road for 2 years.

"Slow down love. Not so fast. I feel what you're saying but you're handling me. You act like the phone can't hang up on its own. I rolled over and it hung up. I like the buck you have but you need to use it when the time is useful. Now meet me at Five Points train station in an hour. Park your car. We're gonna ride the bus and train for the day. You down with that?"

"What do you want me to wear?"

"Whatever fits the weather. It's supposed to be hot. So wear something light. Oh, when is your birthday?"

"My birthday was four days ago. The day I got you out."

"May 12th. Well happy belated birthday. My birthday is September 26th."

"Bye Juan. I'll see you at 12."

"Now see Tasha, it wasn't what you think; you got to give people a chance." He said it not really meaning it, only to show his approval.

"That's the same thang I'm telling you daddy."

She jumped up, ran to the bathroom to run some water in the tub. She thought about what would be the topic of their day. She rushed through her bath, cleaned the tub and went to the mirror, to work on her appearance. Her hair was thrown back in a ponytail. She put on some clear lip gloss and a little blush and walked to her closet flipping through outfits. Once she saw that she couldn't decide, she stopped and called him.

"Juan, what are you wearing today?"

"Some black Levi shorts, a black polo shirt and some black Pumas. Why? What's up?"

"I don't know what to wear."

"Just wear something white or black. I told you we're gonna take some pictures. I think this will be a good time to go shopping so bring some money with you. You should be walking out the door because you don't have long. I can walk downtown from where I stay."

"And where's that?"

"Grady Homes on Hilliard Street apartment 271. So get going I'm leaving out now."

"I'm dressed and I'll meet you at the Foot Locker in the underground. I love you Juan."

She looked in the mirror one last time, looking at the black polo shirt, with the white polo horse, black Gap shorts and black Nike Air. Smiling at her look, she walked out of her room to her mom and asked her how she looked. Nancy gave her the go ahead nod. She went back in her room got her ID and grabbed $300 dollars from her night stand. She ran out of the house and cut through the church yard to McPherson Ave. As she was going across the street, the 7 McAffe was pulling up. She got on the bus paid the $1.25 and sat in the front seat. She thought to herself. If she would've missed the bus, she would've walked to Moreland and caught the 107-48- or 9 to the train station. It seemed like it took forever getting to Inman Park Reynoldstown train station, it was 16 blocks away, but it seemed like 30. She ran up the stairs into the station, ran down the Westbound steps and made it to the train. She was almost there, only 20 minutes away from their first date. *"Five Point."* A man's voice came over the speaker. She was there, she walked up the steps took a right through the ticket gate. When she got outside the station she bought a Coke and a honey bun from the Jamaican stand that sat right in front of the station. She walked across the street to the top of the Underground. People was standing there either waiting on the bus or just enjoying the sight. It was a light skinned brother with a red silk outfit on, with red leather sandals saying, "My pimping is great; my pimping is pimping in all 50 states. Come join my stable. I don't care if you're in perfect health or disabled because all it takes to make money is your back when you're handicapped. You'll sell your soul to join this stable like that. I'll take a bitch from rags to riches all you got to do is listen to this pimping."

He clapped his hands and said now look what I got. About 10 females came from nowhere wearing red silk dresses. She laughed and walked on down the steps. As she entered the underground she saw him already waiting in front of the Foot Locker. She couldn't believe how fast she noticed him. "I guess you can say he's a standout," she thought to herself. When she walked up to him she kissed him and asked him "How did he know to wear his hair in a ponytail?"

"I didn't! It's time to get it fixed. I'm gonna get it fixed tomorrow."

"Who's gonna do it?"

"Cloe!"

"Cloe? Who's she?"

"She works at George Pultman Hair Care, on Flat Shoals up the street from you."

"Well I'll fix it myself."

"Shawty I'm not fix 'en to let you experiment with my hair."

"I can do hair; I do it on the side. That's gonna be my under major."

"Yeah! Let's shop. I got you though."

They walked in the Foot Locker and picked out a pair of shoes for each other. He got her some white Reebok Classic and a pair of black and blue Reebok flip-flops. She got him some all white Fila's and some blue, red and white Fila's flip-flops. They walked through the Underground laughing and holding hands. It was pure happiness going in and out of clothing stores. Buying a little here and a little there, time flew by.

"Juan it's 6:30 and I'm hungry."

"What do you have in store for your stomach?"

As they walked through the upstairs of the Underground she spotted the Subway shop.

"I got a taste for Subway."

They walked in the tiny Subway space. It wasn't like the regular Subways. It was like a little hut that you see on the beach. It was green with little green chairs and table; 5 huts over the small balcony. They walked over to the counter and she ordered a roast beef, ham and white cheese, with lettuce, tomato, green pepper and ranch dressing, some sour cream and onion chips with a large orange Slice drink. He ordered a chicken soup, hot chips and a large grape soda. They ate at the end table that sat next to the guard rail. They could see the top of the street and people coming into the Underground. They talked, learning a great deal about each other. What they wanted out of life. She wanted to be a big time lawyer, a wife and mother of three, all girls. He wanted to have a family and not to struggle. They enjoyed each other honesty. Then afterward they walked out of the Underground to the top of Five Points to take some pictures. They took six pictures for $25, her sitting in his lap on one side of the picture on the other two standing kissing. Each picture had two poses. He paid for them. The pictures were so sweet because on the last one they laid a blanket. On one pose she was laying on top of him kissing him. On the other one, he was on top of her with his right hand on her right breast and his lips on her bare stomach. It was an argument over that picture. So he started to tear it up, but she took it and ran with it. He chased her around the top of Five Point onto the sidewalk. It was so much fun running from him and chasing her. She stopped and put it down her shirt.

"It's mine for life; I keep all my valuable things in here."

"Like what your tits and now my picture?"

"You got that right. So where to now?"

"You can walk me home and I'll walk you to the King Memorial station or drive you home."

"Yeah! I want to see how you live anyway. I bet you dress nice but have a nasty apartment, like most single men."

"Shawty ain't nothing nasty about Juan!"

They walked, ran from each other. It was joy all around. Even the evening air was just right. They finally reached his apartment.

"Hold up Juan, before we go in there I'm a virgin and I don't believe in unmarried sex."

"So I never asked you for sex. I just asked you to walk me home. But it's nice to know where you stand. Now welcome to my home."

She stood on the left side of him as he starts turning the key. When the door open she ran inside and said, "I told you it was nasty in here."

He walked in behind her laughing. He closed the door and it was dark again. He had blinds on the two windows that sat by the door. He reached for the light switch by the doorknob. When the lights came on she said,

"WOW! Juan it's beautiful in here. Your kitchen looks like a TV commercial, it's so clean. Now I like the glass table set. What made you buy this?"

The kitchen had a woman touch. When he got the apartment, he was going with an older woman, so she was the one to pick out everything. The glass table set was placed in the middle of the floor, along with the four chairs; one at the head of the table, two on the side and the other one at the foot of the table. The microwave that sat on the counter next to the stove along with the dish rack, the glasses, plates, forks, silver and gold spoons. The Pots and pans were hung on the left wall. The refrigerator was at the back wall next to the exit and entrance. The tiled floor had a pine scent glow and smile that filled the whole kitchen.

"I know you don't eat here much."

She opened the fridge and was amazed to see real food in it. She thought she was gonna find junk food: hamburgers, hot dogs, ham and so on. But she found some veggies, fruit, eggs, ham so on and so on.

"Come on show me the rest of the house, Juan I've never seen white laca before."

She couldn't believe his living room as they walked in it. The white lacer sofa and chair could be seen as soon as you turn out the kitchen. Passing the steps on the left of the small hallway she stopped in the entrance looking over the living room. The sofa sat in the middle of the floor the Sony entertainment system sat on the left side of the sofa, while four speakers sat in each corner, the two chairs sat in a curve to the sofa on the right side. At the entrance were two table sets with lamps on them. The table on the right had the remote. So he reached and turned on the CD player. Sade, *"Bullet Proof Soul"* came on, humming through the whole apartment. It was a two bedroom apartment. They went upstairs to the guest room which sat on the left at the top of the steps. The door was opened, it was very plain: bed, dresser, night stand and phone. Then he showed her his room that sat across from the guest room. The bed sat in the middle of the room with three dressers and a big mirror on the larger one; which sat on the main wall. Red and blue lights in the light sockets, a small nightstand sat by the bed with a naked lady lamp on it with a see through phone.

"How do you like my home?"

"It's very very nice."

She walked to the bed and sat on it.

"Be careful that's a waterbed."

"Ooh I didn't know. I guess you lay in style also."

She laid back on the bed letting the water comfort her. "Juan these are silk sheets. I didn't know they make these."

"You don't get around much. Let's go back downstairs."

"You're not gonna put your clothes up?"

"Tasha you're making this hard, I'm trying my best to respect you and your belief."

"What do you mean?"

"You're the first girl that ever been here, without getting fucked. So let's head downstairs."

"That's right I'm gonna be the first and the last."

He smiled and grabbed her around the waist. She looked into his eyes and seen his sincerity. She kissed him softly, but he responded hard, so hard her eyes couldn't open. There were too much passion; she wrapped her arms around his neck as he led her back to the bed slowly placing her on it. As her head fell gently on the bed the water rushed to relax her. He moved her closer and higher on the bed. He pulled her shirt from her shorts, ran his hand up her shirt and unbuttons her bra. Her mind told her no but her body told her yes. Confusion took over and she rode with it. He lifted her shirt from her body. The picture fell and he started kissing her stomach from her shirt line. Massaging her breast, he licked her navel line up to the breast. She moaned as he worked his way back down to her shorts. He unbuttoned them and eased them off, slowly kissing between her legs. He kissed her lake of fire through her panties and slowly removed them. She tried to open her eyes but couldn't. She tried to speak but couldn't. She tried to raise her arms but couldn't. She was helpless in the crime of passion. He kissed her inner thighs from left to right, slowly making his way to her fire. He kissed again and again, and then licked it very slow and very hard. She moaned out loud as he stuck his finger in the bottom of her cunt. Sucking on her spur tongue and open her wider with his fingers. Cum ran down his finger as her body shook, tears ran from her eyes. He eased out of his clothes while the anticipation was still there. She moaned his name; she looked up but couldn't see him. But she could feel him easing up and kissing her; grinding hard between her legs. He stopped and looked up at her.

"Are you ready?"

"Yes!"

He slowly enters the head of his dick in her, her eyes widen and she held him tight as he worked his way into her. She cried. She moaned his name once again, as her arms gave out on her, he was so gentle with her, stroking as slowly as he could. The warmth and tightness made him cum faster than usual.

"Please don't take it out let it stay in."

He laughed and kissed her as she moaned out "I can't believe what we just done. Kiss me and let me know this is real." He kissed her and received an erection. They made love all through the night. She woke up in his arms. She stared at him and kissed him. She made her way out of his arms, grabbed a pair of Fila shorts from his dresser and went to cook them breakfast: bacon, eggs, grits, toast and apple juice. Rambling through his cabinets she found a tray and loaded it. He was still on his side of the bed facing the place where she slept on the left. She sat back on the bed and told him to wake up. He just smiled and turned over. Then she leaned over and kissed him on the ear. Wanting to make love again she whispered in his ear "Wake up sleepy head, I made breakfast." He turned over and said, "You cook breakfast too? Praise God!"

They both laughed as they fed each other. Then she put the tray back on the night stand and laid back in his arms.

"When is your birthday Juan?"

"September 26."

"I noticed earlier you don't really believe in God. Why?"

"I believe in God. I'm just not all the way there. I'm unsure about alot of things. I believe in peace, but there's no peace. I believe in love, but love is blind. I believe in life, but we're slowly dying. I pray for power, but I'm only suffering. I pray for wisdom and understanding. Still I'm created in this struggle. I find peace in my heart to maintain, to make it to another day. I find strength to eat, not knowing I'm subject to die. I face fear every time I'm hungry. I face happiness now in my moment with you."

"Juan for a 17 year old you're smart as hell and deep. Why are you in the game, selling dope, robbing and killing all of that nature?"

"Haven't you heard of power? See if I can gain power, I can be like the great blacks that made a difference. My life is based upon a struggle, such life as shaker a born leader, a born king. Now ask yourself who do you believe in? I believe in myself to make a difference. See you, I want a seed from, I want my all to be in you. So my all I'm gonna give you. You're not a bitch in my eyes, you're trust."

With tears in her eyes she asked,

"How could you say that?"

"Your vagina tells me. You've carried it to yourself for so long and open yourself to me to prove love, trust and hope. In such matter I open my heart to you, to build something I've never known. Love."

"I promise to love only you. You're my king."

As time passed they were unstoppable her in her education and him in his crime life.

"What more in life than the happiness we share Natasha?" She smiled as they sat in his bedroom barely dressed. She knew he would be the man she'll marry. She spent most of her time at his apartment, working as her father's assistant and going to school. She thought about her first year with him as she laid in his arms.

"You know it's been almost a year, no let's say a year because we're only a month away. I'm very surprised with you. No cheating, coming home at a reasonable time, you have shown me love Mr. Juan Ellis." But he didn't know how to wake up from the game.

"It's 1994, I have enough money saved up. It's time to retire and dedicate my life to Natasha, go to school and make something out of myself." He smiled because he was finally waking up. Then he said to himself, nall a little more money to be sure. You never know when my seed will come to life. A quarter million ain't much money. He didn't realize he was speaking out until she pouted and rolled over.

As she enrolled in Morris Brown College, she felt her heart skip a beat. She felt like she was leaving him all to himself.

"It's just a job" she thought to herself. "No I'll be the night, I'm gonna leave school and come back when I know he's truly in love with me. Naw he'll get mad because he need this in his lifestyle, I'm his ace in the hole. I wonder if that's his only reason for being with me because my grandfather is a judge and I'll be a lawyer soon. This is his way of gaining power." She sat up in her bed, it didn't feel right. She was alone. In a 3 bedroom apartment with 2 white girls who she barely spoke to. She couldn't take it any longer. The more she thought the madder she got. She thought about when he said "She wasn't his race." She picked up the phone dialed his number. She wasn't afraid to speak her mind to him. But this will be coming from her heart.

"Hello Juan, don't speak just listen."

Tears started to fall because she truly wanted to hang up.

"Okay I'm listening. What are you crying for; I can hear your tears through your breathing. Are you alright? Have any one of them niggas said anything to you out the way? Let me know and I'll come and handle the matter right now!"

She cut him off, the more he talked, she wouldn't be able to tell him what she wanted him to hear. Her heart had to be heard."

"Listen, I been sitting here doing some thinking. How do I know you haven't been using me to gain this power you're always talking about? This power that got you so excited? How do I know you won't change, now that I'll be gone 24 hours 7 days a week. Baby please help me build my confidence. I'm scared."

"You know baby and I've been waiting on this phone call for 3 weeks now, ever since they told you it's best for you to stay on campus, you're acting like you're thousands and thousands of miles away from me. You're only 30 minutes you can come home at will. The only answer I can give you is to follow your heart. Your heart never tells you wrong."

"Do you want me to follow my heart Juan?"

"Yes! Your heart knows best."

Her cries were even harder with that answer. She took in a deep breath and let it run out.

"My heart tells me this is a game you're playing a power move. I think it's best we give each other some space and enough time to think."

"Tasha I said believe in your heart, not in your fears. We've come too far for your heart to talk like that. Search yourself."

"Juan my heart has spoken."

"How do you know?"

"Because my tears are falling like rain, Black rain that stains the heart. Baby I can't breathe bye."

She hung up the phone and fell to her knees.

"God tell me I just done the right thing."

As she cried she heard a voice within her say "I can't make a man love you. Only he can. That's free will and you know his will was free.

CHAPTER 3
Juan

I can't believe this shit, the bitch only been on campus for 3 weeks and has went the other way. I can't trip it, because I knew I couldn't give my all to a sweet talking bitch. My life is dedicated to the streets. I'll never speak to the bitch again. She walked out on me because of fear." He picked the phone up and called Ike, his right hand man.

"Ike this is your boy. It's time to make power moves, I mean, I want to take over Atlanta."

"Juan you're not strong enough to take over this city. You're a nickel and dime pusher to these people. You might got about a quarter million saved up, that's nothing to these people. Just because you're on top of bricks, don't make you strong enough to take over the whole city, not even a third."

"It's enough to make me known!"

"You're already known; where's Natasha, because you're trying to commit suicide?"

"She's no more!"

"This is your reaction, my guy, you're thinking out of hurt. You're 18 years old and you're hurt."

"I'm not hurt. Just because you're 23, you're a love doctor. This city hasn't seen hurt! You're either gonna roll with me or get rolled over!"

"My guy you know I'm down with whatever."

"Okay here's the plan. We disconnect all the telephones and beepers. Sell all the cars and move into hotels."

"Man you're trying to hide from her."

"It's not about her. I don't want nobody having a trace on us. Mothafucka fix 'en to die!"

"So how are we gonna get around?"

"Rental cars for now. It's like we'll be off the face of this earth."

"And when is this going down?"

"It's already going down. Meet me at the Executive Inn on Memorial Drive. Take your cars to the lot and sell them for eight grand apiece. That will give you 24 grand."

"Man I'm not fix 'en to sell my shit for 8 grand. I got a 91 BMW in perfect condition a 92 Caddy in perfect condition and an 86 Chevy in top condition. Man I got to get 15 or better."

"Cool Ike, all I'm saying 6 is the lowest you'll go. But I'm fix 'en to give this Benz up for 10 and this Cutlass up for 3,500. Leave this apartment as is. Okay Ike its show time!"

He phoned AT&T and disconnected everything, got the lights turned off and got his keys left them with the manager. He walked to Bell Street and asked everybody that stood on the corner did they want to buy the Cutlass for 3,500. A young dealer by the name Twon bought it. He jumped in the Benz and drove to Henderson dealership outside of College Park. The dealer looked at the sky blue Benz and said,

"Um this is a 93 with 20 inch rims a nice system. I'll give you 15,000 for it."

He traded to the slim black male in his early 40s and left from there. He took the 91 Shannon Mall bus to Ed rental. There he got a white five, point and drove to the hotel, checked in room 267 and waited out front for Ike to pull up or walk up. 15 minute after Ike was getting off the 121 Memorial Dr. bus. Ike waved at him as he walked to him. Ike stood 6'2" 180 pounds no fat all muscles. Ike was a work out freak. He does 1000 pushup sets. He wore waves always wore Nike outfits and Air Jordan shoes. He was a pretty boy. He wore hazel brown contacts instead of his glasses. Ike was the type of nigga you'll love to have on your team because he's a shoot first and ask questions later. When he reached him Juan was surprised because he didn't have on his Nike outfit or shoes. He had on a black Dickies suit with some black high-tech boots. They got in the car and he asked him how much he came up with. Ike smiled and told him 36,000 plus he brought 50,000 with him. He smiled because together they had over 300,000 they discussed how much money they were gonna spend. They called Lil Gerald and asked him how much his birds were running for in a lump sum. Gerald told them he'll give them a bird for 15,000 apiece. So they told him they wanted 20 plus the 5 he had been promising them. They set their meeting up at East Lake Meadows Park because alot of people be out on Saturdays playing ball around that time 4:30 pm. Gerald told 'em to meet him in the park in 20 minutes. He left the car, ran in, got his money and put the rest inside the mattress. He tore a hole in the side of it and stuffed the money. Walked back to the car and drove down Memorial Dr. While he was driving, Ike was putting the money in a black book bag that he had brought with him. The rest of his money he put in his T-shirt. It took them 5 minutes to get to the park from the hotel. So when they got there, they sat in the parking lot watching everything in the park. There wasn't wood around the park because of the 4 way streets. It had 3 tennis courts that were never used; no one was there so that looked normal. Alot of swings, slides and monkey bars which was all being used by the kids; six basketball courts that had every Saturday's dealers on 'em gambling to impress the Hoes that stood on the sideline cheering. 2 big fields which had kids playing football on 'em, everything looked normal. Gerald pulled up in his green 1500 truck from the Second Ave corner at the front of the park. They were parked side by side when Ike threw the money in the truck. They counted it and threw a brown paper sack to Ike and pulled off. They didn't have to count it because they've been dealing with him for years. Plus they knew where Ms. Ann stayed, his mom. He was Ike's brother; Wicket's partner before Wicket died. When they got back to the hotel, it was 27 bricks in the bags. He had promised them he was gonna look out and he did. He was known for robbing big! Big! Time dealer and had a clique of killers with him. He asked them to join him when Wicket died because he promised to look out for them, once he had seen they wasn't no hoe and will shake something. They hooked up the hot plates and burners whipped up one brick and made it two using B-12 and combat. All together, they whipped up 52 bricks, chopped them down to 10 dollar breakdowns. They sacked up 2.5 million dollars of French Fries sized dimes. When they realized how much time they had spent, they laughed, because they started at 5 pm and it was 8 am the next day.

"Juan if we get off all this dope, boy we'll be so on that we can take over small parts of the city. Then our next re-up we can lock the bitch down."

"Ike you just don't get it. We'll never make it big by selling dimes. We're gonna sell dimes just this one time. Get up enough money and rob big dealers. Like Gerald. Okay! You take the east side and I'm gonna take the west."

"Juan we're still gonna have to make small sales."

"Then we do what it takes!"

He showered then Ike. While Ike showered he counted everything out equally money and dope. They grabbed the dope and put there Glocks in the front part of their pants. Ike had on the same black Dickies suit when he had on a blue Dickies suit with some blue and white Fila's low cut. He didn't know that Ike kept his house on Home Street. But he thought about it when Ike told him to give him his half of the money which was 60 thousand. He locked the door jumped in the 5.0. looking at Ike because he had a feeling Ike would turn on him because neither one of them had ever seen that much money. Then he asked for his half of the money. He tried not to think of it, but it was eating him up, He pulled off and dropped Ike off at Hertz car rental and left. Ike pulled out the entrance in a green Honda followed him to BellSouth and got their phone. Ike was kind a puzzled because he didn't say nothing. He just handed him the phone and drove off. Ike called him and asked him what was up? He just told him I'm serious about this paper. He took the west side off of MLK Blvd to the Boatrock apartment off Boatrock road. Trapping from the 5.O. junkies got to know him fast by the name of "Cash." He phoned Ike 5 hours later and asked him how the East side was doing.

"Boy I got a million dollar trap out here in Scottsdale some apartment called Oak Forest. Toby Grant and Haystack in Clarkston, they know me as "Lil Larry." Business is good out here. I stay in one spot for 30 minute, hit the other two when I get back to my first spot I got a line at the mail box. I'm doing my thing how about you?"

"Cash is the name and I'm on the rise, I trap like you but make house calls. I gave some junkies my number and $10 told them to hit me up when they get enough customers no less than 500."

Days flew by as they trapped; they hardly had time to talk. All they conversed about was re-up. They flipped their first batch in 4 days, met back up at the hotel, took the money and put it in a storage off of Tucker Rd. in Tucker GA. Went back to Gerald and got a 100 bricks same location same process. They whipped up 5 million in French fries. Took the dope to the storage and went back out with the 2.5 apiece like the first time. Each time one wanted to re-up they had to call each other and let them know what time it was. 2 weeks went by this time before they re-upped. They both went by the hotel showered, got dressed in the clothes they had bought for the week. They sat in the room cooking up 100 bricks. Ike looked puzzled but he didn't say much. He asked him how things were going.

Ike replied, "Well. Let's just get this shit cooked up and get back."

It took 5 days for them to cook it all up and chop it up. It was rest that they needed. Ike looked like his normal when they got up. When they got in their cars to go to the storage he noticed that a black car followed Ike. So he called him and told him not to go to the storage because he was being followed. He shot up the exit while Ike parked on the side of the expressway. He told Ike to run in the woods and meet him on top of the street. Ike did it and called Hertz and told 'em the car broke down. He looked at Ike and asked him with a straight face what was going on. He only replied,

"Nothing... nigga's tried to pull a caper."

He just looked at Ike and smiled and told him,

"Some shady shit is going down. Here's a rental car business goes and get another car stop by Hertz and pay for the car. Don't go to the storage. Let me move the money first."

Ike walked into McFurgo and got a black 5.O. He watched Ike as he pulled off and followed him to Haystack apartment. As he followed him he thought about that he hasn't had sex in weeks. He thought about Tasha and then quickly changed his mind. He sat there and looked at the apartments surroundings and said, "Ain't no way in the hell this shit is trapping the way he say it is."

He drove through Toby Grant they were some white brick apartments that sat in circles, then he drove to Oak Forest they were only one way in and one way out. You had to go up a hill to enter the apartment they sat in rows on both sides. When you go to the top of the hill the parking lot was a horse shoe. Still he couldn't see all the money Ike was making. So he drove all over that area. He went through Dekalb Limit, North Decatur Manor, Willow Trace, Carriage Oaks One and Two and Montreal Woods. Still he didn't see the picture Ike drew up. So he got on the expressway on the Clarkston exit and went 20 East. He called Ike and a female answered the phone.

"What up?" her soft voice rung through the receiver.

"Yeah let me speak with Larry."

"Hello."

"Man you ain't got time for no slick bitch, I just rode through your whole set. Ike I just don't see your big picture. Shawty I got an uneasy feeling. What's going on? And who's the bitch?"

"Chill, my guy, she bailed me out."

"Why didn't you tell me you're hot? Change location now."

"Everything is okay I need someone to watch out for big daddy,"

"I know you haven't moved nothing yet, don't sell shit. I want you to relocate to East Point, College Park, Riverdale, West End, Thomasville, Mechanicville, Summer Hill and Fairburn. I got hoes in all these places to start up trap. That's how I get off most of my blow. I'm moving everything from the storage to another storage down Memorial Drive. But don't come to the storage on Memorial Dr. We'll keep this one and I'll just drop dope and money off over here and store it over there. Just ditch the bitch for me. I just don't want no hoe in our business."

He hung up went to the storage, and got all the money and dope. The money was in green trash bags and the dope was in black bags. He wondered how in the hell was they gonna launder 20 million in cash. He drove out the entrance he always goes out; the first entrance. He could see the second entrance because they were on the same road. The only difference was one were a right turn and the other one were a left turn. It depended on which way you came on the street, north or south. As he drove off he saw the same black box Chevy with deep dish Dayton rims. He phoned Ike and told him that he was a mark man and gone make the move to Marietta. But he insisted that everything was cool because they had plenty of chances to hit him. He told him he was paranoid about the white girl Lisa. He assured him that she was cool because she was sucking his dick as they spoke. They both laughed and he said alright you know what you're doing.

Ike didn't worry much about Juan fear because he knew what he was doing. It's mighty hard for the folks to get him. Plus an undercover wouldn't be doing the shit she was doing. They open up trap at 10 pm. Lisa had a red Ford Tempo. He told her to take care of business over here because he had a new trap to look at. He left her with 2,000 dimes and left. As he rode he watched through his rearview mirror to see was he being followed. Then he turned round to check up on Lisa. To see was she a good hustler like she appeared, he drove back to the apartment her Tempo was gone, so he rode through Toby Grant and just like he thought, she was taking care of business. He called him and asked him was he still on Memorial Dr. He told him he just put everything in the storage at Acron. Ike asked him to drive over to Toby Grant and watch Lisa in action. He told him she was in a red Tempo and that he was on his way to Marietta to start a trap in Loveyville apartment.

Juan rode through Toby Grant and seen Lisa serving on Toby Circle. He smiled because the white girl was doing her thing. She had two black guys watching over here. He seen her give them some money and they just stood there with their guns out. He watched her serve for about 10 minute and left. Even though he had seen her in action he still didn't feel right about her. Maybe Tasha had fucked him he thought to himself then he smiled, dropped the dope off in his traps. He had Tara in East Point off Station Rd. Tara is a 10 on any nigga scale; a red bone, 5'7" and 145 pounds with sandy brown long hair and hazel brown eyes. He met her in Magic City Strip Club. She had got into it with a man she was table dancing for. He didn't want to pay her all her money. So he stepped up to her and paid her the money. He knocked her off time to time. Always promised her he'll take her out the club. So when they started their takeover, he went to her with a 70/30 deal. She couldn't turn it down once she seen the size of the work. She always cut a piece of the tip of every sack to make extra money. He knew about it, just didn't care. She turned him on to her cousin Oliva, she came from Dublin GA when she was 12 and moved to College Park to better herself and schooling. She stayed in the Old English apartments. She stood 5 feet flat 130 pound brown eyes short black hair. She needed help she was 24 and on her own. So he gave her the same deal. He gave all his girls the same deal. He told 'em he had someone watching them. But he really didn't. He'll pull up and pay somebody $10 to tell him how things been going.

He made all his drops and went to MLK Boulevard where he trapped in Fairburn Village. Days went by as he trapped he stopped worrying about Ike because Ike was his own man. He really had fallen into a mode of not caring. Ike called him and told him that everything was fine and he needed re-up. He told Ike to take the money and put the money in a trash bag and take it to the dumpster before he could continue.

Ike stopped him and told him he was in Marietta and he hasn't checked on Lisa in 3 days. So he told him to drop the money in a trash bag and put it by the first herbie curbie at the end of the street. He told him to call Lisa and get that money. He'll make the drop at the top of the street. He did everything in order, but he was mad when he turned up Edward Street and seen Lisa and Ike standing on the corner. He just rode up the street dropped the bag on his way out and left he was so mad, that he didn't care about the money anymore. He put in his train of mind that was his money and his dope. He renewed his car not the hotel because Ike was so into the white girl, he didn't care. Besides he was shacked up in her apartment. As he drove down MLK Blvd he noticed that he was being followed, he didn't have to panic because he had just dropped the dope and didn't have no more than 5 grand on him. All his dope was in Wanda apartment. Wanda a thick brown skin older chick with spots in her face. Wanda was a Jay but she could handle business. So he used to give her 200 sacks and hid dope in her toilet top. She never noticed because he always walks out with his clothes in his book bag. Still, he wonders who is this that could be following him. He examined his steps, *"Sat in the hotel, cooked, cut and bagged by myself."* Then he remembered he left 60 grand in the hotel in the mattress. He wondered did they hit the hotel. His thoughts were on

Gerald, even though they knew each other, the game still remains cutthroat. He bought all that dope from him. That extra dope was the bait up. Word was out that they had them Florida French fries. So it's easy to count up their money. He looked out his rearview, the black Benz was still behind him. He took a left on Bakers Ferry Rd. real slow. He speeded up the car and made another quick left, got out the car and ran into the woods on the corner of Bakers Ferry Rd. He hid behind a big oak tree, the Benz stopped and an older black man got out the car. The tall slim older fella looked like he was in his late 40s. He walked to the 5.0. Juan came out the woods with the Glock pointed at the car. Jumped into the passenger seat put the gun to the other older fella in the car and told him to pull off. As they pulled off he looked in the rearview seen the other fella sit on the trunk of the 5.0.

"What's up Pop? Why are y'all following me?"

"Cash, am I right?"

The older black fella was clean shaved, had some cold brown eyes and a very soft voice. He wore a nice white dress shirt and some nice black slacks. He didn't blink. He had no fear in his eyes. He looked like he was in his mid-50s, slick wavy black hair brown skin with a few wrinkles in his face. He liked Pop, because Pop had this coolness about him. He reached in his black Dickies pants and pulled the other Glock 17 out and put the Glock in Pop side.

Pop smiled.

"Okay Mr. Cash, I haven't heard of you."

"And I haven't heard of you."

"Son put the gun down, I mean you no harm. We're in a black Benz and we're black. People look and see the gun we'll be in jail in 5 minute. Beside you already got one in my side. My name is Tony and I'm from Detroit. Have you heard?"

He lowered the gun and said, "I heard y'all boys are putting it down. But what y'all want from me?"

"I want you to play God and condemn someone to hell. See a kid name Anthony Jones ran off with 100 kilos. We know where he's at, can't get to him. He's under federal protection. He's due to testify against a dear friend. We don't want the dope, but we want his life. See if he makes it to the stand everybody fall and a drop will hit everywhere, it will hit Atlanta harder. Now we don't want that either. So I'm gonna give you an address and name and you take him out. They got him on the Morris Brown College campus. He stays on the south part of the campus. He's a dorm leader for Alpha Kappa Alpha. Now the job pays 100 grand plus the 100 kilos if you can get 'em. The dope is 60% pure so you can step on it about 5 times."

"Why me? And when do you want him dead?"

"Let's say I know you'll get the job done. It's in your blood to succeed. I know this and plus you've been chosen. Today is July 18. On July 26 he's due to testify."

"How can I contact you?"

"Don't worry I'll contact you. Believe me I know how to find you. Here's a gun it's a cop. So leave it on the scene along with some drugs. Don't take it from this black bag until you use it. Please wear gloves."

"Don't worry he's in hell already."

"I know!"

He drove him back to Baker Ferry Rd. and dropped him off. He searched the car and couldn't find anything. He went back to Ed Rental and got another car, under the name of Robert Jones. As he left he thought about Ike and Lisa. Ike had over 5.7 million and that much in dope. Thing just didn't feel right. He drove to Moreland Ave. and checked into the Atlanta Motel in room 91. It was downstairs. As he went to the room he noticed a tall slim girl wearing a blue dress standing at the steps leaning on the rail.

"What's up?" the girl asked.

"Nothing what's up with you?"

"Trying to make a lil money!"

"Show and tell!"

She took her hands and grabbed the back of her dress and raised it, showing a back shot of her bare ass and hairless pussy.

"How much?"

"$30 for pussy, $50 for ass, $20 for head."

"That's a $100."

"Yeah!"

"Check this out, come in. Here's the hundred. Stay in the room and don't come out. Order what you want send them at anything. This money here is just for you to stay. You straight with that I know you need the rest anyway."

"Yeah! You right. My name is Me-Me."

He left and went to the Home Depot on Memorial Drive and got some brown work gloves and a box of latex gloves. He went into the TJ Maxx and bought a black skull cap and some black shades. When he got in the car, he put the latex gloves on and drove to the Executive Inn, got his stuff, got the money from the mattress and went back to the Atlanta Motel. Then he gave Me-Me his clothes. He kept the 60 grand and headed for Morris Brown. He called and checked on Ike, Ike was still talking the same talk but he was mad with him because he didn't get the money. They didn't argue, Ike understood and hung up. He knew Ike wasn't working because he heard Lisa moan in the background. That's why he hung up. As he entered Morris Brown parking lot, he thought about Tasha and hoped that they didn't run into each other. Having no picture figure or color, he didn't know how this was gonna go. But he knew he had to do it because this will be a power move, hook up with some big-time people. With just a name he went to work. When he reached the south campus he notices so many beautiful black and white female. A black and a white female walked up to him. He spoke in a proper tone. "Hello my name is Roderick Brit. I'm new here in Georgia, I'm from New York and I'm just visiting the different colleges here in Georgia. I was wondering can you show me where the men's dorms are."

"Why yes, I'll show you. My name is April and I don't have a boy-friend."

April was a beautiful brown skin sister, shoulder length hair, brown eyes and 120 pounds. Just right, but he wasn't really concerned about the brown sister wearing a yellow bathing suit with some yellow shorts and white sandals. He had a mission. The white girl introduced herself as Erica; she was beautiful also blue eyes, 5'4" 130 pounds blond hair that came to her back. She had a white bikini top and some white Gap shorts with some white sandals. She kept looking at him and she told him that she had seen him before. Just couldn't remember when. She told him she was probably sightseeing.

"That sound cool April, when I get settled in we can holla. Right now I'm just checking out the campus. I might get me an apartment I don't know.

"Hey Willie! Hey Willie," April yelled waving her hands in the air. A tall muscular brother walked up wearing an all-white Karl Kani short set.

"Yeah April," he replied as he came up.

"Why don't you show Rod here around? He's new to this state. He's thinking about joining our school and staying on campus."

"Okay."

He extended his hand out to him to shake his hand.

"Hi my name is Willie Maze; I'm the dorm leader and big brother for

Alpha Kappa Alpha. Right now we don't have any room on the south campus. But I'm sure we'll have some in a few weeks."

"A few weeks, man I got to start school now or I'll be behind. Plus I'm trying to holla at April."

She smiled. "Let me get your number and address and I'll call you Mr. Maze." He wanted to hurry up and leave because he seen Tasha coming with books in her arm. He walked off and said this will be an easy 100 grand. The dope will be the tough part. He got in the car and started to back up. He saw Willie getting into a blue Chevy Capri. Willie pulled off and he trailed him. He went I-85 south as going toward College Park. But he rode it out for almost an hour. "Damn where is this nigga going?" Willie stood 6'9" 230 pounds all muscle, low cut hair. He looked very educated. He got off on Flat Shoals Parkway and drove down a road he knew very well, Dotson Drive was where he used to stay with his grandmother. He saw him turn down the dirt road. He drove to the other end of the dirt road. He could hear Jake the Flake from the Chevy. He left his car running put the latex gloves on then the work gloves, grabbed the gun from the bag and ran in the wood, to his car. He got in the back seat on the driver side and knelt down. Willie jumped into the driver seat and threw a black tote bag over the seat. The bag landed on the back seat by the passenger window. He rose up and put the 357 to his head and told 'em to keep it in park.

"Nigga you got one chance of living, where's the dope?"

"I sold 30 bricks I got the other 70 in the tote bag. The money is under the toilet top in a black plastic bag. It's $300,000. I stay in room 112 on the far end of the campus. Please don't kill me, I've told you what you need to know."

He searched the bag with his right hand he felt the dope at the bottom of the bag. He put the bag over his right shoulder and told him to take the apartment key off the key ring. With no hesitation he took the key off the ring and handed it to him.

"I knew it wouldn't be long before y'all found me. Y'all crossed me first. They tried to kill me because of Phillip's nephew. Phillip's nephew killed Spooky, not me. He gave me the dope and the disk and told me to leave and to use the disc if y'all came after me. Spooky found out me and Paul was lovers so he was fix 'en to expose us. So Paul shot him, I tried to tell Phillip what happen but he wasn't gonna believe his nephew shot his brother. He sent the hit man at me. So damn right I ran. The Feds was my only way of living. You got to understand that, Bro, you got to; I can't take on no mob by myself."

"Where is the disk and I'll let you live. Without the disk they have no case. I don't think they knew you had the disk. So where is the disk?"

"It's in the Fruit Loops box on top of the refrigerator. So it's over with right?"

"Yeah man it's over with, all you had to do was tell 'em about the disk and gave it back you wouldn't went through all of this. But I promise you as of right now it's over with."

He lowered the gun and took two deep breaths and shot him in the back of the head two times. His head fell on the horn sounding it. He went in the bag grabbed a brick threw it on the front seat and walked back to his car.

"Where in the hell can I hide 69 bricks? I know one thing I don't really want to see that cat I don't even need his money now. All this dope."

He pulled off real slow, not wanting to seem panicked. He drove off smooth and calm. He was thinking about getting the money. He knew it was 300 grand; He had to get it, because when the Feds find out he's dead. They're gonna find the money and use it to bust a nigger. He drove down Main Street to Washington Road and got on the expressway. His phone rang; he knew who it was, because Ike was the only one with the number.

"Yeah Ike!"

"Man what the hell is going on, I get to the motel and all your shit is gone."

"Man I told you I don't trust Lisa."

"Goddammit I told you she's cool. I done fucked her, did everything to her. She's here right now. She wants to meet you and show you she's cool. She feels like if she was black, then you wouldn't be downing her. So she's fix 'en to prove her loyalty."

"Man I don't give a fuck if that cracka go kill the president. I don't trust her. She's trying too hard Ike. That's what the Feds do they keep on trying till they get you. Man she got to have some good pussy because you're going to jail fucking with that white hoe."

"Look I got the money here with me right now come and get it. "I'ma leave it here."

"Did you bag the money or her?"

"I did. Check the money good for tracers."

"Ike I'll be there to get it, just get the bitch from there.

He hung up and went to the campus. They were partying so this would be an easy lick. He parked on 5th Street the frat house sat on the corner.

The house looked like a regular house with a fence around the yard and green grass. Their sign was on top of the roof. Night was creeping in slowly, people coming from and standing everywhere. He went in and the front room had people standing, talking and sitting. The music was extra loud, he wondered how they heard each other. He blended in and danced with this thick white girl with black hair. She had on some cut-off blue jeans made in to some Dazzy Dukes and a white T-shirt with no bra. They formed a line of slow dancing. She turned and put her ass on him while he held her from behind; she grinded on him hard. She could feel his erect dick pressing through his pants on her ass, as she grinded deep and hard against him. She turned and asked him did he want to go in a room. Wanting to say yes, he smiled and said not right now. He had to stay focused on his mission. Then he locked eyes with Tasha, she started walking toward him. He grabbed the white girl and walked up the stairs smiling. He looked back she still was coming. She started running up the stairs. He made sure she seen him go into the first room on the left side. He pulled his dick out and the white girl started sucking it. She opened the door and liked to dropped she held her heart as he smiled at her. The girl didn't care that she was standing there. She felt the tension in his dick as she sucked it. Tasha just stood there and watched a white girl suck off the only man she ever loved. He wanted her to feel his pain; she wanted to explain her fears. The girl finished smiled at her and said, "I guess she got some explaining to do."

She left and two more people came to the door, asking could they use the room. She couldn't speak because he would've seen that he defeated her every mean. He just walked out and went down the hall looking for room 112. It was the last room facing the whole hallway. He looked behind him and she was right there. For the first time in her life she wanted to commit murder. She had her fists balled and her eyes started to puff up.

"What? Why are you following me? I told you from the beginning you didn't want to get caught up with a nigga like me. I can't feel hurt. All I can do is give it."

Before she knew it she swung her right hand and hit him on his left jaw. It was hard so hard, that he slapped her. This was just perfect he thought. He took the key out, opened the door while she was swinging; hitting him on the back and head crying. He weaved under her and picked her up on his left shoulder and walked in the room. When he turned the lights on, he was amazed. It was a regular room with a bed, sofa, chair, a system and pictures of great blacks; Malcolm, Martin, Ella Fitzgerald, Louis Armstrong, Nelson Mandela, Lionel Hampton and so on. He threw her on the sofa and asked what her problem was. She just looked at him wanting to get up and fight, but she had seen his focus was more on the room. She still jumped up and slapped him.

"How could you come here and let a white bitch suck your dick in my face. You knew I was coming up them steps. You're right! You're a heartless son of a bitch!"

Tears formed and flowed down her face. She took her hands and wiped her tears away. You're not worth my time or my tears. She stood up and walked to the door. She opened it and looked back when he called her name she stood.

"Ain't nothing wrong with crying. Anybody say that they're that strong they're lying. See crying is like taking your soul to the cleaners and getting rebuilt. See Tasha it's like the feeling we had they come naturally like the rain, so go on and cry and you'll be over me. I can't cry, but I know I did love you. Your tears are my tears so go on and cry for the both of us."

She walked out crying her soul out without the tears. He went to the Fruit Loops box and got the disk, looking in the closet found a red book bag. Put the books on the table that sat by the door. Went to the toilet top got the money in the black bag put it in the book bag. Got a rag from the towel holder wiped down the toilet top wiped down the door knob because he didn't want his prints on it. Closed the door with the rag and walked out normal. When he went to his car he threw the bag in his back seat. He heard noise in the car beside him. He looked in and seen Tasha bent over on the floor crying. His heart didn't skip a beat but his eyes teared up. He jumped in the car and pulled off. He was happy because they were finish. He went to the motel and sent Me-Me to Wendy's to get them something to eat. He threw the bag under his pillow. She brought him 2 deluxe burgers, biggie fries and a biggie coke. She had a bacon cheese burger, biggie fries and a biggie coke. As they were eating he thought about fucking her but couldn't get his mind into it. She was lying in the second bed watching "28 Days." She could sense something was troubling him. But she didn't bother to ask question. She was a Hoe and a Hoe stayed in a Hoe place. She was under the covers her clothes was folded neatly on the table in the middle of both beds. He laid there thinking this could be his first good night of sleep in a long time. He couldn't sleep in a room with a stranger with all that dope and money. She would see that he was in a deep sleep and rob him. He told her he no longer needed her and gave her 300 dollars.

"You sure you don't want sex? Because I'm well rested and it will be worth your while I promise you that."

He watched her come from under the cover. He watched her move her cheeks left to right then made them jump. Standing back on her legs she popped her playmate to him, he rose in his pants. She seen it and smiled. He thought if cops come asking question and she say he didn't do nothing that would look bad. So he stood behind her and pulled out. She fell to her knees with her ass pointing upward; he could see her cheeks as she placed him in her mouth. She gave him the best head he ever had. She enjoyed him so much that she stayed there sucking until he received another erection. She pulled out a rubber from her small red purse. Put it on him; put her hands on the bed. Tooting her ass to him and receiving him hitting her from behind. She threw it back to him moaning he came but she wasn't ready to leave. She asked him could she stay the rest of the night because hoes need to be held too. She wanted to make love to him and get a good night sleep. He gave her an extra hundred told her to get a room and come holla at him in the morning. She left the room with a smile on her face and he locked the door put a chair under the doorknob, cut the lights off and closed his eyes.

CHAPTER 4
Ike

Ike did not care no more. He thought Juan was stupid. Lisa was steady filling his head up with the thoughts of him being controlled. He needed to take over and leave his friend alone. He thought about everything she was saying because it was true, Juan didn't want him to wake up. He have a mind of his own also he has a million dollar trap that she helped him build. If she was Fed she would've gotten him by now because she's made 100s of grands; he's paying her well. She should have about a 100 grand herself. So she was in it to win it just like them. He called him but Me-Me picked up the phone.

"Put Cash on the phone."

"Yeah!"

"You can trip me being with a hoe. But you can lay up with a hoe. Man you're backwards. Listen I'm gonna give you this money tonight you take it where ever the rest is and split it. You give me mine and I'll continue to do my thing we're still gonna be tight. It's just got to be like it was before; me and my own dope you and yours because I can't do the shit I wanna do because I'm worrying about what you're gonna say. Man this ain't right. We should have 6.8 million when everything is all sold. So come and get this lil bit. I'll drop it off at the hotel so come and get it don't worry I'm leaving out now and Lisa is leaving out also."

"Ike that cracka got you thinking I'm trying to control you. Man I just hit a lick for 69 bricks plus 300 grand. Shawty how the fuck is you being controlled. Fuck it do as you say. But remember when this shit blow up in your face I'll put you on again because you're my boy. I got mad love for you."

He hung up and a knock came to the door. Me-Me opened the door. They had been sitting there talking. She woke him up at noon with some pancakes, eggs and coffee. He saw that she was cool. He stood behind her as the door came open. He had the Glock 17 hanging in his left hand. Tony came in smiling.

"Cash you can come from behind the door. It's me Tony."

Me-Me closed the door and walked back to the bed. She didn't have to dress because she was already in blue jeans and a black Boss shirt. She didn't hoe during the day, time. that was her sleep time. But she found something that can't come to a dreamer. A young nigga who could fuck and had money. He had put on a blue Nike jogging suit. She came over with some blue and white Jordans. They sat on the first bed. Tony threw the envelope on the bed and said, "Job well done." He threw the money to her and told her to count it. Really the money didn't matter to him. She counted it by laying 100 on the bed in 100 stacks.

"100 grand."

"That's correct, okay Tony, you're a good man!"

Tony started to leave when he said, "Hold up." Tony stopped and looked.

"I got something for you that y'all didn't know the clown had." He went in the book bag and threw the disk to him.

"We knew he had it that's why they're tearing his place up now. I guess you can say you're gonna be one of the best."

Tony left and Juan smiled at her because she's a hoe and about business. He told her to take one of them stacks for herself because he needed her help again. He promised her he'll give her some more of that money before the night was over. "Just stay down." She smiled and told him she wasn't moving until he commanded.

He phoned Ike and told him he was leaving out. Ike told him everything was cool. He put the book bag in the back seat as they got in the front. She wanted to ask him why he was riding in a rental. But that wasn't her business. They rode down Memorial Drive things didn't look right so he parked in the Amoco and just watched the surrounding.

"You're a street hoe, what look out of the norm to you?"

"All these police look at the phone men in the phone truck and the 2 climbing the pole. Look at that black van at the tip of the parking lot with the For Sale sign. I've been hoeing at that hotel ain't that many hoes here. Brave hoes, hoe here because it's a trap and not much money. Now look at Dekalb County, somebody is trying to set you up. I just be damn, they want you bad. Look, there, go a damn cleaning crew turning in the parking lot in that blue truck. Let's go before they peep us."

They pulled off riding down Memorial Drive to make sure nobody seen them or were following him. He called Ike and told him.

"Polices were everywhere to consider that money as a lost." But Ike didn't leave the move in the hotel. He left a bag of clothes.

"My guy I'm at the Olive Garden. I didn't leave it there; I left clothes in that bag. I don't feel right myself. I heard her on the phone and she was like not tonight. She thought I had left the apartment. So I put everything in the black suit case. I got it here at the Olive Garden with me. It's in the front seat. The bitch is in the bathroom. If you come get everything now she won't have a good case. I'ma leave the restaurant when I see you pull up. It's a Burger King across the street park there and get the money. She knows the money is here so she got somebody watching us. I can see a black car in the parking lot. Here she come now."

"Do you think you can make it out of there?"

"No!"

"Dammit what to do! What to do! I'm riding pass the restaurant now I can see the black car. I'm parking in Shell gas station up the street. I'll hit you back when I come up with a plan."

"Me-Me I'm gonna give you another stack but I need you to do some Jane Bond shit. I got a black suit case in the Olive Garden I really need to get. It got my dope in it do you think you can get it."

"It's in a black suit case, go to the mall and buy some clothes and a black suit case. Get me a big ass coat and I'ma get that dope baby."

They drove to South Dekalb Mall and bought the same kind of suitcase Ike had in the room. A big trench London Fall coat. She took her left arms out the sleeve and they took off. He let her out at the Shell station. She walked down the street staggering like a drunk talking all loud bent over carrying the suitcase under the coat. She went in cursing.

"God dammit what a woman got to do to get service."

She walked around to every table cursing I need some service. Everybody looked at her and got closer to the wall. She looked at 'em threw her head up bucked her eyes and said, "Oh my fault I'm not welcome in here. I'll leave since I can't get no service. Oh lord you've took my arm all I want is some to eat."

One of the workers, a white female, came to her aid and sat her in the first seat and asked her what she wanted. She ordered a 12 piece with coleslaw and gave her $20 dollars. She ordered it to go. She looked around and saw everybody was still looking. She noticed the black suit case on the floor. Ike looked up at her and she winked. She seen Ike get up and sit in the same seat with her and put his arms around her. Ike picked up his phone and made a call. She slid the suit case with her right foot and dropped the dummy. The girl came back with her bag and escorted her out the door. The girl apologized to the customers. But Lisa wasn't paying attention to the apology. She thought about the whole play, went in her pocket pulled her badge out and told him to freeze. She hit the window pointing toward the street, grabbed the phone called them and told 'em the lady got the money. She pushed Ike and ran to the front seat. Ike ran and jumped over the counter and ran out the back door. When he jumped over the fence the chopper came from nowhere. He knew he had to buy some time for them to get away. So he ran through the woods with the chopper behind him when he came out by the red light he seen Juan and started to jump in the car but the chopper was over his head. Juan stayed even though the light was green he couldn't let him go out bad but Ike ran the other way, so he pulled off. Ike ran and ran he went into Mountain Villa Apartment and open the first door he ran to. A dark skin heavyset woman with a brown dress on was sitting watching the T.V.; her 2 sons laying on the floor in red and white short sets. Jumped up "Nigga if you don't get your ass out of here I'll kill you myself."

"Ma'am just chill let me catch my breath."

She turned the T.V. to the 11 Alive news and there he was. They knew he was in them apartments and they were begging the residents to lock their doors. They said he was armed and dangerous. She looked at him very startled. Her boys didn't understand so she looked at him. "You know they gonna search every apartment until they find you. So what you gonna do? It's best to gone and run or give up. Whatever you do please don't bring any harm to me or my boys."

He looked at the boys looking at him and said, "Fuck it" and left. He walked down the middle of the street; he knew they didn't have a real case against him because they didn't have all the money or dope. He seen them going home to home they wasn't paying him no mind because they had alot of apartments to search, it was a straight driveway with alot of parking lots plus it had gotten dark. He pulled his cell phone out and dropped it in a dumpster. He made it all the way out the apartment got on the MARTA bus and sat down. He didn't know what to do because he was so mad, at himself. He couldn't see through the money and sex. Juan was so right and because of his dumbness he got his self fucked up and almost got him fucked up. He had 5 grand cash on him he knew he had to get off it because that was their evidence. He saw an older black lady with her kids or grandkids 2 girls and 2 boys. He got up and rang the bell just before the bus got to Avondale train station. He handed her the money and got off the bus. He walked down Dekalb Avenue. He thought about it, it was over for him before it even started because they had him the second day. He should've relocated. Now he got to give him all the connection in Marietta. So he can keep the business going. He walked to Decatur Station and called him.

"Listen I know you want to say I told you so but it's already said. I messed up everything. Listen just break my mom off 1 million and what you wanna do about Marietta?"

"Listen I don't really care about Marietta; where are you so I can come and get you?"

"I'm at the Decatur station."

"I'll be there in 15 minute I'm on Moreland."

They drove to Decatur station to get him but when they pulled up Dekalb County was cuffing him up. They drove off.

Meanwhile, at Dekalb County Jail Ike sat in a detective office. A white officer with a big stomach wearing a black suit named James was standing next to officer Linda Whittus.

"Hi my name is Officer James you already know federal agent Whittus. Mr. Jackson we searched both the apartment and room at the Executive Inn neither in your name. Agent Whittus said you were constantly on the phone with someone. Who's your contact and where's the fucking money? You're facing some big time here son. You need to work with us. You think your people is gonna keep it real with you. They're gonna find someone else to take your place. Keep in contact with you until your trial is over then leave you messed up in some big trouble. We know you're part of some drug ring or you could be part of some terrorist group. We can put so many charges on you that you'll never see daylight. You need to help yourself and help us."

"I don't know what y'all are talking about. I met Lisa in the apartment; I was trying to get some ass. I don't know nothing about no drug ring."

"What if I show you the tapes I got on you?"

"Mr. James look I don't have no money, don't have no drugs. Y'all searched the hotel and didn't find nothing. I'm clean, man. I don't know what Ms. Whittus been telling you, for all I know she could be stealing from y'all, everything that look good ain't good. That's all I got to say. Can I have my phone call now?"

They stepped out of the office, Lisa was very mad because alot of the government money was used as well as street money she made by selling the shit. Money they could've used to bring down more dealers. She really needed the money to bring him down. Without the money the state will take the case and he'll walk in 10 years max.

"Let him make a phone call but monitor it. We got to find that money. We got to find out who he was talking to. He threw his cell phone when he was running. I want you to take his mama into custody if you have to."

"Mr. Jackson you can have your phone call but you have to make it here and give me the name and number."

He gave him his mother name and number.

"Hello am I speaking with Mrs. Betty Jackson?"

"Yes!"

"Ma'am this is Officer James from Dekalb County Jail we have your son Edward in custody, he'd like to speak with you."

He handed him the phone.

"Mom."

"Boy what have you done?"

"I haven't done nothing. They say they got me for drugs and money. But they haven't found nothing on me. I need you to come bond me out. I promise I'll get the money back to you."

"How much is your bond?"

"I haven't went downstairs yet; I mean I haven't been to court yet. Just be on standby."

"Okay."

They took him upstairs to booking where he sat in a holding cell for 3 days. Thinking how stupid he was and how did Juan know Lisa was the Feds.

"Hey who got the phone next?"

"You got it!" somebody yelled out.

With no one to call, he called Tasha, knowing Juan would hate him for it.

"Collect call from Ike."

"Hello, Tasha, this Ike!"

"Ike why are you calling me collect?"

"Tasha I'm locked up, you haven't seen the news?"

"Oh my God! Where is Juan, please tell me he's not in trouble. I've called everywhere looking for him. But I can't find' him. I went by the apartment, he moved Ike where is my baby? I done him wrong. I was scared."

"Tasha here's his cell number, because I got to get out of here. Don't say nothing because he'll hang up. Just call let me talk then you can talk."

"Ike it's 3:40 in the morning he's probably sleep."

"Tasha I need to holla now."

She dialed the number and clicked back over.

"Ike you there?"

"Yes! Be quiet."

"Hello Ike, what are they talking about? And who called me for you. I know you ain't called me on that one call shit."

"Naw I called my mom with that three days ago. Just chill. Someone trustworthy."

"Man you ain't in the best shape to trust nobody. So who called?"

"Hey man I'm due in court in a few hours. If the Feds don't come I'll be going to Decatur my mom is gonna bail me out. I'ma need to meet up with you somewhere. Tasha called."

"Juan, don't hang up, please we need to talk. I'm not mad with you about that frat party we need to talk."

"Man why in the fuck you gave her my number for? I don't want no dealing with you Tasha. And Ike don't call me till you're out. I'm sure them folks got some kinda code to break the phone system. I'll drop your mom that money because you're gonna need it, them crackas ain't fix 'en to let you out. You better holla at Tasha old man."

Juan hung up the phone and turned it off. He couldn't believe Ike had called her. His heart wanted to hear what she had to say. But he didn't need love in his life. He was on a power move.

He woke up at 11:00 am. Me-Me was in his arms, turn on the TV to the news he seen Ike's picture. *"Suspected drug ring member is held without bond."* Then they showed Anthony Young found dead in his car off Dotson Drive. Drugs were found on the scene, along with a murder weapon. Police suspect foul play.

He smiled, turned into Me-Me kissed and had sex.

CHAPTER 5
Tasha Has to Find Juan

"I can't believe Juan is running from me. He's acting as if he never knew me or loved me. How could I hurt someone to the point where he'll let someone go down on him in front of my face? It hurts, yes it do because I know he did it out of hurt. Mrs. Anderson, you're a counselor and people here on campus say you're a good counselor. How?"

"Well, Natasha, I've been a counselor now for twenty years. During my years of counseling I've seen many young talented girls such as yourself drop out because of their mate. It's either a baby is coming or your situation. See, Natasha true love stands the test of time. From the statement you just made, I can see that he never loved you."

"No, Mrs. Anderson, I left him because I got scared."

"Scared of what?"

"Scared of losing him. See Juan is street smart, book smart and religion smart. But he's a loner, he has no family. Nobody now! He told me I was all he had. I've been in love with him since I was thirteen years old. I told myself that he would be my husband. It took five years for us to get together and eleven months for me to destroy everything I've worked so hard to get."

"Natasha, Juan will come back on his own time. He knows you love him. Just give you both the time y'all need."

Mrs. Anderson was a beautiful black female, 5'8" and 125 pounds, with pretty brown skin, long jet black hair, brown eyes and a voice that would melt anybody's fears. She knew what Tasha was going through because her husband had left her out of fear when they were in college, but Paul came back. She only hoped that would happen for Natasha Middle.

Tasha walked out of the office with hope, because it was all she had now. A hope that he would give her enough time to say four heart-felt words: *"Juan, I love you."*

She attended class like always, but this time her Criminal Law Professor, Mrs. Barber Tate, noticed life in her. Mrs. Tate didn't say much about it as Tasha took her seat in the front row and pulled out her books, papers and notes. Usually Tasha would sit in the back. She never smiled and always had her head down. But today it was life, smile, front row and a glow.

Mrs. Tate began her class differently. She talked about the love of law. Was it right to have such laws concerning murder, robbery, drugs, rape, theft and so on? No one raised their hand to answer the question, so she called on Natasha.

"Natasha Middle, you seem to be up in life today. You came from a family with judges and lawyers. How do you feel about this?"

"Mrs. Tate, I feel law is right in a way, only if they get the right people. Then I feel it's wrong. Look at all the people locked up for the things they didn't do. Just because they fit a certain description. So if the law convicts the right person then yes. If they convict the wrong person then no. Laws are good because they teach you how to live in a productive society. I feel God should call you home in a peaceful way. Nobody should be raped or robbed. Drugs are wrong too but that is a personal decision."

Everybody applauded her answer because it was the truth. Mrs. Tate was very surprised with her answer, it had life in it.

"Is it life or something you read about, Natasha?"

"Mrs. Tate, it's very much my life. I'm suffering from it now. I can't tell you why. All I can say is I'm gonna make a difference."

Tears rolled down her cheeks as she spoke about making a difference for Juan.

Mrs. Tate didn't want to push her so she ended class and let her walk on. Tasha walked to her apartment on campus that she shared with two other girls. Erica Wright was a white female from Miami, Florida. She was 5'4" and 130 pounds; she had blonde hair and blue eyes. Tasha called her blue eyes. Sam Fowler was a black female, 110 pounds, 5'7" with jet black hair. She was from New York. She got along well with her roommates. Their apartment was roomy with white carpet, two brown sofas, a brown couch and a Sony stereo. The 3 bedroom, 2 bath apartment had colorful rainbow striped wallpaper and a big white kitchen. She was lucky to get the room with her own bathroom. Tasha walked in, the girls had company. Erica and Sam's boyfriends were there as well as another black male, around 6'2", 190 pounds, waiting on her. She only spoke and walked right to her room. Mike walked to her room and knocked on the door. As he looked in she had laid across the bottom of the bed. He saw her tears from afar. She couldn't help but cry because she destroyed their relationship. She looked up.

"What do you want?"

"Hi Tasha, my name is Mike. May I come in?"

"Look Mike, I'm gay, I'm not looking for no man. So be on your way. As a matter of fact. Sam! Blue eyes! Come here. Look here, I'm not interested in boys, I'm gay okay—so don't try to set me up with nobody else. Y'all got that?"

"Tasha, we are just trying to help," Blue eyes replied.

"Don't! And shut my door."

As the door closed she smiled because if he popped up asking questions, everybody would say she's gay. She could prove to him then that he was the only man in her life. She picked up the phone and called the number Ike had given her. As the phone rang her heart beat so fast that she couldn't sit up. She laid there hoping he'd pick up. The phone had rung 10 times already. She was just about to hang up. She heard his voice.

"Hello Tasha what you want?"

"Juan please don't hang up. Just let me say four words to you. Juan, I love you. Really I do. And I need you in my life. If you don't come back to me I'll kill myself. Please Juan stop being hard on me."

Tears ran down his face then she heard the dial tone...

"What the hell? He hung up on me. He don't care about me at all." With that she cried herself back to sleep. Now she has to live a gay lifestyle on campus. She never told them about him. Now it was finally over between them.

"What kind of game is she playing, calling me, telling me that love shit then hanging up. Haven't really talked to her in 3 months. Ike got 6 years behind some bullshit. Didn't even give his lawyer a chance to fight the case. I guess he was avoiding a federal case. Lord, what part of the game is this. I'm tired of the bitch playing with my emotion. I'm fix 'en to go and kill her."

He jumped into the black AZ Toyota he rented from Ed rental, took the expressway from Moreland to University and drove to the college. As he parked, he loaded the Glock 17, tucked it in his white Tommy jeans and walked to her apartment. It wasn't far from where he parked. He knocked on the door.

A girl's voice said, "Who is it?"

"Juan."

"Juan who?"

"I'm looking for Natasha Middle."

As the door opened he seen Erica, as he walked in he seen Sam and 3 boys.

"Ain't your name Roderick?" Blue asked.

"Nall it's Juan, I was here checking on Tasha, that's all. Where is she?"

"Man, if you're trying to come up with her, you're just wasting your time. She gay," Mike said.

He just looked at them smiled and walked to her room. He knew where it was because she told him it was the only room on the right side of the hallway. He turned the knob, but it was locked. He knocked on the door real hard four times. The people in the living room just watched from the top of the hall. He knocked again, this time the knock scared her.

"Who the fuck is it? I told y'all I'm gay. So leave me the fuck alone."

He looked back at them and smiled then knocked again.

She jumped up and slung the door open.

"What the hell do... baby... baby, I can't believe you're here. Why did you hang up in my face Juan?"

"Don't play games. You hung up in mine!"

"No I didn't. Is your phone charged up?"

"I don't even know. If I hung up then I'm sorry."

"And if I hung up I'm sorry. I love you so much, boy I been so lonely and empty."

He took her in his arms and kissed her hard. He picked her up, walked in the door closed it with his left foot and took her to bed, where they made love. She kept him in her arms, because she knew if she let him go he'd be gone when she woke up. So she held him and fell asleep.

He woke her up by entering her. She kissed him and laid her arms out. He made passionate love to her; he could tell she haven't slept with no one because she felt like a virgin all over again.

"Juan what you been doing these last 3 months, besides getting your dick sucked by the white girl. If I had a gun I would've shot both of y'all. I know I've been a mess since the day I hung up with you and the day I seen you do that. Why?"

"Because I wanted you to see how it felt to be betrayed for nothing. But really you've made my life a living hell. I'm on top of things money-wise. Ike got 6 years. I stay in a motel on Moreland Ave. I drive rental cars. I robbed a Nigga for 69 bricks. Nigga paid me to knock the Nigga off I robbed. I killed him for a 100 grand. I kept coming around here to check up on you. Haven't had no sleep. I paid a lawyer 100 grand for Ike and he pled out for 6 years and gave his mom a million. You won't believe where I was last night. Oh yeah I changed my name to Cash. But anyway,

Shawty I went to church last night. Everybody stared at me, because I jumped up and said, "I thank God for my life, now bring back my wife."

She laughed.

"Baby, that was so sweet. I see you've come to know yourself."

"Naw Tasha, my heart was lonely. I had to go to God, my grandmom told me I can always go to him when I'm in trouble."

"Juan are you in trouble?"

"Naw Shawty my heart was hurting. I thought I was gonna die without you. Shawty you got me pussy whipped, Naw I'm in love."

"I'm in love too!"

"While I was in church, I read the bible. I read 1 Corinthians 3 and James. I mean I read alot of the book in the 3 hours I was there. Everything I read was about love. Sweetheart you're the only love I know. I want to have a baby. Tasha, baby, if you give me a baby, I'll stop everything, I mean that."

"Juan, wow! It's too much to believe one night in church made you believe all that. I mean, in God everything is possible. But I'm not ready for a baby yet. I got to study so I can be your lawyer."

"So you're saying you want me to stay in the game?"

"Hell naw I want you out of it as soon as possible."

"Well, I'm not leaving until we have a baby. Either you give me a child or someone else will."

"Juan you think a baby is gonna change you? Nigga the change got to come from within. When you change within then you'll have a baby. From here on out start wearing a condom or you won't be going up in me."

"Shawty if that's how you see it then fine!"

"Leave now... Juan." Tears running down her face. "I mean it leave now."

"So you're gonna push me away because I got a fucking dream? Because I want a better life for myself? Bitch you've gone crazy. Life ain't about a bitch name Natasha Middle. It's about love, at least that's what you say. How in the fuck can you say you love me when you don't even believe in me?"

Tears were falling from both of their eyes. She saw that this really was his dream, his cry for help. But she wasn't fix 'en to mess up her life at this early age. She was only 19 and he wasn't 19 yet. He looked at her and said, "You're gonna answer my question?"

"Juan you have a beautiful dream, I'm sure you got good means and intentions. But it isn't time for us to have a baby."

"Time! What you're playing God? Time for me to create, then a baby pop up. Bitch you're sick."

"I'm not telling you no more, Get the fuck out! It's over with Juan Ellis. I'll start eating pussy before I fuck you again."

With that statement she started what she wanted, a fight. He was partly dressed, in pants and shoes. He swung and slapped her. The fight was endless. She wouldn't give in nor would he. He never hit her in the face with his fist only slapped her. He had her pent to the bed at 6:40 am.

Her roommates stayed knocking on the door asking her was she alright. She'll yell out "yes" and look up at him.

"Juan it's 6:42 please get off me, we've been fighting for 3 hours. Let's lay down and go to sleep. I'm not bleeding; I just want to go to sleep with you in my arms. I see now with you being mad at me you won't hurt me. Juan can we please go to sleep."

"I'm fix 'en to leave, because as long as you live on this campus we'll get nowhere. We had a perfect life before this college shit. You got to be here another three years, Tasha baby, I love you, but I don't want to ever hit you again. To keep from doing that, I got to leave. So I'm gone." With that he put his shirt on.

"Okay! Okay! Juan, I'll have the baby. I never said no, to it. I said it wasn't the right time."

"Baby Girl, I'm not fix 'en to force a baby on you. I'll call to check up on you. Forever you'll be my love Natasha Middle."

She wasn't hearing that; she grabbed his gun and pointed at him. "Juan you walk out that door your life ends and mine also. Try me!"

"Tasha, you ain't crazy, look I'm grabbing for the knob; oh my God I got the knob in my hand. I'm turning the knob and the door is open."

She was pointing the gun right at his head. Her grip was tight and her eyes were watery because of the tears. He walked in the entrance of the door; she closed her eyes and shot.

"What the hell! Tasha, your roommate is right here."

She jumped up, ran to the door and put the gun to his head. She was still naked and she didn't care who seen her or who were standing there.

"Nigga I mean it. We'll die right here!"

Her roommates just watched; Blue eyes started crying, "Tasha, please don't. Juan, go back in there. Can't you see she love you to death. Do your part, think about it first Juan!"

Blue eyes spoke with sense to him; he walked back in and closed the door.

"Tasha, I guess you're a fool with it."

"Yeah a fool in love with you."

She opened the door and called her roommates in the room. He threw her a long purple and gold 34 Laker jersey. She put it on before the girls got to the door.

"This is my husband Juan Ellis, he's the reason why I said I was gay. I didn't want him to walk up and think that I was cheating on him. This is Blue eyes and this is Sam."

"How are y'all doing? Blue eyes, you made alot of sense. I see these black folks are teaching you something."

"Yes they are. I'm studying to be a counselor; I see I got what it takes." She laughed.

"Tasha, are y'all gonna be alright?" Sam asked.

"Yes! Sam, listen I'm not going to school today, so go to my classes and tell 'em I'm sick. Today is Friday anyway. You got me?"

He looked at the bullet hole in the wall and started playing. "Tasha please don't kill me, take all my money. Please don't rape me. Noooooo!"

She started laughing and jumped in his arms. They kissed and made hard passionate love.

Tasha woke up fixed them some pancakes, OJ, bacon and eggs.

"It's noon and y'all is just now waking up?" Sam asked.

"Girl you might as well cook some more." Blue eyes stated.

"Are y'all really hungry? And why ain't y'all at school?"

"Okay, Mom, yes, we're hungry and some fool started shooting so we came home, Mom." Blue eyes replied.

Blue eyes is 21 and Sam is 23. Sam's last year in college is this year. This will be her fourth year in medicine. She's already an RN. She's studying to be an LRN a licensed registered nurse.

"Tasha, what was that about this morning?" Blue eyes asked.

"Well, we want the same thing, which is a family. But he wants a child so it will change his life. See he's a drug dealer. He feels a baby will make him stop. He's smart as hell, to drop out of school at 14. But his life is the street. He can get his GED at will. He don't have a family so he wants a baby. He's ready to leave the streets but I still got 3 more years in law, I'm not ready for no baby. And I'm sorry for my foolishness this morning. But our relationship was over with. I didn't want it to end like that. So I picked a fight, just to get him to stay and understand my point of view. He wouldn't hit me with his fist. He only sat on top of me slapping me. They weren't hard slaps. Here is y'all lunch and I'm sorry meal." She walked off and went to feed her baby.

"Tasha, I got some shit to do, but I need your help. I got 4 million dollars. I need your help to carry it to Switzerland. The plan is simple. We put all the money in suitcases ride in a rental van and take it through. You can get your roommates in on it too because it will look good if four people had bags. It will be a little vacation; y'all got 5 or 6 days out of school anyway."

"Juan you need to run this down to them and see what they say because I'll go to hell with you. You know that."

She called them in and he gave them the plan. He told 'em they'll get 50 grand apiece up front. To his surprise they were down with the trip, because they knew they don't really search bags only send them through metal detectors.

"When do we leave?" Sam asked.

"We'll leave in a few, y'all gone and get dressed."

They all showered dressed and left for the storage. The money was already in suitcases. In 4 suitcases, really 5 because he were putting 1 million in each one. He was gonna keep the 400 grand to live off and pay them. They all stood in the storage looking; the money was in a corner sitting by itself. While the dope was in a green duffle bag. They didn't rent the van they just left for the airport. He paid for the ticket. The girl was excited and ready to go. But there were one problem; they had to get passports in 12 hours. They headed for the large post office in Atlanta, the Memorial post office on Lee Street.

They walked in and went straight to the passport office; this will be a hard trick to pull off. They all sat in the chairs thinking. As Juan thought, he was approached by a white fellow name John Adam.

"Mr. Ellis, we've been expecting you."

His heart dropped as he stared at the heavyset white guy, about 5'9", 270 pounds with green eyes and brown hair.

"Mr. Ellis my name is John Adam; I understand you paid for four tickets to Berne, Switzerland. Am I correct?"

He didn't say nothing, he just listened.

"Mr. Ellis, I would like for you to come into my office."

Juan walked to his office and sat in the soft-back chair, it was a neat, small office with a laptop computer, picture on the desk and flowers.

"Mr. Adam, you said you've been expecting me. What's up?"

"Well, Mr. Ellis, this is business, I got the names already: Erica Wright, Sam Fowler, Natasha Middle and you. I already have y'all passports made up. Tony need for you to take 30 million over there. They're hot but you're not. The girls are college students. I must say that was very clever. Now, this job pays 3 million because they need the money over there.

"Your money is in this black suitcase and theirs is in them 5 suitcases. Now, the money is well hidden in the suitcases. Once you arrive someone will greet you with a kiss. Nina Jones. She's a banker that we sent over there. So you'll be clean. Nina will monitor your account, ten percent charge. I believe y'all are ready for y'all pictures. I already had you in the computer. I just didn't have the girls."

They walked out and took the girls' pictures. Juan didn't say much but "fun time." He wasn't scared because only a fool would hand over 30 million to bust a nigga.

They went out to eat to pass time at Hard Rock downtown and took in a movie at the Omini off Marietta Street.

"Show time ladies."

When they arrived at the airport a black slim man greeted them, took the bags with a smile and said, "Tony."

He walked them to the gate, no one said a word. They boarded the plane and sat in coach. They all went to sleep. Eleven hours later they were there. As they got off the plane Nina kissed him on the cheek and they walked out of the airport and got into a white limousine.

The girls looked puzzled but didn't say nothing. As they rode, Nina pulled out a counting machine. He was very surprised. They checked in the Switzerland Inn room A12. As they entered, he was checking out Nina. She was 5'11" about 150 pounds Puerto Rican. Nina took the suitcase and started counting the money. The girl eyes were big, never have they seen that much money before. Neither had him. Eight hours later all the money was counted including his 7 million. He filled out the papers to open a joint account with Tasha and they all fell asleep including Nina. The morning came and Nina took them to the bank. Processed the money and told them that the limousine was theirs to keep so they could sight see. They went everywhere and had fun the whole five days.

CHAPTER 6
Two Years Later

$\mathbf{A}$s time passed, Juan was unstoppable and Tasha was studying extra hard to make sure Juan stayed out. The law hadn't even seen him. After the trip to Switzerland, he became very well known as "Cash." Everybody respected him. He was now supplying Scottsdale, East Atlanta, Mcrae, Macon, Valdosta and alot of small counties in Georgia. He made a promise to Tony that he'll never step on their toes. Tony was responsible for his success, because as a nickel and dime pusher and thief this would have taken years. Instead, Juan made hits and put the dope he found on the streets. He was still considered small, even though he was standing on 18 million. Natasha slowly started to transfer some of the money down to Atlanta.

Tony asked him what his goal in life was. He replied, "To have a family and settle down."

Tony wanted him out of the game while he was unknown and on top because he had saw many young people like Juan let fame go to their heads and do stupid stuff. In the end, they would up dead, in prison, or on drugs. Tony didn't want that to happen to him. He understood Juan and knew he had a future. He told Juan to leave the game and go to college. But Juan wasn't hearing anything about college. He was watching his bank account increase. Juan never wrote Ike but he sent packages, money, books and shoes. Ike lived like a king in *"Lee Arrendale"* known as *"Alto."*

One Saturday Juan was up near Alto in "Steusen County." Ike always asked him to come see him, but he always told him "one visit, then a trip for a long time." Anyway Ike was due for parole. It was 1996, Ike was at 2 ½ years. As Juan rode past the prison he thought about how he could be in prison right now, if it was for Ike. He turned the car around and went to see him. Juan was fresh in his Look Polo down. Black Polo shirt, black Polo pants, black Polo jacket, a black Polo skull cap and some black suede Air Jordans; it was kinda cold that morning. He really wanted to check trap and leave. He sat in the parking lot thinking about his greed but Ike is his boy. Plus he don't really believe in bad luck, it was his birthday September 26, he was 21 a grown man.

"I might as well gone in and see my boy, I haven't seen in 2 ½ years."

Despite how cold it was, he went and got in that long line. The two pair of footy socks was holding his toes but not his ankles. As he came to the desk, he handed the lady his ID. The dog came and sniffed him down and he went in. The visitation area was crowded with people but very spacious. It had 3 drink machines and 3 snack machines. Everybody looked at him, as he was looking around he seen some fine females of all races. He waited at a machine until an officer came up to him. It was a black lady officer. She was a redbone stood 6 feet and a 165 pounds looking good with her hair in a bob.

"Excuse me, Sir, but you can't stand here. Who are you here to see?"

"I'm here to see Edward Jackson."

"Well Sir you were supposed to come to the desk, and then I would've shown you to your seat. It's over there, by the way. What's your name?"

"My name is Juan, but I'm called Cash."

"I've heard that name around here, my name is Melissa Horne. What are you doing after you leave here?"

"Going back to Atlanta, but anytime you got something plan for us. We can handle business."

"What kinda car do you drive?"

"I'm driving a black and gold BMW, with 20s on it. You'll see it if you leave before me."

"I'll just wait by it and you can follow me to a motel."

"Sound good Melissa." As she walked off he saw Ike coming through the door.

"Hey Ike!" he yelled waving his hands.

Ike looked up and smiled. After 2 ½ years he finally get to see this person. Juan wouldn't send no picture only pictures of shake dancers. Ike rushed over and gave him a hug. Just as they sat down a brown skin girl walked over and gave him her number. He opened the paper and it read Tab... 404-333-9999. He told her they would hook up. He had seen her in line. She was behind him.

"So Ike how is life treating you?"

"Fine man. What brings you this way?"

"Man I got traps everywhere, I was checking trap in Stenson County and decided to stop. Boy Ms. Horne asked for the dick. How is she?"

"Mean as hell. Drag the bitch, man."

"Man, I got a plan. I'ma get her to bring in some weed for you."
"Boy good plan! How is Tasha?"

"Man she's living swell. She got us a condo. She moved off the campus about a year ago to Club House Condos, in Buckhead. Nice condos. She's studying hard. I make her get up every morning to go to school. Man I'm thinking about going to school now. Everybody is telling me to go. I dropped your mom some more money, so you'll be super straight when you get out. I ought to slap you, man you ain't wished me happy birthday or nothing."

"Happy birthday love. Man I'm just so happy to see you. I can't even talk."

"Ike I see you're getting big as hell. How much do you weigh?"

"Two twenty, all solid. I work out every day, nigga don't give me trouble. They call me Big Ike or Richie Rich. Juan man time fly by when you're excited. It's almost time for you to go. One more hour and this visit will only exist in our memory. Oh yeah boy, I'm in college in here. Small business yeah! So gone and go to school so we can make something out of that money. Juan, man you need to keep your head above water, so we can finish what we started."

"Ike why you didn't tell on me, when you went down, man I thought you was gonna lay it down on me."

"Shawty you don't know why?"

"Why? What's up?"

"Because I got mad love for you. This is a vacation so I can get my mind right. See I slipped one time. Never will I slip again. And that hoe Lisa, she's gonna die. But man you got to handle business with Ms. Horne and bring Natasha to see me. I be writing her mom house. She write backs."

"Yeah she tells me. I read the letters. That's how I know what to send you!"

With that their visit was over with. He rushed out to see if she was waiting on him. She was fine and had a nice ass on her. Just as he expected she were parked beside him in a white Nissan two door sports car. As he followed her, he noticed small spots of Alto County he didn't know. Instead of a motel, she pulled up in front of a blue house. It had a nice yard, wasn't that big, a long driveway and 3 small steps to the front door.

"Melissa what part of the game is this?"

"This is my home, Cash, you don't seem all that bad and I don't want to seem like a cheap trick."

"I feel that, this is a very beautiful place!" He wanted to say small place. But he had to hold it in, she picked up on it because all her friends from Atlanta always say, "Girl this house is beautiful but it's kinda small." She sensed the same thing from him because he looked the house up and down.

"Cash, just because you're from Atlanta doesn't mean that this is a small place. This is considered big, considering that I'm single with no kids. So three bedrooms is big enough for me."

"Well, Love, if it's suitable for you, I can't complain, because I stay in a condo. At least you have a house."

He walked in and true to her words the house was kinda big. The living room was like the average living room. Two sofas, two chairs and an entertainment system. The only thing that really caught his eye was the red carpet. She showed him her bedroom king-size bed in the middle of the floor. Three dressers and mirrors on all of them; and a red blanket on the bed. The house was a home for a young, girl who just got out on her own. But he wasn't judgmental. They sat on the bed and talked for hours. She was so surprised to know that he had a heart and agreed with some of her theories of life, love and pain. She believed one must suffer a great deal of pain in order to live and love. He agreed because blacks suffer a great order every day. He kept in his mind about what Ike said, "Drag her."

So he asked her about the weed. She was down with it. To be truthful she was tired of sleeping alone, she just wanted to be held by someone who wasn't a co-worker or didn't really have to worry about coming back maybe he'll come back maybe he won't. But she didn't want to worry about that. All she thought about was this was her time to be embraced. She thought no one would suspect her because she's a sergeant. And mean as hell. She liked him and it showed. They laughed, and played. She liked his charm and confidence. She fed him pork chops, rice, corn and corn-bread muffins. After dinner they were making love.

She slept in his arms as if he'd leave her. She jumped in her sleep because it had been so long since a man held her. She was only 29 years old and every man she picked turned out to be bad. They beat her and took her money. She thought about being gay. She looked up at him and thought how she could trust so fast. She could only pray he wouldn't treat her wrong. She was putting alot on the line for him; her heart and her job. Beside they wouldn't be tighter that much. She knew he had a lady friend in Atlanta. Their space would make them miss each other. She was so happy in her thoughts that she didn't notice him looking at her. When she seen him looking at her, she became frightened.

"Juan, don't tell me you're fix 'en to leave?" Tears formed in her eyes.

"You could wait till I'm asleep."

"Shorty, you just jump to conclusions. I wish you would've asked me if I were leaving. But it's nice to know where your heart is. What time is it?"

"It's 1:30 am why?"

"Because I got to let my people know where I'm at. You know you're not the only female that betray to care about me."

He told her about Tasha and that she and Ike were his only family. She accepts that with a smile, knowing that she too will soon be part of that family.

"Juan don't you think she'll ask you, where you are?"

"Yes! And I'll tell her, see Shorty I don't hide nothing I do. If I have to hide it, I shouldn't do it."

He grabbed the phone and called Tasha, Melissa showed she was irrational. So she tried to get up, but he held her down with his arms. She looked up at him and he kissed her.

"Hello!" her voice sounded through the receiver.

"Tasha I'm in Alto."

"Why are you up there? Are you in trouble?"

"Nah I'm chilling laid up at this moment. I spent my birthday with Ike and Melissa. Melissa works at the prison."

"You trying to get Ike some dope ain't you? Boy, I can't even be mad because Ike'll do the same for you."

"Shorty you know me like a book."

"How is Ike, Juan?"

"He's fine. I just wanted to let you know, I'm not in trouble. I made it through the day."

"Juan I'm glad you're where you're at, because the police are looking for you. They say you really need to contact them."

"Well I'm fix 'en to see what's up now. Bye, love."

As he hung up, Melissa was smiling. Juan called the Fulton County Police Department.

"Yeah. This is Juan Ellis; I heard y'all was looking for me. What's up?"

"This is detective Jones. Ellis I just need to know where you were yesterday 12 noon."

"I was visiting a friend at Lee Arrendale Prison, in Alto. I was visiting Edward Jackson in case you need a name. I do believe they'll have a record of that." Melissa gave him the number and he hung up the phone.

She still couldn't believe how bold he was at the age of 21 years old. He explained to her that she was part of his family and would lack nothing. They made love once again and fell asleep.

Her alarm clock went off at 4:45 am. She looked at him. He was still there, she dressed got the four ounces of weed from the dresser, stuffed them in her bra and kissed him. She left a key so he could lock the door and went to work. Her ride was faster this morning because of the dope. She got through the gates as usual and went through briefing. She knew she had to act normal; she didn't cut no slack with the inmates or her staff. She was quiet in briefing as the heavyset white Lt. gave everyone their post. Her post wouldn't change for another 10 days so she knew her post. She walked out and went straight to her office which she shared with every Sgt. over E-unit. She only had 4 dorms to overlook. 15-16-17-18. They all were open dorm. Ike was in dorm 15 right next to her office. So she called him to her office. When he came in she gave him four sandwich bags of dope and told him that if he got caught it was on him. She explained that nothing had changed, if he try her with anything she was gonna jail him and get him shipped. She also told him she was going to be a little harder on him and at the same time keep him out of trouble. She told him Juan was still at her house and she really liked him. Ike was happy to hear that because that meant more dope for him. He explained the same thing to her that he did. She's now part of their small family gave her his momma number to call if she ever needed anything. All he need was for someone to reel her in. Now it's over with. But he smiled because he was truly happy. Not for her, but for him, because he was fix 'en to smoke out like on the streets no more skeeter legs for him.

CHAPTER 7
Decision

$\mathbf{J}$uan drove 95 North, trying to make his mind up. He didn't know what he wanted no more. All he knew was the streets. But he knew something was missing in his life. He needed love, not street love, but real love. He was so trapped in his emotions that he didn't know his face was bleeding with tears. He looked at his watch and noticed that he'd been driving for 13 hours. He pulled over and got some gas. As he pumped his gas he saw a graveyard. It was as if the graveyard was calling him. The sun had ended his life cycle for today and started to rest. The breeze picked up a little as the wind blew. His black Tommy jeans started to move his black Tommy thigh-length coat that kept him warm. He looked down at his tan Timberlands and smiled he was dressed for the weather. Tasha had called him and told him to stay where he was for a few weeks, because the police were still asking questions. He had to make a pickup then a drop. He went to Florida picked up 30 bricks from Newkirk, a guy he had met in Atlanta at the Playa's ball last year. He took Tasha and Blue with him as his bitches. Newkirk stepped to him about some business. So he decided to take him up on his offer. Ten grand for a brick. So when he steps to him, he's buying 30 at a time. He'll stop in Valdosta holla at Antwon one of his personnel and Antwon would cook it make all the drops for him around that small area. Once he makes those drops he'll head for Atlanta. Antwon was younger than him but had heart. He told him if anything he'll take the fall for him, because Antwon was only 19. He knew he'll take care of business for him if he got popped. Antwon was a small slim brown skin kid with a little cut to him. He had the eyes of a sparrow forever seeing past the bullshit a nigga brought to him. So that was his young nigga.

He turned and looked at the graveyard. It was like the yard was calling him. So he parked the car and walked in the graveyard. It was like he heard a voice on the inside of him telling him he was gonna lose. As he walked by the graveyard he dropped to his knees at a grave site that said Pearl Talley and asked the grave to speak. With complete silence he listened to his heart. A voice told him it was over. He just kneeled and put the Glock to his head. He clicked the Glock and for the first time it hammed up. What was over? He wonders... He looked up and pointed the

Glock to the sky. He released 17 rounds toward Heaven, hoping Heavens doors would open and give him answers. He believed in God, but he couldn't understand why God brought him into this hateful world.

"I don't like doing wrong but you God! Dealt this hand to me. Why did you take my family? Why did you bring Natasha in my life? When you know I'm gonna end up hurting her? Why all this pain? I'm lost and can't be found."

He reloaded the Glock and put it back to his head. As he pulled the trigger, it started thundering and lightning. The gun wouldn't go off.

He sat there on Mrs. Talley's grave and asked "Are you speaking to me old lady?"

He didn't want to face the fact that the old lady had led him to her gravesite because the old lady was the only soul who cared about him. That was his grandmother, his father's mother. He was forced to stay with her when his parents were killed. She made him one promise that she would always be with him. With that promise she died on this same highway. In a sense he hoped his heart would stop the same way hers had stopped. She had a heart attack and drove off the road and hit the side of an off-ramp guard rail. But he wasn't that lucky as she was. After she died he had faced 3 deaths in 10 years. He was 12 year old then and found himself alone on the streets. He used to go to the Public Library and read book and eat out of Wendy's... Long John Silver's... whatever restaurant he came by. What they threw away was his meal for that night. He would take enough for 3 meals a day. He would bum up two or three dollars a day so he could buy little snacks to take with him to the YMCA, where he'd pay 50 cents so he could play with the other kids and stay clean. Sometimes he'd go back to Dotson Rd. to his grandmamma's house and sleep. But he would find himself struggling to find a new life. One Friday night he found his new life when a drug dealer name Ced who was running from the police. Ced threw a blue book bag in the ditch that he hid in some time fell asleep in to the next morning. When he opened the bag it was filled with money, cocaine and a gun. Juan got on his bike and rode back to Dotson Rd. to hide everything. So he could give it back to Ced. He knew Ced would look out for him then. But Ced never came back, because Ced was dead. He had got shot down by the cops. So he counted the money it came up to be $2,000. So he took pieces out of the money to maintain himself. But he stayed on his grandmamma's property now, so he couldn't help but to think about his family. He had no one and he was so young by himself. How could God leave him like that? The more he thought about his family, the more madder he got. He got so mad that he wanted to kill everybody. He got the gun and the book bag and put up 6 bottles. He pointed the 32 automatic and let off 7 rounds. Out of the seven rounds he only hit one bottle. He reloaded the gun and went at it again and again. After two days of shooting, he felt like he was a born sniper. He named the little black gun "Black viper the rattle snake." He paid a junkie named Tim a bag of cocaine, from the bag he got from Ced, there had to be thousands of thousands of little bags in the book bag. They were little dime bags of crack from what he gathered from Tim and it was some good stuff. Tim made a deal with him that he'd run for him, but Juan didn't know what that meant. So he told him he would sell the dope for him, every hundred he made he'd have to give him $20. Tim explained to him 10 bags were $100. So he went and hid the bag in house in his grandmamma's closet and brought out 60 bags. Tim was tall slim cat 6'5" big mustache cool but his eyes told you he was a snake. He gave Tim 10 bag at a time and watched him sell the dimes at the top of the street. Tim had seen the book bag and money so he decided to sell all the dope and rob Juan in the end. After five days everything was gone. Juan had over $5,000 then Tim tried to make his move. Juan trusted Tim because Tim was nice to him and helped him. He told Tim they needed to get some more dope, so he showed Tim where he hid the money at, in his grandma's closet. Tim grabbed the bag and started running. Juan brought out the viper and walked Tim down with the 7 bullet in the viper. As Tim laid there, breathing looking up at the sky smiling. He looked at Juan and told him "The game is to win all the time. Don't let nobody take nothing from you." Tim smiled and closed his eyes.

Juan had to find another place to stay, because they would soon find Tim's body. He wasn't strong enough to move a dead man. He went back in the house, got his brown book bag, put some clothes in it and left. He went in his pocket and felt the two dime bags he always kept in his pocket for Tim. Tim wasn't gonna get these two sacks he thought, while walking the streets. He saw a man name Wicket; he had seen Wicket and Ced hang together and used to go to the store for them. They'll give him a dollar for going. He told Wicket what he had done to Tim and what he had done and he needed some more cocaine. Wicket looked him in the eyes and called him little killer. That was his new name. Wicket was cool. He was 26, 165 pounds. Tall slim with 4 gold's at the top and two at the bottom on the fronts. Low hair cut with a beard that connected to his side burns. Wicket gave him 4 ½ ounces of crack for $3,500 and a place to stay and trap. He taught him the game since he was already in it too deep. He even taught him about pimping. He taught him how to trick off with junkie hoes for crack. As time passed Juan was unstoppable no one expected a 13-year-old kid to be that strong. But he was with Wicket help. Wicket had a brother name Ike. Ike and Juan became best friends. Ike was 6 ½ years older than him, but age didn't matter because Wicket told them they all was family. They sold dope together even tried to be young pimps. Wicket got their peter sucked every day and let them sleep with any girl they wanted.

A year later Wicket got killed. Somebody came in to rob Wicket apartment on Cushman Circle #211. Not many people knew where they stayed because they sold dope everywhere. Wicket didn't want them to stay in one place, because the robbing crew can set them up by scoping them out. The robber didn't expect Wicket to be home. So when they broke in Wicket bucked and they killed him. They didn't get anything because Wicket always hid stuff at his mom house in the dog house and Juan always kept everything close to him. That's what Wicket liked about him. He was in it to win it. Wicket never let them buy over 2 bricks because he knew niggas talked. So when they got there, Wicket told them who it was and for them to love each other. Wicket told them where his money and dope was. So he left them with everything; three cars, the two traps apartment; one in Edgewood Court the other one in Fairburn Village. Clothes, shoes, dope, money and jewelry. Ike was kinda scared but Juan told him they were on their own, and they had to kill Fred and Bobo. Juan just walked up to Fred one night coming out of Fairburn Village and shot Fred in the head in the middle of the street and ran through the pathway; back to MLK to Cushman Circle. Ike caught Bobo in the trap one morning buying some re-up shot him in the head as soon as he came around the corner of the apartment building, he was trapping in, in Fairburn Village. Nothing could tear them apart; they were in it to win it.

Now Ike is in jail and he's at his granny's gravesite. He's in love and doesn't want to accept it. His mind drifted back to Tasha. He promised her he wouldn't hurt her. He only wanted to make a life for her. She's the one to start his family. She loves him and he needs her in his life. He picked up the phone and called her.

"Tasha, listen. I'm in Forrest Park at my granny's grave site. I was coming back from Miami and the graveyard called me. I finally think I understand life. You are my life. I only want to make things right. I want to make a life for us. I want to love you with all my heart. Tasha, please tell me you love me!"

She was crying so hard you could hear her tears hitting the receiver.

"Juan, you know I'll always love you. But the cops here are talking about you killing a man 3 weeks ago. Juan, please tell me you didn't. I can't go to the water for you because they know we weren't together. Please come home and please turn yourself in. If you didn't do anything, you'll be alright.

"If I turn myself in will you stay by my side?"

"Yes I will. I promise."

"Tell them I'll be at their office in an hour."

With that, he brought everything to life. Tasha was what his granny was telling him. He drove to the Fulton County jail and turned himself in. Tasha, her father, mother and grandfather were there. Her father told him everything would be alright. He explained to them that he had got to the prison around 10 o'clock and a week later he was in front of a judge. Mr. Middle filed a speedy trial motion after he entered his not guilty plea. A month later they found him guilty of murder and this time he didn't do it. He had proof he didn't do it because he was at the prison visiting Ike. Juan didn't have a chance at trial. Mr. Middle didn't do his investigation; he couldn't get the proof. He was railroaded. A week later he was shipped to prison. Tasha and her grandfather knew Richard helped railroad him so he told Tasha not to worry because he was going to handle the case. He promised her he wouldn't do any more than a year. He couldn't believe Richard hated that boy so much that he'd help send him to prison just to protect Tasha from him. Harold didn't approve of the relationship. But he believed in her being happy. He was the reason why Tasha was doing so well in school. He was mad but couldn't show it. She was crying and ran to her father.

"Daddy, twenty years is too much for a murder he didn't do. Daddy, please get him out. I'm pregnant. I can't raise a baby by myself. Daddy, you have to help me; you're his lawyer. Why hasn't he written me? He has money; he went in with five thousand. I know he feels like I betrayed him. Daddy, why ain't you talking?"

Harold looked at him waiting on an answer. Nancy was waiting also. Tasha just hit them with the hard news. No matter how much he hated him, he had to accept him because he was his grandchild's father. Nancy looked even harder after being trapped in thoughts.

"Natasha I'm thinking about a way to get him out. I know you want him home with you and the baby. Didn't daddy just say he's gonna try to get him out in a year's time? Just be patient. We just can't snap our fingers and he'll get out. He needs this time to get his mind together."

Juan wrote three letters his first week in Valdosta State Prison; one to the love of his life, and the other two to Ike and Melissa. He stayed in his two man room which was six by nine feet and had a bunk bed, toilet, sink, two locker boxes on the wall, and had a long three inch tall window in the back wall. His roommate was a cat named Ryan, a high yellow kid 18 years old with a round baby face, thin mustache and hazel eyes. He was considered cute in prison, at least that's what everybody would say when they walk to chow. They gave him a third shift detail-he had to clean the showers. This white thick female 5'5, 140 pounds and blonde named Sandy Brown always talked to him as he cleaned the shower. There were 5 other guys cleaning up at night also. But she talked to him basically because he was new. He tried her and told her he had to write 2 letters and he needed 2 stamps. She got the stamps from a white inmate that she was cool with. She let the inmate whack their penis in front of her. She'll either watch them or turn her ass to them so everybody liked her. He told her it will take two weeks before his money came. But promised her that he'll return the favor. Hopefully they'll get cool, because he truly was lost and needed inside help like Ike got. Ike had told him during his visit that he didn't ask anybody for anything when he first came in. So he's doing the same. Ryan offered but he didn't accept. He wrote and told Ike what was all going on. He thought about how to ask her for help. So, he decided to write her a letter. He tried to give her the letter the next night, but she told him to read it to her, because she didn't want anyone to get jealous and write a letter out on her. He just sat at the table in the drop off with his head down. The drop off had four tables and a wall that blocked the booth from seeing the last two tables. The other orderly was buffing the big floor, TV room, top range and bottom range.

"Look me in my eyes and read the letter to me,"

Sandy was pretty and had some pretty blue eyes. She had a heart and it showed. He looked her in the eyes and balled the letter up.

"Why did you ball it up, Ellis ?"

"Because if I had to look you in your eyes, then the paper does me no good. Listen, I thank you for the two stamps. I plan to pay you back 100 times that, which will be $660. Listen, I'm a millionaire, I just got jammed up. I don't really have any family; I can't take this life anymore. I really need a friend, somebody to do this time with me. I know you don't believe me, but time will tell and show you I'm true."

"Well Mr. Ellis, time will tell. For right now, keep everything on the low and as of now you're my orderly, okay? That way I can keep an eye on you and we can get to know each other a little better. Know one thing-I will be your friend but nothing freaky."

"That's all I'm asking for is a true friend."

"Okay."

Sandy's heart went out to him, because he was 21 years old with no family and she saw the sincerity in his eyes. They put him on mental health but he would not take medication. He had a depression problem as well as a psychotic feature.

Days went by and Sandy was getting pretty cool. She cried when she saw him cry. He was so depressed, and she wondered what she could do. So, she sat and wrote him a letter and dated it October 28, 1996. She went to the front, stamped it and put it in the mailbox the next morning. Time was hard on him until he got Tasha's first letter and his money came. He wrote her and told her the county didn't send his money. She put 2 grand in his envelope, so he had 2 grand and a letter from his girl. He smiled. He had been locked up 69 days. Sandy told him to get in school and work for her at night. Buffing the floors and cleaning the showers was cool because that took his mind off his life. Plus, it made him sleepy. He'll stay up until they called school at 7:45 until 9:45. That way, Ryan had the room to himself. All he did was sleep during the day. He and Ryan barely talked but when they did talk, they talked about his sister Sonya. He didn't like his older sister, so he didn't call her name. Ryan got store restriction for smoking, so when Juan went to the store he'd buy Ryan $20 worth of store goods every week because Ryan tried to look out for him.

Tasha didn't tell him she was pregnant, just that he'll be out real soon. To hold his head, she told him to go to school and get to know God. He showed Sandy the letter and his money order. To his surprise, she went and got a bible. To her surprise he showed her so many bible verses and broke them down to her so that she felt joy. Then he explained that he had been on the streets since he was 12. That's why it's so hard for him to really accept God. He went to his room, got on his top bunk, closed his eyes and pictured how he and Tasha used to make love. Sandy walked up and hit the door. He looked up and she was smiling.

"Sandy, you play like that? You broke my concentration."

He washed up and started playing with her, joking and touching hands at the table. He asked her to help him write Tasha a letter. She couldn't come up with any good suggestions, so she told him to think of his love for her.

Sandy had become a sister to him and somewhat a mother. All he knew was Sandy. He didn't talk to the other inmates because they weren't on his level. He asked Sandy what made her want to help him. She told him she'd seen hurt in his eyes, he was someone who needed help.

She wanted to tell him so much about herself, but she had to keep it professional and care for him at the same time. Juan was the type of kid who had a world full of hate and disappointment, and she knew it. Her family wasn't always there for her, so she understood a little.

"Why don't you talk to your counselor Ms. V.K.?"

"Sandy I don't talk much and I really don't like her. She has a world of hate and hurt built inside of her. So at any golden moment she'll pop. I don't want to be the one she unleashes it on. I'm tired of hurting people and causing family to cry. When my own family can't cry because they're living free up there in Heaven, while I'm suffering in hell. Sandy why did I have a bad life? I don't want to ever get out of prison, if I'ma keep suffering? "Juan you don't mean that. I'm gonna make a promise to you. If I'm here the day you go back to court I'm gonna give you my number and address, deal? But you got to learn to heal yourself. If you don't love you then no one will. And I'm not lying. I'm gonna read you this story I wrote for this short storybook. It's called "Learning to Heal." Please pay attention. It's a Christian story, but it fits your life so listen.

Learning to Heal
"Any name,
Last night was a hard night, because my mind was stuck on why? Why is my family so hard on me? Does my family really care? As tears ran down my eye, I came to find that I couldn't answer that question only my family.

I went to my parent's door. I saw them laughing and my mind told me they were laughing at me. I slowly turned around and walked away. I looked in the mirror and seen a long face. As I moved, my face would stretch. I looked. I heard a voice on the inside of me saying "come."

"Come where?" I asked the voice.

"Come to the mirror."

As I walked to the mirror, I heard another voice, "Why are you crying?"

"No one loves me," I replied and poked out my lips.

The mirror said, "So?" and laughed at me.

"Hey, what are you laughing at?"

"I'm laughing at you. You look so silly, crying with your lips out. Hey I've seen you look so beautiful. Now you look like a mess."

"Don't laugh at me mirror. I'll break you."

"Oh, now you want to get mad at me, because someone has mistreated you. That's wrong because even though you feel don't nobody love you. I love you."

"How can you love me? You're not real."

"Hey! Hey! That's something I don't play. I'm just as real as you are. See, many people I've seen come and go. But you're different, alot different."

"Why am I so different?"

"Because I'm you and your me."

"Hold up mirror, you're trying to trick me."

"Nah but I see you smiling. See, I'm really your reflection, see when you're down, your reflection is down. Only you can pick yourself back up. See, as long as you love yourself, then others will love you. Just because people do you bad, don't mean you stop loving yourself. Now ask yourself, "What am I mad at? Who am I mad at? Do they deserve forgiveness?"

"Well my parents they're always arguing and hitting on me. I feel don't nobody care."

"But they do. Have you ever heard of Jesus?"

"Yes! He died for our sins."

"That's all you know? Well let me tell you a story about a little boy named Eric. Eric was blind, but he had a heart of gold. Every day Eric would get his guide dog Spike and walk the streets. He would hear all the problems of the world beyond his sight. He always says, "Lord God, I wish I could see, by me having my sight I can see what's real and what's fake. If I had my sight I would do my part in helping someone find life and happiness, if only I had my sight."

Eric would start to cry, because he didn't understand how he lost his sight and why he was born blind.

See while Eric mother was carrying him, her husband abused her.

"Why?" she used to always ask. Her husband would only hit her more. Love is blind, and a fool for love is a fool for pain. She thought to herself,

"Maybe he'll stop. Maybe he'll understand he's hurting the baby."

But it only got worse. Finally she got enough courage to leave. Months later Eric was born. When the doctor told her Eric was blind, she cried and cried. Her heart ached with pain; her tears flowed like the rain. She looked at her baby boy and said, "No matter what it takes, I'm gonna be the very best to you." I'm gonna be the very best to you." She held Eric while he cried. She asked the doctor to make him stop crying but the doctor couldn't. As he cried she thought, "I'm not ready to raise a baby. Lord please forgive me; but I got to put him in better hands."

She spoke with the doctor about putting him up for adoption. The doctor explained the procedure to her and told her she was doing the right thing.

As year went by and Eric grew up, he was filled with hatred for both of his parents, without knowing why. All he knew was his parents didn't love him. But that didn't stop him from walking every day to listen to the problems of the world. Eric would pray each night he returned home. One Sunday morning, Eric got up and started for church. As him and Spike walked the sidewalk, a drunk driver ran his car on the sidewalk and hit Eric. Eric was seriously injured that there was no chance of survival, one doctor said. A middle age couple was in the hospital hallway as the doctor discussed Eric's situation. The couple said, "There has to be something we can do. There got to be something y'all can do. Look here we got money. We want the best operation there is and we're gonna stick by the boy's side."

They didn't even know the boy's name, because his chart said, "John Doe."

Day in and Day out the couple sat there and prayed. The day came for the operation. It was hours before the couple heard anything.

"How is he?" they asked.

"Everything is fine. We even restored his sight."

The couple started crying, because truly they had done a good deed. One hour later the couple was allowed to see him. Eric, now able to see asked as he heard them come in, "Are y'all the couple that saved my life?"

The couple answered, "No baby, we just took part in it. God wasn't ready for you to come home. By the way, we're the Flowers."

"My name is Lawanda," the older woman said.

"And my name is Torrey."

"What is your name?" they asked.

"My name is Eric Smith."

"Where is your family?"

"Well my real parent walked out on me at birth and my adopted parent passed."

They cried, "You know Eric, we have a son that we walked out on at birth 20 years ago. I wasn't ready to be a mom and my husband here was a drunk and a woman beater. We just wasn't ready."

Eric began to cry and asked, "What was his name?"

"Eric," Wanda replied.

Eric then looked up with his eye open and said, "Truly God answers prayer."

They asked, "Why would you say that?"

He explained, "All these years I thought my parents didn't love me. Now I see who y'all really are."

I began to cry, because truly all we want our family to do is love, forgive and forget.

"Do you know how to make that happen?" the mirror asked.

"No," I replied.

"Well you wasn't listening to the story. See, if you take it to God he'll deliver you and your family."

"Ok, Juan, what did you get from my story?"

"Sandy your story was cool. It shows you really believe in God, and he'll deliver us from our situation. Sandy, why didn't he deliver me? All the pain I'm going through. No family. No one who really loves me. I'm stuck here for the rest of my life."

"No! You ain't Juan, you got to believe in God and trust in him."

"Trusting in him ain't got me nowhere. I trusted in Him my whole life. What you think I don't know what he's done for y'all? He ain't done Jack for Juan Ellis. But made another option. I must be optimistic that I'm gonna make it out of here, if I have to give up all my money. But waiting on your God is like waiting forever. Someone asked what's a million dollars to you. He said one penny. He asked what's a million years to you. He said one day. So the man asked God can you give me one penny of your wealth. Do you know what God said to him? The Lord said yes, I will one day. So waiting on God is like dying over and over again. His happiness consists of Heaven Sandy. We're here to suffer."

"I noticed as I was reading you was writing. Who were you writing?"

"I was writing Tasha."

"Read it to me please?"

"No!"

"Come on Juan, read it to me. I want to see where your heart is."

"Sandy, where is your heart? Are you pitying me? Because your God says visit the motherless and prisoner?"

She hit the table with her fist.

"God dammit! That's it! Juan, you think you're the only one having or have a bad life? Ha! Let me tell you like this. You don't know how it is to lay beside someone who's abusing you. Rarely love you, I got problems! I need peace! I'm just as locked up as you are. I'm locked up mentally and emotionally! There! Are you happy now? Is this what you want? To see someone else tears besides yours? Well Juan, here my tears. Take them to bed with you. I don't have nothing. Like you don't have nothing! I see my life in you! My heart goes out to you! Anytime you think its pity then screw you Juan Ellis, screw you!"

"Sandy don't cry. Take this to heart, my letter to Tasha and words to you. If life was perfect, everybody will be happy, but nobody is perfect. So we must try to stay strong to what we believe in. I've accepted the things I can't change. Right now I need you more than a Christian prayer to God in hopes of making us stronger."

She cut him off because she saw where he was going. The words she spoke to him, he was putting in his own words only to find her heart. She looked him eye to eye.

"Juan I've never thought about making love to a Black but you've taken control of my mind, body and soul. It's now 3:00 am and everybody is through cleaning up and going to bed. Once I finish counting meet me in my office. I got a special gift to give you."

She rushed her count and waited downstairs in her office which really was the counselor office by the showers. Juan entered the office. Sandy dropped to her knees and took his penis out of his grey gym shorts and placed it in her mouth, sucking at a slow pace. She became hot. She took off her uniform and they made love on top of the brown wooden desk that sat in the middle of the floor. Sandy wanted to lie in his arm, but Juan stood strong and walked out of the office and went to take a shower. The shower had a shower curtain. He didn't close the curtain so she stood and watched him shower. She asked for his rag and stepped in the other shower beside the one he was in and washed herself, not caring who saw her get the rag. She cleaned herself and went in the office and stayed because she couldn't believe that she let herself go so quickly. Juan stood in the door watching her sitting in the dark crying. She told him to go to bed. He blew her a kiss and walked in his room, locked the door, got in his bunk and went to sleep. Sandy walked to his room, opened the door with her key and prayed over him. She took in love for him.

Juan tossed and turned in his sleep and jumped up sweating with tears in his eyes. He couldn't figure out why he was crying or what he was dreaming about, as he sat there lost in space. It hit him real fast that he was really locked up. He looked out the door; he couldn't see anyone out the dormitory for day shift. Everybody must be on wellness walk outside doing daily exercise. He looked at his watch and it read 9:14 Jan 29, 1997. Tears ran down his checks. It had been three months and he had not noticed it because he tried not to think about it. He had school to worry about and sandy was on love time consisted of the raising and setting of the sun. Weeks had turned to months. He cried out with moans. He wanted his family but God had left him alone.

"Why? Why? I didn't even do nothing. God get me out of this mess. I promise I'll change my life. I'm locked away for the rest of my life. What about Tasha? What about my dreams of a family? What about me, God? What are you telling me? You want me to read my bible? You want me to pray? What is it? Why are you awakening me with these dreams of murder? Are you planning to kill me? I don't want to die! I want a family! I want a baby! I want Tasha! I can't bear this any longer. Help me God. Don't take Tasha away!"

Sandy had been off on her 2 week vacation, so all he did was go to school. He knew just about everything they was teaching him. He took a Tab test and past it. Made a 100 on all 5 subjects Math, Reading, Writing, Science and Social Studies. He was ready to take his GED. But he had to wait until the rest of the students were ready. So they moved him into a G-Sam. The next step to GED, there he passed everything because he brought his books back and studied to keep his mid-off of Sandy and Tasha.

Sandy came back to work and things slowed down. She helped him with his math, he was having small problem with Algebra. So she taught him a quick way to do it. By thinking about selling drugs and he got it.

CHAPTER 8
Take My Breath Away

As Tasha drove to her mom's house, tears fell. Tasha's heart was overly happy when she received his letters. It showed and secured her love on his love. She read them over and over again. Telling herself that she must bring her baby's daddy home. Her dad and granddaddy was doing everything in their power to get him out. Richard had to help now that a baby was involved.

Tasha hoped his prison time would change him because he sounded like a changed man in his letters. In many ways she was glad he was there. Being there would give him enough time to think about her and their future. She got a nice apartment for them; in Forest Garden Apartments in Buckhead. It was a 3 bedroom and one bath apartment; with a full living room. She was proud of herself at the same time sad. She had to stay busy, so she wouldn't think about him. She haven't visited him yet. But she had plans. She could only hope God was on the same mind she was on giving him a change of heart.

She wrote him another letter telling him about home and to change his ways because God had given them a blessing. She took pride in him and was gonna take pride in raising their baby. Her mom stood in the doorway of her bedroom while she laid on the bed writing him. She turned and looked at her mama and said, "Juan can be turned from a name Juan to a girl's name Juanna."

Nancy smiled because she had grown to accept him. Richard was slowly accepting but she had already accepted him and Tasha knew it.

"Mama, you know daddy got to give Juan credit. He kept me in school, out of trouble. He didn't beat me, he came home and he didn't bring the drugs around me."

Part of that was the truth she thought to herself because she used to help him bag some of the dope. She always told him if he went down they'll go together. She even sold some weed he had robbed for. He taught her about the street game. They were in a frat party when she heard two white guys say they couldn't find the pot nowhere. They needed two pounds. She told 'em to give her 3 grand and she'll bring them the two pounds. They told her 3 grand was too much for two pounds. She told 'em not if I got to steal them it's not. Juan had weed and dope in the closet.

They gave her the money first. She left Juan and went home and got the two pounds out the closet. He didn't know she knew where the weed was. But as soon as she went in the room with them white boy he was fix 'en to snap. He thought they had drugged her. He went in and seen the dope on the bed and almost lost it. She smiled and kissed him whispered in his ear,

"I got 3 grand so leave me alone."

He smiled because she only supposed to get $1,600.

She snapped back into the conversation that she was having with her mom. She was smiling. Nancy wanted to ask what the smile was for. But she knew how a memory lane smile was.

"Mom, he'll change, because Psalm 37: 4 says if I put Heaven first my eyes on God he'll give me my heart desires. And my whole being is him Juan. I wrote him a very meaningful letter. I told him how God is blessing us. And how God loves him."

"Tasha did you tell him about the baby?"

"No! Because I want him to change, and if anything should happen to me while he's there, it won't hurt him. See, all Juan want is a family. I've produced all of that, I plan on marrying him even if that means I'll have to wait 20 years because he's my better half. I wonder what he's doing now. I bet he's lifting weights trying to get all swole. Hot damn my baby gonna be built."

"Tasha, your daddy says they took weights out of the Georgia prisons."

"Well, he's doing push up trying to get swolled up off hot meals and cold cuts. That's something he said in one of his letter. He promised to write me some poems. He said he's realizing a different part of himself. The part I want open is his heart, everybody got a heart. The doctor said my stomach won't get that fat because of the diet I'm on plus I exercise alot doing sit ups rolling my stomach on that airball. I'm hiding my pregnancy at the same time I'm staying in shape. I look good at five months. Well I got to go back to campus and study these law books. Do you think if I ask my professor to help me with Juan case, he will?"

"Baby just let your father and granddaddy handle it. He'll know you're doing your part. I know you told him your father and granddaddy are working by the hours for him. Oh yeah, your daddy wants to know why are you still living in the apartment on the campus and in Buckhead."

"Yes I did tell him that daddy they is doing their best and I learned that from Juan, to keep two places so no one will know where I lay my head.

That way it will be hard to rob me."

Tasha drove off in the cold December air just smiling and loving the present of Juan through his letters. It was like he was sitting on the passenger seat talking to her. Wearing one of them Fubu suits just like she was wearing. She had the red and blue he probably would've had blue and red or blue and white. With the matching shoes. Like hers.

She stopped at a red light on the corner of Ashby and MLK Drive smiling and enjoying life. A black male put a gun to her face and told her to get out the car. She didn't know what to do. She didn't want to lose the candy apple red painted, 20 inch rim gold grill and gold trimming. She had put a pull out Kenwood CD player and 12 inch woofer and 2 1,000 watts Kenwood amps. Juan told her not to fix the car up. When she begged him for it, she promised she wouldn't fix it up. But did the opposite. Soon as she got it. She took it to Godfather and he hooked it up for 3 grand. Now she's at a red light with a gun in her face.

"Bitch up the car and you'll live. But play super Dave and you'll die trying a silly stunt."

"Okay! Okay! You can have the car just don't kill me."

She began to open the door and stuck her left foot out and with the right one stomped on the gas. The jacker fired two shots at her but missed. He didn't even hit the car, she was so glad, that she felt with Juan's spirit nobody could stop her.

She had parked the car and ran in to tell Blue Eyes what she had done. She had bucked a car jacker. But when she came in her eyes were widen by the surprise she saw on the TV. Somebody had taped the whole thing and turned it into the police. The white female officer said she was lucky to be alive. She stared at the phone because she knows it would ring. But it didn't! Blue Eyes did.

"You stupid bitch! You stupid bitch! I can't afford to lose my sister. You are my sister bitch! You got a baby in you! That boy would've went crazy if you had gotten hurt. You stupid bitch! A car Tasha? You risked your family for a car? When you can get another one! If you don't tell that boy about that baby then I'm gonna tell him. If he don't know about this I'm gonna tell him. You don't buck on no gun. What the hell is wrong with you? Bitch you were face to face with death."

Blue Eyes couldn't finish before the phone rang. She picked it up, accepted the call and handed the phone to Tasha. Tears rolled down her cheeks because she knew he was gonna snap. She held her breath with the phone to her ear.

"Don't go crying now, Super Dave. So you think you're Linda Carter Super Woman, who can out run a bullet? Bitch have you went crazy? That nigga could've hit that gas tank. I told you not to fix the car up you lied to me, Tasha. What were you thinking about? What you think a nigga ain't gonna try that red 400 up? If you wanna play roulette, get a gun and kill yourself, because another stunt like that is gonna take me to the grave with you, and we'll never be 22 years old. I didn't want you to drive to Valdosta, Georgia, but you got to get down here Saturday because I got to put some sense back in your brain. You ain't me! You think cause you my lady Nigga's gonna say that's Juan's lady leave her alone. Hell No!. You're a target whether you like it or not. Now park that gotdamn car and get you a Honda you got that?"

With a trembling voice she answered, "Yes."

With nothing else to say the phone went dead. Juan either hung up or his 15 minutes was up. She dropped the phone, looked around and fell into Blue Eyes' arms. The thick cotton pink DKNY sweater comforted her head. Her hands on Blue Eyes pink GAP pants she spoke,

"I couldn't let him take nothing from Juan. That's all I got of him now. Blue, I love that boy, he just don't know."

"Hell bitch you just don't understand. He loves you and don't want you to get hurt. The letter said, 'Stay safe and protect yourself and heart.' All this will be behind y'all. Y'all will grow from this."

"Blue, I didn't plan our relationship to come to this. But as he says, 'Things happen.' Blue, you're on his visitation list. Are you coming with me Saturday to see him?"

"Yes I want to see how he looks with all those muscles."

"It's all muscle. Well Blue, I'm fix 'en to eat and go to sleep. I was gonna study but I blew that. Plus, we don't need no pressure on his baby."

She fixed a hamburger fries and grape Kool-Aid, she ate showered and went to sleep.

Thursday and Friday went by fast, because the girls stayed in their books. Blue asked over and over again if she was going to buy the Honda. Like he told her. She just smiled and said they would make it through. He would see things her way and let her keep the car. She was pretty sure of that. They got dressed, wearing almost the same thing. Blue had on a black polo shirt and shorts, with some DKNY Reeboks, black and white. Tasha had on a blue polo and blue and white Nike Jordans. They left at 5:00 AM and arrived at the prison at 9:00 AM. They walked into this small room. Some dogs sniffed them and they walked through a metal detector. As soon as they went through the double doors, they saw him sitting by a small wooden table and two chairs.

Tasha ran and fell into his arms, kissed him and told him she loved him. Blue just gave him a hug and a kiss on the cheek. Blue asked him did he want anything out of the food machine. He ordered hot wings and pizza, 2 grape sodas.

"Tasha, you're not the person I fell in love with it's like you're hiding something from me. There's so much I would like to say to you. But I can't because I feel, no I don't really fell close to you anymore."

"I don't know why? Because I'm doing everything in my power to prove my love is real. So what? I lied to you about the car. The reason why I bucked the Jack because I felt like he was taking something from you. I'm sorry I'm not fitting your approval but I do love you."

It was all smiles from there. They ate and joked about a threesome when he came home. Time went by so fast, it was time to go before they knew it. Before Tasha could cry. He walked away and went in the shake down room. When he got back to the dorm, everybody was asking about Tasha and Blue. The ones who went to visitation because he kissed both of them in the mouth when he left. He just laughed and went to his room.

Ryan had his family pictures out looking at them. Juan took a look and saw this redbone he liked and Ryan told him that was Sonya. He told him he had to put him on. So they sat down and wrote. He and Ryan had got cool, once he peeped him out. Juan became depressed and put the cover over his face. Something about seeing a happy family always got to him. Times like this he wished Tasha or Sandy was there. He couldn't wait to see Sandy tonight. He had already planned to make love to her and think about Tasha. So he was straight again.

He fell to sleep thinking about his day before he knew it he felt some lips kissing him. It was 2:00am Sandy asked, "What you're gonna do sleep all night?"

He smiled, got up, brushed his teeth, washed his face and began to clean up. He had that floor buffed in 30 minute. The rest of the orderly was asleep. He went to the off and kissed Sandy. Sandy dropped to her knees and performed like always. They made love for an hour. All of a sudden Ryan was standing in the door crying with his pants down. They jumped up dressed and Sandy ran and cried, "Rape! Help, rape!"

Juan thought, "Damn this bitch done screamed on me."

He asked Ryan what the hell was going on. Ryan explained to him three boys had raped him. Juan ran to calm Sandy down and told her the deal. She acted like she already knew because she had seen it before. Her only concern was, "Will he tell?"

Juan insisted, "In this situation he won't."

The lieutenant came and Ryan told him what happened. The boys waited until Sandy made her rounds, called her count in and then they raped him. He added they put a sock in his mouth. So Juan and Sandy wouldn't get in trouble.

Juan looked at him and told him not to worry because when he comes back the debt will be paid. Juan laid down to think, but Sandy wouldn't let him rest because she seen the killer look in his eyes. So she arranged for Juan to go to lockdown but it was too late. Juan had a buddy name Snap Dog.

"Jesse Parker who had life without parole. Struck his head in the door and Juan told him to kill the boys who raped Ryan. The next day Juan got on the phone with Tasha gave her orders and told her not to put her name on the money order. They locked him down and he wasn't mad, because 'Snap' will take the fall by himself.

They put him in the last cell on the range. The range had bars on them; 21 cells, with only 6 people were in them. They were so spaced out that neither bothered to talk. Three days had passed with no sight of Sandy. He had nothing to do better than read his Bible. His school teacher Ms. Oliver came to see him. She's black short nice tits from the look of her white blouse. She had on a black skirt everybody say she eat it up. But he never tried to ejaculate off of her.

She stood in the bars giving him his books and assignment. She told him she'll come back on Friday to give him his GED test since he had already passed his pre-GED. She kept pushing her breast between the bars and looking down at him smiling. He thought to himself, she must do eat the dick up. He never ejaculated off none of the staff but her breast was getting very enticing. He stood there in his white nylon T-shirt and boxers. She saw him arousing through his boxers because the tip of him was almost out of the split.

She looked at him and said, "It's okay I understand y'all men need to release some pressure. I don't care about jacking."

So he grabbed his baby oil and jacked off her. She stood there fanning herself watching his every stroke. She unbuttoned the top two button of her blouse and let him see her breast smiling. Everybody knew he had money because most of everybody from Atlanta down there knew him or either heard about him. So they talked about him alot. Most women working in a man prison get swept off their feet because it's so easy to see when a female was hurting or lonely. In this case Ms. Oliver was just friendly and freaky. He finished cleaned himself and she stayed a few more minute and told him she'll be back on Friday.

So he started his work and read the Bible for the rest of the day. Mail came late. But it came he received a letter from Sandy six letters from Tasha and one from Blue. Tasha told him to get to know God but he was already doing that. Sandy told him to stay strong and he'll always be the new love of her life, and Blue told him she was dead seriously about the threesome and it would happen.

Ten o'clock came by so fast reading the Bible. He didn't even notice Sandy standing there looking at him. She smiled at him and told him she'll be back later. She had to go pack up the 3 guys that was shipping out. She was the only officer working that range. Her desk sat at the top of the range, she was glad he was in the back because she could talk to him.

She packed them up and walked them to the top of the range another white male came and got them. She made her rounds and opened his cell door. She told him Ryan tried to kill himself but didn't die. Ryan sent his picture and mom address through her. This meant the favor to be returned was to look out for his mother and sister.

Sandy wanted to make love, Juan showing no more concern about Ryan flicked the pictures and address on his shelf, fell into Sandy's arm. Juan had no dick control, he didn't care about nobody but Tasha, not even Sandy. He tried to trick himself, even she knew it was just a jail thing but she didn't care.

Juan had arranged for Tasha to send some weed through the mail in a house coat. The coat came a week later he was happy because he had passed his GED so when Sandy came they celebrated by smoking weed. Laughing at each other. She had really fell in love with him. No men or women ever treated her the way he did. No one never held her so strong and compassionate as him. She wanted him and wanted him right then. For the first time she came out all her clothes sat her radio on the shelf and got in bed with him, where they made mad passionate love to each other. Sandy fell asleep in his arms, not even caring about her marriage or job. She need this affair to give her back her sanity.

As Juan laid there he heard, "Help! Help! G-2. Help! Help! Medical!" over the radio. He woke her up and told her somebody was dying or getting beat pretty bad. The call came again. She jumped up, dressed and walked to the front of the range. She couldn't leave her post. So she called medical, and they told her Ryan had killed himself and somebody in G-2 had killed 3 boys in their sleep. Sandy asked who the killer was? The nurse said they don't know the dorm was on lock down.

She told Juan everything that happen and made him promise that he didn't have nothing to do with it.

He promised and told her,

"This is the favor Ryan wanted me to do, take care of his sister and mother. So I had nothing to do with that."

She kissed him and asked, "Am I going to see you when you get out?"

"Damn right!," he replied.

She had to run to her deck because her L.T. was coming on the range. She heard him answer his radio. She let him in; he was an old white fellow about 50 and skinny. He's had a crush on Sandy for years. Always try to buy it but she'll turn him down. He looked at her and told her he need to see Juan. But he wanted her to know that the walls talk, and they been saying some unusual things. He told her it don't cost much to keep his mouth closed. She just smiled and told him we'll see.

They walked down to Juan cell, he pretended to be sleep. He woke him up and asked how did he know Ryan. Juan replied, "Not that good, but he was cool. He wanted me to go with his sister Sonya that's all."

"Well he's dead."

"What? How can he die on medical?"

"He hung himself."

"Damn!"

"Also the boys who raped him was killed in their sleep."

"Damn, Ryan spirit work fast."

They laughed. "I just wanted you to know, people is gonna ask questions about them."

"Listen I can't answer them, because I'm down here. Ryan people got money. Shit I don't know."

"Well Juan you're right."

"Hell I'm down here and don't know why!"

"Mrs. Brown suggested that you come down here. Something about you're depressed about having no family and your girlfriend broke up with you and you wanted to kill yourself. You blame yourself for what happen to Ryan because you were in the shower. The mental health director suppose to come see you. But she's out. You'll get out soon. Just don't do nothing stupid."

Juan smiled and went to sleep.

A few days turned out to be ninety, because Sandy new 90-day post was there. Juan didn't complain at all. Every night he had free world food, sex and dope. He didn't care. He had his days mapped out he'll smoke weed, read the Bible and write Tasha Bible verses high as hell. "Snap Dog" would send little notes about how the three little pigs cried out. Juan would only laugh, because "Snap Dog" is 30 something and can't spell. He spelled pig, 'big.' Juan would throw the note in the toilet and laugh all night.

Juan got a letter from Ike saying he made parole. He was seeing Tasha every day, but Tasha had made him promise not to say anything about the baby. He told Juan that he was also sleeping with Melissa and she sent the tape and papers to Tasha's pad. Juan just smiled and wrote Ike a letter and gave him Ryan's address. Ike was to give them 50 grand and tell them it was from him for Ryan.

Days went by, and then a letter came from Sonya and her mom thanking him. Sonya told him about her Cuban boyfriend how he was a big time dope dealer and how he treated her. She wanted him to tell Ike to rob and kill him. But Juan didn't respond to that, only to the family on how he'll be out soon and hooking up with Sonya. Juan looked at himself if the mirror he had gotten big eating Sandy's home cooked meals and doing push up.

Tasha came to see him again, for the first time since he had been in locked down. He didn't notice her stomach because it only had a small perk to it. She had it covered good with an extra-large shirt. He went back and jacked off. Tasha had gotten thick; she was coming through her shorts. Sandy agreed to work overtime, because she felt she wasn't gonna see him again. She made love to him that night, stayed in his arms til every count.

At the 5 o'clock count her L.T. came in and counted and told her, she couldn't work the overtime because that first shift officer called in and said she'll make it. But he told her, "I know you're messing around with Ellis. You owe me big."

She looked at him and said, "What? Is this your way of getting some free ass from me?"

"You can call it what you want. But I'll like to see you in my office tomorrow because you won't work this post anymore."

"I can quit right now! This is my body my life, you're not gonna black male me into your bed. So here's my badge sir."

Her captain came to the range door and she popped him in. Her captain was a tall white male in his late 40's. He slept with Sandy when he was a

L.T. at Autry State Prison outside Albany. He transferred to Valdosta just to get the captain position.

"What's going on," the captain asked.

Sandy looked at the L.T. waiting on him to tell on her she wasn't worried because he didn't have any proof.

"Sandy here is sleeping with inmate Ellis in cell 21."

"Do you have any proof of this?"

"Not really sir."

"Well how can you say she's sleeping with him?"

"He's just proposition me for sex and I told her I'll quit before I do something like that. So I gave him my badge."

"Give her back her badge. This isn't necessary because Ellis is fix 'en to go home. Right now, all charges against him have been dropped."

They walked to his cell, she open the door and told him to pack up because he was a free man. He packed all his stuff up and walked out. Sandy heart was beating fast as she watched him get on that van in some brown pants, white shirt, blue jacket and his Jordans. She tailed the van to the bus station and waited. Soon as the bus came they let him out the van and left. She pulled up blew her white V6 Toyota Camry took him to her home made love again and again. Then she took him to Atlanta, he gave her 50 thousand when they got to Ike apartment off Home Street by the Atlanta Zoo. She knew then that she would never see her black love again, so she called him to make love to her again this time they had anal sex.

They showered and she left.

Ike threw him some new Nylon boxers and shirt, a pair of Nike black jogging pant cotton and the shirt to match.

"Boy, Ike it's a new day. It's time to get in these streets."

"Juan you should go see Tasha, the girl loves you. Go check in."

"Man she don't know I'm out. I got some shit to do before I go home, you'll see. When I go I'm retired, and that ain't no bullshit."

"Man take your ass home, it's for the best."

"Nigga , you went to prison and got anti righteous on me? Prison don't change strong niggas. It changes the weak. What, you soft now? Nigga done touched you on your ass or something?"

"Naw man she used to write and tell me small matters that she couldn't tell because you ain't ready to hear them and settle down. You're so into fucking that snow, your eyes are open but you're still dreaming."

"What, you fucking Tasha now?"

"Nigga I ain't touched that girl, open your eyes son. She gonna know you're out since her folks working on your case."

"No she won't."

"I told her Melissa was sending the tape to the police office and DA office."

"Man you fucked up everything! I'm not ready to face Natasha yet. I got alot of shit I want to do and with Tasha holding me down I'll never be able to do them."

"Is that right?"

"Tasha, what's happening? And how long have you been standing there? And why are you over here?"

Ike had seen her when she opened the door. He didn't say nothing because Juan was pointing his finger at him. Juan was standing at the end of the blue velvet sofa which sat in the middle of the small living room; his back was to the door. He looked at Ike then back to Tasha. She was looking so good.

With tears in her eyes and a clog in her throat, she answered, "Long enough to know you really don't love me. Ain't nothing happening now, and I came here because I knew you'll come here first. My dad told me yesterday that you was coming home. All the letters and poems you wrote wasn't about shit. Nigga my folks was right from the start. You ain't shit and ain't never gonna be shit. Right now I wish I was fucking Ike. He's more man than you are."

He slapped her to the floor, for the first time he hit her with all his might.

"Don't you never disrespect me like that. Bitch I'll put hot lead in you and won't lose no sleep."

As she got up he went to hit her again. She backed to the door. Ike held him back and told him not to make that mistake.

"No, Ike let him go. Let him hit me again and again because all he's doing is beating the love out of me. Nobody on earth will ever love you like I love you. All this crying, 'Nobody loves me.' Mothafucka you just slapped it out of me."

Tasha had on a black and blue Polo outfit with some Polo boots and by the door in a bag was the same kind of outfit for him with 20 grand, so he could go shopping.

"Here's your clothes and money. I got to hold my head up high because you ain't hurt me you just hurted yourself. Nigga I'm your investment. Your money is in my hands. So I got your love, your heart and your money, my love for you is real. I'll blow everything you worked hard to get because it's all in Natasha Middle's names, ain't shit in Juan Ellis name. That's right bitch, you taught me good. So start over again and remember hurting me is easy but coming back is harder."

Tasha walked out the door.

"Damn! You know, Ike, I don't need that hoe bitch and I don't need that money. All I need is the 20 grand the hoe left me with, and the 2 sacks."

"Well, I got two twin gold plated 45 and 50 grand to get you back on your feet."

"What? Because I dissed the hoe you turning your back on me. Nigga it's just like I thought you're fucking the hoe. But you know what? My money made both of y'all. Since I don't want to go straight back to the joint both of y'all lives are saved. Just give me what you owe me and stay the fuck out of my face."

Ike gave him the two 45 and 50 grand dropped his head and turned his back on his only family Juan. Juan point the pistol at Ike's head, tears fell and Juan let two rounds off hitting the wall, Ike never looked back. He grabbed the bag and walked off.

He went to a payphone up at the Amoco gas station and call Tony. He explained to Tony what had happen and how he felt about it. His best friend had crossed him for a no good hoe.

Tony told him now you'll find life is mind over matter. Tony told the young killer to stay put and he'll be there in 5 minute. Juan went in the store and got some cheddar cheese Lays chips and a Coke Cola soda. When he walked out he seen Tasha heading back to Ike apartment tears ran down his cheek and pain stained his face. He wiped the tears away as Tony pulled up. He told Tony, to drive down Home Street. As they drove down the street Tony stopped the car because he seen why he wanted him to drive down this street. He saw Ike hugging Tasha as they walked into the apartment.

Tony looked at him and said, "You can't kill pain you can only live to love and to let go."

Juan smiled through his tear and told him,

"The world is not enough someone has to pay for the cards God have dealt me."

They drove off and drove for a long time. Finally not knowing where he was, they turned off the road to a dirt driveway. As they rode up, Juan looked at Tony and said, "You drove up the back way. This is the big white house I used to come see as a child. My grandparent property is on the other side."

Tony smiled and said, "I've always known you. I know your whole family. Your granddaddy and I are blood brothers. I wanted to tell you.

But you're dangerous. Nobody knows you. We're all we got that's why I stayed down with you. I'm not gonna die on you I've made sure you've been on top since you was a child. I know you feel everybody you love die. But not me."

"Nobody never told me about you."

He cut the 500 black Benz off in front of the big white house looked at him.

"Juan nobody never told you about me because they didn't know I was alive. I ran off to Detroit when I was 14 years old. I didn't have time to plow the field."

They got out the car laughing and walked in the house. Juan always wondered what the house inside look like. Now he saw, it had everything, but the only thing mattered to him was a bed because he was sleepy. He went to the first room upstairs by the steps on the left side. Open the door and jumped in the big king size bed with black satin sheets.

Tasha cried to Ike as they sat on the sofa and said, "Ike why did he slap me? Why did he do me like this?"

"I don't know Tasha, all I know is he's hurt. He shot at me put 2 bullet holes in the wall. I wanted to tell him about the baby. I just couldn't so I dropped my head and turned my back. Then he shot. All I know is he think we're sleeping together. Then he just seen us hugged up walking into the house, so who knows what he's thinking. I know alot of people is fix 'en to die, because of the pain he feels."

"Ike I got to find him, because I love him. Maybe I took what he was saying the wrong way because my heart says I'm wrong. He did say he had alot of unfinished business, he wanted to finish and he was going to retire. I took shit the wrong way now that I think about it. He told me in his letters he had a couple things to straighten then he'll ask me to marry him. I'm gonna read this poem he wrote to me. I know he loves me, I just get so unsecure when I hear him talk about them streets. You got to help me find him, if we find him then he'll really believe in love. I really got to find him before this baby is born. I only got one month. I'm not having him by myself I refuse."

"Tasha you might have lil' Juan by yourself. You should've told him while he was locked up. You knew that's all he wanted is a child. I should've told him. That's the only family I got beside my mom. How did I let you talk to me into this? I know that baby will turn him around. What's done is done. We got to find him."

"Ike listens to a side of him you never heard before."

She pulled the poem out her pocket, she had it on both sides of her key ring.

- *How can you love a heart, when you're afraid of that heart.*

- *But you can feel that heart from afar.*

- *It's like it's watching you, guiding you to be free.*

- *Wishing it will return, therefore you'll believe*

- *It's like missing someone that's no longer there.*

- *Why do you miss 'em because in the back of your mind*

- *You'll always care.*

- *If expression can speak a thousand words.*

- *I believe by crying our true needs will be served.*

- *Am I a coward, cause there's things I want to say.*

- *But can't say them because we're not face to face.*

- *I'm afraid because I love to love hurt.*

- *Being gentle creating love from dirt.*

- *I'm being strong taking a stand.*

- *I'm still alone with my heart in my hand.*

- *Take me, touch me and hold me.*

- *Lift me, guide me, I'm free.*

"Nigga, I refuse to fall victim to the system I'll kill up all y'all black crackas. You think y'all are gonna take me alive?" Juan opened up his trench, he had a bomb taped to his body.

"Come on and get me. You'll never take me there enough money in this bank for all of us. I didn't take it all I just took some of it. I'm telling y'all I blow this bitch to pieces and come back and haunt everybody that live… Oh hey Tasha I'm glad to see you came to your senses. I know the road of life is rough and the hills are hard to climb. But you got to always think, don't feel, just think things out. I'm gonna forever love you."

With that he put the gun to his head and pulled the trigga…

"Who are you?"

"I'm Jesus of the ghetto, I understand your problem, my son."

"How can you understand my problem when I haven't told you my problem?"

"You're a young black trying to make it whatsoever you ask for I'll give it because my father has given the world to me. I'm black Jesus."

"Well black Jesus I want my own shake dance club with big booty girls and about 4 million dollars. Problem free."

"But what are you giving in return?"

"I'm giving my soul and taking care of all the ghetto kids."

"My son you are rewarded."

"Oh thank you black Jesus."

Juan woke up smiling because them was some truly stupid dreams with no meaning. He sat there wondering what Tasha was doing. Was she still at Ike crib? So he called and she answered the phone.

"Bitch I knew you wasn't no good, hoe you ain't shit. Tell Ike I'm a real nigga and nigga's don't fall out about a no good ass bitch like you bitch." He hung up.

Tasha screamed! And Ike came running.

"What's wrong Tasha?"

"Juan just called."

"What did he say? Nevermind, the answer machine was on. I'll rewind it."

Ike replayed the message and dropped his head. "Tasha I don't know if this is a game or what. I don't know what to do. If I stay away from him, it will look like we're fucking. If I go to him he'll try to kill me."

"Ike I'm sick of this. Where do you think he's at? Do you know Tony's beeper number? He used to tell me to call Tony alot. Hold on I remember it."

"Tasha just dialed *69."

She dialed *69. "Hello Tony this is Tasha, let me speak to Juan don't tell me he ain't with you because he just called from there. I pressed *69."

"Naw Tasha he's not here he just left heading y'all way."

"So he really do think I'm fucking Ike. I'm not fucking nobody. Tony I didn't want nobody to know this. But I'm 8 months pregnant with his baby. This nut has went crazy, are you sure he's on his way over here?"

"I think so."

Tony hung up and walked upstairs.

"Juan that was Tasha talking about she pregnant. Boy hoes play all kinda games."

"Man you ain't lying. Ain't been pregnant while I was down. I slap her now she's having a baby. Boy hoe's got game. But me I'm sharper than a razor blade."

"That's how you're suppose to be, it's in your blood."

"So what's your plan, Tony? Hold up Tony if you knew I was your blood before, why didn't you proclaim your own style of living?"

"Because it wasn't easy for me. So why should it be easy for you? What you wanted a family to turn you into a gentleman? Man you're a born survivor, no it or be about it. Then too I didn't know how you'll react to blood, knowing you've been on your own for so long. Who say you would've believed me, if I told you that the first day I met you. Man kick that child shit. Your child days are over."

"Tony I had a dream I killed myself. What's up with that?"

"Shit, that might be your death. Did you pray while you were down?"

"Prayed and read the Bible."

"That ain't nothing but you're killing the image God has set you."

"So what's up for today?"

"You got to ask yourself that, because you're your own man you ain't been depending on another to make your day out."

"Yeah you're right, take me to a car lot and let me pick me a car out. You know Tony, I never had anybody to look up to but I look up to you. I'ma be just like you when I grow up. You always wear the flyest slacks keep some fly shoes on, gators, snakes, lamb and you stay with a fresh silk shirt. Rolex and one herringbone and one pinky ring. Man that's fly. I always wanted to say that."

Tony dropped his head because Juan caught him by surprise but it made him feel good. That somebody admired him. He looked at his green gator shoes. Green slacks and green silk shirt. And smiled because he didn't know his wear was fly in the eyes of the young.

"Naw man I got you a brand new Lexus out there. That blue 2 seater is yours. I knew you'll need a fly whip so I got that for you and put them 22 inch rims on it for you. It got a pioneer system in it with 2-12s in the back. 2-1000 watts amps with crossover. Just like the rest of your cars. Enjoy yourself today and don't kill nobody. Don't bring nobody over here."

"Blood that." "Yeah blood that."

Tony walked out the door and threw him a set of keys. Tony felt telling Juan the truth was like being a father to the son he had always wanted. Now they both had a family, they had each other. He wanted to leave the game alone and make a life for him and Juan because like Juan he too was a loner, he knew he was set for the rest of his life. Now he wanted Juan to be set for the rest of his life. He thought back on Tasha's words, as he turned down Highway 91. Boy if she is having a baby that will be the new generation. He got on the phone with Denise a nurse at Grady Hospital and asked her to look up Tasha's record. As she had said she was having blood. Tony changed his whole out look of life right then and there. Wow! He had to turn Juan's life around, which was gonna be super hard. Juan is a young killer and ain't nothing getting in his way.

He went to B&B Insurance Company and took out a million dollar insurance on him, Juan and the baby. He also went to Trust Bank and put 30 million in an account for the expecting baby, leaving him with 10 million in the states. But an hundred million in an account overseas.

"10 million is enough for me and Juan to blow up."

Tony sat in the car and called Philip Nore. Tony told him he was going to retire, but Philip needed him to make one last hit before he retired. HE wasn't hearing it, and then Philip asked him to ask Juan to take out Mike because he was snitching. Tony told him no, he was trying to change him not destroy him. Tony hung up the phone.

He knew the cat Mike and had, had a close look at him before. So he decided to return this last favor and retire. He drove around Moreland Avenue, down Glenwood, around Second Avenue, until he seen Mike in the old East Lake Meadow. He parked the car on Alston Drive and walked around to the first circle. He saw Mike in the parking lot. He took the high power scope and put it on the 30 aught 6 with the silencer. He put the 30 aught 6 in position and fired two rounds, hitting Mike both times before he hit the ground, everybody ran off.

He broke the gun down wiped it down and left it there. He went back to the car and went home. He waited on Juan to come, so he could tell him about the baby and plans he had to fix their family. As he sat in the recliner facing the door, he felt a chill run down his spine. He knew something was wrong, so he clicked the Glock 17 and spun around real fast. But as he turned, bullets from a Mac II started hitting him. He fired three shots killing his killer, and laid there. By the time Juan got there he was almost dead. Juan called the police and told the lady what was up. Two bodies were lying before him. Tony tried to speak, but Juan put his hand over his mouth. Tony moved his hand.

"Blood! Blood love take care of blood. Tasha is blood. Philip. Detroit."

Tony died in Juan arms. When the police came everything was easy to figure out. The other body was a hit man with a hit because he had the address in his pocket.

Juan just looked around, grabbed a mop and bleach and went to work cleaning after the officers left. He looked up to God and said, "I guess it ain't meant for me to… have a family." He just smiled, because he knew God was the reason for him losing Tasha also.

He picked up the phone and dialed a number. It seemed like it rang forever.

"Hello. Hello." A girl voice came through the receiver.

"Hello. Hello, who is this? Fuck it, people always playing on the phone. You better be glad I don't have caller ID." She hung up.

Juan was still holding the phone, listening to the dial tone. Finally he hung up and it ranged.

"Hello."

"May I speak to Tony?," a girl's voice replied.

"I'm sorry but Tony is dead."

"Who is this?" the young lady demanded. "I just talked to Tony this morning, so stop playing."

"Listen I said he's dead! Dammit! Can you get that between your ears?"

"Juan," the voice yelled out.

"What? Who is this?"

"This is Tasha."

"What do you want Tasha? And why are you calling over here?"

"Well you had to just have called her because I dialed *69 and I remembered the number. I called Tony this morning looking for you. Was you there?"

"Yes I was here. Tasha shit is ugly. I got to bury Tony because he's my uncle. I know who killed him. I got to get them back."

"Boy, you're a damn lie, you ain't got to do shit but bring your ass home. Boy I'm fix 'en to have your baby next month. You better bring your ass home and stop all this bullshit. We got enough money to take us for a long time. Juan I'm your family, your only family. I couldn't tell you about the baby while you were locked up. I made everybody promise not to tell you because I didn't want you to worry. That's why you felt I was hiding something from you because I was. You said it yourself I was getting thick. I just exercise alot, so cut the foolishness right now. Juan marry me! Please marry me and come home."

"Tasha, everything is gonna be straight, we'll get married and raise our baby. I'ma be a good dad. What are we having?"

"A little boy. We got to think of something to invest this money in."

"While I was locked up I was thinking about owning my own club and hotel. I've been looking at this three story building on Marietta Street downtown. We can make the first floor a teen club, second floor a baller club and last floor for the rich people, have different entrance."

"Juan where do Tony stay?"

"On Dotson Road next to my grandparent house. You remember that big long dirt driveway that sits in the curve? That's Tony house. Now, my house. This is where we'll stay. I'll clean the land up and connect both of them and build shit on them for us. All these years Tony has kept the land up by paying his taxes."

"I'm on my way. I love you Juan."

For the first time Juan thanked the Lord for his life and Tasha. He sat in the chair next to the chair Tony was killed in and waited for Tasha. Hours went by, Tasha did not call and there were no signs of her. So he called her cellphone. Her mom answered.

"How are you doing Mrs. Middle? Tasha must have stopped by there before she came here."

"Juan I don't know how to tell you this, but Tasha is… no… she's. Juan, I…"

Juan heard the tears and said, "Dead."

Her mom dropped the phone, picked it back up and told him to come to Grady to see his son, "He's barely making it, so come fast."

Juan ran out the house, jumped in his car and made his way to Grady Hospital. It was if his heart told him where she was because he went straight to the 5th floor. He saw Mr. and Mrs. Middle standing there. He also saw Ike mom Betty.

Mrs. Middle hugged him and told him,

"Tasha went to get Ike so they could straighten out, that they wasn't sleeping together. On the way to your house a rig hit them from behind. Tasha had the baby on the scene. Tasha and Ike are both in a coma."

Juan looked at her and asked where is his son, they took a long walk down the hallway to the baby ward and she asked for the Ellis baby. Juan smiled because they thought enough of him to name his son after him. She explained that Tasha named him before she went into her coma. The nurse rolled a glass baby bed to the window. Lil' Juan was all glassed in. Tears rolled down his face. He looked up and asked God,

"Why are you doing this to me? Don't take my family from me."

Mrs. Middle hugged him and told him everything would be okay. Juan looked up and told her,

"If my wife and son die the whole world dies." With that he left and called Sandy.

"Sandy I need you to take off for a few days. We're going to Detroit, Michigan I got to take care of some business. Tasha is in a coma, she had my son and he's living in a glass crib; Ike is in a coma also. You're all I got. So is you game or what?"

"I've been missing you and I'm doing alright. Yes I'm game, and I'm ready to leave whenever."

"We'll leave in the morning you'll be my alibi. I love you."

Juan called and got Sonya, Ryan's sister. She was a flight attendant. He told her the plan and she was down with it and will put 2 Glocks on the plane for him. He went back upstairs and kissed Tasha and Ike. They were in the same room. He looked at his son and went downstairs and asked the coroner for Tony Banks body. It was ruled a none investigation, because they knew the motive for the murder. So he asked that the body be cremated as soon as possible.

Juan waited upstairs, looking at his son. The coroner called a friend that cremated people and told him 5 grand work done right away. Hours went by Juan just stood there staring. His phone rang and it was the call he was waiting for. His uncle was cremated. Now he had to go meet Sandy.

Everything was set on Sandy's end. She met him at the airport at 6:45am.

A redbone female seated them and told him everything was set. He looked at her red thighs and legs as she bent over to buckle Sandy in, she was as beautiful in person then the picture, beautiful green eyes he was dazed because she was a Coke bottle. Sandy asked who she was when she walked away. He told her Ryan's sister.

She smiled at what she just saw, Juan and his two girl clique. The plane took off. It was silence between the two. Sandy stayed on her guard from Sonya, at 9:15 am the plane landed. At 9:45 am they were in a white Ford Taurus. Sonya took care of the rental and the hotel. He had promised to help her rob her boyfriend. When they got to Pontiac Avenue they saw the hotel. Sandy parked in the parking lot of Romainya and changed clothes he dressed in an all black Giovanni suit with some black gator. Sandy dressed in all-white Katherine suit with the matching white jacket and shoes. When they popped the trunk he grabbed the black tote bag with guns in it. Sonya left them in the trunk, went to the desk and asked the white male for the keys for Sam and Tammy Jones. They were sent to 362, a penthouse suite. Sandy couldn't wait to get into the suit once they closed the door she made love to him. An hour later Sonya walked in the room and joined the two. He laid there and gave them the plan.

CHAPTER 9
Tasha

Tasha laid there lifeless with Ike on the other side. No one knew much about the wreck. The driver of the rig shot himself while driving. The people on the scene said the rig just dragged them to the rail. As soon as the officer pulled Tasha free the baby was coming out. They cut her pants open and delivered the baby on the scene. Tasha was completely out. Tasha somehow said, "Juan Ellis Jr." and was out again.

Nancy grabbed her hand and told her to hold on.

"Juan has been here, he saw the baby. I don't think he can take seeing you like this. Baby your face is so beautiful you don't even have a scar on it."

Her tears dropped on her hand while Betty held Ike hand crying because his face was all cut up. Ike was driving, he caught the worst of the wreck.

"You know Nancy I had two sons, and I'm barely holding on to my last one. You know Juan loved Tasha; he used to talk about her so much. He's been through so many deaths; his parent, grandparent, wicked uncle and this all in one day and now to see his wife lifeless and his son barely holding on. That's why he's not here. I wouldn't want to see my life die either. I can't stand to see Ike lay up like this. God needs to open their eyes or lay them to rest. Right now they're suffering, makes you ask, 'Why God? Why my child?' It like you see it every day on the news and say, 'God help that family' and hope it never happens to you. Now it's hitting home and all we can do is say, 'God why?'"

The heart monitor changed it beeps steady to fast an alarm sounded. Nancy screamed, Betty ran to Ike.

"Get a doctor! Get a doctor! Get a doctor!," they both yelled.

The doctor rushed in, cleared Ike chest and picked up the defibrillator.

"One, two, three, clear… one, two, three, clear."

Ike was dead; Betty just looked up and said, "Lord take care of my child."

Tears rolled down her cheeks. "How am I gonna tell Juan Ike is dead?"

Betty cried and looked at Nancy, Nancy held her as they rolled Ike away. She stayed there a while, kissed Tasha and told her to hang in there. Then she left.

Nancy fell on her knees and prayed, while Harold and Richard cried. A day went by and Tasha was still motionless, showing no signs of coming out of her coma. There were also no signs of Juan. At 6:00 pm. Juan called and check on Tasha. Nancy broke the news about Ike and asked him to come to the hospital.

His only reply was, "I can't see Tasha like this."

"She couldn't see you in prison but she came to visit you and waited. Went against her father for you. Nigga you better get your ass to this hospital and see about your family."

In response to that, he had to move his play forward.

"Put the phone to Tasha ear. Tasha, there's somebody out there that will heal you, baby you just got to hold on. I know your faith is strong. When I was locked up you sent me all them verse about faith. Listen to this song baby girl.

"Somebody here need you Lord.

Tasha here need you Lord she needs you right now.

"Baby girl, I don't know if you know it or not, but Ike is dead. I never got the chance to say I'm sorry to him. I'm sorry, Tasha. I'll never hurt you again. If you die I'll kill myself. So wake up."

He hung up and Nancy just prayed over her child. She had wanted another child years back and they tried only to find out her body wasn't strong enough to carry another child. The doctor told her that she was lucky to have given birth to Tasha. Nancy's womb was barren. But she had prayed and prayed for a baby. After 4 years, Tasha was conceived.

She carried Tasha seven months, one night at a party with Richard. Richard just had made partner at Edmond Law Firm. They were strolling through the ballroom at the Hilton Hotel. When she fell to the floor breathing hard. Everyone panicked, yelling, "Call 911! Call 911!"

By the time the EMTs arrived, Tasha was wrapped in a nice Hilton towel. Everybody called her 'Little Hilton.' She made Tasha a promise to be the best momma in the world. So far, she had indeed been the best. Now her little miracle was lying there virtually lifeless.

Nancy jumped up and grabbed a bottle of Motrin and Midol from her purse got some water looked up to the sky and said, "If you take my baby, you might as well take me. She began swallowing pills. Ten minutes later she fell to the floor. The bottles on the floor beside her hand, now she laid on the floor lifeless.

Richard walked in the room and seen her on the floor out cold. He yelled, "No!" and ran out the room screaming for a nurse. IT seemed like no nurse were in sight. He stopped and yelled, "Somebody help me!"

A fat white nurse came to his aid. He yelled and pointed, "Overdose! My wife Oded come now and save her."

The nurse ran in and checked Nancy pulse, she was fading fast. She grabbed the phone and called for help.

"Hurry nurse I can't lose both of them. Help me nurse."

She started trying to induce vomiting by pumping on Nancy stomach with her hands.

"Come on, Nancy! Come on, Nancy! Throw up the pills Nancy!"

The nurse pumped and pumped, but there was no response from Nancy. She checked for a pulse and there were none. Carol started to give up but she pumped 5 more times and gave up. It was clear that she was dead.

"I'm sorry sir but your wife is dead."

Richard grabbed Nancy and lifted her upper body.

"You left me, Nancy. YOU promised to love me forever," with tears in his eyes. He rocked her back and forward.

"Aha, Aha!"

"Throw them up, Nancy. Throw them up, Nancy. I knew you wouldn't leave me."

The nursing crew came and pumped her stomach with the charcoal and all the pills came up. They placed her in the bed that Ike had been in. He made a vow to never leave them while they were there. He only wondered where his son-in-law was.

CHAPTER 10
Revenge

"Sonya, since you know this area good, I need you to find some 'gangsta gang leaders' and bring them here to the hotel. Also Sandy I need you to rent another car get two dresses for you and Sonya. Get me a dinner suit. We're going to the club where Philip eats. Tony said the club is an Italian place. So we'll be there for a while. Tony showed me a picture of Philip once. So I'll know who he is. If this plan goes right we'll be able to leave tomorrow. "Sandy I got to get back because my boy Ike is dead my girl Tasha is in a coma and my son is living in a glass crib. My family needs me."

"You already told me that last night. I'm sorry about Ike though Juan I need you to. I need to know that you'll always be there for me. Like if I want to come and visit, can I? What happen when I need you real bad?"

"I'll be there and yes you can come and visit. As far as I'm concerned you're Juan's godmom. So don't you have the right to see us. If Tasha don't like it, she'll learn to love it because you're apart of me. Anytime she don't make it out of this coma you'll be his stepmom. Only if you'll leave your husband enough of this go on and handle business. Sonya's already gone."

As soon as Sandy left he made a call to check on his son and his wife. He was very disappointed about Nancy but she was coming along as hours passed. Richard asked him when was he coming to the hospital and did he really love his family.

Tears rolled down his face at that question, because Richard really needed him. He didn't even answer; he just hung up the phone and laid down.

When Sonya returned, Juan was asleep. She returned with six fella's wearing black rags on their heads.

"Juan, get up. I found what you were looking for."

As he looked up, he saw a future standing before him. "Hi my name is Juan. I got you boys here on business matter and an act of trust. So tell me who's who and let's get down to business."

They just looked at him in silence. Finally a big muscular dark skin guy spoke, "I'm Smoky AKA Killer Kid this is my man Clique; right hand man Leo; bodyguard Baby James; chief of violation CJ AKA Cateye;

Knight Bump; footsoldier Pale."

All the guys were dark skin and muscular, except Leo and CJ. Leo was pecan tan slim fellow who looked like Juan, and CJ was brown skin a pretty boy. So far Juan liked what he saw.

"OK Gangsta, here the plan. I want you and about 10 of your men to shoot up Club Faryo at exactly 8:30 pm sharp. At 9:20 I want 40 of your men at 191 Bannery St. I don't want no shooting unless we have to. Now this job pays a hundred grand. So, are you down or what?"

Smokey replied, "I like the pay. Also I do favor for favor. Sonya tells me you're from Atlanta and you have major cheese. Money, if y'all don't say cheese. Now we're hot up here and we need to relocate. So I can help you out now, and you help relocate my crew which is a 150 deep."

"Well, well, I might can return that favor, but I'll need another favor, you and your clique roll with me and we'll take over Atlanta. Those that don't roll with us will get rolled over."

"Sound like a perfect plan to me Smokey," Leo replied.

"Then Lil' Juan you have a deal."

"Smokey how old is you?"

"23, and you?"

"21."

"I heard y'all boys be doing it big down there," Smokey replied.

"Well, Smokey, it's like this. I be doing my thing. Hold on, Smokey."

Juan made a phone call to John. Juan never asked him for anything not even the day he first met him. He met John through Tony on the Willie job. Now John had to return the favor. John just remodeled the old East Lake Meadows Apartment and it was badly in need of a resident. They worked a deal that all 150 could stay at the cost of $800 a month. Juan explained to Smokey what was up his heart jumped, and they left to prepare for the job.

Sandy came back with two Tommy Hill dresses with white matching shoes for her and Sonya. She gave Juan an all-white Sean John suit and all while showering together Sandy made a comment a serious one.

"Juan if this don't show you how much I love you, I don't know what will. I'm doing a crime for you and eating pussy for you."

"Yeah me too," Sonya replied.

Juan just laughed and said, "Believe this, this will pay off everything right."

At 7:50 Smokey called.

"We're all geared up and ready to move out."

They left after the phone call. Sonya had a Mac II in her white tote bag. Sandy had two 357s in her black bag and Juan had two Glocks 17s. They left the hotel in a 1996 dark blue Luxury Lincoln. As Sonya drove off with Sandy in the passenger seat and Juan in the back seat, she kept her eyes on him through the mirror. She noticed that he showed no signs of worrying or fear, knowing he was going up against a mob boss. She only saw a desire for blood. This was the guy she always wanted a nigga that'll shake something. She told herself nobody was gonna get in her way. Not this bitch Sandy nor the bitch Tasha, Juan belonged to her. She looked at Sandy and said, "Death becomes you."

Sandy laughed and said, "Love is something to die for."

IT was as if she knew what Sonya was thinking and talking about.

Sonya parked the car twenty steps from the club, "Just like Tony said, it's open."

It wasn't really a club, it was really a nice restaurant

Juan saw Philip as he walked in the door. Philip was sitting right in view of the window. They were seated in the back of the restaurant. Philip was a goofy looking old black man. Tall with broad shoulders. He wore a black and white pin stripe suit. Low hair cut with thin rim glasses. He had to be smart to develop a clique strong as his.

"May I take y'all order please?," an Italian male asked.

Sandy replied, "Yes! We'll have the special whatever it is."

They sat and conversed about whatever the girls had on their chest. Really nothing because neither liked each other. When the waiter came back, bullet started flying everywhere. The waiter dropped the plate and ran for cover.

Juan heard Phillip yell out, "I'm hit! I'm hit!"

Juan and the girl quickly rushed to Philip aid.

"Come sir," Sandy suggested. "We'll lead you outside."

Dragging Philip by his arms was easy as they thought his men were still in clover with the table flipped up shooting. Philip had been hit in his right shoulder and both of his thighs. They put him in the car and drove off.

"Where to sir?," Sonya asked looking at him through the mirror.

"1623 Lifithed Avenue."

"I know exactly where that is."

When they passed the first light 3 black vans pulled off behind them. Sonya drove fast on the open street now that they were shielded. Cops were coming from everywhere. When they finally reached the house

Sonya drove in the driveway. They vans parked outside the house a little bit up from the driveway. They dragged him into the house, into the living room. It was very big with plastic over all the chairs and sofas. Alot of pictures on the walls of famous people.

Sandy and Sonya ran in the kitchen grabbed beach and towel a big pot with water and cleaned the car. Philip was sitting on a long sofa facing the door, the lights were still off.

"Listen pimp I'm very well-known my name is Philip you saved my life. I'll forever be in your debt, you and your brave girls. I'm rich I promise you'll be a millionaire after tonight."

"Philip you're not worried about your shoulder and legs?"

"No I have a personal doctor. I'm fix 'en to call him right now. What's your name pimpin?"

"Philip I got to go I'll holla back later."

The siren really took him out his thinking. He turned to walk away. Then he thought about Tony and took out the 17s. He turned and said, "Philip, my name is Juan." Pointing the Glocks in his face, "and you know why I'm here. You had Tony killed. That was my only family I had alive. Now you must die unless you can come up with something fast."

"Hold up Juan, I got hundreds of hundreds of kilos of heroin in my storm shelter in the backyard. If you and your girls will help me out there I'll give it to you. I know I done wrong for killing Tony so I'll pay for his life with the kilos."

"Girls come in here, help him walk."

Although the pain was hard on Philip, he walked. He led them to the backyard by an oak tree and told them to kneel down and grab the hatch to the storm shelter. As the IBH watched them go underground they noticed Philip men coming so they opened fire on them.

Underground Philip had a built-in tunnel. They walked to the iron door. Philip hit his code and they walked in. The girls dropped him on the floor and went to fill the green duffle bags up which laid on the 3 tables on top of the dope. Juan walked in another room that had money on 3 tables. Philip was reaching in his right pocket for his 357 derringer and pointed it at Juan, but his arm fell.

There were duffle bags everywhere, Philip was an easy asset, Juan thought. He filled five duffle bags with all the money and walked out. Philip let off a round with the derringer but he missed because he couldn't raise his arm high enough. When he shot his arm was dropping.

Sonya and Sandy unloaded on him.

They hurried out the tunnel dragging bags. Juan drug three bags with two on his shoulders. Sonya and Sandy draggled one with two on their shoulders. When they got to the yard they saw an all-out war. They managed to make it to the car by going through the house. After they pulled off, Smokey called off his men only to realize they were shooting at each other because all Philip men were dead.

Everyone returned to the hotel Smokey and his five, Juan put all the bags, on the bed and when they opened the bags Smokey eyes widen. Juan handed him a duffle bag full of money and counted out 30 kilos of heroin.

"Smokey go buy alot of books and boxes. Since you're a 150 deep have your clique to tear the inside of the book and tape the dope and y'all money in the boxes. Sonya I trust you'll handle our money and the dope right?"

"Right! Smokey I'ma need to know all your people name so I can get y'all ticket or if y'all are that hot y'all will come out better driving so what's up?"

"Give me a number and address Juan, we're gonna drive."

They checked out the hotel and went to the IBH home where they met everyone and talked about the future. Juan saw a young pretty red bone that looked so innocent. He asked her for her name, she said Cindy. Cindy was a younger version of Sonya. He noticed that Sonya and her was close so he thought they were family. Just didn't say nothing.

By 5:45 am Juan was ready to go. Smokey them where packed and ready they had the dope hid well. So they started for Atlanta in seven U-Haul trucks. By 6:20 Juan them were on the plane. By 9:50 they were in Atlanta. By 11:20 Juan them rode to East Lake Meadows took care of the business and went to his house. Sandy followed while Sonya rode in the car with him. He put the dope in the house gave them a duffle bag a piece full of money.

Sandy told him she was feeling freaky, so they went upstairs and had a threesome. When they woke up, he left a note telling them to take care and he'll holla later he had something to look into. By 4:30 pm he was in the hospital bed with Tasha sleep. He didn't even know the girls had brought flowers to the room. Richard accepts them while he laid beside Nancy which was better just restless.

Juan slept the whole day and night, when he woke up and he saw that it was 10:30 am. He heard a baby crying but couldn't see the baby, so he jumped up and saw Nancy and Richard with the baby in the glass crib. They rolled him in the room.

"Look little baby there goes your daddy," Nancy said with a smile. She was happy first to be alive, second to hear that her grandchild was going to make it, third to see Juan and fourth to have her family all in one room together.

Juan fussed at her for trying to kill herself and promised that he'll tell Tasha. She just laughed and thanked God for seeing that Saturday.

The days went by so fast with the baby getting out the crib. Everything went well. But he had to stay in the hospital in another baby crib because he had a small hold in his heart. Tasha still haven't said a word or moved. He talked to her every night. Telling her his plans to change his prints so they can go places and live. He let the baby lay on her and slob all over her. Just something to give her hope. He got scared because it was Saturday again a whole week. He offered a doctor a million dollars to wake her up. Give her a shock treatment. But the doctor told him she got to wake up herself.

"It's now 10 am Ike funeral is in an hour. Are y'all coming?"

Nancy and Richard replied, "Yes."

They all got ready to leave, but first went to check on the baby and walked back in, to check on Tasha and kissed her. As they were walking out the door she whispered, "Juan," but no one heard her. She whispered again, "Juan stop them from taking the baby."

She jumped breathing hard snatching tubes out her nose and mouth. Almost throwing up. Her face was pale and her head was pounding. She looked around for her clothes; she started to cry because Juan had left her and had taken everything. She looked in the drawer and saw Juan clothes; she put on his white pants and white dress coat, found her shoes and ran to the nursery.

She found lil' Juan and headed out the hospital. She headed out the double doors and looked around in fear. She covered him up and began her journey although she didn't know where she was going, she knew that Juan didn't love her and the baby. He had left them. As she though she began to run. She ran toward things that started to look familiar to her.

Before she knew it, she had walked down Memorial Drive, to Moreland Ave, down McPherson, down Eastside on Marbut and ended at her mom house. She was home safe with the baby. Where she knew they were loved. She tried to open the door, but it was locked. She had prepared to tell her daddy he was right about Juan and she was sorry. She pounded on the door yelling for her mom. She knew her daddy was out of town.

"Mom! Mom! Mom!"

Since there was no answer, she picked up a brick and threw it through the window. She opened it and climbed through it. Somehow Juan found her breast and started sucking it. She laid on the floor curled up with him and blacked out.

Ike funeral was sad and bright. Alot of people showed up. Ike laid in a white and gold casket. The preacher was Bishop H. Johnson. He's been their Pastor forever. They sung, "All I want to be is a Christian falling on my knees praising the Lord. All I want to do is magnify your name because serving my God is so wonderful."

Juan once again thanked the Lord and blessed Ike into Heaven. He spoke about their friendship, how wonderful it was and how much he was gonna miss his only brother. After they buried him in 7th Heaven off Calander Rd they went back to the hospital. They walked in the room and Tasha was gone. He went to the nurse station and asked what happen to Natasha Middle.

The nurse replied, "She's still in her room, she's in a coma."

He ran to the nursery and Juan was gone. He called Smokey and told him to come to the hospital because Philip men had grabbed Tasha. He needed help finding her.

He ran to his Lexus grabbed the Glock 17 walked back in the hospital and demanded the nurse to seal the doors. "Philip boys knew it was me and now they got my family. He didn't want to point the gun so he yelled, "Bitch I said seal the doors! My wife and kid is missing!"

With that the nurse sealed the doors and hit the panic button. Richard came out the elevator and grabbed him. The guards and nurses was running while on the 5th floor.

"Think Juan, think. She ain't in no trouble. Don't nobody have her. The doctor say they come out of their coma and wonder around when no one is there. That's all she's done. Don't get yourself in no trouble. She'll be found. I can't get you out of trouble if you nut up in this public place. Just listen to me. I'm not gonna tell you nothing wrong. Get on this elevator with me and let these folks do their job."

They got on the elevator and went back to the 5th floor. He wanted to pull that Glock out so bad because he knew what it was. But he was gonna play around with Richard for now. As soon as the gang comes it was on because they supposed to have nurses watching them. When they got off the elevator Richard pointed to a slim white nurse standing by the nursing station, and told him that was the nurse in charge. He snapped because she was smiling and drinking a cup of coffee. He reached for the Glock. But Richard jumped in front of him. Took the gun out of his hand and tucked it in his coat. Juan walked over to her and slapped the cut of coffee out of her hand.

"You think it's funny bitch? You're the reason why she's missing." He raised his hand to punch her but Richard grabbed his hand.

"Please sir," she said with the fear of God in her eyes. "Please sir." She threw her hands up.

"We're gonna find your wife and son I put my life on it. Just please don't hit me. I'm a good nurse and a good wife and good mom. I know you're the same. Please be patient. I got people everywhere looking for her. I got to stay her in case something happen to the other patient I swear."

The media moved in quickly. Every station was covering the news. This was the first time a person walked away from a coma, and haven't been found; especially with a child. Even the media suspected foul play.

Once they saw they weren't in the hospital the city organized a search for them. But Juan wasn't satisfied. He wanted them found and found now. He told Richard they got 30 minute or he'll do things his way. Richard told him to have faith. For the first time he seen his love for his family also for the first time he seen how dangerous the kid is. IF he wasn't with him he knew 10 people would've been dead by now.

Ms. Emma, their next door neighbor, had seen Tasha climb through the window. When she seen the story on TV she called the police.

A black detective walked into the room where they all were knelt down praying. When they finished praying he said, "Mr. Ellis your wife and son have been found. They're at home. The lady next door called the station and said she saw them go through the window. Right now your wife is unconscious. You son was found feeding from her breast. She must have laid down and started to feed him before she went out."

"Thanks Officer," they all replied.

Smokey came up to him and asked him to step in the hallway. Told him that they had surrounded the area and there was no sign of them. Juan only smiled because Smokey was on top of things. He explained to him that somehow Tasha made it home. "She's on her way back to the hospital."

"Smokey listen I want you to spread your men out all over Atlanta. Also go to Macon with some troops. Make more soldiers. That way we can grow. Put the dope down, once you feel you've put it down there move to the next town. Stay in contact with me every 4 hours. I want you to open up crack spot heroin spots and weed spots. Listen be careful and stay unseen. Send the new troops out on these mission. In 2 weeks I want y'all back up here. Sonya got a lick set up in Florida Key West. We're gonna intercept the deal and kill everybody. We got to kill 'em because they're Cuban. Take the money from Detroit buy 6 bricks of cocaine. Get 2 bricks of heroin and buy 2 bales of weed take that to Macon with you. I'll buy 50 bricks from my uncle people. When you come back up I'll have all that ready for you the 50 bricks or send a soldier up to get. However you feel at the time look man be careful and one love."

"Yeah one love, why is we buying dope when we got dope?"

"Because Phillip just got murdered, if we pop up with dope out of the blue, everyone will know we did it. Think my man."

CHAPTER 11
The Making

Things went as Juan planned; Smokey gave the order and went to Macon. Smokey set up shop in 4 Hill on the east side of Macon on the east side the IBH hang hard so Smokey and his 6 men clique blended in good. The IBH there took them in and gave them a home. Smokey was used to staying in rundown apartment but this one was run to the ground. It was a 3 bedroom with one bed in each room one chair and one white sofa. It also had a small Kenwood radio set. Out of all the places Smokey every stayed, this was the worst. It belonged to a junky. There was no gang leader their leader Polo just got 30 years. Nobody stepped up to take charge so they all ran free without order or law. It hurt him to see a clique he gave his life to go out so bad with no direction.

The next morning Smokey called his 6 man clique all geared up in black Dickies suit; told 'em to gather everybody up. Once everybody was gathered Smokey stacked rank and told 'em he was now their leader.

"All this banging is uncalled for. We don't bang we put it down. This is unnecessary heat. We're about making money, have y'all forgotten all y'all knowledge, I was always told y'all didn't understand what Insane Brother Hood was about down her in Georgia. Now I see with my own eyes, it's clearly a shame. I see y'all running around her abusing rank. Using your rank to sleep with underage kids. That's a violation from this day forth robbing is a violation, gang raping is a violation. We're gonna put it down on the dope tip. We're gonna supply all of Macon. Every gang will have no choice but to get down with us because I'm the truth. So if you want to keep your rank from here on out you got to show me because I don't think none of you can beat my 6 man clique."

He looked around at all the men women and kids there in the circle. They were all listening. He looked up in the sky at the trees surrounding them at the sliding boards' swings and they pulled out their Glocks and pointed.

"Listen this here is what I got. If you're not down with what I'm about to say then push on now because it's death before dishonor. I brung 2 kilo of heroin 6 kilo of cocaine 2 bales of weed with me. Everything are in those 2 black box Chevy's. Each member of my 6 man clique is now in charge of his own 50 man clique. That's all 300 of y'all. Again if anybody don't see this clear, you can drop your rags and go color blind right now. Understand it will be hard for us at first, because I didn't roll down here with much. But if y'all want the up to date shit. Y'all got to avoid the law. Let them other banger do their thing. While they're banging we're putting it down. While they're getting prison time, we're making million we're a cash money clique now."

Smokey gave them no time for question. He sent them to the cars and he came back with 3 duffle bags divided the dope between them and sent them out. The heroin was mounted up to a million dollar 1$ 25$ bags. The 6 kilos was of cocaine was whipped up to crack cut down to 10 dollars bags. The rocks wasn't no bigger than the tips of your pinky finger. So that gave them 350, every 2 kilos the whipped them into 5. So that gave them 2.3 million in crack. The bales were bagged in 5$ bags came out to 600,000, so that gave them 3.9 million. He only looked for 3 million back. He figured he'll have half of everything sold in two weeks. Before the big score. Money went progressing and days went flying. Smokey name got big in Macon, but he didn't let it make him think more of himself because he knew he was on a mission.

IT was time for him to contact Juan, he worried when nobody answered or nobody in the apartments had contacted him. He called Leo and got no answer. It had been six days. Smokey wanted to turn it in and check on his fam, with no one else to call he called Sonya because he knew she'll know what's going on. She was Juan second lady, so he'll get the info from her. Juan told him to call her only in an emergency.

"Sonya, this Smokey. Have you heard from Juan or the family?"

"Yeah, Juan is at the hospital with that dead as bitch. She need to gone head and die. Your family is putting it down everywhere. Juan sent Leo them to Valdosta. Rome, Savannah, Waycross, Albany and Griffin. Man he's just spreading everybody out. We're doing all the work while he's laying up crying over a dead bitch. Then there's the bitch Sandy; Sandy he cares so much about. Smokey that nigga will cross us over them two bitches."

"Sonya what have Juan done to make you so mad? He's gonna take care of the Cuban for you."

"I just don't like to see him like his is. I mean that bitch been in a coma for almost three weeks. They need to pull the plug. Sandy laid the cross in Detroit. I didn't tell Juan. I heard her on the phone telling somebody that he was bring them damn gang member down here. Smokey y'all need to do something about this; I believe the bitch is the Feds. If you don't do something we'll be in prison before we set up."

"You're right I never trusted the hoe anyway. I'll have Leo to take the hoe out. He used to be in the army until they discharged him. They got caught making bombs and selling them. They didn't catch him. He just got ratted on."

"I think he's at this number (912 878 4606). Take care of this Smokey. Maybe Juan will get back on track; I asked the nigga about the lick on them damn Cubans he didn't say nothing. The deal is going down in 3 days. I'm tired of this fat Cuban Mothafucka laying on top of me slapping my ass and shit. Man I'm getting mad! Because Juan is suppose to be handling this shit for me. He's talking about I'm his family. Smokey you got to do something."

"I'll take care of Sandy and I'll tell Juan what's up with the Cuban. We're gonna get the Cuban. Just chill out, everything takes time."

Smokey called Leo and gave order for Sandy's life, and Leo gave word that it would be done because he was with Sandy at the time, she was showing him alot of spots outside Valdosta before he hung up he told him death before dishonor.

Smokey headed for Atlanta to check Juan, on slipping. He made up his mind that he wasn't gonna tell him about Sandy. He just wanted him to stay on top of paper. When he arrived at Grady it was 7:30 pm. He wondered how he was gonna get Juan away from Tasha and his mind back on business.

As he walked into her room he saw Juan lying under her sleep. She was still out. But his baby had progressed because he was in a regular crib at the side of the bed. He called Juan name and he woke up and hugged him and said, "What's up Ike?"

"Juan Ike is dead; you got to let the dead stay dead."

"Yeah! You're right. It's just you're just like Ike. Man I got so much to do. But I ain't got my mind straight. Sonya is coming up here every day bugging me about the Cuban. The Middle family keeps bugging me about staying. I'm surprise they're gone now. Man it's like I'm in the coma because they keep throwing my son in my face every time I'm about to leave and get right. I don't want to leave Tasha, because she might wake up again. Man I know I've been slipping and I hate I brung you and your crew into this situation. But you got to understand you're my right hand man. When my mind is going left you're going right. Yes I know I'm slipping."

"Nall man I'm here to let you know that everything is well in Macon and I don't want to be seen down there. That's it, I've spread everybody out, and that was cool. What are the doctors talking about?"

"Right now they don't know. Mrs. Middle is coming to get Juan today. He can go home, that's a blessing. Sandy is giving Leo the rundown and everybody else is doing good. Your girl Toccara been coming up, she wanted to go to Macon. I told her to wait, so you gone and spend time with your girl. Man really all we got to do is chill and let them make the money. Oh yell. Get Leo and about 10 more men to go with Sonya so she'll leave me alone about that Cuban."

"Hold up Smokey! Turn the TV up!"

"Newsdate! Valdosta Prison guard Sandy Brown was called to work early. As she arrived at the prison, her 1996 Toyota exploded. Officer Anderson, a L.T. said no one called her, it was a set up. He said he had spoken with her family and they said she was called to work. No one saw anything. The guard in the towel said she waved as she pulled in and the car blew up. More details on Officer Sandy Brown tonight at 11 pm on Channel Five Eyewitness News."

"I'll just be got damn! Smokey get Leo on this shit right now! I want some answers."

"Juan, what's wrong?"

"My friend just got blown up Mrs. Middle."

"Who's your friend here?"

"This is Smokey, he's just checking on Tasha. He went to school with her."

"Well I'm fix 'en to take the baby, I would stay, but I'm tired plus Richard is coming up. So bring the baby to the car and I'll call you when we get home."

Juan grabbed the baby and his bags and they all walked them to Nancy car in the hospital parking lot. He tucked the baby in the car seat and fasten the seatbelt. He kissed Nancy and watched the white 1995 Lexus pull off. They went into the McDonalds and got 2 Big Macs large fries and grape soda. They ate and headed back to the room to make plans for the trip to Florida. When they walked back into the hospital they heard, "Code Red! Code Red!" on the 5th floor.

They ran to Tasha room only to find that she wasn't there. Her machine was unplugged and there was blood on the floor. They ran out the room to the nurse station.

"Where is Natasha Middle?," Juan asked.

"Calm down sir, we've moved her. Someone came in her room, shot her daddy in the shoulder trying to shoot her. All we know is it was a white nurse that did it, and she is still in the hospital. She's a white female wearing a blue uniform."

Smokey pulled out two 357's from his white Tommy jeans and told Juan he would check downstairs. Juan ran back to the room grabbed the Glock 17 out the closet from his Atlanta Falcon Chalk Line Jacket, and ran wildly through the hallway.

As he made his way to the fourth floor, he saw a white nurse in an all blue uniform coming out of a room.

He pointed the Glock and yelled, "Hey you stop!"

The nurse fainted when she turned and saw him approaching, her with a gun.

Juan slapped her. "Don't die now bitch."

She woke up and screamed, "Please sir don't kill me. All my money is in my locker. It ain't much I'll take you to it without no noise. I promise sir."

He grabbed her from the floor and took her back to the 5th floor nursing station. He saw Richard at the station with his arm in a sling. The left side of his blue shirt was blooded. His blue pants had blood on them also.

"Is this her Richard?"

"No Juan, it's not her, let her go and calm down."

The nurse asked what had happen once Juan let her go. Richard explained to her a white nurse ran in Tasha room and shot him trying to shoot Tasha. Saying this is payback bitch. He explained the only reason why he got shot because he dived over Tasha. He also explained to Juan that Tasha had been moved to a private place where he's not allowed to come near and she was out of her coma.

Juan looked at the lady and apologized offered her 5 grand not to press charges. She accepted the money, Smokey gave her and they left. He explained to Smokey how it had to be Philip folks who killed Sandy and tried to kill Tasha. He looked at Smokey and said, "It's time to take over this shit."

As they walked out the hospital to the parking lot Smokey went to his Chevy as Juan was walking toward his Lexus they saw Sonya red Honda Accord coming toward them.

She stopped, "What's up fellas?"

Smokey thought back on their conversation and knew it was Sonya who tried to kill Tasha. He didn't say nothing because her motive were on the level he was on, no play all work.

"Nothing, just on our way to see you," Smokey replied.

"Well there's a hotel up the street, I'll check in and we can come up with a plan. Follow me."

They jumped in their cars and followed her to the Hyatt Hotel she checked into room 221 and walked up. When they entered Sonya jumped on the bed. The room was big and spacey with a king size bed, a full living room, white wall, a dining table and a 60 inch Toshiba screen TV. Sonya patted the bed and told Juan to come and lay down.

"No time for that Sonya, tell me about your boyfriend."

"His name is Alex Hindu. He's 5'11" and 262 pound mostly fat. He's head of the C.A.P. the Cuban America Posse. They're based in Miami Florida. In three days his uncle Carlos is sending two 55 gallon drums of cocaine and two 55 gallon drums of heroin over here by boat. They have been on the water now for 11 days. They're on a Catalina 470 yacht. They been on the water for so long because they're fooling the National Guard. By stopping at different island getting off touring. From the conversation I overheard it's an all-white yacht with 6 to 8 people. There will be one steering the boat and three guards with M-16s so they ain't bullshitting. If we hurry down there we can catch them off the rip."

"Sonya you ain't gave us no plan, listen we're gonna go down there and check things out that way we'll be able to hit them the next go round. So if you want this lick it will have to wait. I'm not fix 'en to go down there half stepping and get myself killed."

"If you wouldn't been laying up with that dead bitch." He slapped her to the floor. "Don't you ever disrespect Tasha. She hasn't done shit to you. As a matter of fact, what was you doing at the hospital?"

"I was coming to see you and see what was up with the lick. Since you never say much when I come up there. I was looking for a parking space when I saw y'all sir."

Sonya had ditched the uniform when she ran out the room. She ran up the stairs and went in an empty room on the 6th floor took the blonde wig off wiped the pale color blush off her face. Fixed her black blouse took her low heel black shoes from her blouse put them on and went down the elevator. She left everything in a trash bag in the bathroom tied up.

He looked at her and told her he was sorry and he'll handle Alex for her because she was all he had. Sandy got blown up, Tasha liked to got killed. Her pop moved her so she was all he had. He told her not to worry they'll fly out to Key West today.

"As soon as we got some ticket. As a matter of fact get me a ticket to Nigeria. Smokey you and Sonya drive to Key West in 2 U-Haul's. Smokey do whatever you see fit. If you feel like the lick can be hit then hit it. If not don't worry about it."

"Cool Smokey, I'll get some C-4 and put it on the bottom of the boat. I was in the Navy for 4 years learned how to build bombs. I just left the Navy because my mom got sick. Make sure you bring Leo with us."

"Sound like you got a plan Sonya."

"Yeah I do."

Sonya and Smokey left to gather up stuff for their lick. He didn't want to go, shit didn't feel right plus he had to change his prints to attempt the shit they had plan. He had to go get a quarter million for the doctor. He laid down and called Nancy.

"Nancy this is Juan I'm calling to check on you and my son. Richard moved Tasha and told me to stay away from her. So how is he responding to his crib?"

"He's doing fine. You know something I notice about that boy he don't cry much. It's like he just look into the sky, like he's praying like he know something is wrong. I kissed him when we got home he just smiled and reached for the sky. Tasha is doing well, she's out of her coma. She's talking and asking question. Richard says she's talking about her life dying, her mate dying, but she don't remember names. All she's doing is talking. Richard said the doctor said at the rate she's going her memory will be back soon. They're trying to keep her up. Richard was shot with a 380 in the left shoulder. The bullet has been removed. He's doing fine. He says he's gonna take his arm out of the sling. He's stubborn. I got to give it to you. When you handled your business, you stayed faithful. Juan promise me your life of crime is over."

"Does she remember the baby or me?"

"Sorry she don't really remember nothing."

"Well Richard don't want me around y'all. I'm fix 'en to go to Nigeria for two weeks. I know Richard is gonna try to erase me from her memory. Well kiss my son tell 'em his daddy love him."

He laid down and fell asleep. Six hours later, Sonya came into the room. She saw him sound asleep. She undressed and got into bed with him. She kissed him and he called out "Tasha." She kissed him again and he woke up.

"I'm sorry Sonya I thought you was Tasha."

"Yeah you called me her."

"I can't explain."

They kissed and made love. Lying on his chest she told him she loved him and nothing or nobody would come between that. Juan kissed her and went into her again. As they laid there he looked at his Rolex it was already 8 am. He asked her about the ticket. She jumped up.

"Oh shit you ain't got but 2 hours to go handle business. Your plane leaves at 10 am."

"Let's get dressed."

They showered and dressed. Juan went back to the mansion packed got the money and called a cab. He got 10 extra grand out of the safe that sat in Tony's room, the master bedroom. He didn't want to sleep in the room so he left the big king size bed with the white satin sheets and pillow case just as they were. The dressers like he left them one on the back wall with a mirror on it and the other one by the window with all kinda cologne on top of it. The back wall turned inside out. The bottom was on the bottom right side of the mirror frame. His room was the last room at the end of the hallway facing the hallway.

The cab driver blew and he looked out the window and seen the yellow cab. He walked out the door and a white slim young cab driver opened the passenger side door. He sat in the back seat and closed his eyes. He was only 30 minute away from the airport he could've drove. He didn't want nobody to steal neither one of the cars because Tony left all kinda cars. Limousines, Caddy's, Lexus's, Benzes, BMWs, Jags. IT was about 20 cars parked on that property with 1 bike. He couldn't risk none of them getting stole. Not many people knew about that house. Plus the house had cameras around it. That's something he didn't understand about Tony. How he let the dude kill him because the laptop sit on the stand right by the door. "Tony got too comfortable that's all." he thought.

He saw Smokey and Sonya waiting on him at the airport. Sonya killed him and told him he had a day and a half trip. So get plenty of rest. He boarded the plane got in his seat. The pilot told everybody, "Thanks for flying with Delta and he hopes they enjoy their flight."

He put his portable CD player on Stuck Sade Love Deluxe in and fell asleep.

CHAPTER 12
The Betrayal

"**D**addy, who is Juan?"

"That's your baby."

"I have a baby?"

"Yes you're a mom he's only a month old."

"Where is his daddy? And what's his daddy name and where is my baby?"

"Tasha your baby daddy name is Juan Ellis. He's the same age as you 21. At this time I don't know where he's at. I heard he got locked up then I heard he was dead. He was a loser any way Tasha you don't need him. Your baby is home."

Tasha laid there in her private room on the 8th floor of Grady. He had put her on the mental ward floor. Where alot of guards patrolled the floor. Richard sat on the corner of the bed with his arm in the sling. He had spent the night with her. He got his clothes from the 5th floor room. He showered and put on some blue slacks with a white cotton button-down shirt. He had his laptop on the bed typing with his right hand. She raised the head of the bed up. He looked back at her, she had tears in her eyes.

"What's wrong princess?"

"Daddy things are flashing so fast in my head didn't I love him? Did he love me? Wasn't he there with the baby? I remember he loved me. He can't be dead, Daddy. I think I loved him. I do love him. He just can't be dead. Help me remember where he's at. Help me find my life. Pay the doctor to get me back my memory. I need to see my baby. Where is my baby? Do I have a mommy?"

"Yes I'm calling her right now. She also have your baby."

He called Nancy and told her to bring the baby before Tasha go in shock. He also asked about Juan, she replied, "He's in Nigeria."

"Why did he go there?"

"He didn't say. All he said was he knew you were gonna try to erase him from Tasha memory. Richard don't do that. They have a child together plus they have a life also. You know he love her. He stayed in the hospital night and day. You said it yourself he really do love her. One thing I do know and believe that boy really loves her and that baby. So whatever you do try to put him more into her memory. You got to admit

Tasha have slowed that boy down. He don't even sell drugs no more. Plus I've grown to love that boy. He's always been there for her. So don't take away what she tried so hard to build. Me and the baby will be there shortly."

Richard thought on Nancy's words very hard. But he couldn't let his baby fall into the hands of Juan again because of him she can't remember; now he's being a coward and running to Africa. As he ponder on Juan in his mind he looked at his only child laying there in another world with her hands over her eyes trying to remember. He hated every being of Juan Ellis. He knows he had to do something to tear him from her. He almost had him if it hadn't been for his daddy. His thoughts were broken when Tasha jumped up in excitement.

"I remember! I remember! I remember!"

"You remember what sweetheart?"

Juan ain't my baby, he's my husband. My name is Natasha Ellis, not Middle."

"Hold up baby, you're moving too fast. You're not married and Juan's your baby."

"So why do I keep seeing us getting married? I can't marry a dead man." She started hitting her head with her hands screaming, "Think, Tasha, Think!"

Richard grabbed her and calmed her down; Nancy walked through the door with Juan cuddled in his white Wendy the Pooh baby blanket.

"Tasha, here's your mommy and baby."

Tasha looked at her looked at the baby. Something about Nancy red shirt with one love written in cursive all black letters made her stare harder. She was remembering but couldn't figure out what it was. So she asked her mom was that Juan. Nancy smiled and told her yes and tried to give the baby to her. She folded her arms.

"I don't want no baby! Why did daddy kill Juan?"

She started crying and screaming, "I hate you daddy! I hate you!"

Juan started crying so Nancy handed him to Richard and she hugged Tasha. She cuddles her and started to rock her.

"Listen baby, I'm your mom and I can't tell you a lie. I don't know what your daddy told you about Juan. But listen Juan ain't dead. As a matter of fact, he just left you a day ago. Someone came into your room and tried to kill you."

"I remember the shots yesterday."

"Yes, so your daddy moved you here. He told Juan not to come around you while you're unstable. Right now Juan is heading to Africa."

"Africa! Africa! Nigeria!"

"Yes! How do you know, Tasha?"

"I don't remember."

Things started to flashing in her head. "Oh! Oh! I see Momma! But what do I see? Africa! Prints! Africa! Finger! Fingerprints. He's going to get his fingerprints changed. Yeah that's it. He's going to Africa to get his fingerprints changed. Oh NO!"

"What Tasha?" Richard asked.

"Oh no! No baby, I'm not dead. He thinks I'm dead. He's fix 'en to take over Atlanta. Lord have mercy, alot of people fix 'en to die. He got a gang IBH. Do he know about the baby? Naw he don't."

"Yes he do. He just walked me and the baby to the car yesterday. Before the shooting."

"Mom I remember he kept telling me something. I remember he used to wake me up and tell me if I die he's gonna kill himself. But why is he changing his prints?"

"Richard think with her!"

"I can't think because Juan never talked to me. Hold up, you remember when Tasha left and went home them gang members was surrounding the hospital?"

"That's right he's gonna fake his death and come back as Ravenion. He told me all of this when he used to wake me up."

"What did he say about you and the baby?"

"I don't remember Mommy. I'm sleepy now. Can I have my baby?"

She hugged Juan and said, "Everything is gonna be alright." She pulled her left breast out and started to feed him. In ten minute she was asleep and Juan still feeding.

CHAPTER 13
Ravenion

As Juan left the airport in a green cab he looked at his driver. He had a low nappy haircut. Kept bobbing his head to a tune on the radio. Juan smile, he was amazed at what he saw as they rode. Cars, trucks and vans. He told the cabdriver,

"I thought I was in Africa, this looks like the city. They don't show all this in the history books. Y'all are wearing clothes like we wear in the State. I thought I'll be seeing females with their breast out."

The cabdriver just laughed.

"I will take you to see Dr. McCray, he's good doctor. I will also let you stay in my home for a small fee. One hundred American dollars."

Juan smiled and asked him his name.

He replied, "Me-chell."

"Okay Mr. Me-chell here's 300 American dollars make sure I have the best stay in Africa: big booty female that will dance and have sex. Can you handle good food and American fun."

"Yes I can. Will find you the best of everything."

They rode the rest of the way in silence. Juan looked left to right enjoying the sight of small stores and big building. Me-chell turned left down one street and he seen regular apartments, set up like New York city apartments. All binded together in rows. Me-chell drove and turned left again and Juan saw small huts-like home. As they rode he had seen people walking the side of the streets with food over their heads kids walking in line behind their mom or dad. Then he seen young pretty ebony women around his ages and titties that hung. Me-chell looked in the mirror and said, "You like? I can stop car and you can have anyone you like. You know you can pay family and she'll be yours. You can take any woman or child back to the state with you. For small price."

Me-chell had slowed the car down for him to get a good look at the young female passing by. One of the female had her head bent down as she walked by. She was topless and had on a green looking skirt like bottom.

"Her with her head down."

Me-chell called her and pulled the car around to her. The girl mom turned and made her hold her head up. When she looked at him, her look was breath taking. She was so beautiful; pretty brown eyes, nice shining skin, no stomach fat, nice round breast that stood and her nipple stood also. She smiled and her teeth were white and perfect. He looked down at her bare feet he couldn't really see because she had been walking on that dirt road. Me-chell got out the car and gave the mom a hundred dollar bill and the girl got in the car. She sat in the back seat with her head dropped.

"What's your name?"

She looked up at him and said, "Kau."

"My name is Ravenion what's wrong?"

"Nothing Mr. Ravenion I just a little shy."

"You don't like doing this type of thing do you?"

She raised her head and looked at him. "No! I mean Yes! I really don't have a choice as of now."

She dropped her head, he kinda felt sorry for her he told her Me-chell will take her back home. He gave Me-chell his money back and told him to take her home, Me-chell just looked at her in the mirror with his cold eyes. She dropped her eyes again.

They pulled up to a brick building with a sign, "Dr. McCray."

"Leave your bags. Me-chell will take good care of them. Take her home and be back and wait right here. He went in his back with his clothes in them got his passport; opened the bag with the money in it. She caught a quick glimpse of the money and smiled. He closed the bag, one thing he knew about women they loved money. No woman will turn down money. He got the tote bag put it on his shoulder and walked into the office. As he entered the building, he noticed that this was a regular hospital. He went to the desk that sat in the middle of the hallway. An older black woman sat behind the desk with glasses hanging on her nose.

"May I help you sir?"

"Dr. McCray?"

She pointed him to the right hall and told him the last door on the right. He walked the hall it wasn't long at all he went in and seen a short fat white man with black hair and green eyes. He was standing waiting on him.

"Hi Doctor McCray my name is Juan.

"Oh yes, I believe we spoke over the phone months back. Juan Ellis."

"Yeah."

"You're here to get your prints changed over. I got your message two weeks ago. Do you have the money?"

"Yes. The whole quarter million."

"Well hand it over and we can get to it today."

Juan handed him the money and he counted it by the stacks they were in. He looked at him and said follow me. They walked through some wooden double doors, out the back of the hospital to a small hut. Juan walked in first then the Dr. He shut the door and hit the lights.

"Gotdamn, this shit look like Emory."

"Let's get you finished."

He sat Juan in a chair, strapped his arms down and shot something in his vein that made his hands go numb. He left his hands and told him the procedure is very simple.

"I'm gonna take the center of each finger and put implants in them. Then I'm gonna tattoo your fingers."

He gave him another shot hooked the IV in and shot something in the IV and he was out in 10 second.

3 hours later he woke him up with his hands in bandages.

"How do you feel Mr. Ravenion Nalls? Here's your passport and you're ready to go. Your hands should be healed in four days. Here's some bandages to rewrap your hands some ointment to keep from getting contact of any disease. Wash your hands in sterile water which is in your bag. I talked to Me-chell your cabdriver and he'll have you on the plan in 4 days. It's best you stay here until your hands heals. Me-chell and Kau said they'll take good care of you. Don't worry about Kau I've paid her. Oh I put some Tylox in your bag for pain."

The Dr. helped him put the bad on his shoulder and helped him to the car. Kau put him behind the passenger seat and she got behind the driver seat. She let him rest his head on her lap as they rode to Me-chell house.

Juan thought he was gonna see a hut. But Me-chell lived in a house a big pretty white house outside the city. He had about 15 cabs in his yard. So he musta owned his own cab company.

Juan was still kinda out of it. So they help him up the steps onto the wooden porch in the house. They took him upstairs, to the best room in the house, the last room in the back. The upstairs were made like a horseshoe. That connected at the back. Kau laid him on the bed and he fell asleep. She undressed him and seen that he had alot of money stashed in the front of his pants. She put it in the dresser on the left side of the bed. Got the key from the dresser and locked it. Went downstairs and told Me-chell to bring some potatoes chops and chicken to the room.

She looked very interested in doing her job. She wasn't a hooker, but her mom had tried to sell her a couple of times. She only gave lazy sex and back talk, so they always sent her back. She was only 19. Most of her buyers were white old and thought like slave master. She didn't know what to think about Ravenion because he was young and good looking. She knew she had to do her best, because not many young American males come to Africa. She had looked at his passport and seen that he was 23 years old. From Cleveland, Ohio.

She looked at the other girls there walking around naked and letting the men of all color touch on them. This was truly a brothel and she didn't like being there. Me-chell was a rich African enslaving the women for a small percentage of their earning. She was happy because the doctor paid them both so she can take her $1200 dollars home to her family. Me-chell gave her two plates and told her don't mess this us. He reminded her that she had a 4 day gig…

She went back to the room undressed and woke him. He looked at her out of a blurry eyesight. Then he became focus. He liked what he seen. She model for him walking back and forth. Me-chell had sent 10 girls to the room with water to bathe with. They filled the tub and left, the water was hot you could see the steam raising. She smiled at him and said, "Too hot right now. Let me feed you."

She feed him with her hands. He had sat up on the twin mattress which had no head board. His back was against the wall. She was sitting in between his legs with her legs open, leaning her body towards him to feed him. He just looked at the hairless clit that sat before him. Her lips wasn't puffed or abused. So he could tell that she wasn't a hoe or hooker. She looked like she took care of herself. She finished feeding him and sat him in the tub. She stepped in the small can tub and rubbed his muscular chest. She smiled at him leaned forward and kissed him.

"I'm gonna treat you very special. I promise. I've never been with a young man before. So this is gonna be very wonderful. Tomorrow I take you around okay?"

He nodded and let her bathe him and watched her bathe. Then got out of the tub she dried him with a white towel then dried herself. He laid on the bed and watched her put the towels back on the racks. She turned, sat on the bed and took him in her mouth. He came in her mouth and she spitted it in the tub water. She went back at it until he erected and she crawled over him and sat on it and started to ride him. He enjoyed the ebony love he was getting. He couldn't make love to her because of his hands. So he enjoyed her. She came before him and started getting into it more. She turned herself around while he was still inside of her. Leaned backward and rode him til they both came. She stood up smiling turned to face him kneeled back over him and licked him from his navel to his lips and kissed him. She covered them and fell asleep on top of him.

They were awoke by one of the Me-chell girls a slim brown female which were naked to serve them breakfast. Fish and grits with coffee. Kau was upset because the girl came in naked. That was disrespect! They ate and she told him to get dressed and get his bags. She put one of his white t-shirt on. Her green skirt and walked out the door. She asked one of Me-chell driver and older black man with gray hair to take her home.

As they got in the car she told him not to speak. She stayed in the city with her mom, 2 little sisters, father and 1 younger brother. They stayed in a small house made out of oak wood. When the driver let them out. She told him her father is an officer that's how they got lucky to own a house. She walked in the small house, the living room were spacey it had fur sofas all with blue sheets over them chairs and a TV. Her mom was the first lady at the front of the crowd yesterday with the big breast.

"Why did you bring your company here? You know your father rules."

"I had no other place to take him. I fear something would happen to him there. One of Me-chell women enter the room naked. Showing me all disrespect. When we left alot of hostiles were downstairs. This is Mr. Ravenion, so can he stay?"

"Why are you wearing that shirt? Have he offered to take you with him?"

"No!"

He just looked at them talk while the mom sat in front of the TV. He sat in one of the chairs next to the mom and told her,

"Ma'am I pay whatever to stay for the next 3 days. I just want to stay somewhere safe. Right now I'm kinda handicap."

He held up his hands.

"Oh, I forgot I got to change your bandages, come with me to the backyard."

They walked through the kitchen which was small. It had alot of pots and pans. They walked out to the back yard, he looked at the wooden fence that surrounded the yard. He didn't hear or see the kids. So he asked her where was her sisters and brother. She told him school like every kid should be. She spit a razor out her mouth and cut the bandage.

His hand was purple, bluish and red. She poured the water from the bag on his hand then put the ointment on both hands and wrapped them. She walked him to her room which was beside the kitchen. She had her own room with a door on it. The kids room were across from hers had a blanket nailed to both walls. Her room was pretty she had flowers on stands and a small mirror. Her bed was a twin bed with a homemade quilt on it. She laid him down and told him to rest. She gave him 2 pills and laid beside him. Her father came in the room a tall dark male with a little afro. All brown police suit.

"Mr. Ravenion, this is very rare in my home. I have small kids here. I don't like this at all. But my wife said you were in danger there. I don't approve of my wife and daughter living but we have to survive. We only have enough for ourselves. So you'll have to pull your own weight the next three days. Kau give me your earning."

She gave him the whole $1200, and looked at him.

"I have to put this in the bank, you do want to go to college don't you? I haven't heard from the exchange people yet. So we need every penny."

"I have contacts in the states, I'll talk to my people and get her in a college. And I have my own money so I can pull my own weight."

The pills had started to kick in. He told Kau to go to the market and buy the best meat, fresh fruit, fresh veggies and whatever else she wants. He told her to get $300 out his bag.

When the father seen the money he smiled at him and said, "Indeed you do have your own money."

He went to sleep and woke up to 3 small kids looking at him. He liked kids and they looked so innocent. The smallest girl was sitting on the bed Indian style the little boy was standing by the other girl. They were the same height. The girls wore braids and the boy had a low haircut. They all wore shorts the little girls were bare chest.

He felt bad because they were living like that, he stood and dressed. The little boy helped him button his black jeans while the two girls tied his Air Nikes. He put on a black T-shirt and the little girl unzipped the bag he gave them a hundred dollars apiece and got 5 hundred for himself and they went shopping. Kau was in the kitchen with her mom cooking. They didn't even see them leave out.

The kids took him to the many booths and stores he bought a few necklaces made with gold and different stones for Tasha, Sonya and Nancy. The kids bought toys. So he bought toys for Juan. The kids had bought 3 wagons and the baby girl got her a little bike. He liked that. To his surprise they bought him a dashiki.

They spent all their money, but they were all happy. They rolled everything on their wagon. A man approached him with a ring and necklace 14K. He bought them for 100.00 dollars. The baby girl walked beside him. When they got to the porch they heard their daddy saying, "What do y'all mean, y'all didn't see them leave. It's dark outdoor and they ain't back yet. No telling what have happened."

The kids laughed and they helped each other push their red wagon into the house. One by one right behind each other, in a line youngest to the oldest. The boy was at the end of the line. They rolled through the kitchen to their bedroom. The father just looked and smiled because he seen the joy in their faces, especially his baby girl who's always whining.

Juan stopped and gave Kau the ring and necklace. She liked to drop to her knees. The necklace was a figure link and the ring had a diamond in the middle of a heart. She put it on her ring finger. He told her mom to go in his pocket because he had something for her also. She looked at her husband and he nodded. It was a pair of earrings.

He looked at the husband and said, "I didn't know what to get you. But I'ma set you straight before I leave."

The husband laughed and said, "My name is Manni and my wife is Kendra and we appreciate what you did for the kids."

He put his stuff in the room and walked in the kid's room. Manni was there looking over everything. Baby girl ran and jumped in his arms.

"My name is Mayya."

She kissed his cheek. The boy name Emmanual and the older girl name Sasha. Manni asked him to step out they walked to the front porch and he asked him to take a seat. They sat in a swing chair and Manni asked him to be serious.

"What do you do in the United States?"

Juan smiled and said, "I'm a freelancer. I help develop homes."

"Mr. Nalls I checked you out, you're a drug dealer. Me and Mr. McCroy is good friend. He tells me you're down with this big drug dealer. Also y'all have many companies there. You're from Atlanta. What are your plans for my daughter?"

"Sir I have no plans for your daughter. I think she's a very beautiful young lady. One that deserve a chance at life. I don't have no plans of involving her in nothing I do. When I leave her I'll never see her again. Unless we run into each other in the state. Or she contacts me."

"You don't think my daughter is marriageable?"

"Yes I do, but I'm not looking for a wife, my life is chopped and screwed."

"But I do have your word, on helping her get into school?"

"Yes you have that, as a matter of fact I can make the call today."

"Not today because it's late, I trust that you'll keep your word."

They went back in and sat at the table. Kau had bought steaks and cooked them for the whole family. Also she baked potatoes and served them. Baby girl sat by him and held his hand while they prayed. They ate and he played with the kids. Finally around 10 pm, Manni sent them to bed.

Juan just looked up in the sky and she came behind him with her bare chest put her arms around him and said, "The sky is beautiful it tells you so much. It guides you to safety, also guides you home. Home in being love. If you take me back with you I promise to be faithful, understandable and tolerable. I'll worship the ground you walk on."

"I believe that Kau! I really do. I already have 2 females in my life. I don't want to get you involved in my style of living. I'm a drug dealer back in the state; a gangsta. I'm subject to die any day. If I did your life will never be completed it will be filled with street thugs that will only abuse you and use you. I can't do you like that. I can only help you go to school and hope you don't try to contact me when you come to the States. I'm gonna send you somewhere far from me because I don't want you to get killed. You have a lovely family and that's something I don't have. I just really want to give you a chance. You're my people in order for me to be a great I must give a future. So you're my gift to the world. What are you studying? "

She smiled and told him she wanted to be a doctor, so she can help her people. She also told him that she'll find him once she gets in the States. She pointed to the sky and told him, "My life runs with the stars and planets so I'll find you. And my love will be with you. Come let's go to bed. On my God I got to change your bandages."

"Naw they're straight until tomorrow."

They went in and got into bed. She made hard passionate love to him. When he woke the next morning she had the water ready and his breakfast: eggs, bacon and toast, with goat milk. She feed him and bathes him. Changed his bandage and walked with him around the town. He saw all kinda business. Again he was amazed to see Africa wasn't' like the movies or books. They walked in the police station and he made the call to John, John told him her tuition at Emory will be a hundred and 20 grand without grants and student loans. He asked him could he help her with a student loan. He told him it would take about a month and a half and could get under one-ten.

He turned and looked at her and said, "You'll be in college next month, I'm not gonna tell you where, you'll know when you get your letter and plane ticket."

They walked out and he told her he had to get back to the States. He had business to handle. She kissed him and hauled him a cab. She hated to see him go. Tears were in her eyes. She gave him the address and he left.

The cab driver took him back to Me-chell because his plane were gonna leave first thing in the morning. So he sent for her, when she got there she didn't want to sleep with him, just lay under him. She told him her little sister cried and missed him. They laid there just enjoying each other and fell asleep. The next morning Me-chell sent food he ate kissed her gave her the money he had left 8 grand and left.

He was in a rush to get back to Atlanta. Atlanta was his life and city to be. Once again he was on his day and a half trip. He watched the clouds this time wondering how far is Heaven. The small tune of J.T. Hatten song kept running through his mind. He wondered if he and Tasha would make it to Heaven together. Then he closed his eyes and prayed for his mom, dad, Ike, grandmom and Tony.

When he opened his eyes it was like he saw an image of everyone he just prayed for smiling. Then Kau words came to remembrance. He knew everything was gonna be alright. He wonder was that God way of showing him his people were okay. He ate steak eggs and orange juice half way through his trip. He thought about making things right with the Middle's being a good father and husband. As he thought about this he fell to sleep, when he woke up he was at the Hartsfield Airport. He was home.

He phoned Sonya but Smokey answered. He wasn't surprised because a bitch is gonna be a bitch.

"Smokey I'm at the airport come and get me."

With that he hung up walked to the bathroom and cut the bandages off. His hand had a little swelling but they were straight. He put some of the ointment on and walked out front to wait.

When Smokey arrived, Juan was nowhere in sight. He had walked to the train station, and was about to catch the train when Sonya walked up behind him and kissed him.

"Come on baby, I got some shit to tell you. Some real shit."

When they had reached Smokey, she got all happy and told him, "We did it! We did it!"

"Slow down Sonya. Tell me later. I need to see how Tasha and Juan is doing."

She looked at him in disgrace, "Oh you're so caught up in them, that you ain't concerned about your real family."

Sonya couldn't understand if he told her. Every time he seen a happy family he gets depressed so he told her, "They are my real family."

As they got in Smokey Chevy, he told Smokey to take him home so he could get his car. As they rode off Smokey started telling him about Key West.

"Man, it took 16 hours to get down there. Boy we went about 50 deep man. We saw how sweet the shit was. Boy we hit that bitch like missionary boy. We were under water putting bombs on the bottom of the boat. By the time they could see what was happening, Sonya walked in with the hidden microphone. Boy!"

"Hold up Smokey. All I need to know is y'all got the dope and did y'all kill everybody."

"Man we got the dope and the money about three hundred thousand it was only two 55 drums of cocaine. Yes we killed everybody. We rented another apartment and the dope is there."

They pulled up in his driveway. He threw his bags in the front door turned around going back toward the car. Then he remembered he had to get that money to John. He ran back upstairs to Tony room counted out 200 grand and closed the door. He didn't even look at them as he got in the car. Sonya was standing by the driver door.

"Something musta went wrong in Africa, because he don't even look concerned about the dope, I got him. Look at how he was holding his head down." Sonya stated.

He backed out past them and went to the airport to drop John the money. He told John to make sure her tuition was paid she had a 40 grand account and her family got the rest. As he was leaving to go check the dope out and apologize to Smokey and Sonya, his phone rang.

"Hello Sonya what's up?"

"That's what I'm trying to figure out with you."

"I'm on my way to check trap. I just got to check on my son and her. That's all tell Smokey that I apologize to the both of y'all."

He phoned Richard, he didn't know what to say. So he just calmed himself down and spoke.

"Richard, I'm just calling to check up on my son and Tasha. How are they coming alone?"

"Juan where are you?"

"I'm in my car heading downtown why? What's up?"

"You need to come over and see your son. I thought you went to Africa? But anyway come over I got something to talk with you about."

He rode past the downtown exit heading for Moreland. He didn't even notice that Sonya and Smokey were following him. As he was getting off the Moreland exit he saw a car wreck on the 20 west the Moreland off ramp. It looked like the blue Lexus was flipped over. He rode down the street in silence; try to capture at least one of his thoughts. All he thought about was taking over Atlanta. How he would be on top of the game like the mayor of Atlanta at the age 21. The thought thrilled him as he parked his car on the curb of Marbut Ave. He sat there thinking that it been a long time since he's been at 1482 Marbut Ave. He never had been inside.

"I must be gaining Mr. Middle trust."

He sat there and thought of the kind of house him and Tasha would have. It would have lots of trees and flowers. The house was white with a screen porch added now.

He rang the doorbell, because the porch was locked. Richard let him in with the baby in his arms. He handed him the baby as they walked in. The house was nice a wooden floor, fireplace and nice anti furniture.

They sat on the sofa, he was amazed how the baby had grown in 2½ months. He just cuddled him and rocked him.

"Juan, I didn't want to tell you this over the phone, I wanted to tell you this is in person. Juan isn't your child. He's Ike child. The blood test came back yesterday."

"So I was right about Tasha and Ike?"

"I guess you was. The reason why I'm telling you this is because Tasha passed the day you left. We're having her cremated so she'll always be with us. I was hoping you had Betty number, so we can tell her about her grandson."

With tears in his eyes, he asked Richard for the blood test results. Richard went and got them. As he had said the baby was Edward Jackson.

"Mr. Richard, I'm sorry about your daughter. Betty got her number changed, so I can't help you with that. But if you need any help just call me. He's still my blood, he's Ike son and Ike would take care of mine if I was dead."

Juan kissed the baby and got up and walked out the door.

Richard came to the door and asked him, "Do you want the baby to keep your name?"

"No give him his daddy name."

Nancy was pulling up, so he stopped and spoke.

"I'm sorry about Tasha. Everything will be fine."

"She just asked about you alot, Juan, really she did. You needed to have been there beside of her, instead of taking all them trips."

He got in the car and put the Glock to his head.

"Tasha, I know you're in Heaven with Ike. I tried my best to keep my word. I told you if you die I'll kill myself. All I want to know is why? I guess I'll never know."

Nancy opened the door and took the gun.

"Boy, what the fuck is wrong with you? Tasha didn't kill herself. So why should you? If you're gonna die let God call you home. Boy, with God everything is possible."

He closed the door and drove off. Nancy kept the gun he was mad. I'll find another gun and take myself out. Ain't no life here for me. As he thought his tears got bigger. He reached in the glove department and got the 357 out.

"Richard what's wrong with Juan? He just tried to kill himself. What did you tell him Richard? What did you tell him?"

With a look of humbleness, he said, "Nothing I just showed him this blood test say the baby isn't his and I told him Tasha was dead. I did it to protect Tasha. She fix 'en to come home tomorrow. She don't need him in her life."

Nancy picked up the phone and called Tasha. Yelling at Richard.

"You're wrong for that Richard you should've let Tasha done all of that now that boy might kill himself."

"Who gonna kill themself mom?"

"Juan!"

"I know like hell he ain't. He told me if I die, he'll kill himself. I'm not dead."

"Your daddy told him the baby ain't his and you're dead even got a fake blood test. I just stopped the boy from killing himself. I just took one gun from him who knows he might have another one."

"Call him mom. Call him now!"

Nancy clicked over and called him. She clicked back over.

"Hello who is this?"

"Juan, this is Nancy and Tasha."

"I'm sorry ma'am this is Officer James Kemp. Ma'am I don't know how to tell you this, but I caught Juan speeding up McPherson, so I put the lights on him and he took a right on Moreland and then a left on I-20 going toward town. As I pulled in closer to him he switched to the caution lane as if he were gonna pull over. As his car came to a stop, I approached the car. He rolled down the window and said, 'I don't have nothing to live for,' and shot himself in the head."

"Officer where is his body?"

"It's laying on the stretcher, covered up."

"Can you place the phone to his ear please?"

The officer took the phone and said, "Ma'am I'm putting it to his ear now."

"Juan, I never had joy until I found you, never smiled over pain till I said I love you."

She was crying hard now and it was hard for her to speak.

"Never dreamed that one of these days you'll love me, so I promised to give my heart, my hopes and dreams! Juan now that we're apart no matter where you choose to be in my heart I'll see you everywhere, because of the day you said you love me. And because of your love, I will forever travel the world rain, hail and snow to hold your heart because I'll see you everywhere I go. I love you Juan Ellis."

"Excuse me Ma'am but can you give me some information?"

"Sir I rather not let in rest in peace. Thank you. Bye bye."

"Well mom since daddy want me dead, I might as well be dead. Mom take care of my son."

"Tasha don't do nothing stupid. Don't do nothing stupid."

Tasha hung the phone up.

"Richard, you see what you done. Juan killed himself and now Tasha is fix 'en to kill herself."

They ran out the house and got into her blue Lincoln and rode to Grady as they got on the expressway. They saw a blue Lexus with police and ambulance pulling off.

"Well there goes Juan. Thanks to you his daddy is dead."

Richard had tears in his eyes and asked Nancy, "What am I to do? Tasha is gonna hate me for the rest of her life. How can I explain my reason? What am I gonna tell his son? Nancy I only wanted the best? I can't face Tasha!"

When they walked in her room she was fighting with the nurses.

"What's going on?," Richard asked.

The nurse standing with a needle in her hand trying to stick Tasha answered, "She went in the room next door and stole some Nitro Glycerin heart pills from Mrs. Fan. Mrs. Fan said her and Tasha talked every day. She said Tasha asked, 'Will these pills kill you quiet?' That's when she walked out of Mrs. Fan room and Mrs. Fan called us. We got here just in time. She only took one and one of the nurses slapped the pills out of her hand. She's been struggling with us ever since. Maybe y'all can calm her down."

Tasha looked over and saw Richard. She held her hands out to him and ran to him saying "Daddy."

He opened his arms to embrace her. Tasha started choking him saying, "You killed Juan! You killed Juan!"

The nurses grabbed her again, but that wasn't calming her. Nancy gave her the baby.

"Look Tasha, Juan will live through him, he left you with a blessing and you know he left you with millions, so you know y'all will be okay."

A white slim male walked in with a brown suit and asked, "Is Natasha Middle present?"

"Yes. I'm her."

"My name is Ben Franklin. I'm a probate lawyer. Do you know Tony Banks?"

"Yes that's my son uncle."

"So you do have Juan Ellis son?"

"Yes."

"In his will Tony left him $30 million. I need you to sign all these papers and put his name on the Red Xs and your name on the black Xs and I'll be on my way. Here your check."

As Tasha signed the papers, she looked at Richard and said, "If you hadn't told him that bullshit he'll be alive to see this and he would have straightened his act. All he ever wanted was to make sure that we were secure. You killed my family! I hate you for this! I hate you for this! I will not go home with you. Give me my baby. We're going back to my apartment."

She signed herself out the hospital and went to the apartment she shared with Blue Eyes. Erica had moved out, Blue was also moving, so the apartment would belong to her and the baby. As she took the cab home (she had no remembrance of her condo in Buckhead that she hoped to share with Juan), she looked out the window and saw many smiling couple and cried, she looked at the couples and said, "That will be us soon." Then she'll rub her stomach. Now he's dead. She would live for herself and her son. No man alive would touch her, take his place or their riches.

When she walked in the apartment, Blue ran and hugged her and the baby. The apartment hadn't changed at all. She walked to her room with head down. Blue came behind her.

"What's up girl? You look like you just lost your best friend. You should be happy you've recovered."

"Blue, baby I wish I was dead."

"Tasha you know what? At times you can act like a selfish bitch. Do you know how many girls would love to have had that boy son and be his girl?"

She started crying saying, "Blue he's dead Blue! He's dead Blue! I wish I was dead Blue! He's dead Blue!"

"No! No! He ain't he can't be Tasha, I just seen him coming out the airport earlier today. Someone is lying to you."

"My dad told him the baby wasn't' his and I was dead. So he killed himself."

Tears fell hard as she sat Juan on the pillow and laid beside him. She couldn't think of a life without him. He was her everything and now he's dead.

Blue started to leave the room and turned around and said, "Why would a man who's on top of his game kill himself. That don't make any sense. He's used to people leaving him I mean dying on him. So being alone isn't nothing new to him. Tasha that boy ain't dead, you remember when we took that money across the world for him?"

"Yes!"

"His passport didn't say Juan Ellis, it said Ravenion Nalls."

"You know what Blue when I left the hospital the first time, I remember he said he was gonna change his print and now, so in other words he ain't dead, that's why he went to Africa."

She jumped up in joy, picked the phone up and called her mom. The phone rang three times before she picked up.

"Hello."

"Moma, he ain't dead. That couldn't been him. Do you remember why he went to Africa. He changed his prints and name. When we went to Switzerland his passport said Ravenion Nalls not Juan Ellis. Call the hospital and see was that him on that Moreland exit."

Nancy called Grady and clicked over.

"Grady Memorial Hospital," a female voice answered.

"Yes my name is Nancy Middle my stepson has a blue Lexus and I was just told about an accident on the Moreland exit. That's where I stay. Please tell me that wasn't my stepson."

"What's his name, ma'am?"

"Juan Ellis, he's 21 years old."

"Hold for a minute ma'am"

A few minute later she came back with the sad new, she said, "I'm sorry ma'am but it was him.

Tasha yelled out, "No! It can't be him."

"Ma'am I'm not suppose to give that information out. I'm sorry," and she hung up.

Without saying goodbye to her mom she hung up the phone, looked at Blue dropping her head and said "It was him."

"It can't be Tasha, I just don't believe in my heart that it was him. My heart won't let me accept it. It just can't be him. Let's go down there and check the body."

"Blue give it up he's dead, you act like you was fucking him! He's dead!"

CHAPTER 14
Blown

As Ravenion and Sonya sat in the information booth in Grady, Sonya turned to her friend and said, "Good looking girl, you just don't know how much you helped me out. Now they won't bother my baby no more."

He looked at Sonya and said, "You got to make sure the body is taken care of."

"Don't worry about that I got you covered."

She looked at Kym golden brown face into her brown eyes in disgrace and said, "I can bring your 30 grand to your house or give it to you now."

"I need it now I got bills to catch up on."

Sonya looked at him then her and said, "I'll be right back I left my purse in the car. I don't know what I was thinking."

She left the room and went downstairs thinking to herself.

"How could this bitch charge me, when I saved her damn life? If it wasn't for me the big boned bitch would be in prison. A high price booster, ungrateful bitch, I'm the one who got the bitch the job."

When she got to the parking lot Malice opened her eyes toward her ungrateful friend. She thought for herself and him when she looked at thing in this prospective. This was a stupid bitch that loved money, "Black male would be on her mind."

She opened the door to her blue 500 Benz and went inside her glove department. Inside her purse was a chrome 45 with a silencer on it with some cyanide that she was gonna use to knock Tasha off with. Now she got to use it on her ungrateful friend. She walked into McDonalds and ordered coffee and then she went back to the hospital. While walking back to the booth, she sat the coffee carrier down, opened it and put the cyanide in Kym's cup. Kym seen her coming and popped the door. She handed him the first cup in the front on the right side. Kym the one on the left and she took the last one.

Kym sipped her coffee and said, "Girl this is a good hot cup. Just what I needed."

Kym noticed he wasn't drinking his and asked was he gonna drink it. He just smiled and handed her the coffee. He wasn't much of a coffee drinker.

"Can't let a good cup go to waste."

Kym needed the coffee to stay awake. She had told Sonya she had a long night. Sonya handed her the money and Kym popped them out. For a moment Sonya wanted to turn around and shoot her. But she looked and seen so many people walking around and standing looking. She just said have a nice day girl. He spoke for the first time walking to the parking lot.

"Sonya how do you know we can trust her?"

"Remember that coffee she's drinking? Cyanide is in her cup. She'll be dead soon."

"You know nobody can know about Ravenion but you. Not even the gang. I don't trust nobody. I want to move in a house, I'm tired of staying in apartments and hotels."

Sonya smiled as they pulled out the parking lot. She knew she was the only woman in his life now. That was her dream and she's seeing it with her eyes open. They rode the downtown area passing store such as: Walton, What's Happening, Lanes Clothing for Men, Sport Shoe and so on and so on.

As she drove she thought to herself how it would be to get him out the city. Into a rich environment around rich people. So they could experience the upper living where they both belong. With hopes of him getting a real look at life and want to settle down and have a family. She knew she could make all this happen and protect him at the same time, even if it meant losing everything she owned.

The drive seemed forever as they rode in silent. No music, just a classic drive they were both trying to get their thoughts together.

"You know I wish I can make enough money, so I'll be able to raise a family and leave this street shit alone. That's all I ever wanted to see families together really depress me. Sonya ain't no real future in these streets you and I both know that."

A smile came across her face; it was like he was reading her mind.

"I'm just tired of living this life alone; I'm scared if I get close to you, you'll die like Tony and Tasha. I never even told Tasha that. I look at you as my friend someone I'ma try very hard to protect."

Tears filled her eyes; she was moved by his words. Her whole body went into heat then shivered. Not knowing what to say, she said the most common words to suit the situation.

"I love you."

She turned on Powell Rd. and stopped in front of a big white house with a beautiful rose garden growing on the right side of the house. There were all colored roses: red, pink, yellow and white. One would kill if one of those beauties was not taken care of. On the left side of the house was honey sets and shrubs. With all this, this was the most beautiful home he'd ever seen.

"Sonya I'm in love with this house. The yard displays the whole house. The nice cut green grass reflects the white wooden home, with the blue brick porch. I got to have this house. Find out what's the price and I'll buy it for us."

"I know the person who owns it and it's priceless."

The boyish smile dropped from his face.

"Everything and every person can be bought. Sonya, you just got to throw the right price."

"So you're saying the great Ravenion Nalls can be bought?"

"Yes because his existence was bought. I really want to live here, away from the world one can write books and poems by sitting in the front yard. Sure we got neighbor but look and listen to the quietness. Won't none of them gang member come here."

"Well I talked with the owner of this house and with the price that was set you can't pay. But you can obtain it with your hear, that's all it cost."

The car pulled up into the drive way, they stepped out and walked over to the roses.

"See baby everything can't be bought. This house was left to me by my grandmother. Just like you all I want is someone to love me. Let's forget about the gang and them streets. Let's grow old together you and me right here."

Her true feelings, wants and desires to her motives and means.

The thought of a family brought a smile to his face. One couldn't describe it; it was like seeing Heaven open and the face of his mother, father and grandmother. Before he could respond to her request she tipped on her toes and kissed him very hard. They laid in the grass, with her on top of him hugging and kissing. Then his cell phone rang.

"This is Smokey; I just heard you died in a car wreck. Listen man you need to get to Evanlane and let's put this clique together. We're down here and got everything we need. Now it's time to do this."

"You're right I've been tripping alot lately I'll be there in 2 hours. Just get everything cooked up bagged up and we'll get shit straight. No more talk from here on."

She had gotten up and started walking in the house. She had pulled her phone and dialed a number. By the time he caught up with her, he heard her say, "I'll get you all the names."

She turned as he walked onto the last step of the porch. She keyed the lock waiting to hear him ask what was that about. But he didn't ask as they walked in the most (beautiful) living room one could see. It had painting of a great painter on both sides of the walls, fire place sat on the left side of the living room, stairs which sat on the right side of the door with Asian carpeting coming down the steps. You could smell the cedar wood the house was built upon. The Asian antifurniture set the living room off.

Traveling to the den was even more outrageous. The wooden floor smiled at you, the shine was so beautiful, and it gave the den and living room life. The drape gave character as they sprung light onto the softly laid pillow.

"Girl your grandmother must been Chinese?"

"Yes I'm mixed!"

That respond sent him to one of the huge pillow laughing.

"I'm just playing," she stated and fell into his arms.

"Make love to me. Right here now" and kissed him.

"Baby I got to tend to the gang, the set up."

"Dammit, do I have to beg?"

She raised up to her knees and softly asked, "Please spend some time with me. Massage my inner thighs. Become to know the real woman in me. The woman that truly loves you and will kill for you."

With that she lowered herself and put her mouth to his zipper kissing him around the area. Taking her hands and undoing his black Sean John belt and the black Sean John pants. As she kissed his massager she unbutton the last button and released his massager from the nylon holder and placed it into her mouth. The warmth of her inner mouth soften the massager outer layer and it grew in her upper womanly. With his eyes closed he moaned out her name. Lifting himself to her every downward motion.

Then suddenly her cell phone rang twice then stopped and rung again. She jumped up and disappeared into another room. He snapped out of the moment, jumping to his feet putting himself back into his pants and walked to the edge of the room. Waiting at the entrance of the den, behind the small wall. She walked back into the den to finish what she had started. Only to find a barrel of a Glock 40 in her face. He took her by the back of her long hair and clipped her face forward. He put his knee in her back and grabbed a handful of her hair and put the Glock to her head.

"The first jump you made with that phone I let go. Then you jump up with another call. What's going on Sonya?"

"Nothing that was my sister calling my private line."

"What's so important about that line, that I don't have the number? Give me the phone."

She took her left hand reached down to her skirt pocket and handed him the phone, he snatched her up and they walked through the living room and up the stairs. Once they got to the top of the stairs he seen many rooms and opened the first door to the right. When he opened the door it stunned him. The downstairs was from Asia and had cedar wood. This room was made out of cherry oak wood. He threw her to the floor and made her get naked. He thought about shooting her, but she probably told whoever she was talking to he was with her.

"Sonya I'm gonna ask you again who was you talking to?"

"I told you my sister. My mom is suffering from C-O-P-D. It's a breathing disease that kills over a million American."

There were no fear in her eyes no tremble in her voice.

"Well tell me why the phone rang 2 times and stopped and run again? That's how the Feds contact each other."

Her eyes widen for the first time, he knew he hit a nerve. He looked over and seen the ironing board in the hallway. He went to retrieve the iron. She just laid there with her hands over her eyes. Trying to think letting him know that she had nothing to hide. It was her sister she knew it and would die with the truth.

He plugged the iron up and put it to the max, while the iron was heating up, she just laid there. She looked up and said, "If you burn me Naw! Naw! If burning me proves to you that I love you and I'm telling the truth, and then burn me. That's how much I love you I'm willing to get burned."

Deep down inside she prayed that he believe her, because this ain't worth getting burned for a phone call.

"Sonya I go with gut feelings not my heart, my gut tells me you're Feds."

He put the iron close to her face.

"Now tell me who you were talking to."

He was bending over her so she could move. The heat from the iron was burning her face. Still no tear dropped.

"Just press *69 you'll see for yourself. IF you scar me I'll hate you for the rest of my life. Then I'll be the Feds for real I'll tell them on your ass quick and fast. You won't be able to blank. I'm telling you the truth."

He put the tip of the iron on her face. She screamed in pain then she broke. "Okay! Okay!"

He moved the iron and sat on top of her.

"When we went to Key West Smokey and Leo raped me."

Tears were coming down her eyes and he sat the iron on the floor.

"Everybody is against you but me. Yes I am a federal agent. I've been on Smokey them for 3 years now. But I'm dirty the lick at Key West suppose to been a bust. But I turned it into a murder, look I never loved anybody in my life. But I love you; you killed for my little brother. Plus you sent my mom that money. 46 thousand a year ain't worth this. I was in for the good but when my brother died I lost it. My momma can't except he's dead. I'm losing everybody to this job. If you don't believe me I have you listed as my informant. Baby I killed my best friend for you. Don't that mean anything to you. I'm doing all I can to protect you. I'm not after you, Smokey killed my sister son in a shootout. I'm after him and he's after you. That first phone call was them. The phone is tapped; they want you on Evan Lane. I'm not gonna let nothing happen to you. Everything is on the table now. You can kill me or trust me. This whole house is bugged. I blew my cover for love they know what's going on."

"Why did you bring me to this house?"

"It's my safe house, it's the only place I can protect you. IF anything happen here they'll be at that front door in 5 second. Look out the window you're surrounded now. I love you enough to let you know you're safe."

He looked out the window and seen unmarked cars everywhere.

"Sonya I can't be your snitch, I'm sorry it's not in my blood."

She came off the floor and pulled the black 357 from under the mattress and said, "Well then Mr. Ellis you're under arrest."

Before he could turn around four male agents rushed in and took him down. They cuffed him and escorted him to a white crown Victoria, placed him in the back seat and closed the door. He looked at her being rushed by the arriving paramedics with tears in her eyes. She came by the car window with her back turned and asked her captain what charge to put on him.

"There's no case you blew your cover. All we can do is go after the gang. But we'll hold him 72 hours. Book him and just watch him."

The car pulled off carrying him to the old pretrial; once again God has allowed him to fall when he was doing so well. He just lost Tasha and now his freedom is gone. When they pulled in pretrial he thought about his prints.

"Did she tell them about Ravenion?"

As he went through the booking procedure, they printed him and asked him his name. He told them Ravenion Nalls. They put him in a cell by himself; he asked could he call his lawyer. But they refused. He noticed they had carpet and a TV inside the cell. He just laid down and fell to sleep. He heard somebody talking outside his cell. He seen a small time hustler him and Ike knew name James. He came to the bars and called out his name.

"Say James."

When James looked up a smile came to his face he was on the phone. He dropped the phone and came to the bars.

"Juan, boy I thought you were out the game. I haven't seen you in so long."

"Say call this number for me and repeat everything I tell you."

He got his people to make the call. Tell whoever picks up to relocate. He repeated and said, "Anything else?"

"Tell 'em Sonya is the Feds and she's trying to take them down."

"He said Sonya is here now worried about you."

"Tell 'em I know what happen in Key West and about the rape and them siding against me for the goods. Sonya is the Feds. Tell 'em I'm in the Feds right now."

Second later he stated, "They hung up."

He said thanks and laid back down and said, "I tried to tell 'em."

He thought about calling Nancy but that would mess things up. He knew Tasha was alive. But she's dead, in his heart because of that baby. But the truth will always come out. He's just happy it came out when it did. He fell back to sleep as if he was on sleeping pills. He had hoped for a dream and to wake up to yesterday. But instead he woke up to the big tall black captain that came into the cell and cuffed him. They walked down this hall that led to a door. When the captain opened it, it was the back door to the jail.

"What's going on?" he asked.

"You see we can't hold you and since you won't talk to us or work with us, we decided to let you go and let the gang have you for breakfast, lunch and dinner. It's already being stated that you're telling so when they see you on the news being took down and out before a court appearance you'll be a dead man. So help me and I'll help you."

"I guess they'll try to catch me medium rare because real nigga don't die."

With that statement he let him free. He went to a pay phone to call

Smokey.

"Smokey did you get my message?"

"All I got were you're trying to bring us down. What's up Juan? Where are you?"

"I'm at the Garnet train station."

"I thought you was locked up!"

"Listen man Sonya is trying to take y'all down. Stay away from her."

"Naw you stay out of sight because you're a marked man."

He looked at his watch; it was 9:45 pm. He took a cab back to the house. Tony house was his new home, when he stepped in the house he sat in the chair Tony died in and said, "Speak to me Tony."

CHAPTER 15
Get Back

"**T**asha I told you he wasn't dead. That's him right there they just busted him."

She jumped out of the bed and ran to the living room. She saw him with her own eyes.

"Big time drug dealer/gang leader has been taken into federal custody."

Yep that's him.

"I got to get him out again."

By the time she could finish her statement the phone rang.

"Hello, baby before you get your hopes up high your daddy is already checking things out. He's down there right now trying to get him out. So meet us at the pretrial."

She slammed the phone down.

"Come on Blue we're going to get my baby he's at the old pretrial on Jefferson St."

She grabbed the baby and ran to a blue white Lexus. They speeded off, once reaching pretrial she seen her folks through the glass door. They walked in and she hugged her mom. Richard stood there looking at her. She didn't even acknowledge him. He walked in front of her.

"Tasha baby I made a mistake, but I'm gonna correct it now."

They heard a voice come over an intercom.

"Captain Mathis please come to booking."

It was an hour before anyone came to talk to them. When they complained for the last time the big tall bald head man came out.

"Ma'am, sir it been a mistake, we thought we had Juan Ellis in custody but it wasn't him. It was someone using his name."

"But we seen him on the news today," Richard replied.

Sorry people it wasn't him, the prints came back and it wasn't him.

"Was his name Ravenion Nalls?" Tasha asked.

"As a matter of fact that's who we had. How did you know that?"

"Because that's his real name."

They got up and left. When they reached the parking lot Richard asked her what that was about.

"Juan isn't dead he's in trouble, you remember when he went to Africa he went to Africa to change his prints and name. Nobody knows that but me. He killed Juan, but not himself. Put two and two together. He says if I die he'll die. He thinks I'm dead. He sees a wreck on the express way same car. Okay the hospital has nobody. No name no nothing. The information lady we talked to this morning pops up dead. Now look at all that protection he had at that hospital when he thought I was missing. Tony get killed. Ike told me he's in over his head. So what do that tells you? He's in trouble. I know I seen him with my own eyes."

"Well Tasha let me see what I can do. Don't get in over your head because whoever is out to get him might get you. Tasha I love you you're my only child. I'll do anything to make you happy."

"I love you too daddy. I know where he's at; either at his grand mom house or his uncle house my bet is he's at Tony house. I know how he thinks nobody knew he's Tony nephew. That's the uncle that left the baby all that money. But where do Tony stay."

"Tasha don't he have a phone?" Blue asked.

"Yeah."

She got her daddy cellphone and called Tony house the phone just rang. Just as she was gonna hang up he picked up and said, "Who is this?"

"Hi baby I can't call your name because I'm in front of pretrial. I knew you wasn't dead. Mr. Mathis assured that when he called your other name. I love you with all my heart. I'll never sleep around on you. This is your son my dad had the results drawn up. I'm willing to help you with whatever. Just tell me what's going on."

"Baby right now I'm in hiding no one knows I'm here. So it's best you don't contact me. I'll contact you. Where is my son?"

"He's right here."

"The Feds and the gang are after me. The Feds are on my grandmoms property now. I have to go and hide. Listen stay close to your folks."

"You know Tony left 30 million in Juan's account."

"Yes I know I'm also receiving money from him. I just got to get back to Africa to make things right. Everything has blown up in my face. Tasha things is fix 'en to get ugly so stay close to home. I love you."

"Let's go he's cool! Moma I got to move back home and go to school from home."

They got in the Lexus and her parents and the baby got in the Lincoln.

"Blue we're going to Dotson Rd. off Hwy. 91; I know where he's at. It's a big white house in the woods beside his grandmother house. The driveway sits in the curve."

As they pulled toward the express way the Lincoln went 20 East and they went 20 West to the west end exit took a left on Lee Street and rode it out to they came to Hwy 91 four way and took a right on 91 and another quick right in front of the old red farm house that sat on the corner. Blue were amazed at all the pretty houses and yards on both sides of the road.

"When you get in the curve stop, it's an opening in the woods. I'll have to move the chain and you hurry in, if the road was clean, if not we'll just keep going down the road and turn around."

As they drove into the curve there wasn't a car in sight so she jumped out and moved the chain and Blue drove in. She fixed the chain back and jumped in. As they rode up the driveway everything was so calm when they came to a stop they seen all kinda cars: BMWs, Benzes, Jags, Caddy's, Lexus, motorcycle, vans and trucks. They got out and ran to the back of the house. He told her about a crawl through window, he used to crawl through as a child. She crawled through, and then Blue; she turned and told her to feel for a hatch on the floor because he's in the basement.

Blue asked her how did she know all this?

Tasha turned and told her, "He use to tell me things, just crawl and search for a hatch. I don't know rather it's in the center or by the wall. You take the left and I'll take the right."

"Tasha I have a little lighter I can strike it and we can find it."

"No need to y'all talk so loud. Remember the door to the wine cellar is 19 steps away from the window in the center of the floor, you'll never find the hatch if I'm down there, it's covered by wood also."

As they got to their feet Tasha, grabbed the back of his shirt and Blue grabbed hers. He led them down the steps once they were at the bottom he went back upstairs and hatched the door.

"Juan is it any lights down here?" Blue asked.

"Yes the switch is on the rail of the step right here under the left rail. No one would think to look here. Tony had a good hideout, it's cool down here. You can see the lights upstairs, plus he got little hot plates to cook your food with."

He took them on a tour of the cellar, Tasha was amazed at how it looked like a small apartment. With small swimming pool chairs with soft pillows on them, little pool table sets to match the chairs. A 50 inch screen TV. A shelf that had can goods on them another shelf with cookie cakes and chips. A small refrigerator and a twin bed set that sat at the end of both walls.

"Wow! Tasha, I think I can live down here forever." Blue stated.

"Juan why did you fake your death?"

"With your pop saying you're dead the baby ain't mine. There was no reason for Juan to keep on living. Plus I still want to take over Atlanta. So if I came up with an identity that no one knew about, I could do something positive with my life in the end."

"You still can Tony left us 30 million I signed the papers today."

"Listen until I get this Fed and gang shit straight, you got to live your life without me. Pray to your God that I make it no more visit or calls. I'll call and visit you. Take the 300 grand and hold it 'til I come for it. Tell my son I love him. Tell your dad I'm fix 'en to bring down the IBH and Sonya. That's the only way I can live a happy life. Sonya is the Feds."

"Make love to me."

She kissed him and he looked at Blue.

"Don't mind me I'm fix 'en to watch TV."

She sat in the chair next to the bed and cut the TV on. As they made love she looked at them a time or two.

"You promise me you'll come back to me safe."

"I promise you I won't die."

Blue got in the other bed and went to sleep. While they slept they heard a noise upstairs. He jumped up and grabbed the Mac-11 from under the pillow and told them to be quiet. Tasha whispered to him, to put on his pants and shirt; as she was getting into hers. He slid into his clothes, walked toward the steps, and pointed the weapon. He heard Sonya calling him,

"Juan I know you're here. I'm alone we just need to talk."

He caught Tasha hand waving at him. When he looked at her she pointed on top of her. Telling him she wasn't alone, he quickly returned to the bed and grabbed the black computer from under it. He opened it and typed in the view of the yard and seen the house was surrounded. She had come to take him down for burning her with that iron.

"Listen it's a storm shelter that connects to this house that will lead us to my grand mom yard. Me and my cousin came down here through the barn. No one knows about this escape route but y'all. So keep it to y'all self. Let's go."

He grabbed the computer his coat and a book bag that had guns and money in it. The opening of the tunnel starts behind the steps. You couldn't tell it because it was a brick wall.

The door hasn't been opened in so long; it took all three of them to push it open. They enter and closed it back, walked about a mile 'til they seen the steps. He walked up first, turned the lock cracked it and looked around. He didn't see any shadows and opened it all the way. The girls came out and locked the door.

"Listen we're going straight to the woods, it's a dirt road there. Tony left a Suburban hid in a barn at the end of the road it's gonna be a walk, about a 30 minute walk so let's go."

They ran into the woods and walked with haste. No one said a word.

"Tasha them folk's is gonna be watching you. Blue your car, forget about it. Tasha get her another one. Y'all remember I love y'all. Listen Tasha I'ma need that cash, because this ain't gonna last long I had just went in my room and got the 60 grand Tony had put on my night stand. I'll be seeing you when I can."

They made it to the barn and the truck was all gassed up. The black truck had a little dust on the windows but that didn't matter. It was ready to be drove that's all that mattered. They drove off Tasha cut the computer on to see what was going on in the house and the yard. They were searching the house high and low but never went in the cellar. They bugged all the cars that were in the yard. Then she saw Sonya opened the cellar door with a crowbar and close it back. She called off the search by waving her hand.

"Why didn't she go down there," she thought to herself.

Not wanting to make a fuss with him right now she held her tongue. But she knew why she closed the entrance because he was sleeping with her.

"Juan the girl who's leading the investigation is the one who came to the hospital and shot at me. That's the nurse."

"I figured she was the one I just couldn't get my head together to see shit clearly. Listen I know you got question and you want answers but now is not the time to nut up. We got to keep a positive mind. That's the only way I can stay alive."

"Is she part of this gang you're running from?"

"Tasha not now!"

"Because I already know you've been fucking her. She's the agent that suppose to be bringing y'all down. But she fell in love with you, she knew with me out the way she'll have you to herself."

"Let's say you're right!"

"Then I can slow her down and get her off the case against you. That way she'll go after you and they'll nail her. You forgot I got power too!"

"Well you get your people to see what they can do and see what y'all can pull off. Don't contact the Feds, contact Internal Affairs and see what's up."

He dropped them off at the College Park train station and went to the United Postal Service on Grant St. To the same office he went to before. When he went in it wasn't like before.

"Juan I'm surprise to see you here again."

"Listen my uncle Tony is dead I heard the people who's responsible is in Cuba. I need a passport so I can get in Cuba."

"You already have a passport under Nalls and Ellis. What you need is a sure way in Cuba. What's wrong?"

"Man alot of shit went wrong but I'm fix 'en to fix the shit now because if I don't I'ma either be locked up or dead. Either way I'm looking at death."

"Listen I play favor for favor, that's how me and Tony ran business. I'm gonna hook everything up like last time and have you in good protection. But you got to bring back a kilo of heroin on your return. That's 56 bullets if you swallow, and I'll have someone to pick you up from the airport."

"Deal but I need you to get me to the Fambros family."

"That's the family you'll be going to see. Well not really the Fambros but the Martinzs. The two families are large suppliers over here. But Nikko Escarbar is the man. It's like they're shipping together through him. So I'll have them meet you at the airport."

"I don't need to stay there long I need to leave as soon as possible. I got the Feds behind me."

"You'll be able to leave at 5:45 am be at the airport at 5 sharp your supplies will be waiting along with 20 grand and four hundred thousand when you return with all 56 bullets. Oh by the way take alot of acid pills the day you get ready to leave."

He walked out and seen one of the gang girls name Cindy leaving her post. Him and her had a thang for each other so he knew he could win her over, all she ever wanted was a life. He remember when she came to him in Detroit asking for a way out once they hit Atlanta, she was so innocent with big green eyes, a red bone slim just right for any man. She had realized that she had made a mistake and she wanted to go home. He promised her he would help her because if you realize that the streets were a mistake then you should leave. Seeing her walk made him remember his promise. At least she's working and trying to do right. So an escape route would do her good. He watched her get into a black Kia and followed her.

He noticed the route she was taking and it wasn't to her family. It was a route of her own or did they relocate?

"Naw not that quick!"

He followed her to a white house off Riverdale Rd. He watched her get out the car and looked up at the sky as she was enjoying life or praying. It looked like a friendly quiet neighborhood. Eight houses on the block four houses on both sides. Her house was the third one on the left side; it looked like a sweet dream home. Trees big yards woods behind every house. The common peaceful neighborhood. She unlocked the door and went inside.

He saw her open the curtain in the living room and kitchen. No one seemed to be there but her. So he walked to the door and knocked. With a black 9MM in his right hand hid between his leg and the door.

"Who is it?"

"It's Mr. Parker from the Post Office."

"Okay hold for a second."

She opened the door and seen him her eyes widen by the sight of the gun, she tried to close the door but he forced his way into the house.

"Juan I don't know what's going on but please don't shoot me."

"Can I come on in and close the door?"

"Oh yes!"

She stepped aside and he seen a beautiful living room set. The setting in this living room wasn't the setting of a 23 year old. He seen this style somewhere before. It's the setting of money. Either she's tricking a rich guy or she's turned herself.

His thoughts ran wild as she returned to the living room with a large red t-shirt on, something wasn't right. She stood by the Lazy Boy chair he was sitting in.

"What's up Juan?"

Her voice was clearer now.

"I've figured it out, you've turned on your family, you're fix 'en to bring them down."

He thought to himself, "She can nail me for Phillip murder, so I got to play my cards right."

"Listen Cindy I didn't come here to harm you, because I'm not in the gang anyway. I've never been in the gang. It's Sonya who's behind everything and she's fix 'en to bring y'all down. Now I know this may sound strange but I care alot about you. Just haven't had the time to spend with you. Trying to get my own life in order, so let's take the tape recorder off. I'm with you. I know you got to report back to them or blow your cover."

"What are you talking about? I don't have no recorder!"

He jumped up grabbed her by the arm, clipped her, put his knee in her chest, lifted her shirt and got the recorder. He turned it off and helped her back up.

"Listen Cindy I'm no fool. I know you want a new life a safer one. But listen you're going by this the wrong way. They haven't even coached you on how to act normal. You never return with a longer shirt. On top of that, your gang don't wear red. I know you're going to meet your superiors here today. When are they coming? Those people don't care about you. Just think if it wasn't me. You'll be dead sweetheart and you know I'm telling you the truth."

He sat back down rewinding the tape to record over it. She thought about what just happen and what he said. She sat at his feet and placed her head on his legs.

"In about an hour."

"Are you fucking him or her?"

She answered slowly and said, "No I'm not fucking her. I was told that I have an agent watching me. But she don't act like she's watching me. I know who it is though. It's Sonya, because I followed her one day and seen the two of them meet."

"Have she ever bugged you before?"

"Yes, she bugged me through a pair of glasses. She says that she can see everything through my eyes."

"Do they know where the money and dope is?"

"Nobody knows where nothing is but Smokey, Leo and me."

"Where is it?"

"It's here! Smokey took your advice and came to me. He thinks this is my grandmother house. No other member knows about this house but us four. But you're the only one knows about the Feds."

"Cindy I need to know what happen when y'all went to Key West."

"Okay, that night we were in the big apartment. Me, Smokey, Leo and Sonya. She was giving us the plans. Her and Leo were making bombs out of C-4. After she gave the plan and the bombs were made I left. When I came back I heard screaming. So when I looked in the door Smokey and Leo was beating her in the body. She asked what about you I heard their plan to take you out. They told her she's now one of us. She took her beat down and they raped her. I walked in the room after they raped her. She was balled up on the bed naked. She said, 'If I'm one of y'all, why y'all raped me?' I helped her to the bathroom and bath her. I got her clothes and helped her back in her skirt got one of Smokey shirt and gave it to her. She left, so I thought the mission was over, but she came back the next morning. I heard her on the phone saying they raped me I want out. Second later she had a clear head, I told her I know how much you mean to her to continue out with this after the rape. She said she had just finished talking to you. She told me about her brother and how she promised to protect you, if this is what it took to prove her love then she just proved it. She was so happy about putting you on top.

We loaded up U-Hauls about 50 deeps 4 trucks. Once we got there he sent 2 swim teams to plant the bombs on the boat. Me, Smokey, Leo and Sonya went in the boat. The guy was so happy to see Sonya that he introduced her to his mom. We danced for him, and then we went to killing everybody that had life in them. We loaded the U-Hauls, blew the boat up and left. Soon as we got back Sonya distanced herself, she didn't come around until you were due back. Ever since then she's been on this strange rage of power. Smokey knew something wasn't right, but said it don't matter because in the end he'll have everything. That's when Quin came and talked to me right after Sonya got raped. That's why I always wore those glasses. She told me that this was almost over. Just another month or two.

"Here comes Quin with Sonya, hide in the kitchen closet so you can hear everything."

He hid in the closet and watched them enter the house they hugged each other.

"Sonya where did you get that Victoria Secret Dress from?," Cindy asked.

It was black with the shoulder lace and a split came to her thigh Sonya had a small band-aid over her right cheek. Quin is peacantan 5'11" 145 pounds with green contact. She wore blue jeans and a black jacket they walked to the kitchen sat at the table and begin to talk.

"I have y'all to know I seen Juan today he came in the post office and mailed a letter off."

Sonya looked at her with a smile and asked, "Was he okay?"

"Yeah Sonya he asked about everyone and told me you were Feds and had him locked up for burning you with an iron."

Cindy had seen her yesterday when he first got locked up.

"Yes we got into a fight. I told him I was Federal and trying to protect him."

"Sonya that bastard burned you with an iron."

"Quin it's not what you think. We're a couple and couples fight. I threw a knife at him and he pent me down and put the iron close to my face. I kneed him in the nuts. He went forward and the iron hit me in the face. I did a report on it and they let him go, and now he feels I'm out to get him. But I just want him safe, I love him. I told him we can protect him he just won't help out. Listen Cindy, he ain't no gang member your case ain't on him. You got that?"

"I'll personally make sure he's protected. After all I never saw him give any orders or nothing. Personally I like him; I thought he was just a smart ass foot soldier."

"This is bullshit! Y'all know this nigga is head of this shit. As y'all commanding officer y'all need to stay away from him. Sonya you've blown your cover and case on him. You probably lose your life, he don't care about neither one of y'all. Especially you Sonya, when he finds out that you tried to kill Tasha in that hospital."

"For you to be a commanding officer, you put your neck on the line for her. I mean you know about all her dirt and you still give her assignment. Y'all must be in a girl-girl relationship."

Sonya looked at Quin and smiled.

"Is it that appealing? If I'm madly in love with him, what make you think I'm bumping pussy with her?"

"Don't go there Sonya, Sonya is my kid sister, we might as well feel her in on everything. Cindy I'm not a commanding officer, but Sonya is an agent and she got you protected. When y'all were in Detroit years ago, Smokey shot my son in a shootout. All y'all took 3 to 5 million when y'all came down here. I don't think Juan know how much money were in them duffle bags. Smoke and Leo raped my sister and probably had something to do with my brother death. Now you can see why I want them dead. But Sonya got to make a case on him, so she does got you listed as a witness. I'm just not your commanding officer she is. She just get over emotional when it comes to Juan. Now Smokey I know got his hand on the money because Juan haven't been around y'all. We don't know where none of it's at. That's where you come in at, you help us and we'll split everything. That way when you start your new life you won't start it broke."

"I can feel that and I'm down with it. But Smokey ain't gonna let me know where that money is at right off hand, I got to make a plan. But I do know somebody who knows where it's at."

They both said, "Who?"

"Juan hand is over all money made and all dope issued. He got alot of money in different accounts."

"But how are we gonna get him to tell us where the money is?," Quin asked.

"If Sonya wouldn't blew her cover and got the boy locked up she could've gotten the money; because it's clear that he cares about her. So Sonya you played your cards wrong."

"It's a fact that I can't do it. He will never trust me again. He don't know Quin, so that leaves you Cindy."

"Yeah that do, I'll do whatever it take even if it means sleeping with him."

They all laughed and left the room. They told her to do her best because the gang is after him and left. She went to the closet and opened the door.

"You know they're gonna keep pressuring me about this money."

"Then I'll let you talk to a real commanding officer and tell you where the rest of the money is."

"Naw then they'll come after you. See the trick is to let me trick them and we'll split everything. Man I'm just trying to look out for myself. I don't want to struggle when I start over."

"Listen I got people working, the Feds won't even have a case in a few more days. I'm going out of town. Stop coming to this house. When this is all over you'll have a Swiss account I'm doing this because I like you."

"Well then make love to me."

She eased out of her shirt he seen the tape recorder off. She pulled it out of her pants.

"I got myself protected I recorder our whole conversation."

She walked over to kiss him.

"Cindy this is the time I need you to think safe and stay safe. Think with your head not with your legs. Just be ready when I call you."

He left driving back to Decatur he thought about Tasha, his son and his life. He wanted a life of love so bad. Now he just wanted them safe. He stopped at a BP gas station and called her to tell her just have the money on standby; because he had put the money from Detroit in Tony's room with Tony's money. Also he still had 50 bricks from Detroit in Tony room. So he was straight. Just couldn't get to it because he knew Sonya had someone watching the house if she bugged the cars.

She told him to come to her dad house because he needed to talk to him. He thought that was cool her old man wanted to talk probably help him. He hung up the phone and it hit him why John wanted him to swallow 56 bullets. He knew something was odd in the midst of this. So he had to play his way in it or keep it all. He drove to Marbut Ave. sat in the truck for a minute and got out.

Tasha was at the door when he walked up. They kissed walked through the living room to the dining room. Juan was sitting in his high chair making noise with his fist balled. Mr. Middle sat at the end of the table his wife sat to the left of Blue to the right of Tasha. Tasha on the other end and Blue on the left side. He sat at the end of the table facing the door. Put his hand together and said, "What's up Mr. Middle?"

"Tasha said you're in alot of trouble with the Feds and that IBH gang. Tell me what's going on so I can help you."

He explained to him about Sonya being a money hunger agent and how he brought the gang to Atlanta, Sonya turned against him. The Feds wanted him for drug trafficking, murder, robbery and a whole list of charges. He also explained that he was afraid that she was gonna tell the Escarbar family that he ordered the hit. He had to straighten things up because he didn't need Cuban on his back because they'll harm Tasha and Juan. He turned to Richard and said, "I can see why you tried so hard to keep Tasha away from me. Ain't no future in this life for me. The only way out is to turn myself in and spend the rest of my life in prison. Or fight them. Either way I'm gonna lose my family."

He turned to Tasha and said, "Tasha as much as it hurts me to say this but I think it's best you go on with your life. Move on y'all are well taken care of. I know it's enough money for us to run away sooner or later they're gonna find us by tracking the money. I love you too much to let you die for my silliness. Juan is dead now the only way back is to go to them folks and I'm not gonna do that. Unless your dad can work something out. Now I'll do that for the love of you and Juan."

The telephone rang; no one seemed to care to answer it. They were all amazed by his words, which were telling her to move on. Nancy finally picked up the phone after six rings. It was a man voice on the other end of the phone asking to speak with Erica. She turned and looked puzzled and handed the phone to Blue. Everybody looked at her as she said hello.

"Yes! Yes! Yes! Yes! No he don't know and I don't want to be the one to tell him. He's going through alot right now and telling him now will only burden him more. I feel it's best he don't know."

She paused then said, "If you want him to know then you tell him."

Everybody stared while confused, who was she talking to and about? She was looking Juan eye to eye. Then tears started to roll.

He knew then that she was the Feds and was fix 'en to turn him in. His life was over she knew everything. He got up went to the truck, and got the tote bag, came back and sat the bag on the table and then stood by the chair. He told Tasha to go get the money. She sprinted up to her room got the money off the bed and quickly got back downstairs.

Blue still held the phone looking at her when she handed him the red pocketbook the money was in. He dumped the money in the tote bag and told the Middles he was sorry for what they were about to see. He pulled the 9MM out and pointed it to Blue head. Everybody screamed, "Juan! No!"

The baby started crying. Blue looked him in the eyes and handed him the phone.

He gave the phone to Tasha and she said, hello who is this. Her eyes widen as the voice went on, she handed the phone back to him and looked at Blue in amazement.

"Juan I think you need to hear what he got to say."

He got the phone and said, "Hello."

"Juan take the gun from your sister head."

The voice sounded familiar but it couldn't be Kerry it couldn't be his pop.

"Juan I know you're confused and you're in alot of trouble. But listen, your mom died in that accident with another man. No one never told you that I'm a government agent. I always told Erica she had a younger brother. She's named after her mom because I was always on the go. Your mom and I had separate lives. She was an agent and so was I. On many trips, Salley and I became intimate before you were born and we had her. When your mom died I was on a mission, when they found her, I was instructed to leave everything and be dead to keep cover. It's been hard knowing you've been living alone. I tried to offer help but my mom turned it down. Then she died and you went on your own. When I found you again you was a rap sheet the few times you got in trouble. Then Erica was like I met my baby brother and she was so happy, but I told her not to tell you because you wouldn't have believed her. Plus I didn't want Tony to find out about her or me. She called and told me that you're in big trouble and your plans to take down the Feds and that gang. I'm gonna pull some strings and clear up you faking your death. Whatever you got planned out you need to continue with it under my supervision. Keep me in touch with your every move. I've never stopped loving you. Love you son."

Then the phone hung up and like that he was gone again.

He looked at Blue pointed the gun at her and started fussing at her.

"I didn't need this Blue. You knew who I was all along. You played me Blue."

She stood and yelled back, "But I done everything you told me to do. Why do you think I was so eager to help you? I'm not afraid of you Juan, go ahead and shoot me Juan. Shoot me for loving my baby brother."

Nancy and Richard looked as she started to walk around the table.

"Go ahead Juan shoot me."

The tears were rolling hard; she threw her hands up when she got on him the gun still pointed at her.

"This isn't real Blue."

"Then shoot me Juan, you always wanted a family. All you got is me pop and the Middles. I love you Juan."

She threw her arms around his neck and cried.

"I always wanted to be around you. You're my little brother. That's why I came here to go to school. I was born in Florida I could've went to any college down there. But I choose here to find you. Ain't nothing changed. I'm still gonna believe in everything you do."

The Middles stood up and rushed them.

"Put the gun down son," Nancy commanded.

"Accept change, life is always changing you out of all people should know that."

He dropped the gun down by his right side and hugged her with his left arm and kissed her cheek told her to take care of herself because they'll never be sister and brother. Juan is dead.

With no good byes he just up and left. He got in the truck and thought about it for a minute. He didn't even hug his son. He looked and seen them standing in the doorway, pulled off and went to the airport. He stopped at Buddy gas station on Moreland and called Cindy. He told her to take the money and go home, back to Alabama start over and live, he told her how proud of her he was. Even though she ran away from home, she never told that gang where she was from or her real name. She told him her moma's address and she'll 4 ever love him and to be careful.

Before she hung up, she asked him how he knows so much about her. He just laughed and told her money let you know about everything and he'll stay in contact with her. He walked in Buddy bought him some Ranch Lay chips a coke and headed nonstop to the airport.

As he rode, he thought more about the 56 bullet balloon. This had to be something ole boy had on the low or was this a set up for what happen in Detroit. His thoughts went from situation to situation. Then he thought about his sister, his pop, his girl and his son. How could he get under this bullshit and live his life. He took in a deep breath and asked the Lord did he have any answer to this situation.

Something in his mind told him to think about his wrong doing and then think about his family. He thought about Tasha and how brave she was. He smiled because Blue been by his side since day one. He should've known something wasn't right about her loyalty. He parked in the airport parking lot went to gate 16 and was prepared to enter the gate when a guy in a black suit called his name. He acted as he didn't hear him. Then he heard it again:

"Ravenion."

He turned and faced him and the guy said, "Not this plane, come on you're going on a jet."

He followed, just as they turned he seen two federal officers go to that same gate.

"What's up my man," he asked.

The golden skin guy just smiled and said, "Don't worry you'll get to Cuba safe. Big people are expecting you."

They entered the jet and were greeted by some of the most beautiful girls he had seen, someone musta really liked him or wanted to make sure he was comforted. Once he was seated, one of the pretty golden skin Cubans wearing a blue dress went to her knees and enjoyed herself with his penis. The jet took off and he enjoyed himself with all of the beautiful ladies kissing him and sucking him. Finally he fell to sleep and was there in no time.

Once the plane landed he notice some men wearing black suit and three black Benzes waiting. They exited the plane and got in separate cars. The ladies got in the first car, him and the man from the airport got in the middle car. No one got in the last car but the driver. He didn't ask no question, he just rode in silence.

They arrived at this golden gate, once it opened he saw a palace for the first time in his life. Guards at the gate on both sides with 2 AK's gardens of all kinda plants leading to the door cars everywhere.

"Whoever crib this is had loot," he thought to himself.

When the car stopped another beautiful female opened the door, greeted him and escorted him into the house. Once inside the house he was taken by all the gold, every statue was made out of gold. The floor was made out of gold. Famous pictures on the walls of people who he didn't know; all he knew was this was money and the way to live. Also there were maids and servants walking around.

When he walked in the dining room, he saw a table that seemed to be 10 feet long; with alot of males and females sitting watching him. He felt odd because all of them had on suits and dresses. He was dressed in street gear. Finally a guy got up in his early thirties with a gray Dolce & Gabbana suit.

"Hello Juan my name is Nikko Escarbar, and this is the head of the Fambros family."

He pointed to the gentleman sitting to the left of him. An older guy got up with a gray silk pinstripe dress suit on.

"And to the right of me is the Martinz head man."

He stood wearing a brown pinstripe.

"We understand that you have some information containing the hit on the Fambros family and Alex."

Still standing he said, "That's correct."

"Then be seated and eat and we'll discuss this later tomorrow. It's late already. We just wanted to greet you and feed you. It will be very disrespectful to treat you any other way."

He pointed to the third chair to the right of him. All kinda food was on the table. Someone blessed the meal and they waited to a servant came and placed food on their plate. He was so hungry he took a bit out of one of the bread stick. That sat on the side of his plate in the small gold bread holder. The only meal he ate was the steak and potatoes and the salad.

After dinner everyone conversed about their area, how much money they're bring in, their plans for the future and how wonderful it was to touch base again. He noticed alot of the older women were looking at him. Not wanting any of their men to think awkward, he raised his hand and asked Nikko could he be excused.

He pushed his chair back as Nikko waved to a beautiful lady wearing an all gold dress, beautiful wavy hair, pretty brown eyes, small face and a knockout figure in her dress. She quickly assisted him to his room. When they exit the room they took a left down the hallway with the many statues and pictures. Finally a door was at the end of the hallway, she opened it and they were outside. He just looked and didn't say anything. Then she spoke, "That's where you'll return to for every meal. This is where the guest stays."

Beyond the dining room sat many guest houses, they were lined in rows with a wall beyond the perimeter. No cars, many females stood in the doorways of the houses.

"How many houses are back here?"

"It's 40 then the big house that Nikko stays in."

Then he saw alot of armed guards as he got closer to the houses. It was like they were walking a prison gate to make sure no one ran or enter.

"Do they walk around every house?"

"Yes they scale the land to make sure we're safe. If anyone of us screams, a guard will be at the door in a second. Nikko keep us safe and at peace. This is our world beyond the real world. Everything we could every want is here. Just over the wall we have our own little stores where we get our clothes from, we don't need money here, but we have it to send to our family. We shop with our deeds and our deeds are our work."

"What's work?"

"Cooking, cleaning, gardening, babysitting. There's alot of ways to earn good deeds here, I can no longer talk beyond this point."

They had reached her home which was the third house in the front row. One of the guards searched him and they entered her home. She had purple and gold curtain, white leather sofa and chairs, white carpet, a big screen TV in the middle of the room and chairs. He couldn't even pronounce the name of the entertainment system. She too had pictures on her walls of popstar and movies stars. The house was a two bedroom one bathroom and a kitchen that sat off the living room. The house was very small, but it was nicely furnished and very clean. The bathroom sat on the left side of the hallway, both rooms sat across from each other.

He walked down the hall and looked in both rooms. They were like every house hold room in the States. Dresser, queen size bed, mirrors with bulbs, plus she shared the house with someone else.

He asked was it any kinda way he could take a warm bath. Then he remembered he didn't even bring any clothes to change out in. His plan was to buy clothes on his way to his hotel. He looked startled because he had left his bags on the jet.

She smiled and said, "Don't worry he already have your clothes didn't the guy on the jet tell you, you've been expected? Your money is in my closet."

He smiled and went in the room on the right, laid on the sheet only to find that they were silk sheets. He thought about his life everything that took place that day. Then she entered and said, "Your water is ready."

She led him to the tub undressed him starting with his white t-shirt then the black sweatpants. As he stepped out his white Nikes and footies and he stepped in the tub, the water was warm just right. He relaxed himself closed his eyes again still thinking on his day. Then he felt a body standing over him. It was her naked getting in the tub. He looked at her Coke Cola bottle frame, perky tits and aroused immediately.

She dropped between his legs and started making love to the tip of his cox with her mouth. She spread her legs and sat on his cox. She moaned as she was seated as comfortably as possible for herself, with a deep arch in her back. She began to massage his temple, and then she spoke.

"You're very tensed right now. Relax yourself and let Gloria please you."

"So Gloria is your name?"

"Yes."

"How old is Gloria?"

"I just turned 18."

"You're very calm and good at what you're doing."

"Yes we go in training at the age 16; we get the job at the age 18. All of our virginity is given to Nikko. If we can please him then our training was a success."

She moved her body with the flow of her hands. Her hands were soft and her inside was tight like a washboard. He thought very hard on her, all his worries were in the hands and cunt of an 18 year old.

As the water cooled she stood, neither one of them released a load. It was just the stillness of knowing each other. Something she was told not to do. Something that would get her killed if she ran her mouth. It was something about him, his style or could it be that he was her first one and the one she's really proving herself to. His body spoke a language she longed for during her two years of training. Her mother always told her, her first one would be rememberable, one she wouldn't want to let go.

Like her, her mom was a servant also. Her mom met her dad the same way. She washed him and to her surprise he washed her. They got out and he watched her as she cleaned the tub. They dried each other, walked to the room and closed the door. This time he made love to her, in a way he never made love before.

As they laid there and talked the door came open and four girls walked into the room undressed and got in the bed. She closed her eyes to hide the hurt, because if they saw it, they reported it, she would be dead in the morning. She opened her eyes to make sure his eyes weren't on her. Just as she hoped they were closed. She kissed his lips and went into the other room.

The new girl was kissing him everywhere while one had him in her mouth. He heard a click of a gun. When he opened his eyes he saw Nikko, Mr. Frambo and Mr. Martinz standing there pointing the gun at him. The girls cleared the room; he just looked at them as the light of the moon shined on their face. Martinz and Frambo stood on the left of him Nikko stood in front of him on the right side.

"Get up Juan," Nikko ordered.

He stood naked.

"Were you enjoying yourself?"

"Not really I've had better."

"Good let's take a walk,"

As he stood he reached for his clothes.

"No clothes, Nikko!" Frambro expressed.

"Well then Juan no clothes let's walk."

They walked out the front door, back through the dining room, back through the yard and out the gate. This time he noticed a field as they walked straight into the field across from the palace, it wasn't trees he saw, it was a cornfield. As they walked no one said a word, it seems as they had been walking for what seemed like an hour, before they came to an opening which had many graves dug. All three of them had their gun pointed at him now. He thought to himself, "I guess this is the way it ends."

He dropped to his knees put his hand behind his head and said, "If y'all gonna shoot, then shoot because this ain't scaring me. We're born to die. But know this you'll never meet a nigga like me. I'm about living and getting to the money, I try not to make the same mistake twice. Since I didn't see it coming head on then I deserve to die."

Edrundo Frambo got in front of him; put the gun to his head.

"Why did you order the hit on my family?"

"If you were sure that I ordered the hit on your family, I would have never made it to Cuba. So don't ask me why I ordered the hit because I didn't order nothing. I was in Africa getting my prints changed over."

"Yes Edrundo I can speak on that," Nikko stated.

"Well then tell me what you know!"

"All I know is I met this cat in the joint name Ryan, he put me on with his sister Sonya."

"Yes! I know Sonya, she's dead too."

"Well, well I guess you don't know shit, Sonya is the one that ordered the hit, see my uncle Tony was killed in a hit. I went to Detroit I killed the cat that called the hit."

Nikko said, "Phillip! Yes I know."

"I brung the IBH down to Atlanta for helping me pull the hit. Sonya is the Feds, instead of giving them the bust she took the dope for herself. Now her and the gang got everythang."

"What about your girl Kizzy AKA Cindy in Alabama?" Nikko asked.

"I just got word that she contacted a Swiss banker wanting to know how could she open an account for five million dollars. Easily I could've gotten that money. But I wanted to hear from you what she's doing with that much money."

"Nikko I'm on the run from the Feds and that gang. I need money everywhere. Anyway that's all the gang had made by my knowledge. So I took it. She's young she don't deserve the cards she's playin."

"So she betray them what makes you think she won't betray you?"

"You know Edrundo that's a chance I had to take. I can't lose nothing that I never had."

"You know Juan I really want to kill you," Edrundo expressed.

Before he could say another word Juan told him,

"Either let me fly or let me die. It really doesn't matter because I'ma die anyway, it's a curse for you if I live another day."

Edrundo looked in his eyes he seen that this kid is the truth to only be 21 years old. And not scared to die. He yelled out something in Spanish and pulled the trigger. The gun went off and he seen the kid never blanked. He started laughing.

"Hey Nikko he's better than any one of them."

Nikko smiled and told him to get off his knees when he got up they all laughed and hugged him.

"You're as brave as your uncle Tony," Mandai Martinz told him.

"Tony was right; you're a heartless son of a bitch. But you know what Juan, you got one problem you're soft for a female. You need to learn to control your dick when you leave here you'll be ready. You see Juan Sonya didn't kill my family. She only helped my family. The Government wanted my brother so we sent a look alike to the state for him to take the rap for him. So Sonya did us two favors. She stopped my brother from going to prison and led you to us. You see Juan we promised Tony that we'll look out for you. The boy you killed he had too much on us. Somehow Philip let him get copies of records. Philip thought he was the kid to handle business. But he slipped and let the kid in on alot of shit, Philip was gonna die, just not then. Tony told us not to worry because he knew his blood would handle business. Philip was getting old so it was time we retire him. But you handle it for us, I'm 37, Edrundo is 48 and Mandai is 53. I have to answer to them they're the ones who lead me to take over. But you're gonna have to take over there, just like God has a plan for everybody, you're plan is to get money. Now let's walk and get you back in the arms of Gloria. She's a good girl and if you treat her right she'll forever be faithful to you. No man beside me has ever touched her; she's part of my first to you. You can keep her here getting money for you or put her in training to be your gansta bus as y'all call them in the States or take her with you."

He knew this was a test so he told him to put her in combat he's gonna need a killer no man can refuse.

When they returned to the palace it was daybreak everybody were beginning to get up. The servant was up and about, none of them dared to look at his naked body. When he returned to the house she was waiting for him. She was still naked when the door came open and Nikko order that she bathed him and fed him in bed also make sure he's well rested.

When they left and they were all alone she kissed him and ran to the bathroom to make bath water. He was right behind her, he told her to let him use the bathroom. When she closed the door, he quickly sat on the toilet and he pissed and shitted at the same time. When he finished he hopped in the tub and relaxed. She came in and cleaned him without getting in the tub.

"Did you enter anyone of them?"

"No that was a set up. I'm putting you in combat training you'll be coming in and out of the state to handle business for me. You'll my girl and you'll be very well tooken care of. We're gonna train together."

She smiled and got in the tub, kissed him and laid in his arms. The water was cold when they woke. She cleaned the tub and hurried him to the bed.

A knock came to the door, she was heading out the room he stopped her and made her put a blue house coat on. When she opened the door it was another female servant with their breakfast. She brought it in and said, "Breakfast is served."

When she opened it, it was a breakfast she never ate. It was waffles, sausage links, eggs, toast, jelly and apple juice with coffee. She fed herself more than she fed him. She smiled as he laughed. She tried to explain that,

that was her first time eating that. He was sleepy anyway. They ate she sat the plate on the small tray it rolled in on and rested in his arms. He didn't dare have sex with what he had just learned; after all he didn't have dick control, not even his emotion even though he's in love with Tasha. It's always a number two girl in every man life. He thought to himself and went to sleep.

CHAPTER 16
Death

"**B**lue, if you knew he was your brother all this time, why didn't you say nothing?"

They all sat at the table and looked at her.

"Look at my uncle Tony, look at you, you almost died. Tasha I really don't know. I guess I thought he wouldn't believe me anyway. I don't think he believe me now. Tasha I have feeling for my brother. It's all confusing. I love my brother that's why I was so quick to go to Switzerland I stuck by your side because I love you. It's like I don't have a family either. My folks are never there for me. We both caught the shit in of the stick. All that matter is I'm here for him and I can do all I can for him."

"Daddy what's your plan?"

"I really don't know, I got to make some phone calls and see what my peoples talking about. See if my people can strike a deal on his behalf."

"My dad is down with the government maybe he's gonna help. I'm sure he got something plan."

"Blue I don't believe your dad is gonna help him because when he fell on that murder case he didn't help him all he had was me, my dad and my granddad."

"That's because I kept him informed and told him y'all were handling everything."

"Enough of this Tasha, all that matters is she told him can't nothing y'all do change the past, y'all got to focus on the future."

"But momma, all I'm saying!"

"It don't matter what you'll saying all that matter is us staying strong. If we fall apart now then everything we strive for is no good. Y'all were best of friends before y'all knew and y'all will be even more closer. Oh God my head hurt."

They sat and stared and each other. Then Richard stood and told everybody to get in the car. He was taking them out to eat. As they enter the car Nancy said a quick prayer, then he put it in reverse. As he was backing out a green Nova came rushing up the street. He slammed on breaks.

"Damn! Now you see why I want to move out this neighborhood?"

"Richard we talked about this time and time before. My father gave us this house for a wedding present."

"It's not safe in this neighborhood anybody can come and get us. That's right, Juan told me long ago if I want to keep Tasha from thugs like him move to an uppity neighborhood because this neighborhood is wide open; a cop isn't safe here."

His heart just didn't feel safe it was Juan in away. He still hated him and if something was to happen to his family because of him he'll kill him. But the truth of the matter is he's been getting death threats from someone he put away years ago. His hand shook as he gripped the stirring wheel. Nancy noticed it but keep her peace. Even she was afraid.

He backed out and drove to Moreland. His thoughts were set on taking them downtown on Buckhead. But his hand was shaking so badly, so he took a left on Moreland and rode down to Long John Silver. He parked and opened the door for everybody. When he opened the door for Nancy she noticed that he had a gun in a holster on the right side of his pants and jacket. She wanted answers but couldn't cause an argument.

He buttoned the blue blazer up and escorted the girls in the restaurant. They went right to the counter and order fish, shrimps, fries, coleslaw and a big pitcher of tea. They sat the baby in a high chair and started eating. It was small talk about school, Nancy wanted to break the silence and take away the tension of the day. The girls started laughing when they joked about being Drs. And lawyers. Like some law firm would hire Tasha or a big name hospital or even an accounting firm were gonna hire Blue.

Richard noticed the same green Nova come into the parking lot that speeded down his street. He put in his mind that he were gonna speak with the fellow. Once the fellow came in he noticed that it was Travis Barber a dealer and murderer he had put away 20 years ago. When he was on the D.A. team. His eyes widen as Travis walked by. He acted like he didn't even see Richard. Then two black vans pulled up only 3 people got of both of them. The men were wearing black and blue; he took in a deep breath and exhaled out relief because surely he knew a robbery were about to go down and they're gonna be witness.

He stood and told them let's leave. As soon as they stood up, the six men pulled out black masks and black automatic and started shooting in the air. Not a word was said from either guy. The middles and the rest of the customer were ducking under the table. As Tasha were snatching Juan from the high chair the robber snatched the money from the register and started shooting above everyone head saying, "Stay ducked off and you won't get hurt."

Then one of the gunmen stood over Tasha and asked for the baby.

"You're gonna have to kill me before I let you take my baby."

Nancy yelled at Richard.

"Do something, you got a gun too! Protect us!"

Then another gunman walked up and said, "Just give us the baby, we're gonna lay it on the sidewalk once we're out safe."

Siren started sounded.

"Take me leave my baby alone."

Before she could say another word the second gunman shot her in the head with a Tech 9.

"Noooo!" Richard yelled, stood shooting the 357 Magnum. He let out 3 rounds hitting the two gunmen. Before he could check on her, Travis stood and said, "You remember me Richard Middle and them 20 years you got me?"

He fired a black 9MM two times hitting Richard in the chest. When Richard fell the gun fell on the floor in front of Blue. She picked it up and hit Travis in the shoulder one time. The big frame man fell to his seat and got up and started running. Another gunman snatched the baby out of Tasha arms and started running. She fired the last two shots but missed. Then Nancy told her to get down. Men in blue and black were standing outside the window with automatic pointed at the window. No one fired once they got out the door. They all ran to the side of the building. Then one guy lit two cocktails and threw them in the vans. Travis pulled off in the Nova.

Blue hollered out,

"Somebody call the police! Somebody call for help!"

Nancy didn't know what to do; she just lost her whole family. She cuddled Richard while Blue cuddled Tasha. All that ran in both of their heads were "Richard Middle you remember me and them 20 years you got me."

When the police and ambulance came they pronounced Richard and Tasha dead at the scene. The few people that were in the restaurant gave statements. While Nancy and Blue sat at the table, Nancy was speechless and shaking while Blue explained what happened. A black female officer tried to comfort Nancy by giving her a blanket and lifting her to her feet, so she can go to the hospital and be checked. Nancy took three steps and passed out.

"We have one down get some help over here."

Nobody could describe either of the gunmen. The two gunmen Richard shot didn't have I.D. Barber got away. Nobody knows what the gunmen got away in. Blue didn't know how to begin to tell them about Juan, so she told them, "I'm all the baby got healthy right now."

They put Nancy on a stretcher and wheeled her out. Blue got in the Lincoln and drove to Grady behind the ambulance. Once they got there they took Nancy to the E.R. Blue sat in the waiting room crying. She saw it on the news, no picture of her nephew. Just pictures of Tasha and her dad cause of murder (revenge of a prison sentence).

She sat there wondering about what Juan said to her long ago. It made sense.

"It seems as every time I find out I have a family member they up and die."

She touched her face because she was so helpless.

"If Juan was here none of this would've happen."

That thought kept running through her head over and over again.

"When he comes back I'ma go all out just like my lil' brother, ain't gone care for nothing because life don't care for us."

She walked to a phone and picked up the receiver. When she went in her pocket she felt Tasha blood or was she shot. A pain went to her thigh. She looked at her blue jeans and seen the whole left side soaked. She was trying to remember what leg she cradled Tasha with. Then she said, "Fuck it" and checked her leg.

It was Tasha blood. She took a breath of relief, got a couple of quarters out her pocket put them in the phone and called her dad. Her mom put her on hold and then she heard her dad say, "Hello."

She started crying telling him they kidnap lil' Juan killed Tasha and her father. She didn't know what to do. Nancy flipped out and passed out. She didn't know how to contact Juan.

"I'm so confused," was all she could say.

She listened to him and then said, "I love you" and hung up.

It was two hours later before she could see Nancy. They had put her on the third floor room 324. She had a stroke and a mild heart attack.

When she walked to the elevator she thought she had seen Tasha walked out the elevator when the door opened. She called her name and the girl looked back. It wasn't her.

"Get yourself together Blue."

She shook her head and pushed the button for the third floor. As she thought about it she knew she saw Tasha she just had on different clothes and a different hair style.

"Girl you're really losing it you really are. The girl turned around and looked at you. You're just missing her Blue."

The door opened and she took a left, she thought about what she was gonna say to Mrs. Middle. She saw a bunch of nurses and doctor running past her. When she got to room 324 the door was opened; she saw the nurses and doctor working on Mrs. Middle. Seconds later someone said she's dead. They put a white sheet over her face and rolled her out.

"Damn, a whole family died in one day. Mrs. Middle musta couldn't take being left alone. She should've fought for my nephew."

She walked back to the elevator and pressed the down button; when the door opened she pressed the first floor button and just closed her eyes.

"Now how am I gonna find my nephew with his whole family being dead. Juan faked his death, he won't be able to get his own son, yep they're either gonna kill him or sell him. Don't nobody know I'm his aunt. Damn! Damn! Damn!"

She opened her eyes when the door opened, she walked out and went to the car. When she got inside the car she cried more, started it and drove to the police station off Memorial Dr. turned the car in and asked for a ride back to the campus. She was going to get her car in the morning from Tony house she'll snatch the wires off herself.

CHAPTER 17
No Understanding

It was around 12 when he woke up. A servant came in and told him that he had been summoned. He got up took a shower and dressed in some black slacks, black dress shirt with some black block gator. She had picked him out a gold watch while she was out shopping for him.

When he finished dressing they walked out to the dining room. She had a frown on her face because he didn't compliment her blue and gold body dress she picked out for him. When he sat at the table he noticed her ass was wearing that dress. Not wanting to get her into any trouble or make himself look stupid, he just kept his mouth closed.

There were alot of salad on the table; the servants along with Gloria appeared with golden trays in their hands. One of the male servant poured wine in everybody glass. Then Gloria sat his meal in front of him. When he opened the tray it was a note in it. He removed the note and placed it in his lap. When everybody started eating, he read it.

"Don't get too attached to your servant because you're just work to her. She'll be on the next dick when you leave."

He removed the top from his tray and ate his steak and potatoes he wonder who sent the note or was it a set up. When he looked up and scanned the table he seen a beautiful Latino at the far end of the table smiling and blinking as something was in her eye. Then she wiped them with a wave to him. She sat by this older cat that never said much last night. So he guessed he were her old, old man. He finished his meal and started to eat some salad. Gloria whispered something in Nikko ear and Nikko said, "Please excuse Mr. Ravenion Nalls from the table."

He stood and wondered why he didn't call him Juan. He nodded his head and walked back to her house. Once they got inside she kissed him and said, "I understand you got a note about me."

"Yes! You want to read it?"

"Yes!"

He handed it to her she read it and smiled.

"Do you have any ideal who sent this?"

"No!"

"Well I do and I'm gonna confront her after lunch. This is total disrespect. I didn't bring you here for this. I brung you here so you can see it with your own eyes."

"See what?"

She cut the TV on and flipped it to channel 3 the American news. He watched for a minute then it came on.

"Mr. Richard Middle and daughter Ms. Natasha Middle were murder last night at the Long John Silver on Moreland Ave. Along with the murder, infant Juan Ellis Jr. was kidnapped. This is the only footage that we have."

It showed the shooting and burning of the van he dropped his head and said, "Damn!"

No tears dropped and that puzzled her. A knock came to the door and a voice came behind it.

"It's me Nikko."

When Nikko came in he wasn't surprise that Juan wasn't crying.

"Ravenion, Juan has no life no more, that's way I called you Ravenion and plus I just found out that it's two informants sitting among us. We can't' figure neither one of them because everybody here has been here for years. This is where you come in at. You remember those graves you seen this morning. Well here's the gun a black 9MM which shot 18 times."

He handed him a pair of gloves to put on, then handed him the gun. They walked out to the cornfield. Everybody that sat at the table was there; all 21 of them. Nikko, Edrunda, Mandai, Gloria, and he made 26 people. Mandai Edrunda stood beside them. He told everybody to line up in groups of threes because he had a speech to make.

He called Helen away from the group. She was the Latino who sent Ravenion the note. When he seen how she was sporting that brown dress he understood why Nikko wanted her spared. When everybody lined up side by side in groups of threes, Gloria waved her hand and 5 more guards came out of the stocks with AKs.

"I'm sorry to inform the group about these graves. There are seven graves here and they're dug about 15 feet but these graves today won't all get filled, only two of them. We have two informants among us; the sad part about it is we don't know who they are. So we're gonna play any meeny miny moe to find the right one."

Ravenion being upset with the news he just seen smiled and whispered in Nikko ears, "Since we don't know which ones they are we might as well kill all of them."

"This is your problem now Ravenion you do things different from me. Whatever you see fit then that's what you see. Me I like to torture but whatever you see fit do it. It's easy to get someone to replace them."

He pulled the clip out and said, "I only have one shot and I plan to make this one count. Everybody get naked."

After 5 minute everybody was undressed. He ordered everybody to line up by a grave, in groups of threes, while the five guards gather up their clothes and started to search them.

Thinking about Tasha and Juan he started at the end. It was two men, and one woman. He put the clip back in and said, "Forgive them Father for they know not the sin they've committed."

He shot all of them and walked over to the next grave. There were two females and one male.

"It's a shame God gift has to be put to waste," and shot all three of them in the head.

The guards were behind him throwing them in the grave. One of the men from the first grave fell sideway one of the guards shot him and threw him in the grave. The other 13 people were breathing harder than ever. The older guy with the Latino standing at the second grave said, "Nikko I thought it was only two? How can you kill seven people?"

Nikko smiled and said, "When you don't know who to kill you kill everyone to make sure you got the right ones."

"I'm not fix 'en to let you, young mothafucka kill me."

He ran toward Nikko, all the guards started shooting everyone including him.

Gloria looked at Helen and said, "You speak bad about me in note?"

Nikko took the 9 from Ravenion and gave it to Gloria, with her eyes open looking her eye to eye. She pulled the trigger and shot her in the head. The guards placed all the bodies in the grave and started burning them. They stood and watched them replant the stocks over the dead. Then Nikko ordered them to dig 7 more.

They left and returned back to the lunch that they didn't finish. He finished his salad without saying a word about the news. Nikko sensed that something was wrong.

"Is your lost troubling you?"

"No I'm thinking about my son, a bitch I will always have in my life. She's dead, my son ain't."

"Don't worry about your son, he has your blood in his vein, you know he's gonna be okay. They want you not your son let's ride."

They all got into a black Benz and rode down a dirt road about 10 miles away from the palace, to a red farm house. When they got out, all four of them put on masks and walked in the farm house.

"This my friend is gonna make me a trillionaire and the three of you billionaires. This is called meth."

When they went behind the plastic curtains they saw 300 workers. Some at a table panning the meth, some bagging the meth and the rest cooking the meth. They all had insulation suit on. Meth is gonna be the fastest growing drug in the US. Some will get this confused with crack or heroin. Once they hit it they'll know the difference. We're only selling 31 ounces in a kilo for 36 thousand, no deals. We're gonna put 5,000 kilos in 10 states. How you sell them is on you as long as you get 36 thousands back to us. Come and let's go on a second ride.

They drove farther south to an office building. When they got out he looked at the 4 window building, it wasn't an office building it was a warehouse. When they walked in Nikko said, "This my friend is ecstasy, the next fastest growing drug in the US. We're gonna put these pills in night clubs in the south. If the owners are not with it, then make him with it."

They went back to the car and drove farther south to a private own airport. The jet was white, Nikko and Mandai got in the pilot seats.

"Where to Nikko?" Mandai asked.

"Brazil. Ravenion alot of professional ballplayers come to Brazil, they come here to train alot of them have marijuana problem and we have this weed called Hydro, that everyone love, we're gonna check out the growth. Mandai is behind this. Edrundo have people transferring the heroin and cain over now. When you get back to the state everything will be at your grandmother house don't worry we already took care of the bugs. We're building pathways to the house now. Something like the tunnel y'all already got. It's gonna be a tunnel from Florida to GA that leads to a new warehouse outside your grandmother property the trucks will come up to the barn and drop things off. Not the barn you already got but the barn in the race track. You do know where the College Park driver license place is? Well that's where the path start. But any way you'll have to haul the work to the house from the barn that way no one will know. You'll never touch any of the dope. You're leaving with a 65 man clique. Four men will be around you at all times don't worry about that gang. What they got they can have we'll take everybody out of business. Cocaine will go 12 thousand a kilo. You'll have 5,000 in every state. You'd have 5 Cubans in every state. The 5 in Georgia will be with you. These are the 10 states I have someone on the forces. Dallas TX, Memphis TN, Atlanta GA,

Birmingham AL, Jackson MS, Baton Rouge LA, Louisville KY, Raleigh SC and Charlotte NC, these are the 10 states you'll work, we're looking at 4 billion dollars' worth of dope. You'll have a month and a half to report back. The money is shipped the same way, but will be sent to Switzerland. Any problem you have let your army fix it, if you feel uncomfortable about a situation phone me and I'll send an enforcer to straighten things out. If one of my men gets out of hand kill them and I'll send a replacement. No Cuban like to be ran by an American. Like I said everything will be at your grandmother house. Every shipment will come to you truckloads at a time. Once the shipment is dropped the money will be picked up on that same truck. We're loaded and unloading in the air that way we'll have enough time to beat air patrol.

The plane landed, they got into a black tinted window limousine and rode down the coastline to a white house with guards at the gate. There were no grass in the front yard, no stairs to the porch, only a wheelchair ramp. When they walked into the house there was nothing there but blue lights and plants. They went into one of the rooms on the left, took their clothes off and put on swimsuits, goggles and air tanks. Walked out the back door to the beach and went swimming.

They swam two miles away from the beach and went 10 feet under the water to watch how the "HyDro" was being tended to. They saw 10 men tending to the plants three men taking them up. There were miles of plants and they tended to check all the plants. As they swam, they seen at least two men checking each plant after checking all the plants they went up and met a white speed boat. Climbed on and rode back to the house. As they entered the house they washed their face and put their clothes back on. Then they walked to the room on the right across from the first one and seen a man controlling a camera of everything going on underwater.

"A pound of this cost $6,500."

They walked in the last room and seen them spraying some chemical on the weed that made it turn color. After seeing everything was well, Nikko asked one of the workers for a tester. The worker pulled out four cigars from his blue jumpsuit pocket, dumped the tobacco out and filled them with HyDro when Ravenion took two puffs, he put it out a.s.a.p. It had him higher than he ever been.

When they reached the car, they waved bye to the guards and visited Hector. Hector was a young Brazilian who supplied the professionals with all the weed they wanted. When they got to the beaches, they saw faces from TV, which they knew walking around naked, laughing and talking to

Hector.

Hector was a slim Brazilian with short wavy black hair walking toward them with two naked ladies on both sides of him. A fine white one with blue eyes brown hair round tits and a black one with a figure most females would die for.

"Hey Nikko what brings you here?"

"I come here because we're in town and wanted to have a good time."

"Okay Nikko I will have ladies come to y'all suites."

They departed and went into the Hilton and checked in four different suites and waited on Hector. Ravenion just laid in the bed not caring how the suite looked. A hotel was all the same to him; one TV, two sofas, one bed, and a phone to call room service. He couldn't get his son off his mind. A knock came to the door. He didn't answer, and then a female voice said, "Hector sent me."

When he opened the door, it wasn't a Brazilian it was Janet Daws a member of the New York basketball team. She was fine he liked to see her hoop. He never imagined he'll have her naked he never thought she was a prostitute. She came in wearing a red tight body dress. She unclothed herself and he looked at the 6'1" slim figure and smiled. Then he laid on the bed and let her went to work with her mouth on his cock.

She was on him 30 minute he just couldn't get his mind in it. He stopped her and told her thanks, "But I have alot on my mind and sex is nowhere near it." She didn't care she had a job to do, so she went back to work. She undressed him and sat on his cock and went up and down pleasing herself. She came and laid on top of him, kissed him and begged him to relieve his mind, so she started massaging his temples still moving in, an up and down motion. Then she remembered what Hector told her a trick like to be controlled or in control. So she looked in his eyes and saw murder. As she motioned herself she whispered in his ear, "Kill him, shoot him in the head; ain't no justice behind his action."

The more she spoke the more he got into it then she screamed, "No! No! Don't kill me!"

He flipped her over and started fucking her to his own hate, he pounded hard. Her scream became real because it hurt. Finally feeling as he has killed his enemy; he came.

She said, "Wow! That was the best fuck in my life."

Sweating he just looked at her rolled off her and closed his eyes. He hated that it took thinking about killing someone to get his rocks off. What was he becoming a killing machine.

She went back to work on his cock while he rested. She wanted him again and she was determined to get it. She felt him rise in her mouth, she began her talk again. This time he fucked her from the back, pulling her hair as he was shooting her in the back of the head. The more she talked the more he wanted to kill her. She screamed at the top of her lungs, "Please don't kill me. You're killing me."

He busted and laid on top of her and went to sleep. He tossed and turned. He was dreaming about Juan crying and reaching for his momma.

Then he jumped up sweating. Janet was still lying there with her breast uncovered. So he put his face in the middle of her breast and silently wept.

He never meant for Tasha to get hurt, all the times he was there to protect her. All he wanted was for them to be secure. Everything he fought hard for, he lost, lost his respect and his family. Then he thought about his money in Tasha name how was he gonna get his money. He rose up looked down on her sleeping body and got up.

He dressed himself looked at his watch it was 5:46 am. He needed to walk he needed peace. So he walked to the beach and walked to the shoreline. All he could do was ask why. Knowing he wouldn't get an answer he decided to call Blue. He went to the room picked the phone up dialed zero when the operator came on, he gave her the number and waited. The phone rung 10 times and the operator asked did he want to try to make this call later. He told her to try 10 more time they just had death in their family.

She placed the call again this time she picked up on the fifth ring.

"Blue this is your lil' brother. I got word on what happen. I need to know how you're taking it."

She explained to him that she was scared and needed him there to protect her.

"Blue it's best you finish your schooling out and forget about me you're my family, I will find Juan really I will. Just promise me when I find him you'll take care of him. I got to find a way to get my money out of Tasha account."

She explained to him that will be easy because the money wasn't completely transferred. Tasha was only getting money out the account.

"You see a big sister is good for something."

He smiled.

Then she explained that their dad was hooking things up against the gang and Sonya, all he needed him to do was testify and he'll be granted immunity.

He told her to tell him to hook it up and he'll do it. He told her he'll do anything to live his life with his son. He hung up, got undressed, got back in the bed, and made mad passionate love to her. His mind was clear and she could tell by the way held her.

Room service woke them with breakfast; Hector had ordered them a small breakfast Danishes and coffee. He looked at his watch it was 10:20 AM. They showered together she dried off and hopped back in bed. Waiting to him to come back to bed, so she could speak with him and learn things about him. When he came back in the room she smiled as he sat on the bed. He dressed and she asked was the morning still young? He smiled and told her he can't say.

He picked up the phone and gave the operator the number to the Swiss Bank. He spoke with Nina and she transferred everything into Ravenion account. He smiled, hung up and walked out the room. Nikko suite was down the hall to the left of his room. He walked right into his suite. He was puzzled because the door was open. So he called his name.

"Nikko! Nikko!"

After getting no answer he walked through the suite the bed was made and the bathroom was clear so he walked to the beach. He saw talking through his hands at Hector between the bar and the shower. So he jogged down to see what the problem was, then he notice Edrundo and Mandai wasn't there. When he walked up he heard Nikko say,

"I'm no punk Hector! You blew lots of money Hector!"

He looked around the beach, it was still young. Not many people were out and about. He pulled out the 9 and said, Nikko your problem is you talk too much. People is always gonna take you for a joke. Ain't no heart or emotion in this life."

With that he shot Hector in the head two times. Nikko jumped back, smiled and said, "You're fucking crazy."

They turned and walked back to the hotel people was looking but still walking. They got Edrundo and Mandai and left. No word was said about Hector, they drove to the jet and left.

"You know Ravenion you're very crazy. I hate to get on your bad side because there's no telling what you'll do. When we get back I'm gonna give you 65 of my best men, and get you back to the US before you kill everybody. I'm even sending Gloria with you to get you calm."

"No let her train."

They all laughed knowing he learned a lesson from the rude awaken.

When they landed Gloria was standing by the third Benz wearing a purple dress. She greeted him with a kiss and a hug. She opened the door for him and ran to the other side. When she got inside he complimented her dress and told her she looked nice in all her dresses especially the one yesterday. She smiled and kissed him again and told him she missed him. He explained to her how important it was for her to train because he didn't need nothing soft beside him. He thought about Tasha and said, "Sholl don't need nothing soft."

She told him not to worry; she'll be whatever he wanted. But deep down inside she was sad. She was ready to leave Cuba she wanted to be beside him. She asked him to promise she won't have to have sex with nobody and he promised and told her train and train only.

When they arrived at the palace she had him a black jacket white T-shirt and some black slacks. He dressed and told her he'll send for her. She got on her knees and begged him to stay the night and be with her one more time.

"At least stay for dinner," she requested.

She knew Nikko owed her a favor and that was gonna be her favor. As they sat for dinner she whispered in Nikko ear, he smiled. Minutes later he asked him to stay for one night and leave tomorrow. He smiled and looked at Gloria and declined.

"I have something to look into immediately."

Nikko looked at Gloria and "I tried."

They ate and he called her. He picked her up and walked to the car. He sat her on the hood and kissed her. Told her to train hard and he loved her. Tears rolled down her eyes. As she jumped off the hood and held him and told him she won't let him down. They kissed for the last time, he got in the car and the driver started to pull off. He told him to stop and he called her to the car. She got in and he held her all the way to the airport. He told her to keep that money for an emergency.

CHAPTER 18
Ravenion Empire

He drove to the campus and beated on Blue's door. He heard her say, "I'm coming"

When she opened the door she hugged him and said, "It's 2:20 am in the morning. Why didn't you come in the morning?"

He looked at her in a brotherly view; because of what she had on. Before his thoughts strayed. She had on a pair of cut off blue jean that showed her inner thigh and the bottom of her cheeks a white cut off tank top and some pink bunny slippers.

She turned around to walk to her room, when he locked the door. He got a good look at her; the brotherly look diminished, all he saw were her cheeks moving. She hopped back in bed and he pulled his coat off and hopped beside her. She jumped up and said, "Boy I'm your sister!"

"Relax Blue, I just want to lie under my big sister even though y'all white folks are down with that incest." He started laughing but she wasn't.

"You're sick you know that!"

But deep down inside, she always liked him and wanted him. They laid there then she cuddled into him and said, "I'm scared for you," and started crying.

"I can't die Blue remember that. I'm gonna live to be 101. So don't be scared for me be brave for me."

He knew the Cubans were due in at 1:00 o'clock, so he was gonna get rested and pain the world Friday. He was gonna let them rest all Thursday. Friday was gonna be the day business was going down. He wasn't gonna touch the dope he was going to East Lake Meadows and find his son. He rubbed his hand through her blonde hair and said, "Everything is gonna be alright."

He fell asleep surprised that he didn't try her because in his heart he didn't have no family. Even though he wanted a family he just couldn't accept it. He felt her moving around in his arms. So he opened his eyes to see what was causing her to toss. When he looked at her he saw that she had took her top off. He closed his eyes trying not to get himself aroused. But how could he not when her breast was rubbing his chest and rib. Then she pulled herself on top of him. He studied her to see will her eyes open or was she still sleep and not doing this purposely. Her eyes never opened, she was rubbing him on his chest moaning and breathing hard. Wanting to respond he just bald his fist and said, "This is what Nikko and them talk about no dick control."

She was freaking him in her dreams and it was nothing he could do about it. Have she really accepted the fact that they were brothers and sisters or did she care. His thoughts was interrupted when she kissed him and said, "Take me Juan!" He looked at her she had positioned herself to sitting on top of him grinding him but her eyes was still closed. He couldn't take it anymore, so he woke her and told her to look at herself. She looked down and looked at him jumped off him and ran to the bathroom, truly she had made love to him and they both had their clothes on. When she returned to the room with a towel on she fussed at him.

"You know I liked you, you had no reason getting in the bed with me." She stood there pointing and fussing her towel dropped and she just stood there. So he jumped up and kissed her and walked into Tasha's old room. Her things were still there and they picture still hung on the mirror. Her make up still on the dresser and her teddy bears still on the bed in the same place she always put them on the pillow. He laid on his end of the bed and fell back to sleep.

She was still wearing the clothes she wore the night before she woke him up and told him some men was in the living room. He jumped up and looked at the clock it was 3:30 pm.

"Are they Cuban?"

"Yes."

He went in the bathroom grabbed Tasha red rag washed his face, grabbed her red tooth brush and brushed his teeth with the Crest sitting on the sink. When he walked in and he saw Alex, Arod, Nigerz, and Gino standing in front of the door. Alex was Nikko's pride and joy. He stood 6"2, 230 pounds all muscle bald head and always kept a pair of shades on. Arod was 6"0, 165 pounds loves to kill with knives. Now Gino thought he was Gino from Scarface. He always says,

"You see him that's my pops they look just alike. In real life pop wouldn't slipped like that me I'll never slip and let my people die. I'ma always stay focus."

Nikko had to meet the four men that he knew would keep him alive. Nikko had their family in deep debt, all four of them loved Nikko for not killing them, but giving them a life. All of them were older than Ravenion by years. Alex is 29, Arod is 33, Nigerz 30 and Gino 30. Gino and Arod are brothers. So he knew he was safe with them. All four of them knew Atlanta well. He used to send them in the states to knock off folks with Tony. He called Blue back into the living room. She had put on some purple Morris Brown jogging pants and a blue shirt to match.

"This is my big sister she's off limits to any of you. I'm trying my best to protect her she's all I got you guys feel me?"

They all agreed then Alex spoke.

"We've been to the house everything is in order. We got here at 9, so we already set things up. We have 10 blue Yukons with the dope all ready to be transported to the states. Nikko said you're just to look after the money and find good spots. We're gonna make sure everything else is tooken care of. We already have people in the states. So all we'll doing is collecting and protecting. We'll jump things off in GA and take care of that gang. I already got 10 men in the meadows trying to get all the information they can find. I don't think they have your son there because that will be the first place you'll look."

"So let's ride to the house since y'all have tooken care of everything."

"Juan I know you're an understanding man."

"What's up Alex?"

"Man our families is 30 million put together in the hole with Nikko. My old man is dying I promised him before he die I'll have our family out of debt. I'm willing to go to the grave to keep that promise."

The other three looked at him and nodded their head. He told 'em he's down with whatever.

Alex told him he know how to make meth and before the men leave out he needed his permission to send the men out to rob pharmacies and stores that sold lithium battery everything else they could buy. The pharmacy held the Benadryl and Sudafed they needed. He told him his uncle showed him how to make it and gave him a recipe he gave him a piece of paper and he looked at it.

"So all y'all need is some clear alcohol, Primestar starter fluid liquid fire, Sudafed, Actifed, Benadryl, lithium battery strips, three jars, some tub and coffee filter. Two large jars with a hole to run to the small jar table spoon of rock salt to bring smoke and blow it 3x, some ammonia nitrate and stir it in the woods with a wooden spoon. Why do it say no sweat?"

"Because it will blow your ass up!" Alex replied with laughter.

"Shid I don't care man go and handle y'all business when y'all get everything right and cooked up y'all come and get me. Now if shit don't go right don't tell Nikko I gave y'all the order on the silly ideal, deal?"

"Deal!" They all agreed.

They left and Blue came back into the room.

"Do you want to talk about what happen last night Blue?"

"No I don't. You know you act like you're God Gift to women. In a way I wish you never knew I was your sister. I liked you better then."

"What makes me so different now? What happen to I'm so scared for you?"

"You want to know huh? I'm in love with you. I've always been in love with you, is that what you wanted to hear. It's hard being in love with my own brother. I wanted to tell you long ago, but I believed in my heart something would happen between us. After all you didn't know, I can see if we were raised together, I don't know what I was thinking.

He sat down on the sofa shaking his head looking at her. She sat beside him placed her leg on the sofa and her head in his lap? She asked him what was they gonna do and where was he gonna stay. In her heart she wanted him to stay there with her. But that wouldn't be a good idea with the trouble he's in. She was surprised nobody came there yet. Knowing how she and Tasha hung together. If those Cubans knew where she stayed then somebody knew about her.

"You stay in school I'ma be straight. Me and Tasha have a place in Buckhead. I thought about going there but Sonya knows about that. Since I got these Cuban I might get a house in Ravenion name or stay at grandmamma house. That's where I'm gonna stay that way I can see 'em coming at me."

"You know you're gonna have to put Cameras' up like Tony had."

"Yeah they're supposed to be doing that now so we can keep track on the dope. One man is gonna stay back and watch everything. He's hooking Tony system to my system that way I can see everything. I'm gonna continue to hide out there. I don't want to live like this Blue, I really don't but I'm forced. I'm gonna have somebody watching you. Not a Cuban but a bodyguard."

"No let me live."

"You know you won't be able to come to me after today we'll barely see each other."

"See I'm losing you again, that's why I didn't want to tell you I was your sister because we'll never be a family."

She started crying tucking her head in his stomach.

"Why?" she asked.

"Blue we're a family right now!"

"No we can't my brother is dead you're Ravenion my kid brother is dead."

He leaned back and put his head on the rest and thought about what she said. Really she was right. Her brother is "dead" he thought to himself rubbing his hand through her hair. Without a doubt Juan was dead.

She knew she had touched him deep, how deep she didn't know. All she knew was she was confused, had mixed feeling about a guy that thrilled her, then a love that a sister would have for a brother.

As he adjusted himself she felt him on the side of her face. "He musta feel the same way to be hard" not being able to control herself any longer, she pulled his shirt up and started kissing his stomach. She knew a family they never will be. So she took her tongue and licked his stomach line.

She looked up at him his eyes was close. That was the go ahead sign she wanted. She took him out of his pants and put him in her mouth. She wanted to know what had Tasha so powerfully in love with him. Stroking him in an up and down motion with her mouth looking up at him. He opened his eyes and they looked eye to eye. It was like she was searching his soul. Her motion never changed it was a slow pace. She wanted him to enjoy her. He grabbed her in his arms and took her to the bedroom. There were no sister and brother bonding. She was right her brother was dead she stood there while he took her shirt off and help her out of her jogging pants and red thongs. He looked at her stacked body. Her body would put alot of blacks to shame. She undressed him and they laid each other down with him on top of her. He kissed her responding to the heat she was in last night. He kissed her breast, her stomach and then put his tongue in her Love Lake. She screamed and moaned. He was gonna make her remember this for the rest of his life. He stuck his ring finger in her anis. She lifted herself to his rhythm she cried when he enter her. She was so tight her wall was right there. She was closed built, so he took his time slowly grinding in her pushing deep and deeper. She whispered, "I love you Ravenion" gripping his back begging him to love her. Her body shook and then started shaking. She throws her head back when he lifted her. They came together and he laid inside of her. She sucked on his neck and repeated in his ear that she loved him. They fell asleep with her in his arms. Hours later he woke up and made love to her again, got up and showered, she fixed him chicken and fries while he showered. She stood over the stove in the nude feeling good about herself. She went to the living room and cut the TV on. When she flipped it to the news they were talking about the many robberies that took place today in the last 6 hours.

She walked back into the kitchen and went into the refrigerator got the Kool-Aid jar to make some more. When he walked up in his shirt and slacks he saw her bending over putting water in something so he walked up and kissed her buttock. She smiled and said, "I got some chicken, fries and cherry Kool-Aid. But you really need to check that new out. Your boys ain't bullshitting. They robbed Grady, GA Baptist. They robbed a whole bunch of places in 6 hours. How many of them is it?"

"65, put your clothes back on in case they pop up back here."

She ran and dressed herself while he tended to the chicken. When she got back he was taking the chicken out the pan and putting it in a napkin covered wooded bowl she had on the counter. The fries sat in another wooden napkin covered bowl. She sat in his lap and poured catch up over the chicken and fries. They fed each other; a knock came to the door. She answered.

"Who is it?"

"Alex."

She opened the door and the four of them walked in. When they saw the news, they started jumping and laughing, "We did it and no one got caught."

You see Ravenion, we're the best. We walked in them hospital and walked out nobody knew nothing. The stores was the same way. We got everything we need. Enough to make more than enough money, we're gonna get to the money."

"Where is everybody Alex?"

"They're at your grandmother house."

"Where in the hell is everyone gonna sleep?"

"On the floor all the Yukan is packed with the dope."

"What the hell y'all went robbing in?"

"The Yukon I was willing to take the blame for everything if anything went wrong. No nuts no glory ha?"

He kissed her on the forehead, gave her the keys to the Suburban, and they walked out. Arod opened the passenger door for him and they loaded up, Alex drove off.

"We got to go shopping when we send everybody out in the morning. Do you need anybody beside y'all four to make the meth?"

"No! Everybody knows what to do. It should be easy because we got people in all these states pushing the cain. So it should be easy. You just got to tell them how you want it sold."

They came up through the back of the property. The pathway wasn't all that knew because he knew it already. It was the path that leads to the driver license place that his granddaddy used to run the moon shine through that path. The land consisted of alot of trees, automobiles, grave yards, a dirt bike, race track, and four houses all empty because they were hundreds of yards apart from each other. A clever place to start a lab, when they got to the race track he seen the other 9 trucks parked and a guard watching them. They got out and walked to the house. When they got to the house he saw all 59 men sitting in the front yard eating taco and drinking all kinda beer. Men were walking around the house checking guard points. They walked in the house to his grandmother room and he saw the computer wiz watching both lands.

"Poco this is Ravenion."

She turned and stood, he was surprised to see it was a female. Nikko was really trying him on the dick control.

"Hi Ravenion I'm Linda but they call me Poco. So everybody would think of a man." I found the house up from us system and hooked everything up Nikko said, "This is your land so I figured everything was alright to hook up. I trust that you have the computer."

"Damn I left that with Blue I got to get to a phone."

Alex handed him a phone. This is your phone it's untraceable. He called Blue and told her he'll be by in the morning to get that computer. When he hung up Poco continued to explain her duty to monitor and report any foul play. He stepped in the hallway and called Alex.

"What's the deal with her? Is she in debt to?"

"I don't know."

"Trust, this Nikko knows about your set up."

"Not really because it's a house across the street the house on the hill with the rocky driveway. I didn't trust her from the jump so everything we push got to be placed up there. And the money got to be wired to your account in Switzerland. Nina got to get a heavy cut so she won't tell Nikko. I took care of Mr. Adam. It was a kilo of meth."

"That fat bastard lied to me, anyway I hear you man I'm with you all the way. Is the lab set up?"

"We set it up before we came to you. We're looking to make a hundred and fifty million to free all 64 of us. I don't know about her. The extra 15 men is to guard the house, only 50 of them is going out. Rav everybody wants to be free even if it means killing this hoe. You got to play under her and see what her intention. We're depending on you because she'll be able to hear all the conversation she don't know we know this my uncle told me everything."

"Listen, tell everybody to destroy these phone I'm fix 'en to order Nextel walkie talkie phone. But make sure they destroy them phones pass the word. How do you know one of these niggas ain't down with her?"

"I don't!"

They rubbed their head they never thought about that.

"Don't worry Alex, nothing is gonna go wrong. We'll just have to start paying your people. We'll pay them what we think they deserve."

"Don't worry my friend let's get to the money."

Alex waved for the rest of them to come to the yard. Alex assembled them together.

"Listen up! Listen up! This is Ravenion our reporting officer; Nikko has put him in charge of us. I've explained to all of you that he's fair and reasonable. I think y'all already know that. Listen to what he got to say."

He looked around and seen Poco, standing on the porch. He ordered her back inside.

"Okay! Okay! This is not about me, it's about y'all and y'all family I don't have a family. My first intention was to send y'all about to fight my war, know that my war will fight itself. I understand y'all got to do what y'all go to do. But we're gonna do it in the most respectable way that everybody would want to deal with us. Understand that the Dro will sell faster, each one of y'all have 30 thousand pounds in each truck. So when y'all get where y'all are going that truck don't mean nothing. Y'all also got 30 thousand dollars a group. So y'all have money to buy what y'all need to get comfortable. Pretty soon y'all will have money to bail out. The Dro is $20 and up, ounce, $500, pounds, $6,500 of the meth will be sold just like cocaine, matter of fact we're gonna make them think it's a new cocaine. That way we can sow the south up quicker. Me I want to sow all 52 states. But we'll get there, meth sells $25 bags, $50 bags, $100 8 balls, and ounce $1,300. No kilos on the ex-pills, I'm sending y'all away with 50 thousand pills. Each night club get 500 pills free. $20 a pill, I want this and the meth in every bar and every club, also around colleges. Like I said the Dro will sell itself."

He turned and looked at Alex and told him to pass the word around about the phone.

"When Alex word get around to y'all, y'all will see that I'm with y'all 100 percent. What y'all do is on y'all I can't control y'all life and I won't try. But we'll control any mothafucka life that rise up against up. I mean babies in the oven, kidnapping families any mean necessary to get our products sold. If you get hot switch out with another group and keep on rolling. Understand there's only one leader and that's me. Cross me and you'll see that I'm worse than Nikko. Nikko can't help you over here. So if you cross me, I'm taking it to heart because I'm for y'all. Now y'all pick who y'all want to ride with y'all. If trap rolling good and one decide he don't want to do nothing, call me and I'll be down and do the unthinkable for my trip. Clique up and roll out may the Lord be with y'all. All y'all stop by Nextel and get the walkie talkie phone."

They all started to fall out in their groups of five, while they walked back into the house.

"Tomorrow we're going into every project and whoever we see getting to the money. That's who we're putting down. They'll report to y'all not me. We're gonna put one on with the meth another with the dro. Leave weapon with them and tell 'em whoever they have problem with to let y'all know and y'all will take care of them. The pills will be sold everywhere? Be on the road. While y'all are in the lab, I'll be raping this hoe mind."

"We're still gonna look for your son,"

"Alex you're a good man, I'm fix 'en to find my son now."

He called Sonya, her phone rang three times and she picked it up.

"Hello." Her voice came from her end of the phone, sounding steepest.

"Sonya, where's my son at?"

"I knew you was gonna think it was me. But I swear to God I don't know nothing. When are you coming in from Cuba? Because we need to talk."

"Next week, Sonya tell that gang I'm nothing to be played with."

"I don't think that they had anything to do with that. They got their own problem. Cindy ran off with 5 million dollars. When you left. So they're focusing on that money."

"Where's my money? If you want to get things right with me get my son back and my money."

"I love you to death Ravenion, nobody know that name but me the feds don't even know it. I'm still protecting you the best way I can. They think that you're dead. At least that's what the hospital report says. I fixed that that day they let you out of holding. I have a small scar on my face and I've been raped. All of this to show you that I love you. I'm the one for you. I'm sorry about Tasha, but I'm your girl. Ravenion what happen to the money and dope you got from Detroit? You put it in your house remember? If I was dirty I could've gotten that money because it's still there. I could've went into that wine cellar also the revolving wall in Tony room where the dope and money is. That's more than 3 million in cash and about a million and a half worth of dope."

"Sonya where is Smokey?"

"I told you, they're trying to get up what they lost and find Cindy they still have dope and money. But that was a major blow. So he's keeping everything close to him."

"Sonya I know you're in this for the money. How much will it take for you to live comfortably?"

"I'm aiming at 10 million."

"Well I'll get you 3 million of the money if you keep me protected from the law. Find out where my son is, deal?"

"Deal. How can I contact you?"

"I'll contact you" and he hung up.

"Now how in the hell are we're suppose to get around if y'all got all the dope in the truck?"

The four of them looked around at each other and dropped their head.

"Just like I thought don't worry. I'm just gonna show you four guys my hide out."

He walked them to the barn on the left side of the house. They all looked at him and said, "This your hide out sure they're gonna find you" they laughed.

"Y'all laugh now."

They walked in and he pulled the storm shelter door opened and they walked in. They all looked around in amazement, and then they walked through the tunnel not saying a word. They came to the brick door and he asked them to help him open it. They pushed it open and entered the cellar, his hideout. They lights and TV was still on for a minute he stood there and thought about Tasha that was the last place they made love. He grabbed his keys off the top of the TV and led them to the stairs. Arod cut the lights off. When they all got up to the kitchen the house was very dark. Gino, asked him who "crib this was?"

As he lead them to the same window Tasha and Blue came through he said "mine."

He climbed through the window and walked to the right side of the house. He stopped and told Gino to close the window back. When they got to the front yard they saw all the cars to pick from. He went to Blue; Lexus took the tracker from under the distributing cap.

"Damn that bitch got all this on camera call her and tell her to erase the shit right now."

Nigerz called and told her but she declined. When he told him they jumped in the Lexus backed out remove the chain, drove around the curb and turned right down the driveway. He slammed on brakes jumped out the car. They were right behind him running in the house. When they got to the room she was on the phone. He walked up behind her and slapped her out the chair; she was still holding the phone.

"He just slapped me Nikko."

She handed him the phone and he yanked it from her.

"I don't need no reporter with me. I run shit the way I run shit you better tell this bitch who's in control or I'll send her ass back to Cuba in a box."

She got off the floor fixed her brown shirt, lined it with her slacks and sat back in the chair.

"Ravenion I don't know what you're doing up there, I'm letting you know I don't like it. She told me you ordered everybody to throw the phones away. I know you like the movie Scarface don't end up like Tony Montana!"

"Who in the hell you think you talking to? As long as I send you 50 million every week you don't worry about what I'm doing or how I'm doing it. I'll never let you slip and let the feds come in and bust the whole clique because they got us on the phone or camera. This is my last time explaining myself to you. If you ever threaten me again I'll kill you, you know I don't bullshit, and get this untained bitch before I kill her."

He handed her the phone and she begged for him to send for her. She handed him back the phone.

"I told her to do whatever you say. If you tell her to walk back to Cuba she better get to walking. I apologize for trying you because I know you're gonna handle business. Just understand the Hector situation. I lost out on 15 million. This phone is being canceled. But the camera must stay for your safety. What she got will be erased, if she starts cajoling you kill her because she's trying to get some get back for you slapping her. Tell her if she dreams a cricket thought. I'll kill her whole family."

He hung up and repeated what Nikko said. She looked him straight in the eyes and smiled. "So you're the one Gloria talked about. She never said a name she just said she's in training because that's what her man wanted."

She also told him she seen tears in Nikko eyes when he saw the two of them together. Also that she heard Nikko joke about him saying he was soft. His upsetness turned to a smile and she stood and bowed her head and apologized. She went about erasing the tape showing him so he wouldn't second guess her. Then he asked her can she trace a call. She nodded yes. He called Smokey when the phone started ringing she punched in the tracer.

"Hello."

"Smokey I never meant for us to become enemies. I've always showed the up most respect to your ever decision. I always thought that you had the smarts of a supreme leader. Man you can't see that Sonya is using you. She's in it for the money. She's gonna be the fall for everything you've built. You never crossed the man that made you. Not to a no good ass bitch. She's a federal agent I'm telling you this because I have mad love and respect for you. You've allowed her to in flick a war between us that you don't have a chance in the world of winning. The same way I found you and your clique. I can always find one bigger and better. But I don't want to war with you. It's all about getting money. Now y'all have took life from me, my child's mother, her family, my son and my money. I can't bring the middle family back but my money and my son I won't back!"

"This war shit we're in is too far, to call truths. It hurts me to my heart to war with you because we're two of the same kinda niggas, Sonya if she's the feds it really don't matter. I'ma die anyway, ah G life is what I choose and a G is the way I'll fly. In this life we live by any means the same way you believe I have your son, is the same way I believe you got my money. I believe where ever you at Cindy's at. She don't have the nerves to up and leave without being coached. I wish it could be a fair exchange. But I don't have your son. I tote Glocks and sell drugs. I never been a kidnapper. I'm sorry for your lost but in life we die, so there's no pity for the living or the dead. Get me my money and I'll help you find your child and make sure he's alive and well and that's how we'll make amends." He hung up.

"Poco phone Nikko and tell him I need an explosive expert over here in the next 24 hours and you send him or her to the address, Gino you Alex and four other men go strip the truck. Nigerz you and Arod take these keys and go get that maroon Suzuki SUV out of my yard. Snatch the wires from under the distributing cap. Load the Benz and the SUV up with the dope and we'll ride like that tomorrow. Poco stated that she had a red 4runner on the side of the house. He nodded and said, "Good we'll use your car to go shopping in, in the morning. After today the four of us will ride in Tony presidential car. It's a black Benz bullet proof. I don't know how Tony cocked it but I know it's safe."

He walked out to his old room straight along the wall from his grandmother room by the bathroom. Laid on his bed smiling Poco came to the door and told him that she was really sorry and she'll never disrespect his mind. She heard how he killed in the corn field.

He looked at her and said cool. He got up and walked in the T-shaped hallway to the kitchen. He was surprise to see the Cuban had made a home out the house. The kitchen was clean and had food in it. The fridge was full of meat, cheese, beer and so on. The cabinet was full of bread, can goods, chips and sweets. He opened the freezer and saw all kinda meat. Now all they needed was a cook. He wasn't always gonna be there or eat there. So he grabbed a big bag of lays cheddar cheese chips and walked back into his room. The room still had the six drawer white dresser with the big mirror on top of it. Still had his batman blanket and batman pillow case. Then he remembered the big hole in the closet that lead to his grandmother room. He crawled through it, moving the dresses and coat real slow. Cracked the door and spied on her. She wasn't doing nothing to turn her back. He closed the door and locked it, turned the lights off and cuddled into bed.

"Juan! Juan!"

When he looked up he saw a man he never seen before standing in front of him. The man was old, had on a white suit. Brown complexion and gray hair. He just looked at the man.

"Don't be scared my son, I remember you were always brave as a child. Oh how I wish I never left you. Your grandmamma is upset with you, but she sends her love."

"Grandpa!"

"Yeah you remember me now listen danger is coming your way real soon. The one you feel is out to hurt you is the one that will save your life and give you life. Remember there's no greater love then this one lay down his life for a friend."

"Grandpa! Wait! Wait! Is my son with you?"

"No he's with you."

He slept on until he heard a knock on the door.

"Yeah! Yeah!"

"Man lets get to the bacon."

"Gino y'all go to the store and get 3000 thousand zero bags a toothbrush and some toothpaste."

He thought about his son while he just laid there then he remembered that he had clothes over Tony house. So he got up got Poco keys, jumped in her 4runner and went to the big house when he looked at his watch it was 10:35 am. He ran upstairs got a couple pair of slacks, a couple of black nylon boxers, two black jackets, two belts, some socks and a pair of black gators. Then he ran to the bathroom and got a rag, a towel, a toothbrush, toothpaste and Speed Stick deodorant. He ran to Tony's room and hit the wall, got 50 grand out and hit the steps; he wanted to get out the house. Knowing Sonya knew about the downstairs and she'll pop up anytime. So he locked the door, jumped back in the 4runner pulled off and raced back to the house. When he walked in he got into the shower and showered for about 30 minutes brushed his teeth, brushed his hair and got dressed. When he opened the door Poco was standing there in a black robe with her hair hanging long. She untied the robe and it flew open. Her body spoke in a language of its on. He shook it off and walked passed her. The guy's finally got back with the sack. He was standing on the porch; he noticed all of them had changed clothes. Hey all worse black slacks and had a black jacket with black dress shoes. Arod had on a blue shirt Alex had a white one, Gino had on a black one, Nigerz had on a black one, also, when they came up. He sent them to go get two kilos a piece. He took the brown paper sack and took it to the dining room. He sat at the big pine wood four glass table. He sat the bag and began opening the zero bags. He jumped up and got 5 spoons and sat back down started back opening the sacks. When they came back they sat two in front of him and Alex and Gino got Arod and Nigerz got the rest. Gino pulled out a hunting knife and opened them. Poco came in with five mask and said, "Y'all dummies couldn't have gotten addicted to this shit always wear a mask hold up let me get y'all some gloves."

She had on a mask with gloves she returned from her room with the latex blue gloves. She still had on her robe he nodded and she left. They went to bagging the dope by the spoon full.

These are 25$ sacks quarter sack we're putting these in the project and clubs."

They sat for hours bagging up dope then he sent Poco to get some saran wrap. They were still bagging when she came back. He told her to go sit at the round table and weigh up the Dro and wrap it in 1 gram balls. She was mad but couldn't let it show. They put all the meth in brown paper bags and went to the table with here. She was exhausted when they finished balling up 50 pounds. Night fall grew near Poco was laying down when the red light on the camera started flashing. She ran in the kitchen where they were sitting drinking. He had a pack of Sonny D orange juice, turning it up laughing.

"We got problems."

When they went to look at the camera he just smiled it was Sonya looking around by herself. It was so funny because she was dressed in all black like a cat burglar. Then she pulled out her lock lit and went in the house. She went inside the cellar looked around and smelled the sheets, she went back up to the kitchen and looked around the whole house. She went in Tony room hit the wall and said something.

Once again he found himself thinking about sex or was he missing her.

She got some paper off the message pad on the wall by the phone and wrote something on it. He went back to the cellar and laid it on his pillow and kissed it, then left.

Everybody turned and looked at him then Poco said, "I don't see her as your enemy. She's in love with you."

He smiled and told Gino to go get the note and told everybody else to get some rest because they had a long day ahead of them. When Gino came back and handed him the letter he read it out loud.

"My love for you goes deeper than the ocean. I've checked around for your son and I haven't seen any sign of him. But I do know they're planning to kill you. I also know you're still trying to convince them that I'm an agent I wish you'll stop that, that's my only way of protecting you. I still dream of us and a family. When all this is over you'll see money ain't everything to me only security. I long to make love to you. I'm still at the house love always your girl."

Nobody said nothing then Alex spoke, "I agree with Poco she's in love with you. Only time will tell though."

"Okay tomorrow this is how things is going down; one car will carry the Dro and one will carry the meth. Fill the truck with the meth, the SUV with the Dro, and Alex will ride in the Lexus. Projects Perry Holmes, Capital Holmes, Grade Holmes, Bon Holmes, Hollywood Court, Simpson Valley, Scottsdale, Bankhead Court and Edgewood. The Bounce, 555, Body Tap, Magic City, ½ Jazzy T's and whatever night club y'all think is jumping. Oh I forgot, Boatrock and the Pink Lounge on Fulton Industrial. Everything will be in 5 thousand dollars bombs. The Ex will be in the same clubs. But we're gonna hit the college also Georgia Tech, Georgia, Georgia State and whatever else we can find. We're gonna get a booth in the five point Flea Market and Candler Road Flea Market. I wanted to pass the pill out tonight but I'm sleepy. Now if y'all want to hit the club tonight we'll go. Don't forget we got to buy our phones and hit everybody else."

They wanted to hit the club. So they all showered got dressed in Versace, got in the Lexus with 100 thousand pills and Dro. They hit the 559 first. Girls were walking all around in G-string. They all sat at different tables and pulled out big stacks and sat the money on the table. Girls came running to them. They ordered drinks and enjoyed themselves with lap dances. Ravenion had Peaches a find red-bone dancing for him. He asked her to get him in VIP and bring the owner. They walked and paid 100$ and she gave him his private dance he showed her the pills and asked her to work for him, showed her 10 grand and told her 5 grand up top and the other 5 when she call him. He gave her Poco cell and told her to contact Poco. When the owner came in he showed him the pills and the Dro and told him 60/40 the owner jumped on it. He gave him Poco number. He told him to watch Peach back. They all walked to the Lexus and he gave them 30 thousands worth of dope and pills. Then Big Nod told him to leave everything and he'll call him in 5 days. Nod was known around Atlanta. He was a big nigga 6/5 320 pound heavy in the game. Ravenion looked him up and down and said alright Nod I don't play about this money. I haven't heard nothing foul about you but if something go wrong you'll be 100 grand in the whole." The big black fat nigga just looked at him and smiled.

"Juan you're crazy I know you're about business boy. I see you've came up hard and I want to be apart of it because this will make my club jump harder."

He only wanted to fuck with clubs people knew him at. He looked at his men and said, "Let's start over."

They went back this time got 200 thousand and hit the Body Tap every club they went to that night was down with it he gave the same speech and same deal. They stayed at Magic City until 4:30 because all the dope they bagged up was distributed.

When they got back they were high and drunk. Poco was at the door waiting on them. Some of the men were in the house sleep while some were walking guard. Alex then went and laid in Poco room on the king size bed and fell asleep. Alex and Nigerz were on the bed and Arod and Gino were on the floor. He looked at Poco she looked at him and smile. He kissed her and they walked to his room she closed the door. They laid in the bed, she told him that tonight she wanted to get to know his mental. So they laid under each other, she needed the comfort because she never felt free comfort or real comfort. She didn't have a boyfriend in Cuba because they were always working. Now she knew why Gloria fell for him because he was gentle and soft. She melted into his caress and fell asleep.

When they got up that afternoon everybody was waiting by the door when it opened she smiled and laughed.

Alex told him they had all chipped in and bagged up the dope. He told him that the men wanted to go out and have a good time. He told them okay but they'll have to go in groups one night at a time. They showered together and he dressed in black slacks again. They left the first apartment they got to was Hollywood Court. They drove around a couple of time then they saw a brown skin fat girl with gold in her hair and white pants and shirt. He liked how she appeared she was standing between a green box Chevy with 20 inch rims on it. They pulled up and parked beside her. He was in the passenger seat he rolled his window down and asked her, her name.

"Tabatha" she responded.

"Is this your car?"

"Yes."

He looked at Alex and watched Gino and Arod pull up and get out with their hands opening their jackets. They showed her their Glocks 40s. They closed their jackets and told her to get in the drivers seat. All four of them got in the Chevy. He told them to go get that, Arod got out he told her to stay calm. When Arod jumped in the back seat with the meth her hands went to shaking. She looked at them through the rearview. He watched her she didn't want to panic. So him and Alex got back in the Lexus and backed out then the Chevy backed out she drove out the apartment and took a left. She drove calmly to the Oakland City train station. Then parked, they pulled up beside her so they could talk face to face. He rolled down his window and just stared. She rolled hers down after a minute or two.

"Tab, how are you holding up so far?"

She was sweating and about to cry. But a tear didn't drop. She was brave. And that's what he was looking for.

"Fine! Fine!" She took in a deep breath closed her eyes and relaxed. "What's up?"

"Tab get in the car let me explain to you what just took place. Gino will drive your car back to the apartment."

She got out the car and got in his back seat by the driver side window she looked at Alex looking at her in the rearview then Nigerz got in the car on the passenger side. This was confusing her because they allowed her to sit by the door. One thing she knew was she had to be brave to stay alive. That meant do whatever they say. To her surprise nobody said nothing they just rode back to the apartment. They parked and all got out. Everybody was looking at them but didn't say nothing. She stayed in the down stair apartment A-R. She let them into the 3 bedroom apartment without screaming or trying to run. They smiled because she was living an okay life. She has a 3 piece velvet furniture set, a Sony entertainment system, and two python snakes in different tank. And she has wall to wall carpet and gold armoire; end table sitting in the middle of the living room, a 60 inch screen TV in the middle of the floor.

He cut the TV on and turned it on B.E.T videos. Biggie Small *"You're Nobody to Somebody Kill You"* video was on. So he turned it up. He sent Nigerz in the kitchen to see was it clear Arod and Gino upstairs. He pulled out a chrome 45 and pointed it at her and told her to get undressed.

She was holding it together until then tears started dropping and she started crying out, "Please don't rape me."

"Just undress like he said," Nigerz said as he returned from the kitchen. He pulled his knife out a Rambo blade and smiled at her.

She stood and undressed herself all four of them were looking confused.

"Hand me the bag Arod."

He handed him the bag. "Upstairs Tab"

She walked passed them very slow moaning under her breath, about to fall because her knees was going weak. When she walked passed him he put the gun in her back and followed her up the stairs to the last room on the right. The room was cool with a nice breeze. It had wall to wall carpet a full poster queen size bed two night stands on both side of the bed. A vanity mirror on the Chester drawer and a sitting chair in front of it.

She stood on the side of the bed.

"Lie down on the bed Tab and relax yourself."

She laid down and prayed with her eyes open. She started to think if he was gonna rape me he'll been done it by now" so she relaxed herself until he had started to rub his hand around her right nipple as he talked to her.

"Tab you're cool as hell I thought you was gonna crack but you didn't. You see this is what I want you to do, if a nigga try to jack you stay calm because we'll get everything back. How much do you push?"

"Two ounce of hard"

"How long do it take you to push them?"

"In a day or two."

"Well I'm giving you 5 thousand dollars' worth of meth. Sell it like powder, quarter sacks. Just to see how it sell over here. Also how do weed sell over here?"

"It sell good." She had a smile on her face.

"Do you think you can handle meth and Dro?"

"Yes."

He called Arod and told him to go get the Dro. He continued rubbing her nipple to see if she was freaky and easy to fuck. Basically to see how she'll react under pressure. Most women would try to sell their self once they see gain and know they're out of danger. But she held up good and still is holding up with him playing with her nipples.

They walked up the steps just to see what he was doing when they walked in and seen him rubbing her nipple they didn't know what to think.

"A female nipple is her comfort zone it tells her she not in harm it gives her strength. Remember that, see how comfortable she is?"

"Tab I want 3,500 a piece I don't care how you sell it just get my money. If you run I'll find you, if you get any beef them Cubans will handle your beef. That's Alex Arod Nigerz and Gino. Here's the number to call when you're out. Just let whoever answer the phone know you're out and your apartment another thing have you ever heard of ex pills before?

"Yes they sell 'em in clubs my sister go to Clark, she be asking me to get 'em for them 25$ a pill. Student pay 35$ for 'em."

"Good tell your sister to be here tomorrow."

He walked out and they left.

Alex didn't say nothing as they rode across Atlanta finding soldier mostly female. When they got to Bon Holmes it was so big they had to get a female and a boy to serve the top and the bottom. Jon was 16 running cars so he gave the kid work. Told him to meet him at the gas station around one o'clock after he dropped off all the meth. He went and got their cell phone walkie talkie and went back to the house and got the double stacks of ex pills. Trying to catch some more clubs before they opened, 731, Silver Fox, Blue Flame, Gentlemen Club, Favors Nikki's and Club Eshilum. He dropped off 10 thousand pills at all the night club and gave them the same deal 60/40 as he made his stops he told them about the meth and the Dro. He knew he had to give just to get, and in the long run he'll end up on top because all the dope was free.

Everybody would soon know Ravenion. It wasn't a night spot that he didn't hit. He kept going back and forth delivering the ex-pills. He didn't won't to make everything to fast. They gave out their cell number; everything was on track just like he had planned. He never got out the car while it was being reloaded. He went to the colleges throughout Atlanta with the meth and ex, finding whites and blacks struggling with their tuition. Before he turned in he stopped at clubs just to see how things were going. His dreams were coming to life. The king of Atlanta, pretty soon it will be the king of the south. When they returned home after a day event he went in to check on Poco because he haven't too much seen her. They were coming and going, night will be days and days will be nights. When he walked in he saw Gloria sitting on the bed. When she seen him she hopped up hugged and kissed him.

"Everything has been done I tried to weave out the good people from the gang. I'm set to leave in the morning. Here's your kill switch whenever you want to blow 'em up hit this button."

It was a car alarm made out of a kill switch for the bomb she had planted on the apartments.

She whispered in his ear that she was on her period."

He laughed it off because sex wasn't on his mind no way. She was wearing a blue telephone suit, with some black boot. She explained that she went in every apartment checking telephone jack and looking for his son. None of the gang apartment had a baby in them. "Oh I forgot hit this button the red light is gonna blink 8 times, letting you know all eight apartment building has been blown up."

With no hesitation he hit the button and threw the remote on the bed and walked in his room. He undressed and took a shower. She joined him and sucked him off. She invited him to have anal sex. But he wasn't with it, his mind was on passing that dope out. They jumped in the bed playing with each other then she cuddled under him. When he awoke the next morning she was gone. No note no nothing. He got dressed in some blue slacks, a blue shirt, no jacket and then some gators. When he finished washing his face and brushing his teeth he walked in the kitchen it was noon they were bagging up dope with their phones on the table. Alex gave the day's report that everybody was set up in all 9 states. Everything was running smooth, he explained he checked all the traps in Atlanta, every-thing was smooth. He passed the Dro out to everyone he had promised. All they had to do now was travel to the small town.

Since everybody knew about the dope they was selling it was the matter of beating everyone out." He asked about their product and they explained they hit the lab early that morning around 4 am they whipped up 10 kilos and had a buyer for all 10 at 35 grand a piece Nigerz was gonna meet him behind city hall. He expressed it could be a set up, but they was willing to shoot it out if it was. He told them that he was down with whatever. Gino told him that the 50 caliber was in the Suzuki and it was Arod deal. Poco came in with five Wendy's bags. They departed went to the porch and ate, he looked over the land, the guard took turn and ate. He saw the streets were still the same no cars riding up or down the street. No cars had a reason to come this far anyway

CHAPTER 19
Street Talk

Days went well they travel to Athens, Savannah, Valdosta, Hall County, Alto, Albany, Cordele they traveled the whole state, finding people and dropping off dope. Everybody was well off reporting to Alex, every day they were robbing hospital along the way. They rode in the Suzuki and the Yukon, while he rode in the presidential behind them with Alex. Watching their backs while they robbed being the getaway driver. He wanted them to know he was down with them no matter what. They stayed in top name hotels; Hilton, Trump Plaza, Marriot and Comfort Inn. He phoned Poco and gave her every address and number and told her to go drop off and pick up. Take some men and tell 'em to help her bag and protect her, kill anybody that talked crazy. Their days were taken by the highway dropping kilos to other Cuban and workers they knew in state up north. He didn't want to put kilos in everybody hands in Atlanta because he needed an army, just in case Smokey caught him slipping. Sonya called him and told him they missed Smokey and Leo. But they took down over a hundred of them. She told him to watch out while he was on the road because they was collecting and recruiting to rebuild. They paths never crossed. After riding for a month they returned back to the house. Poco had an account of every state. She reported that there was no problem in any state and that she had reported to Nikko the amount and what they had left. He looked at her and asked her why didn't he get that amount first. She dropped her head and thought quickly.

"I didn't want to have such a long conversation over the phone. I gave him all the information over the computer." She showed him the report, it read: TX 20 million, TN 25 million, GA 50 million, FL 80 million, AL 15 million, MS 10 million, LA 25 million, KY 20 million, SC 20 million and NC 15 million total of 280 million ready to be shipped ex count 1 million dro count 500,000 pounds meth count 250,000. At the end of the report was a little note that read,

"Nikko I'm doing the best that I can. But I'm afraid of Ravenion. He don't trust me and I don't know how to gain it. I tried to share my body with him but he's colder than ice. No emotion. I heard in the streets that, that gang was planning to war with him so send more men for his safety."

He turned and kissed her on the forehead and told her not to worry about him, he's well protected. He wanted to know was this report weekly or monthly? She replied weekly. He figured about 1.2 billion has been made since they started.

CHAPTER 20
Forgiveness

Smokey was pacing his floor in his suite in the Trump Plaza trying to figure out Juan next move because the kid was making moves. He wondered where he was hiding at. He noticed Sonya wasn't coming around that much and she suddenly has become very secretive. Maybe she was the Feds. If she was he couldn't begin to explain how he allowed her to make him cross a real G, he thought back on everything. When Tasha was in the hospital how she just popped up how she told him Sandy was the Feds. How she knew so much about the Cuban and how she knew them Cuban had something to do with the apartment blowing up. How she knew Cindy had the money. How she knew he got locked up. That bitch knew too much.

Just as he was thinking a knock came to the door. It was Leo. When he came in he dropped his head and said, "We got trouble Chris got locked up for 5 bricks he's telling every-thing to cut a deal. Qwen the police I copped showed me a picture of Sonya. Her name is Sandra Anderson she's a federal agent everything Juan was telling us was true. Now we're in an all-out war with him because he thinks we got his son."

Smokey picked up his phone and called him. Its 1:15 in the morning his phone just rang. He got dressed and told Leo,

"He got a girl in Hollywood court. Let's go over there."

They got into a black 1500 truck and drove to Tab apartment. When they knocked on the door no one answered but they saw movement through the window. They took their Glocks 9 out and kicked in the door she was being robbed. She was taped lying on the floor, they started shooting and the three robbers returned fire and started running out the back door. Leo ran to the window, using it for cover and started shooting out it. He hit two of them while the other one dropped the bag and ran. Smokey held Siren, so he grabbed the bag from the sidewalk ran back in the apartment throw the money under the sofa, ran and jumped in the 1500.

"Damn he's gonna think we had something to do with that because we left the money, he's gonna think that we're trying to run him off or something. Leo to be honest with you, I don't want to war with him. We got to leave man and start over. Damn I can't kill Sonya, cause they got too much on us. We'll be on the American Most Wanted. I don't want to kill him because he kept it real. We're gonna take these 4 million and leave. What you say about that?"

"No we ain't leaving, we're gonna make amends and get things back the way it was. We can beat Sonya, all we got to do is fake our death."

Smokey phoned him again this time he picked up.

"Yeah!"

"You were right about everything Sonya name is Sandra Anderson and she's the Feds. I don't have your son and didn't have nothing to do with his disappearance. I want to make amends, I went to your girl Tab house she was being robbed ducked taped on the floor we stopped it killed two but one got away. I threw the money under the sofa we need to meet I'm staying at the Trump Plaza 20th floor room 424.

He hung up and drove to the Plaza. When they got there the Feds was just pulling up. He jumped out the truck and ran to the elevator. There was no way in the hell they was gonna get his money. It was like fate because the elevator went straight to the 20th floor. He ran in the room grab the two army duffle bag from the master closet. Closed the door and took the stairs with the bags on his shoulder. He threw the bags a head each flight and jumped the steps. When he opened the stairwell door he saw them taking position. He called the bellboy that was walking past the door and told him to take the bags to the black 1500. He knew he could make the straight away, but he waited on the bellboy to return.

He looked at Slim's shape wondering could he fit Slim's clothes. Being that he was black, a grand could easily get that uniform. So he called him back, when the two of them were in the stairwell, he pulled out the gold money clip with nothing but hundreds in it. He told him he needs his uniform, the bellboy told him he need three grand because he'll get in trouble too. He didn't want to tell him they keep an extra suit in their locker. He counted the money and gave it to him they switched clothes and he walked out. The bellboy told him to grab a buggy and walk out. Everything went as plan the Feds was on the outside in black suit waiting by the door. As he sat the buggy outside by the door he seen the Benz pull up he stopped and flagged it down. When the window rolled down he saw Juan face to face. He dropped his head.

"The Feds is inside the building now. Let your driver walk in the hotel I'll drive the Benz to the truck you come back and get him and I'll follow behind y'all."

Alex got out and walked in. Smokey drove the Benz passed the truck and blew the horn and went out the parking lot. He parked the car on the side of the road up from the hotel and jumped out Ravenion switched seats and pulled in front of him. He turned around in an open parking lot and went back to the hotel. He seen Sonya, at the door asking people have they seen this man. Alex shook his head and walked to the car. They passed the truck and the truck followed him to his grandmother house.

When they came down the driveway the guards had AKs pointed at the cars. He rolled down the window and said, "It's me."

But the guard still approached the car opening the doors and the trunk, the last guard left standing in front of the Benz moved. They checked the truck, Smokey still holding both of the bags to his shoulders walked in amazement when they walked in the house Smokey asked, "Boy what you got going on in here? You were right I didn't want to war with you."

They laughed and walked in Poco room, she was on the phone.

"Poco who are you talking to?"

"Tab she want to relocate or you to get her some guards to protect her. He looked at Smokey and told him to order two of his men to go stay with her.

"If they put a hand on her I'll kill 'em!"

He called Ghost and Yum and instructed them and hung up.

"They're on the way now."

Tell her she got two bodyguards coming she'll have to give them 5 hundred a week I need her to check out Fairburn Village. I want her to put 10 pounds with whoever."

Before he could finish Smokey told him to put 'em in Candyman's hand apartment 4-B. Poco relayed the message and hung up.

"We got a problem the club owner of Rolex has decline to give us our pay and is trying to keep a half of million dollars worth of Dro and a half million worth of Ex what do you want me to tell them?"

"We're on our way. Dave County right?"

"Right!"

"Alex go load the Suzuki get Gino, Nigerz and Arod and tell 'em we got a problem."

"Smokey if I put you in California do you think you can handle 20 million with of Dro, Ex and Meth?"

"I took care of the heroin and cain so you know I owe you my life so it's tooken care of."

"I'm gonna set you up in Crenshaw you'll have to mingle in with Crips you'll leave from FL. Leave your money here and when you make all the money take your 4 out of it and send back 16 million. You'll have more than 20 million with of dope. So you'll be straight. It will be a guy name Neill Hatton at the Los Angeles Airport that you'll take the money to. He'll know what to do."

"Poco have you set up the rest of the airport like Nikko commanded you to?"

"Yes. And I spoke with Nina and she understands that 70/30 cut with everything your 30 percent is being transferred to your account here in the state."

He kissed her and told her he'll be back in three days when they got in the SUV, Alex told him that they needed more Meth and it would be best to leave in the morning. Him, Smokey and Leo went back in the house. He knew he had to sleep with her to keep her out of their business. Smokey wanted to talk. But he told him the past is the past and if they want anything to smoke or eat. The Dro was in the freezer of the refrigerator; and the food is where it always is in every kitchen. He told them to sleep in the middle room.

When he turned around she was in the doorway looking. He walked up to her and she asked what was he still doing here and where was Alex them going? He kissed her and took her in his arm, he kicked the door close. Put her on the bed and they shared four play. He know he had to put all he had in her to ease her mind. So he made love to her, licking and sucking her toes, hitting her from behind pulling her hair. While she moaned,

"Ravenion yes! Ravenion more... more."

He pulled out of her and explored her hottest love which had never been explored before. She screamed, he was pushing hard and deep. She screamed,

"I got to use the bathroom."

She ran and sat on the toilet. She didn't want to come straight out; she wiped herself and looked at herself in the mirror. She was confused she didn't know rather to be happy or frighten. Her leg was weak so she went back to the sink to clean the ring. She wanted to relieve some of his tension. She went back and laid the warm rag on his head.

"Ravenion why are you fucking? Make love to me like at first. Never have a man enter my anal. Take your time."

She kissed him to reunite the mood this time he made mad passionate love to her.

She slept while he got up and shower dressed and left. He drove to KFC and got some chicken boxes. Smokey took over the wheel hit 95 south and drove the whole way to South Beach. They discussed the plan. Just going in and shooting up the whole club was Smokey and Leo idea. Shooting up the club wouldn't get the money. So he told them to come up with another plan. So they all stated what they would do.

In the end the plan was to kill him. But he had another plan when they got there. They phoned Vince he gave them Ricky Brown home address and the club address. He told 'em Brown wouldn't expect nobody to know where he live because he change cars three times and drive in a circle two times. Smokey drove to Biscayne Blvd. to Club Rolex, when they parked they watched the security and the surrounding of the club. It had alot of people inside and a long line outside. So he called Vince again and told 'em they were out there. They spotted him and walked up to him.

Once in he took them to his VIP booth, the club was really nice. It had alot of important people there about 50 dancers on the table and walking the floor. Vince had four females working the VIP booth. He told them to come back later he had business. He told them what was up and pointed Ricky out.

Ricky was an ex-football player for the Miami Dolphins, defensive end. So he was a pretty big brother wearing alot of jewelry, a red Coogi and fitted cap. He stood at the bar with two more big muscular blacks with bald heads wearing black shades. You could see their gun holsters hanging from their shoulders through the opening of their black jackets.

"Call him and tell him we're ready to discuss business."

He made the call and told 'em they was in the booth waiting. Being a very important man, it wasn't that easy for him to walk straight to the booth. People were stopping him. But he made his way to the booth. When he walked in he went to talking,

"I hope y'all boys are enjoying y'all self" and grinned.

"Mr. Brown, I'm hoping we can come to an agreement without many lives being tooken. Just return the money and product and I'll be on my way back to Atlanta."

"Look here I don't know who you think you are. But I'm Ricky Brown. I know for fact that you made over 15, million last month; .collecting from the clubs and colleges. I don't think you know the past in this situation. I'll never let a weak ass Atlanta boy come to Miami and run shit. If anything I will get a bigger cut, I want half of everything you bring to Miami and I'll make sure everything goes right with the product and money shipping. I'm gonna give you some time to think about this because it sound sweet to me. You can't beat it, the girls is on the house."

He left and sent eight girls in ready to serve them. They sat there for a minute as the girls dance. He politely stood and walked out.

When they got in the SUV, nobody said anything. He turned the OnStar on and pressed 251 Hillard Ave. and they drove off. Vince followed behind them in a red Mazda 6. When they arrived they saw a tall fence around the yard. Vince got out and deactivated the alarm system. In seconds the gate opened. They drove up the circle driveway onto the grass, to the side of the house into the backyard. Vince picked the lock and the 8 of them searched the downstairs of the house and found nothing.

As they walked up the stairs they heard a crack in the middle of the platform of the steps. They all looked at each other thinking the same thing,

"Ain't no way in the hell these stairs suppose to crack like this."

Vince searched for an opening of the carpet and it was at the edge of the front door. He pulled it back and found the opening of the wood. They stood 3 down and 4 up looking in all directions with pistol pointed. So no one would surprise them. When he opened them they found two safes, they pulled them up and sat them on the kitchen table.

He and Vince sat in the kitchen while the others searched the upstairs for anybody sleeping. They brought his wife and two kids in the kitchen. While they were opening the safes. Gino ducked taped her to the chair while the little boy looked. Alex carried the infant in his arms. He made Alex put the infant in the microwave and told Arod to put the boy in the oven. The woman begged them not to harm her children. But he only smiled.

"Your husband shouldn't took this to this level, understand I went to him like a man asking for my money and dope 1.5 million has cost him his whole family. What time is he expected in?"

"6!," she cried out. "Listen! Listen! I know that it's more than a million in them safes. Take everything! He also have two safes in the bedroom. Behind the mirror on the base wall and behind the mirror on the back wall. The code to them is "Badcall" the black one and the silver one is 9-9-2-9. There's money in my mattress; unzip the mattress. There's some large black trash bags in that cabinet by the stove. There I've told you everything please don't hurt my children. Get them out that microwave and stove."

"I don't think you get it ma'am but your husband asked for this I got to do this for Atlanta. Every lost soul that went down in that Miami Error is fix 'en to rest in peace because a message got to be sent out to whoever else try to buck on Atlanta."

Her eyes filled with tears, and then she said, "Okay! Okay! Okay! I'll withdraw all the money from the bank we're worth 10 million."

"Ma'am it's not about the money it's about respect."

Nigerz and Leo came down the steps dragging 4 big glad bags of money. He told Leo to take 40 grand out for their trip.

"Okay! Okay! I have condoms in my drawer the first dresser you come to in the top drawer. I'll shave and give y'all all the hair I swear! I'll even rush in y'all face. Please spare me and my kids."

Vince opened the safe he would've been opened it but he was listening to a desperate woman plea for her kids. They all felt bad because he was going too far by putting these kids in an oven and microwave. The kids had nothing to do with this. They all looked at him with fear because the point was proven you can't escape wrong. They all would've gotten the money and left while it was still dark. He's putting all of them at risk. But he had a point to prove.

The safe carried alot more money, they cleaned all the safes then Vince finally breaking said, "We've got more than enough let's go."

He replied, "Ms. Brown sure you're a very fair lady even beautiful golden skin pretty brown eyes. But we're not rapist and I respect your plea for your kids. But I still haven't found my drugs!"

She started crying even harder because she didn't even know Ricky was a drug dealer. Given all that she could think of. She yelled out, "Lord it is written whatever we ask for in your son name you'll give it. In Jesus name please don't let them kill me and my kids. Move on their heart Lord. Let them know I don't know nothing about none of this. Jesus please spare me and my kids."

That prayer touched everybody heart but his, they all wanted to go. Smokey stated, "Man just leave them like they are he'll come home and find them like this. I'm sure she's gonna let him have it."

"Man don't let one prayer make you soft. Ms. Brown I've been a praying man my whole life one thing I learned God comes when he wants. To make your husband understand that I mean business your kids will die before his eyes. I can blindfold you if you like."

"No I want to be able to talk to him I want him to see pain I want him to see what he's done to me and his kids. From here on out I won't beg or cry I want him to know I gave him the best of me."

She held her breath; he sat in a chair until they heard his car pull up. He took out his Glock while the rest of them formed a half circle around him. They heard him scream,

"Hell naw them sonofabitches been in my house. Jackie! Jackie!" he called out.

"I'm in the kitchen tied up."

They ran in the kitchen and stopped there were eight guns pointed at them.

"Drop y'all weapons or I'll plug her right now."

They looked at him. He ordered them to drop their weapon and he dropped his. They all had chrome revolvers.

"Ricky this man said that you took drugs from him. He got all the money but he's not pleased. He said it's a point he has to prove why are you selling drug? You don't give a got damn about us. Do you know where Lil' Ricky is? He's in that got damn stove. Do you know where Lakeisha is? In that got dame microwave. Look what you have done. You've murdered your kids over 1.5 million dollars. What in the hell do you have to say for yourself?"

"My kids are dead?"

"Yes your kids are dead."

Tears fell down his eyes, his guards looked at him and dropped their heads.

"This man don't even fear God Ricky. Ricky you've fucked over the wrong man. Where is his drugs at Ricky?"

"Why did you bring my family in this? You didn't have to kill my kids. I got your drugs man. You should've handled this at the club. This is street business."

"Give this got damn man his drugs."

"It's at the club. I promise you all of it is at the club."

He pointed at Gino and Arod and told them to escort him to the club and get the dope. They left his guard didn't say much, but,

"Spare us we told him he was fucking with the wrong crew. We've heard about y'all throughout the South."

His phone rang and it was Poco letting him know that the shipment has arrived and she was calling up everybody to pick up. He kissed at her through the phone and told her she was a big help. She wanted to take Gloria spot, she let him know that. He just laughed and told her how does she know she already haven't. He hung up and smiled.

They came back 45 minute later with the dope.

"It's all counted for" Arod told him.

"Now Ricky I'm not done with you."

He pointed at Alex and told him to open the microwave. When he opened it the baby started crying. Then he pointed at the oven and he opened it. Lil' Ricky got out looked at his dad and started crying.

"Now which one of these lil' motherfucker you value the most?"

Everybody looked at him.

"I already told her both of these kids are dying."

"Please! Please! Mr., don't kill 'em, I gave you everything. Kill him don't kill my kids. Please you can take us with you and I'll work for you, I'll sell pussy I'll do whatever just let us live."

"Vince tell your boss to kill me."

"Killing you is not good enough Ricky. What's that shit you said in the club, oh yeah didn't he send us 8 girl saying enjoy y'all selves? Well enjoy this motherfucker put tha little bitch in there for three minutes."

Alex closed the door and started it up for three minutes. They yelled, "No! No! No! Why are you doing this?"

Smokey looked at him with all the fear in the world.

"This nigga mean business," he thought to himself.

He wanted everybody in the room to know he didn't give a fuck. God took his son. It didn't matter no more.

"Are you enjoying yourself Ricky are you enjoying the smell of your flesh-n-blood burning you son of a bitch? Don't you drop your head motherfucker."

He dropped his head again.

"I see that you're hard headed put that little bastard back in that oven."

The little boy fought with all his might kicking punching screaming, "Daddy help me!" He looked at Leo and he assisted Alex in putting him in the oven. He yelled and screamed "Daddy, please help me!" Alex turned the oven on 500. The whole Brown family screamed. His wife passed out. The bell said ding and Alex opened the door. The baby nose was bleeding and she was crying and shaking.

Alex felt sorry behind the sight. He couldn't take it anymore. He cut the oven off took the baby out the microwave threw cold water on Jackie to wake her up and untapped her, so she could tend to her kids. Pulled his gun out and killed all three of them. Then told her to clean the whole kitchen up. He stood and watched her clean everything they touched even the door handle. Then he made her clean the alarm system.

Once she was back in he watched them leave out the gate, told her to take the baby straight to the hospital and ran out the yard. He jumped in the SUV and they rode out South Miami.

Vince went to Liberty City; they stopped at the airport and sent Smokey and Leo to Cali. They stopped at a Huddle House and seen it on the news, the baby were in critical condition. If she would've stayed another minute she would've died. Jackie told everything that happened risking losing everything. They jumped in the SUV and rode home.

He checked the inventory and made sure Smokey and they were taken care of. When he went to check on Alex and them, they were asleep in the middle room. He felt sorry for them, because they had no life. The house wasn't big enough for all of them, he wanted them to enjoy themselves even the guards. He knew it wasn't always about him, they were human also. Everyman are entitled to have fun. He thought about the days he led Smokey them and they all were free. All had their own home to go to at the end of the day.

He went in Poco room she was wearing white jeans and a black shirt. She was lying down on her stomach. He started massaging her shoulder telling her, his thoughts. She relaxed herself and told him he had good intention. But this is the way them guys are used to living. He asked her how many Yukons they had. He never really looked at the whole yard. She told him four new one came in today so they have 5. He asked her how many rooms does the Motel 6 have. She got up and checked the computer. She checked for the nearest one which would be on Washington Rd. She turned and told 'em more than enough.

"Call 'em and tell 'em we want 20 rooms for 3 days."

She made the order he looked at her and asked,

"Do we have a large amount on the land?"

"No I shipped everything out with that going to Cali. I had to double the order which will be here in about 4 days."

"What about you? Do you want to go clubbin, fuckin or shoppin?"

"I want to go clubbin and shoppin. I want to be with you."

"Count out 200 grand, and divide it up with all of them. Get what you need to enjoy yourself and y'all have fun. Oh buy me some clothes also."

He kissed her hand and left. He jumped in the Presidential called Blue and told her to meet him at the Hunting Inn in Kennesaw. As he drove he called Sonya, when she picked up, he laughed because she was sleep. He knew everything about her. He knew she had a powder spring resident and that was where he was headed.

"Are you sleeping?"

"Yeah its 11:30, I can sleep can I?"

"Well I'll hit you back I just wanted to talk. I'll catch you later."

"No! No! I'm up now!"

He hung up. Phoned the Hunting Inn made reservation and told them to give the keys to the young lady Erica Wright. He gave his account number. When he turned left on Arrington Dr. he cut his lights, off 442 was in the middle of the street on the right side. She had two Benzes in her driveway. The lights was out so he parked on the curb walked to the back of the house picked the lock and went in. Being careful not to hit anything he phoned her again, using the little light from the phone to find the stairs.

"You must be very tired?"

"Yes I am."

"Your old man must be really relaxing you."

"Don't try me like that you know don't no nigga stay with me."

He eased up the steps it was a big house too big for one person, so he opened every door to the 5 bedroom house. When he got to the last room he seen a crack in the door. He saw that she was in the bed alone, from the street light reflecting in the window.

"The truth of the matter is I miss you."

He laid back on the door frame watching her reaction. She smiled grabbed the extra pillow and hugged it. She was lying with her back to the door with the cover pulled up to her chest. He could've shot her right then and walked out the house.

"I miss you too; I wish you were here right now making love to me."

"Where are you?"

She paused for a minute and asked,

"Where are you?"

"I'm on Bankhead checking traps."

She knew it would take her 30 minutes to get to Sandy Springs so she told him Sandy Spring and she'll be waiting. He okayed it and hung up.

She jumped out of the bed with a white lace silk nightgown on and ran to her bedroom bathroom. He walked into the bedroom and sat on her bed facing the bathroom. When she came out she jumped back and fell to her knees.

"Jesus Christ boy you scared me. If you knew where I was all this time why would you play with me?"

"I thought we were on common grounds Sandra Anderson?"

She dropped her head.

"Sonya is my middle name me and Ryan have different pops. You knew all this about me from day one?"

"What's going on?"

"Smokey and Leo and about 6 more of his boys are wanted for murder and kidnap also robbery. For something they did in Florida. They're looking for them now in the Florida area. They have no case on you, but they're trying to build one. They know you ain't dead. They checked the dental record and found that it wasn't you. All they know is you've dropped off the face of the earth. They got people looking for you in Africa, because that's the only place they have you at. They think you've been kidnapped. I'm doing all I can to keep you safe."

"Why all the lies? Why not tell me shit heads up. You know I was in the house when you and Quin was talking to Cindy. She have y'all on tape. One favor deserves another."

"Let's work together and get all the money. You know I'll never cross you."

He kissed her, she fell into his arms. She knew he was a head man so she gave him all of her and thought for the first time a man made love to her not her work. She enjoyed herself sucking him. Then he placed her in the bed and made hard love to her.

He showered while she slept dressed and left. He went straight to Kennesaw, Blue was sleeping so he left and went shopping. He bought some clothes and boots for both of them. Went to Kroger bought enough food for them to eat on their hike. Went to Wal-Mart bought blanket and sleeping bags. When he got back she was sitting on the end of the bed pouting in a long Atlanta Hawks throw back jersey.

"Where have you been?"

"Shopping! I've been here and left I got us some stuff for a picnic hiking and camping. I come to have fun with you spend some time with you. I want to learn you."

"You know that I love you that's all that matters."

She helped him with the bags and made love to him afterwards. They showered together ate hamburgers and hot dogs and started their hike.

They wore matching white Fubu outfits some white Tims. White skull caps and had a white sleeping bag. They drove to the mountains; parked in the half empty parking lot and hit the trail. It wasn't cold out it was cool, they held hands laughing and talking, then a ranger met them coming up. He was a tall slim white guy wearing a brown ranger suit.

"Hi my name is Ranger Joe and I'll be y'all guide. We have a small group here already about four couple."

They hiked up to the campsite settle in. The other four couples were white. They all looked at them with smiles and gave hellos. The ranger asked did they have a tent. That was what he forgot to get. He told him no they plan to picnic and go back. The couples looked sad at the ranger, so he told them a tent cost 30 dollars to rent for 3 days. He paid the ranger and he sent for the tent. He sat on a rock and she sat in his lap.

"Baby I never camped outside all night."

He laughed and said, "I never camped period."

The whole camp side laughed, and then they started introducing themselves. There were Harry and Jill, they were the oldest. Emily and Jason were newlyweds. Fred and Bonnie both sold insurance and probably cheating on their mate. Then you had Reda and Johnny, they were young like them. The tent came and they just looked at it. Then she got up and said, "Ain't you gonna help me fix it?"

"I don't know how to fix no tent; I didn't know they came broke."

Everybody laughed, so he got up and looked for the instruction. This is something him, Tasha and Juan would've done. Now he's doing it with his half-sister, half lover. They looked at the instruction and pulled it out the box. They both looked dumbfounded at the blue tent because they didn't see no sticks like on TV. Then Reda and Johnny got up and pulled the cord and it popped up. Scared the shit out of both of them. Everybody laughed. It was fun and funny to see two surprised couple.

They shared food and said at least we knew how to shop. They shared a little story around the fire sung camp song roasting marshmallow. A tear formed in his eyes as they sung *On Top of Spaghetti All Covered with Cheese.* This was a childhood dream. He hummed along when they sung *London Bridge is Falling Down.* He walked in then tent and did something he normally wouldn't do. He thanked God for the moment.

He called her and she zipped the tent got in the same sleeping bag made love and talked about the future. She wanted him at the point he didn't care who knew he was her brother. She expressed how she loved the idea of coming up here. Just hated spending time apart from him. He just laughed and told her he don't know if he'll ever be able to settle down in a normal life. But if he could it would be with her, because she knew him and how to take care of him. They made love again and fell to sleep.

They woke up early then usual Harry gave him some Scope to gargle with. They ate eggs and bacon, drank coffee, packed up and hiked. It was fun going on and off the trail until they ran into a snake. Jill was hollering,

"Snake! Snake! Snake!"

The ranger told 'em to be still and don't move. He pulled out a net from his brown ranger bag and swooped the yellow and black snake up. When they got back on the trail he set the snake free.

"Why would you set that snake free? That snake tried to bite me!"

"No it didn't Jill," everybody yelled.

Harry told her, "If anything you scared the snake, the snake dropped dead in his tracks. You're a bad lady ma'am."

Everybody laughed but her, they restarted their hike she wandered off the trail again, they wandered right behind her. Somebody yelled, "Bear"

And they dropped everything and took off running back down the trail. Then the ranger said, "What are we running for ain't no bear in these mountains. I've been over this whole mountain more than one could count. I ain't never seen a bear."

Then Jason looked at him and said, "You just seen one now" and took off running.

When everybody looked toward the ranger and seen the bear. They all ran down the trail all the way to the parking lot and started walking, but the bear came out with them. They ran to their cars laughing and pulling off.

They all met back up at the Inn only to find out that the bear escaped from the Atlanta Zoo and the local official was tending to it now. They called to the Inn and told 'em the bear was back in the zoo. They all went to visit the bear before it would be returned back to Atlanta. He stepped to the feeding flap and said, "Damn lil' buddy I hate I was a part of getting you capture. Did you have fun while you was free? I bet you wanted to play with us, not scare us. You know we're taught to be scared of y'all. It's best you're here though, because one of these trigger happy hunters probably would've shot you for game. I hope you'll understand that."

The keeper gave him a fish and he stuck his hand in the cage and fed him. He patted him on the head. He was mad because the damn bear was friendly; he went in his pocket and pulled out some money. Trying to pay for the bear next meal, but the keep couldn't accept the money. He promised the bear a visit on his way out.

They left and returned back to the mountain, their belonging wasn't even bothered. They got their stuff and went to the top of the mountain. They laughed and talked about the event. Then he told Jill it was her fault the bear got caught. Everybody laughed at her, but he was really mad. But deep down inside he wanted all of them to see how it felt to be locked up.

They all looked at each other nodding and blinking their eyes at each other. Alot of the women looked at him. Jill blew him a kiss. He looked at Blue, they knew they wanted to sleep with them. But he wasn't no swinger nor was he about to let her become one. She cuddled in his lap to assure him that he was the only man for her. They went in the tent and made love, while everybody else switched partners. Then she confessed to him that her life was constantly on the move. Her going to college was her way of living her life. She told him many boys she's talked to but he was her first one. He held her even gentle that time around and she enjoyed every bit of the moment. She was sleep and he had to pee so he got dressed grabbed his phone and peed behind a tree. Walked off the trail and sat on a rock and called Poco.

"How is everything going?"

"Fine! And where are you when is you coming back?"

"I'm having fun, I'm in Kennesaw at the mountains. Did everybody enjoy themselves?"

"Yes Alex them is very upset because you haven't called they were having fun then they went to worrying."

"Tell 'em I'll be home soon."

He heard steps and leaves being stepped on. He looked back and it was Emily, she came around him dropped between his legs and started giving him some head. He hung up and started paying attention to her. He pulled her around and lift her skirt and hit her from behind, she moaned softly and felled to the ground. He fixed his pants help her up and left. She came back just as he was getting into the tent. She ran over and kissed him that was the first time she'd ever been with a black man and she let him know it by her kiss.

The morning came and she just stared at him, Blue looked at him and he just humped his shoulder. They all packed and walked down the trail. They hugged and drove off. They went back to the Inn showered and brushed their teeth. He put on some Coogi wear and she put on Baby Fat. They went to visit the bear and left.

She raced him in the truck but the Benz past her. He slowed down honked at her as she hit another exit. She called him they laughed all the way to their destination. She asked him did he sleep with Emily he lied and said, "No."

He asked her did she sleep with Jason.

She said, "Well."

And he said, "What?"

She laughed and said, "Boy you know I didn't."

He turned into the driveway, told her he loved her. When he parked everybody was standing beside the car. Alex opened the door hugged him and they talked. They walked around the land, seeing the racetrack all the woods and trucks. Alex told him everything was going well and a couple of the guys say he can run the operation better than Nikko.

"You know if you say it they'll kill 'em they're tired of him and his family. Nobody wants to go back."

"Then nobody will have to go back. You know I'm gonna get some houses built on this land so they can live right. I hate y'all have to sleep four deep. Y'all should have a hoe with y'all or something."

"All we're worrying about is getting up his money."

"Once y'all pay him then what?"

"Our family will be free and I guess we'll work for you."

"Doing what?"

"Hell I don't know!"

"I just don't want y'all to go to prison or nothing like that. I tell you what if anything fucked up happen we'll blow the courthouse up and take these folks to war. Have Castro send for y'all or something, because I'm not going to jail and y'all ain't either. I put my life on it."

They shook hands and jogged back to the house. He made calls setting up houses for the land. It would cost 3 million to fill the whole land up. He didn't care, he was gonna make a home for his crew. He set an appointment for the builders in 3 days. He hoped they'll be like Habitat and have them done in two to three months' time.

CHAPTER 21
The Lesson

"I got some good news and bad news to tell you so get over here."

With no words at all, he got up and dressed in a white and blue Pelle Pelle outfit and left. Still driving the Presidential, he saw a car following him. He picked up the phone and called Alex. The car started following him as soon as he hit Hwy 91, three blocks away from the house. He explained that to Alex and told him he was gonna ride down Fulton Industrial, to catch the car between Boat Rock Rd. and Fulton Industrial. He rode around the Perimeter for 30 minutes, and then Alex called back and said they were set.

He took off to Fulton Industrial. Once he passed them, they went to shooting. He didn't stop at all; he called Sonya and asked her was the Feds tracking him? She told him no, so he went to her house. When he got there she was at the door with a red silk robe on. She kissed him as he walked in the door. He closed and locked it, picked her up and took her to her room. While she was in his arms, she looked at him, "No, Rav, I know you just didn't get up from sleeping with her and came here!"

She walked in the bathroom turned on the shower, came to the door and pointed to the shower. He undressed and showered with her.

"Just so you won't think stupid, I didn't sleep with her. I was laying down when she laid on top of me, I wouldn't disrespect you like that. I would've told you I'll catch you in the morning."

She smiled as they dried each other and laid in bed. She kissed him from head to toe then from toe to his joy stick and took him in her mouth. After a few minutes, she got on top of him riding him. After sex she popped in his favorite song, *"2 Pac Thug Mansion."* He cuddled her in his arms as the CD went on repeat.

"You said you had some news to tell me."

"Yes. Bad news first. They got Mandai and Edrundo in Cali with Smokey and Pretarell.

He didn't recall the meeting.

"They also got them on tape talking about the operation. They didn't call no names. So tell Nikko to be careful, you too. Now for the good news. You fix 'en to be a daddy."

He looked at her thinking back on the dream he had of his granddaddy.

That is what he meant.

"I'm 4 months. I've waited for this day, now we can be a family. Let's go away from here and live.

He kissed her.

"I don't want you working no more."

"How am I gonna keep you on point on what's going on? Don't make me stop working please!"

"I can't risk you losing y'all lives, do this for me."

She looked at him with tears in her eye and started crying.

"This is suppose to be a happy moment. I can't quit! I just can't! You mean more to me than anything in this world. More than this little girl. I'm sorry. I just can't quit!"

"Sonya, you got over 4 million dollars!"

"It's not about the money, can't you see? It's been about you all this time. I will live in a cardboard box with you if I have to. I can't picture you in a cell or your grave. The only way I can make sure of this is to stay on. I promise I won't come around because I know that's what you're afraid of. Somebody using me to get to you. I'll just work and have the baby I promise. I'm leaving the field because that's how much I'm in love with you"

He smiled, made love to her and they fell to sleep in each other's arms. That morning she made sure she got up before he left. Made him breakfast oatmeal, eggs, patties and pancakes. She woke him and fed him.

"Get used to this because this is our lives. This will be my loving vow to you to be the best lady I can be. I promise I'll humble down to your every word be the best momma too."

She looked at him.

"Nidyah."

"Yeah, Nidyah Simmone Ellis, that's your baby name."

He just looked at her and laughed.

"You just make sure you have Nidyah"

"I will, I promise"

He ate, showered, brush his teeth and left. When he got back, Alex told him, them were two Atlanta cops. He told him not to worry, them was the cops that tried to get their hands in the action. He laughed and said, "The only action they got were them AK bullets. Their whole car blown up so we're straight."

Poco came in the living room.

"We got problems. The zone one polices is planning to bust Bon

Holmes and a new gang is trying to claim Perry Holmes. In the 2000 area."

"I'm gonna handle the 2000 area myself, I want the zone one department blown up before 11:30. It's 10:20 now. Alex get a Yukon and 5 AKs we got to pay a visit to these gang boys. Poco I want 100 pounds of C4 on that building."

He walked over to her and asked her what was wrong with her. She told him he just got up and left. He kissed her and told her to contact Nikko and tell him the Feds got Mandai and Edrundo on tape and pictures with Smokey in Cali. So check that out.

"That's where I went so smile"

He dressed in black with a black ski mask, the truck rolled around, with his four man clique. She ran out the house and kissed him. He really started to like her because she was fly. Her dress code stayed up to par with the latest design, she kept her hair hanging long. She was about that business. He hit her on the ass and they rode to Perry Holmes.

He called T-Baby and asked was they out now. He told him a couple of them were out harassing the tenants; they took up the first four apartments on 2000. L-1 to L-4. They drove down Kerry Dr. and turned into 2000. They saw about 8 of them drinking on the curb cursing the old people out. Alex blew the truck horn, stopped the truck and got out. Alex then pulled down the mask and stated "Don't move."

He looked at Ravenion and said, "Give us the count of 30 before you do anything."

They all had their mask down. He told the people to go inside their apartment. As they cleared out he started counting as each man went to a door and knocked. When the first gun went off they ringed possessive. After gunning down everyone in the street, He jumped in the truck and waited on them to come out. They ran out and jumped in the truck laughing. He backed out slow put it in drive and drove off. When he looked at his watch he drove toward the police station and stopped.

He looked at his watch again, it was 11:29. When he looked at the station it blew up falling inward. He pulled off telling them to tear down the guns and call Poco, told her to send the explosive team to Washington Rd. She told him they had to use two hundred pounds and go into the station to control the blast and fell off the building. So they didn't have anything but 5 pounds left. He just told her to get some more and make sure the team come to Washington Road.

They waited on Washington Rd off camp when the crew pulled up in the Yukon they also wore black masks. They attached the C4, hopped back in the truck and it blew.

They drove back to the house and chilled. He thought about what Sonya said about leaving and living. Alex came up in his thought about freeing their people. They had the money now so he jumped up and said, "After today y'all don't owe Nikko nothing, I'm fix 'en to take care of the problem."

He called and got the Jet fueled up, they dropped him off and he went to sleep enjoying his ride. He was gonna free his people. When the plane landed Gloria was there waiting on him. She twirled herself around showing off her red Christian Dior dress with the matching shoes. He kissed her as one of the men opened the door to the Benz. He got in first and she slide in beside him. It was late when they arrived to the palace. So she took him home, fed him and enjoyed him sexually.

When he woke up she had him a white Sean Jon suit with a pair of white Stacy Adams to match her white JLo dress. She escorted him to lunch. He was surprised to see Nikko and his date. When they got up and greeted him Nikko, had the same kinda suit as him but his were black. And his date had the same kinda dress as Gloria but black. They ate the lobster and shrimp and talked about the profit. Nikko asked him to take a ride with him. He wanted him to see how the people were living. They got in a gold Lexus SUV and drove off.

"Nikko, I didn't know you drive."

"From time to time I like to be alone."

"Nikko I come here with an offer."

"I already know. Poco told her family and her family told this family and so and so on. Word got to me. That's why I'm showing you how they live. You see people ain't trying to change their way of living, they just want to be free."

He stopped at a store.

"You see money ain't no good in this part of Cuba."

"But what if they want to leave this part of Cuba. They have no money. Your card ain't no good in the US or another country. These people are trapped and forced to live here. That's why they train so they can leave; it beat trying to escape and risking their lives. I don't want them to try to kill you because you could've easily killed me and they wouldn't had this chance. You're a smart man that's why you wanted to control everything at first because you know I'm an equal man."

They went back to the SUV and rode in the neighborhoods. In which they was living okay, they had their own houses, grass in the front and back yard. They even had cars. Kia's, some even had Lexus's. They stopped at Alex family house, a yellow 4 bedroom house. They opened the gate, a little dog came running out, behind him was two little boys wearing brown and green short outfits. They grabbed the puppy and greeted Nikko with a big smile and hello.

"Momma! Momma!," they both called, "Nikko is here!"
She came to the door wearing a purple dress and greeted him.
"This is Alex mother Freeda and this is Ravenion."
"Oh Ravenion, Ravenion, it's you. Come, come in. Alex tell me so many great things about you."
They had the average family living room suit. His father came down the stairs in some overall.
"Mr. Nikko I'm ready to go back to work."
He coughed and that tore him on the inside.
"You're not ready to go back to work sir, you're ready to get back in bed. Alex is taking care of y'all as of right now. Just make sure these boys go to school and get educated."
"You see Nikko, people shouldn't fear or risk losing their lives just because you pop up. I have the 150 million."
He called Nina and told her to transfer 200 million in Nikko account.
"The other 50 million is to take care of these people, pay them like they pay in the US eight dollars an hour forty hours a week. Let 'em get medical benefits and stuff like that. That 50 million is for them to be paid."
"So you're saying just add them to a payroll?"
"Now we're on the same page. Just let 'em know they're free. They still have to work for a living. They just got 320 dollars a week to look forward to. How you tax them is on you. But paying them will make them want to work more because they'll know they can give their kids a better life."
"You're right, so I'll take up every family name and put 'em on payroll send them they check in the mail with a letter telling them their debt has been paid they're free to change jobs but they still have to work."
"Yeah."
They rode back to the palace, word got out fast. Gloria ran and hugged him, she thanked him. Nikko told her to get up a team and get right on it. They sat at the table across from each other.

"I have this problem; my team in Mexico is shorting the money. His name is Louis. He sent 30 million when he's suppose to send 50 million. He's built an army that no one can touch. He has a General on his side, that destroy everything that rise up against them. I can't send no troops because he's too powerful."

"Do he expect you to try anything?"

"No he gives me this sad story how he's paying for this and that I got Nina to tap into his account he's loaded about a half billion strong. He has another banker."

"What we get we split right?"

"Yeah!"

"Okay whoever his right hand man is will be the new leader, since you're protected better than me I'm gonna need a mask and gloves. Call everybody and tell 'em you want them here by the morning. Get your guys to get me a tub of honey and 4 gallon of gas. We're going to strip him, sit him in the honey and place him in the room full of bees. If he don't give up the money I'm gonna put this gas up his ass. And on them bee stings. After that I'ma set him on fire. I want everyone to watch this so they'll know you're not to be fucked with."

Nikko got up and left he made the phone calls while he went to Gloria. She was on the phone calling up a work crew to send out payroll. He was afraid to use the phone in Cuba so he laid out and watched movie. He dozed off and dreamed about Juan. He saw him growing up being just like him. But worst. He jumped up and said, "He can't be dead, where the hell is my son? Why ain't nobody contacted me?"

He told Gloria to call Nikko. He didn't want to walk all the way to Nikko house because that was a long walk. He looked at Nikko like a punk living off his family name. When he think about how he's treating these people. They were right; he could've taken over this part of Cuba, because Nikko ain't got heart to match his.

She handed him the phone.

"Nikko I need to holla."

He hung up and waited. A knock came to the door, Gloria let him in. He sat on the sofa waiting for him to come out. When he came out he looked at the TV. The city of Atlanta was in a panic. Locking down the airport to tighten up the security, police patrolling the streets looking for terrorist. Nikko looked at him and said, "I guess you got your city on fire."

"As long as they're looking for terrorist they have no need to bust my dealer right? Nikko I'm doing all I can to help you and I know you got an eye and ear in every state and country. Nikko help me find my son."

"Is that what makes you kill the way you do? I've been wondering about you, why don't you stay over here with me? Be my right hand man, it will be 50/50. Alex them is doing well, Poco can't really expect y'all fling to go on. Your sister will be well tooken care of and your son will fall right in your hands."

"Nikko, you said that like you know things I don't know, I swear if you got my girl and her family killed. I swear I'll kill you."

"Calm down, I don't have the heart to cross a friend; I cross those who cross me. I don't know nothing about your son, what I was saying is we'll buy him back."

"Then I'll be enslaved to you. Come on Nikko this is favor for favor."

"Gloria go get your laptop."

She went and got her laptop and opened it. She showed him where Nikko has placed a hundred million reward for his son worldwide. He looked at Nikko and hugged him; Nikko told him he got nothing but love for him and left.

He and Gloria went to sleep. The next morning she had him an all black suit with black gloves and a black mask. They put a tub of honey in the very last room of the eating area with a 4 gallon can of gas beside the tub. They hooked a camera on the ceiling viewing all angles of the room. A monitor hung from the ceiling of the dining room. On the table where they sat was Gloria laptop. He waiting in the room with 4 other men dressed in black. So he'll have no idea of who they were. He was the only one with a weapon in the room, in case things got out of line.

It was noon when all the guests arrived; they sat at the table conversing, men and women. About their trip and what was going on in their city and country. Mandai and Erunda asked about Ravenion as the food was being served. Since everybody else was there he should be also.

They ate lamb and drank mumm wine then Gloria went to Louy. He was sitting next to Nikko, explaining his idea of making a new drug when Gloria whispered in his ear and he stood up and said, "Please excuse me." Nikko hit the monitor and told 'em this is what happens when you take from him. Gloria escorted him to the room and Ravenion put the gun to his head, told him to strip. Carlos, his right hand man wanted to get up. But one of the guards put a chrome 45 to his head and told him to be seated. Louy was naked when Ravenion slapped him in the face with the black 9 MM. Instantly his nose started bleeding. He yelled out.

"You broke my fucking nose! What is this about?"

Then Nikko came over the P.A.

"You've been stealing from me Louy. Give me the account number so I can get my money and you'll live."

"I don't have no account number."

Ravenion went to work on him kicking him all over his body. The other men picking him up and throwing him all over the room. He still wouldn't give up the number.

"Send me a hot iron."

Gloria brought the hot iron and he put it on his chest. He screamed and squirmed on the floor.

"Put him in the tub."

They sat him in the tub of honey and sat him back on the floor. He prayed in Spanish.

Gloria opened the door and handed him the bees laughing. It was a cage full of bees protected by a 4 wall screen with a hook on the front wall. He opened it and walked back to the door. The bees piled over his body from his thighs on up. Some went below. He was hollering and screaming, "Oh Jesus," in English and Spanish. The pain was so intense he passed out.

Gloria came back to the door with a pot of hot water. He poured it on his face. Carlos perked when he seen the brutal torture. Louy couldn't move all he could do was mumble "SSR." Then he stopped his eyes all swollen.

Ravenion asked for the account number one last time. He tried to open his mouth and his eyes. He laid his head back down in hope they'll see that they were wrong. He just didn't know they already knew about the account. Ravenion grabbed the gas and poured it on him. He jumped from the floor and ran to the door. Ravenion shot him in both thighs before he could grab the door knob, he fell to the floor bent over on his hands and knees.

Ravenion poured the gas down the crack of his ass. He screamed out, "SSR 42A1."

He fell face first on the floor, but they picked him up and put him back in the tub. Poured the rest of the gas on him and set him on fire. Carlos looked horrified and scared for his life. Nikko transferred the account and told him, "You're now the new leader, you have money in your account. So you're already paid for the 100 million worth of drugs already over there and the 100 million I'm sending today. You see Louy built himself an army that he thought no man can touch. Don't get that same idea because that movie star you just seen will come to Mexico and get you better yet any of you."

He looked at everybody, stood up and said, "I hope y'all movie, think before y'all try something stupid and y'all are now excused to go home. Thanks for having lunch with me."

Everybody stood and rushed to the cars that picked them up. Nikko went to Gloria after his guards had cleaned up the mess to check on him only to find that he was already gone.

CHAPTER 22
Will I Live

"Damn Sonya, time is flying by, two more months and Nidyah, will be born."

She kissed him and laid on his chest.

"I don't want you to ever leave this house. I'll love you forever. Nobody knows where I stay. You can leave that clique right now and they won't find you. They think Smokey is doing everything. You have him hid well in Cali. The money is good, you can bring Alex there with you, they can stay here also. Here's the way I look at it; as long as you're happy then I'm happy. I know you want your boys, safe and with you. So they can live here because its houses up for sell, or you can send them back. They already have freed their family and sent money to them. Beside Alex is happy over here, he don't even live on the land no more. Matter of fact don't none of your body guards lives on that land no more. They have their own houses, Poco got a man that she's seeing. She told me just last week she want to get married. So what's holding you up from being a family man?"

"To be honest with you, I'm scared every person I've ever loved has been murder or died. Look at my son, he's been missing over a year. He's 1 years old, with a 100 million dollar reward for him, in every country and there's no sign of him. The only reason why you and Blue is still living because we share a long distance love. I'm thinking about moving to Simi Valley or Ventura California. Somewhere I can buy a big ranch and leave Alex in charge of everything so I can be a father and a husband to you and Nidyah when I make my mind up I'll move you. But until then you keep your ass in this house. Walk around your hood go shipping or to the park."

"All them places I want to go with you. So you take me to the park tomorrow."

He smiled and made love to her, after he was in a good sleep she looked at the clock. It was 3 am and she eased out the bed grabbed a pink silk robe, cell phone and went down stairs. She called her contact.

"This is Wolf. I have a Johnny Coldding and Leo Shame in these two area Simi Valley or Ventura, yes he's here with me now. No he don't know I'm still using him. I do know this they're all riding in black presidential Benzes. How they got them cars I don't know. So I don't see y'all catching them on the road. Yes sir! Yes sir! Try to get the exact location. I don't think he'll give me that. They ride by jets when they fly and I don't know where their jet is. All I know is Coldding got a head on his shoulder and he won't go down easy neither will Ellis. Just remember your promise to me."

She hung up ran in the kitchen grabbed two pickles grape Kool-Aid and some cherry ice cream. She carried them back up the steps into the room and sat on the bed. She got back in bed just in time because he was rolling over. She knew he'll roll over in 3 or 10 minute, if he didn't feel her he'll be on her like a hound. He didn't really trust nobody, not even Alex them, so the little trust she had, she had to keep for her and her baby safety. He sat up and looked at her.

"You just ate not even 4 hours ago you can't be hungry, you're just eating shit because you know it's down there."

"No I don't want to feel no kicks so I feed her. She hasn't been kicking lately, an old lady told me this so I'm doing it."

"You're gonna be big ass a house; I want that weight off you in 90 days because you're eating just to be eating."

She kissed him and told him not to worry it will be gone, if she have to smoke crack. She laughed and said, "I'll be smoking for love." They laughed. He watched her eat all of it, the sad part about it was, she didn't offer him none. She sat on top of him putting him inside of her and her hand on his chest and rode him until she came; she laid on top of him with him inside of her and went to sleep. She woke him with a nice breakfast: grits, eggs, fried ham, biscuits and pineapple juice. She fed him in bed then she dropped her robe walking to the bathroom. Got the water ready and told him to come on because they had a date. They played in the water like kids laughing and enjoying each other. Deep down inside she knew he loved her. That's why she had to protect him and do her job at the same time. She looked in his eyes and started crying on the inside because she was so confused. Her job, her love, her life and more important her family. He seen the confusion in her eyes kissed her on the forehead.

"Sandra, I know you like a book what have you done?"

"Nothing just thinking about what's more important you and my family or my job and this bust. Juan I don't want to bust you, I really don't; you gave me everything you said you'll give me. But I haven't gave you all of me. Last night I reported y'all last night. They want to know Smokey and Leo location. Juan if you give it to me I'll make away we walk away from everything. Please I'm now giving you all of me. I'm on the line, my family means more."

"I told you I can't do it; let's just go to the park."

She had to get him in the park so they could take picture of him, plus she really wanted to spend time with him. Her captain told her, he'll only get two years. That was the only way he could protect her. Juan Ellis had to get convicted. She made him promise, that's the only time he'll get. Because she didn't want to raise Nidyah alone. He promised her the bust won't go down until she had the baby. But the more she thinks about it the more she wants to pull out. Then she thought about her brother.

"We're not going to the park just leave."
So you're gonna get mad at me because I won't give them up. I promised to take you to the park. So I'm gonna start keeping my word to you."

"Got dammit out of all times you want to keep your word now."

"Well then tell me what you've done!"

She got out the tub crying dried off and walked in the room, he was right behind her. She picked up the phone and called contact. She showed him the number as she dialed.

"This is Wolf, abandon that mission. He has left. Yes sir, I'll have him at Six Flags tomorrow. Why can't I just take the pictures for evidence? Okay sir."

"They wanted your picture to prove that you're in the states and that you've changed your prints over. Now we can go to the park tomorrow don't call or come near me."

She put on a blue and white JLo sundress with the matching sandals. He put on a white and blue king throw back Jersey some white Reebok's shorts and some white Reebok's classic with the blue rim. They jumped in her Benz and rode to the park. He noticed alot of families were there as he got out the car. She had parked in the shade under this big oak tree with alot of branches and leaves the grass was green and freshly cut. They walked through the park holding hands passing people on picnic, little kids running around. He pushed her on the swing, trying to keep view of everything going on. People taking pictures but not zooming in on them. She hopped off the swing and ran to the sliding board. He'll catch her as she slide down, they'll slide together. Then they left and rode to White Waters. He bought her a black bikini swim suit, him some black trunks with Fila flip flops for both of them. They slid down the big yellow sliding board together into the water. They were having so much fun. He got a little black tube and they cruised around the park. She whispered to him how much she loved him and hopes he would never leave her. They ate pretzels and nachos. They stayed to 10:30 and left.

When they pulled up he noticed cars on the street that haven't been there, he thought to his self this could be the end. He looked out the window and seen people getting out the car. She went in the bathroom and he ran out the back door, jumped her fence and called Alex. He told him to meet him on the 400 exit, he hung up, called a cab, told him what he had on and he'll be walking down Ponder Rd. He told the cab company that he wanted to go to the coffee shop right next to the 400 exit. He walked about 5 minute before the yellow cab met him. He called her as they rode.

"What's up? You wanted me to stay there so your people could bust me right? Why your people was there waiting? What are you trying to do?"

"Slow down let me answer your question one at a time. Ain't nothing up, I'm glad you left; because they're throwing me a baby shower, everybody here knows it was you. They respect the fact that my baby daddy is a drug lord. They're just surprised at how you left. I came down stair calling your name and seen them. I'm glad you left I'll see you tomorrow!"

"You know what you think, I'ma dumbass; hell earlier you told me not to even call you tomorrow. Sandra it's like this. Fuck you fuck that baby. If you cross my path again I'm gonna kill you."

"Juan no! Listen I won't do anything against you. You know I'm expecting in the matter of weeks."

"I guess you'll have your baby by yourself bye bitch."

He hung up paid the $39.20 with a hundred dollar bill told him keep the change and walked in the coffee shop. As soon as the cab pulled off, he walked to the exit. He called and got the jet fueled up for Ventura. He went up and down the exit a dozen times, before Alex pulled up. He jumped in and told him what happen, when they got off the exit they rode passed her house. No one was outside they were all inside; he took the wheel and dropped Alex off halfway from her house. He watched him run to the car with a tracker device. His car was on the side of the curb. He hit the car high and low, just as he was sitting in, he saw somebody looking out the window. He jumped in the car pulled off, passed him speeding. Nobody came out the house Ravenion noticed as he passed the house, he called Alex and told him to go to Charlie Brown Airport, they were going to Cali. They met up parked and flew to Cali, they landed in Simi Valley. They were gonna pay Smokey and Leo a surprise visit. They grabbed two 18 shot Glocks from the plane because they never been to Ventura before. Rented a black 5.0 and drove the 45 minute trip to Ventura, they talked about the future. He told him how he want him to take over for a while, so he could find Sonya and Nidyah a place to stay. Even though Sonya was no good, she still has his child. He couldn't turn his back on Tasha and Juan, so he ain't gonna turn his back on them. He told him he just got to make sure they're safe, even if he has to kidnap her. He should've done that to Tasha and Juan.

"Since Nikko trust you so much you're gonna be in charge."

"Believe this I won't let you down."

His phone rang and it was Smokey. He told him to hold the shipment because they're hot and he'll ship the money off. He told him that he see 'em outside the house. Also told him he'll be shipped his money to, keep an eye on it.

He hung up in case they're trying to set a trace, he told Alex what time it was as they rode up and seen the two cars on both sides of the road. One was a red BMW with two passengers and the other one was a green Jag with two passengers. They rode up the block seeing all the big houses. He thought, "Damn these fool was living swell in a nice hood."

They didn't see any more cars so they rode down the back street and seen two white vans with people in 'em. As they drove back to their street Alex looked at him.

"I know you ain't fix 'en to try to save these fools?"

"Alex, be cool we're gonna do this shit simple. Put the silencers on the Glock. You walk up one side of the street and I'll walk the other one; drive back up the street and we're gonna walk down the street. No words just pull the trigga. It's two men in both cars so you got to release fast and get back up the street, I'ma go and get them hopefully Leo is with him and we'll get back to Atlanta."

They drove up the side street parked the car up on the hill and walked down the street. As soon as Alex got to the Jag he opened fire. Ravenion had to run a couple steps to match the gun fire on the BWM. Alex waited while he ran up the driveway. He hit the door but no one answered, so he called and Smokey picked up.

"Damn Nigga you can't answer your door, come on let's go."

He walked back down the driveway as they ran behind him. As they hit the street, they saw lights so they took off up the street. Jumped in the car and backed off, put the car in first and went to the airport dropping them off, went to turn the car in and walked back to the jet. They were all laughing about the situation, talking about relocating and laying low when they get back to Atlanta. His phone rang and it was Cindy.

"It's been a long time since I've heard from you. What made you decide to hit me up now?"

"I had a dream that they got you, I've been having this dream that you got killed for about a month. My grandmamma told me to contact you. I keep seeing you fall in your grave. Come live with me. Nobody knows where I am, you gave me life, let me give it back to you."

"I'm okay baby girl, I'm gonna live to see 101. So don't worry I'll be to see you in a few days. I've been thinking about you anyway."

He blew her a kiss and hung up, Smokey looked at him and said, "Man, if I had that much care in my life, I would leave the gang. That's all a nigga need is a family, someone to care for him."

Everybody smiled and out the blue he had to perk. He jumped up and ran to the bathroom and perked. Something was wrong and he knew if he washed his mouth out, drunk a cup of water and walked back to his seat. He looked at his watched it was 2:30 in the morning. He stood, thought he had to perk again, his head was spinning he took 3 steps toward Alex's seat and fell in the middle of the aisles. He wasn't sick, he couldn't grip it. They formed a circle around him asking what was wrong. He stood up and said I'm fine, he looked out the window. The clouds opened up and he saw his granddaddy and mother. He closed his eyes and asked them to talk to him. Everybody was looking at him. He saw himself falling and missing the grave over and over again. The last time he fell he looked in the grave. He saw Nidyah and Juan, Tasha and Sonya, he reached for them. They disappeared and he fell in the grave. He was shot but he didn't know where, he tried to stand when the angel started to cover him with dirt. He opened his eyes and looked at them, he was sweating tear drops, everybody looked at him then he picked up the phone and called Blue. She picked up and he told her he loved her. Gave her an account number and told her she had 10 million in it. It was the money Tony left him. He told her no matter what happen to him she'll always be the love of his life and hung up. He called Sonya and told her he loved her for the first time and to take care of Nidyah. He told her if he died her and Nidyah will receive all his money. She screamed and asked him where he was. She could hear death in his voice. She begged him not to hang up. She could hear them in the background asking him is he alright was he hit. Smokey asked did they return fire she heard Smokey voice and yelled, "Reroute the plane they're waiting on y'all."

He hung up and called Arod and told him to get all the men to Charlie Brown Airport. He heard Smokey phone ring, then he heard him yell to the pilot, "Reroute the plane! Reroute the plane!"

The pilot came over the speaker and told 'em they were low on fuel.

Smokey called his men and told 'em to come to Charlie Brown Airport ready for war. Smokey looked at him and asked him was he ready to die?

He looked up with red eyes dropped his head and told 'em, "I'll see y'all in thug mansion."

Then he start singing,

"Ain't no place I rather be, children dead homies and family, sky high iced out paradise in the sky, can't be no place I rather be, cause it's the only place that's right for me. Gold out mansion in paradise up there in them skies."

Alex grabbed the 35 pound vests and handed them to everybody. They strapped up with A-K-s he was loaded down with two Glocks singing the thug mansion song. The call came to Smokey saying everybody was there including his men. The plane landed when they looked out the windows they seen all the different cars on both sides of the plane, with men holding different kinda machine guns in the air. The door open and they got out first. They escorted him to the Benz and put him in the back seat. Leo and Smokey took the car behind him, while Arod drove off, Alex waited to every car had left the airport heading to the expressway, before he came out. He saw them pull in two cars behind him. He called the troops on the land and told 'em it's going down. He sent them to the land so they could ambush them on both sides of the street and to shoot every car that came behind him. They were coming down exit 91 when Poco called him and told him the land was surrounded not to come. He knew this would be the only day he'll die. So he told her to call Nina and tell her if he dies to transfer his money to Gloria, Eric Wright and Sandra Anderson name, to destroy all the disks and the computer. Then she told him Gloria was there with her. She handed her the phone and she told him she believe God had them a spot in thug mansion. She heard *"thug mansion"* in the background. She knew he was coming to the land. He told her to put the vest on and get ready for war. He hung up as they turned on the street. He was in the 6th car they pulled down the driveway and into the yard. The car came to a stop he heard gun shots. Then two helicopters came up from nowhere. They came from everywhere shooting. His soldiers were holding up through the battle. They were coming out the cars taking position from the passenger side, shooting at the copters. The copters were shining light over the land. He couldn't pull out because they had them surrounded. All the houses blocked alot of the getaway. He thought to himself because of his heart he was gonna die. They wouldn't let him leave the car; they wouldn't open the door or roll down the window. He had to watch both crews hold down the attack from a car window, it hurt him because if he was going down it was without a fight. He wondered what would happen when they ran out of bullets, so far they were locking and loading. Then they saw Poco window open so they rode to her window and rolled down the window she yelled, "I'm coming out."

She climbed through the Benz window and told them to pull around the front. As they pulled to the front, Gloria came out with two hand grenades in her hand. She pulled the pen out and threw them at the helicopter. She jumped in the back seat and Poco gave her a mini 14. They headed for the pathway, but they were coming up through the back in two hummers blocking the pathway. Not wanting to waste any bullets they rode around looking for Alex Nigerz and Gino. They saw Alex ducking and running toward the Benz by the house. They stopped and he got in the front seat putting Poco in his lap. He told 'em the tunnel was the only way out so Arod drove toward the barn.

"Hold it Arod. We got two more men out there I'm not going nowhere without my men."

Alex told Arod to get to that damn barn, as they drove he stopped because they were coming.

"I'm tired of this we're getting nowhere. I'm not going to prison…? Let's do this shit."

They got leveled with the house and opened the door, Poco and Gloria came out first with 3 extra clips. Gloria took the rear and Poco took the front; they took down on-coming shooter and yelled to get him out of here. Wanting them to move the car, so he could get there safe. They came out. Arod and Alex took a position at the top. Gloria yelled out, "No! No! Drive him."

They ignored her and started shooting shooter coming in the direction of the car, trying to clear out the path to the barn. Gino and Nigerz came up shooting MP4s they threw a MP5 to Alex, they started winning the war, because the feds started backing down. Sonya open the barn with an AR15 with a launcher on it yelled, "Send him now!"

He got out on the passenger side; and then Smokey and Leo opened the doors to the driver's side and started shooting walking toward the barn. Sonya shot her way to meet them; he came behind Alex, Arod, Gloria and Poco. The feds started shooting again and pressing forward. He ran and got in the middle of them, leaving a small gap so he can shoot the side view. Shooting the two Glocks, turning side to side a bullet came straight and hit him in the back of the neck, and he fell face first in the dirt. Gloria yelled, "He's hit! He's been hit!"

Alex and Arod dropped back and grabbed him putting him over his shoulder. They were at a standstill, Sonya started crying looking in the direction the bullet came from and fired the launcher and yelled, "Push on! Push on! We can't let him die! Push on!"

They shot their way into the barn. Sonya and Gloria had started taking him through the tunnel when Smokey told 'em to leave all their guns, they wanted them to get him to Grady.

Poco called the street rider and told 'em to make away for them. She asked Sonya what kinda car she was in? And Sonya said a blue Benz. When they came up through the tunnel Alex and Arod stopped and rested. Nigerz and Gino took him and went through the house. They saw that the sun started to rise, when they got to the Benz. Poco open her lap top and seen they had the barn surrounded, she called and told 'em they were fix 'en to bomb the barn. They open the door and threw gas bombs in the barn. Smokey and Leo open fired on them. As they rode down the street she saw the gas and Smokey and Leo come out with their hands up. They held fire and walked toward them to make the arrest. They dropped their hands and started kneeling toward the ground, came up with two Glocks from behind their backs shooting and running to the Benz, but the Benz were surrounded, so they gave up and dropped to their knees, once they took them into custody they searched the barn and seen somehow the rest had got away. Sonya locked the seal to the tunnel. They started wrapping things up trying to figure out where the rest of 'em went. They pulled up to the Grady Emergency Exit with hand guns out asking for a doctor. Sonya showed her badge and a white male doctor came and took him into surgery. They walked around with their gun up, his blood on them for two hours. The doctor came out and said he'll be fine. They're putting him in the intensive care unit. One of the nurses walked up and she was a Cuban. She told her not to worry Nikko was taking care of everything. She gave her an envelope and said I think Nikko faxed this. It came an hour ago, it's for Juan Ellis. She was just waiting for the perfect time to give it to them. The letter wasn't supposed to go to her. It was supposed to go to another agent that's been working in Grady since all the robbery took place. Since she was on the fax machine she got it and sealed it. Somebody said, "Damn look at all them polices coming. They jumped up and ran to the intensive care unit and got him."

"Put him in that wheel chair and bring the IV pole also," Sonya said.

Alex called and got the jet fueled up and walked to the elevator. The Cuban nurse ran up with two IV bags. When the door open Sonya looked back down the hallway and saw the Middle family going into the intensive care unit. Tasha had his son in her arms. That puzzle Sonya, but she went on and pushed the button to the ground floor. They hurried to the Benz letting him lay in their lap and rode to Charlie Brown Airport, heading to Cuba. When they got in the air Gloria laid beside him on the floor while Poco went and got all the pillows from the seats, laying them on the floor so he can lay in comfort. Sonya sat in a seat and opened the envelope. It was a photo copy of his family and the middle family, Blue, his dad and her mom. She opened the letter and read it.

"Dear Son, I'm very proud of you, you helped us take down some important people. When you and Nikko started dealing, Nikko went to Washington and somehow got diplomatic immunity. They cut some kinda deal. Anyway Nikko gave up Mandai and Erundo and Carlos. Once I learned that Sandra already had your back, I had to fake the middles family death just in case the gang intervened. In a way Juan the U.S. and Nikko used you like a pawn in their chess game. What they're getting from Cuba only Nikko them know. I don't really trust Nikko. I've made a way that you can return to Africa and got your prints back, come back home and fly straight. Sandra had cut a deal where you would've done 2 years. But I can't let you do a day for the people you brung down. You can keep all your business and live your life. Tasha said she's gonna help you run all the business. I feel the only reason why Nikko gave them up because a scientist that went missing. I don't know. Nikko said he wanted to keep your word to your men. They all are gonna be returned back to Cuba. So I'll be seeing you in a couple hours. I love you son. In hopes of letting the past be the past and we can live as a family. I'm fix 'en to retire so I can be a part of y'all lives. Blue loves you she told me about how you protected her and took her on trips. Now we all can go as a family.

Love always your dad.

Sonya tore the picture and letter up. She laid beside him, looked at Gloria while smiling and said, "We're all he got. Smiling."

"For now," Gloria thought.

THE END